# DIG

**L.A. FERRO**

DIG: by L.A. FERRO Published by Pine Hollow Publishing



Cover by K.B. Barrett Designs

Published by Pine Hollow Publishing

Proofreading & Editing by Chrisandra's Corrections

Cataloging-in-Publication data is on file with the Library of Congress.

Created with Vellum

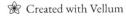

## NOTE TO READERS

*The characters found within these pages are unapologetically dramatic, the scenes are steamy, and the road to a happily ever after is sordid. This book is meant for audiences 18 years and older. A list of potentially triggering themes can be found on my website.*

*Please read responsibly.*

*https://www.authorlaferro.com*

# 1

## BAIT

ARIA

"Aria, I know you're in here somewhere. Come out, come out, wherever you are." Immediately, I startle, dropping the pens and paperclips I had been searching for in the supply closet. But, of course, the supply closet at Callahan Brothers & Associates would be the size of a conference room, jam-packed with row upon row of shelving units stacked high with old paper filings, no windows, and crappy lighting, making it creepier than shit to step foot in. I get chills every time I have to fetch supplies. I'm always waiting for someone to pop out and grab me—and not in a good way.

"Kris, you fucking scared the piss out of me! You couldn't wait until I got back to my desk for whatever conversation we're about to have?"

My hand is still firmly placed against my chest when I bend down to retrieve the supplies I dropped. It's just my luck that the flimsy box the paperclips came in would bust open, and now I have to spend even more time in this dank room. Seriously, this is a multi-million-dollar law firm, for crying out loud. I look up to see Kris peering down at me with a smile plastered across her face.

"Are you going to just stand there and watch me clean this mess up? This is your fault, you know."

I'm scowling while I angrily jam paper clips back into the stupid piece of shit box. Kris taps her black stiletto twice before saying, "I would help you, but seeing as how I need to talk to you, letting you clean up this mess means I'll have your undivided attention a little longer."

"Whatever you have to say better be good. These are brand new slacks I'm wearing, and crawling around on this dirty-ass floor was not in my plans. So, if it's not good, you owe me a pair of pants."

Throwing her head back, Kris lets out the loudest laugh. I swear she has the most audible voice of anyone I know. It's one of those voices that carries no matter how hard she might try to stifle it. Kris is the person you ask to give an announcement when there's no microphone. I, on the other hand, have always been asked to speak up.

"Well, whether you'll want to hear what I have to say is up for interpretation. I told you a month ago, I'm having a huge party for my twenty-first. That party is this Saturday, and you said you'd be there."

I pick up the last of the ten million paperclips before rising and meeting her big, blue, questioning gaze. I've never seen someone have actual puppy dog eyes. Her eyes are currently conveying their genuine emotion. Right now, she's begging. The problem is, I don't know why.

"Yes, and a month ago, I told you I would come. In fact, I'm pretty sure we've talked about it at least twice a week on our lunch breaks." I quirk a brow at her in question before setting the supplies down on a nearby shelf and dusting off my pants. *Great.* Now my hands are black from the floor. Once I'm satisfied that all the dust is off my knees, I delicately re-tuck my white blouse in, making sure not to get any of the dirt from my hands on its silky material. I spend good money on my work clothes, knowing it's required and expected that we dress professionally, not to mention, being a woman in a man's world is rough. An excellent wardrobe goes a long way toward earning respect.

"Aria, you look fine. You can stop obsessing over your outfit for one second."

Dropping my hands to my sides, I purse my lips and drag my eyes down Kris's attire. "Easy for you to say. All you have to do is show a little boob, and men are all ears." She's wearing a tight-fitting blue dress cut low enough in the front to show off her assets without being too risqué or inappropriate. Kris was blessed with a set of tits most women pay for. I, on the other hand, was blessed with a handful, and that's about it.

"You're being ridiculous. I catch one of the lawyers checking you out on the daily. No man in this building walks by the reception desk without doing a double take. Now, on to more important things. I don't want you to be mad but—"

Holding up my hand, I stop her from continuing. "That sentence never ends well for anyone. Whatever you were about to ask, no."

Picking up the supplies, I start heading toward the door. That's when Kris grabs my shoulder. "Aria, wait. Just hear me out before you say no. One of my really good guy friends will be there, and he hasn't come out in a while, but he RSVP'd this morning that he'd stop by. That's when it dawned on me that you two need to meet. I hadn't thought about him for you—"

"Kris, stop right there. Why would you be thinking about a guy for me anyway? You know I'm still involved with Logan."

"Yes, but you and Logan have been on and off again for months. Not to mention you said involved. You didn't call him your boyfriend."

"That's beside the point. I said I'd come to your birthday. I didn't agree to a blind date." I watch as all her enthusiasm diminishes. I'm not sure how she saw this conversation playing out in her head. *Who jumps for joy over a blind date?* I start heading back to the reception area with Kris on my heels, this time silent, which is new for her. The woman can't keep her mouth shut, which has me wondering.

"You already told the guy I was coming, didn't you?" When I

suddenly stop to face her, she thins her lips before they turn into a small apologetic smile.

"Okay, fine. You may have been the carrot I dangled to get him to come to the party." I feel my eyes bugging out of my head.

"You what? You realize that puts me on the spot big time. When you said you had someone you wanted me to meet, that's one thing, but telling the guy I'm there for him is another." I'm fuming inside now. The last thing I need right now is a man. Men are shit, and I have enough of my own crap to deal with. I don't need the added stress of being what someone else wants.

"I know. I'm sorry. It's just, Holden is a really great guy. One of the best actually, but he got screwed over by an ex and hasn't dated since. Honestly, I figured he didn't care to since it's been months. He's thrown himself into baseball, work, and school, and blown off everyone else in the process. You being there was honestly my last-ditch attempt to persuade him to come out. I didn't think it would work, but then it did." My shoulders slump at her admission.

"Great. Glad I could be someone's backup plan. That means he's just looking for a quick lay." When I start heading back to my desk, she doesn't follow. *Thank god.*

Kris just started working here a little over two months ago. Her mother, Catherine, is the HR Manager and got her on as a temp for the summer. We became fast friends. Kristine is very easy to talk to—mostly because she does all the talking—but the woman is also an open book. Her only problem is that her mouth never stops, which seems to land her in more trouble than not. Case in point: my current predicament. I'm sure she wasn't scheming to set me up. Most likely, she was in the middle of texting and had an idea flash through her mind and ran with it rather than thinking it through.

The problem is, now I have to deal with the fallout of a half-baked idea. *Perfect.*

~

My stomach is growling, and I'm starving. The only reason I haven't left for lunch yet is because I'm waiting for it to be 11:30 am on the dot. That's when the phone system automatically switches to our Boston location, where the receptionist answers the phone while I take my lunch. The time difference between my office in Chesterfield, Missouri, and corporate in Boston, Massachusetts, works perfectly for our lunch breaks. I've been a receptionist at Callahan Brothers & Associates for over a year now. This is the first real job I've ever had, and I lucked into it. Callahan Brothers & Associates is a highly sought-after law firm. Many third- and fourth-year law students would kill for my position just to get their foot in the door. I know I could easily be replaced, so I've dressed the part and worked my butt off since day one. I make damn good money here, money that helps pay for college.

Currently, I work full-time during the day and go to school at night. The best assistance my parents can offer me with paying for school is continuing to put a roof over my head. I always knew they wouldn't be able to pay for my college tuition. They never hid their financial struggles from my brother, Spencer, and me. Spencer and I both knew whatever future we wanted for ourselves would be one we chased. There would be no handouts. In high school, we both worked our asses off to get good grades and community college scholarships that would help pay for our first two years of school. Spencer needed all the scholarships he could get because he decided to go to med school, and everyone knows that's not cheap. I, on the other hand, just finished up my second year of community college, where I got all my prerequisites out of the way. Now, all I need to do is decide what the hell I want to major in at university this fall.

My issue is that, mentally, I've been struggling for quite some time and focusing hasn't been easy. Garrett, one of the lead partners of Callahan & Brothers, has said that, should I decide to pursue legal studies, the company would reimburse me for every A I earn. *No pressure there.*

When I finally pull my eyes from the window wall that lines the front of the reception area, I notice it's 11:35 am. *Great.* I've wasted five minutes of lunchtime daydreaming about my craptastic life goals. Grabbing my purse and phone, I quickly tidy up my desk before making my way out to my car. In the past, I would grab a bag of pretzels and a Diet Coke from the vending machine and work through my lunch, but I know that's not healthy, and the crash from the caffeine high with little food in my stomach sucks. But eating hasn't come easily lately; like many things, it makes me feel worse.

I'm just pushing through the front door when I collide with a hard chest. "Christ! I'm sorry." I was looking down as I went through the doors, lost in my thoughts, but when I look up, I come face to face with Logan, my ex-boyfriend.

"Geez, Aria, are you okay?" His tattooed arms are still firmly gripping my shoulders to ensure I don't lose my footing. He knows I've been weak lately.

"Logan, what are you doing here?"

His eyebrows pinch together before he pulls me over to the side and out of the way of the revolving glass door. "I wanted to surprise you and take you out to lunch today. I would have been here earlier, but a car accident down the road had traffic backed up."

When I meet his onyx gaze, I see true sentiment in his words. He's trying, I'll give him that. It's hard to stay mad at someone when they go out of their way to make up for the shitty thing they did. It's even more complicated when that someone is six-foot-tall with naturally tanned skin, jet-black hair, and a gym body to die for. Throw in his fully sleeved arms and back tats that leave no patch of skin unmarked, and he's any woman's bad boy fantasy.

My eyes soften to his sweet talk, even though I know it will be short-lived, and he pounces. The moment my eyes collide with his, he's reaching for my hand and bringing it to his full lips to kiss before pulling me with him toward his car.

We've just reached the car when he opens the door and says,

"How about burritos? You can order yours without a tortilla." I risk a glance up at him before sliding into his classic Camaro, of which I know he's told me the year a thousand times, but I never remember because cars aren't my thing. As soon as my eyes meet his, he averts his gaze and closes the door. Without words, he realized his mistake.

Once he's in the car, the apologies immediately start flying out of his mouth. "Aria, I'm sorry. Seriously, babe, I'm just worried about you. It's hard being the only one who knows how bad things are. I just want to help. Please don't overthink my comment." His eyes are pleading for forgiveness that my fucked-up brain can't give. There are times I wish I never confided in him. Hell, half the time, I'm trying to figure out why I did at all. These days, I can't figure out what's the sickness, what's my heart, and what's just me, and it fucking sucks.

Either way, I don't have time to dwell on it because, before I can even grant him a morsel of forgiveness, he's gripping my face and forcing my eyes to focus on his. "Aria, you are so beautiful. Do you understand me? Please let me help. Don't shut me out." His eyes are darting between mine, waiting for a signal that I'm not only listening but feeling the conviction in his words. I want to feel it so bad, I really do, but I can't feel anything anymore. When his eyes don't find what he was hoping for, he releases my face and starts the car.

We drive in silence to his favorite spot. It's a food truck park, but it does have great variety. Exiting the car, I come around to meet him before heading to the outdoor garden to grab a table. Usually, we pick our table before we get our food so we can scope out what trucks we want to visit. Today is no different. As we take our seats at a picnic table beneath a maple tree, he starts his scan. I'm just about to get out my phone to check the time when Logan smacks my arm to grab my attention.

"Babe, look, there's a Crazy Wraps truck here. They have lettuce veggie wraps. I can dig that."

I don't even get a chance to respond before he's taking off

toward the wrap truck. Drawing in a deep breath, I try to find my Zen. Reminding myself he's only trying to be supportive, and I really need to try and eat lunch today.

When he returns to the table loaded with food options, he looks pleased as pie. I can't help but stifle a smirk. Logan is very attractive. If women knew I wasn't jumping his bones every night, they'd think I was nuts, but somewhere along the line, the feelings I had stopped, and I don't know why. He should do it for me; he has the looks, and he has the parts I like, but something is missing, and that's one of the reasons I ended it.

He catches my failed attempt to hide my smirk and quickly places all the food on the table before coming around and straddling the bench I'm sitting on. Leaning in, he grabs my chin and pulls my mouth to his. He has some of the fullest lips I've ever kissed, lips I used to get lost in for hours. When his tongue seeks entrance, I grant it, knowing I need to show some signs of life.

Logan has never been gentle. He takes what he wants as if it's always been his. Plunging his tongue into my mouth, he hungrily swipes it against mine, and I let him take it. I give him all that he's seeking because I don't know what's wrong with me, but I do know it's not all his fault. I'm just as much to blame for the status of our relationship now. Pulling back, he smiles against my mouth before saying, "There she is. I love that smile, babe."

He grasps the back of my neck and kisses my forehead before turning back to the table to open all the food boxes. I swear he bought one of everything on the truck, and I should be so grateful. A small part of me is. *So why isn't it enough?*

"What looks good, babe? I got veggie wraps, shrimp wraps, hummus with fresh vegetables, and these veggie bowls with brown rice and blackened salmon." His eyes are downcast toward the food as he lays out all the options. Sweet moments like this make me doubt my decision to take a break in the first place.

"Thanks, Logan. I think I'll try the salmon bowl." Without hesitation, he reaches across the table and places it in front of me before handing me a plastic fork from his back pocket. I've actually surprised myself with this choice.

"Friday night, there's a concert at Riverport. I was wondering if you wanted to be my plus one?"

For once, I'm glad to have food in my mouth, as it gives me an excuse not to immediately respond. I cover my mouth and chew slowly, choosing my next words carefully. Logan has become a little obsessed recently. I'm not sure what's changed to make him that way, but he has me on a short leash—or, rather, he tries to keep me on a short leash. I may be weak and easily persuaded as of late, but I'm not dumb enough to let a man control me. He doesn't have to like my choices, but they are still mine to make.

"Actually, my friend Kristine from work is having her twenty-first birthday party this Friday, and I promised her over a month ago I would be there." I shrug my shoulders and keep my eyes down on my food, not wanting to meet his gaze, which I'm sure would just confirm what I already know. *He's pissed.*

"How come you didn't mention it before now?"

Thinning my lips, I push the food around my bowl, searching for the right words but finding none. I have no good reason for not mentioning it, other than I didn't feel like I needed to. We are not currently boyfriend and girlfriend. That title was stripped away three months ago. We'd been dating for almost six months when I told him I thought we needed to take a break. Logan didn't want to take a break. He acted as if I was fucking breaking his heart when I sat him down to have the conversation. Hell, maybe I was, but I was tired, and I felt like he was demanding too much of what little energy I had for myself.

After a month of being on a break, he showed up on my doorstep demanding I talk to him in person. It's easy to hide behind texts and phone calls, but face to face is a lot harder.

I'm unsure why I divulged all my secrets to him that night. Looking back, I think he caught me on one of my bad days. I shared with him all the demons I'd been struggling with for quite some time, and how, slowly, they crept up on me and morphed into a sickness I couldn't contain. Whenever I think I'm getting better or have a handle on the situation, the poison running in my veins rears its ugly head and reminds me that I'm not. I'll never forget the blank expression that was on his face after I shared my darkness with him. His expression was unreadable. At first, I thought he didn't believe me, and thought I was making it up.

I hadn't put much thought into how someone would react upon finding out that I was sick, but I didn't anticipate anger. After I confessed my struggles, he stood up and punched the wall, hitting a stud and breaking his hand. As we sat in the ER waiting to get his hand x-rayed and fixed up, he confessed his indiscretions and admitted he hooked up with some girl he met at a bar–not once, but twice. He said when he went out the night I asked for a break, he didn't have plans to find a hookup. She came onto him, and he was angry about how things were between us. You know, the standard male excuse for sticking their dick where it doesn't belong. It was a revenge fuck. Some would say that, since we were technically on a break, he should get a free pass, but for me, it felt like a slap in the face. Now here we are, three months later, doing whatever this is.

"Logan, I'm allowed to do things without you. We aren't an official couple anymore. Kris and I have become close friends over the past few months, and I told her I would go. That's all there is to it. Nothing more, nothing less."

He throws his fork down and shakes his head. "Aria, we aren't a couple by *your* choice. You know this isn't what I want. I fucking want my girlfriend back. Babe, it's been three months since I've been inside you, two since you let me back in, and one since you let me have your mouth again. What do I have to do? What do you want from me?"

Times like this are when I can't find it in me to care anymore. He's listened, and now he's taking advantage of my sick heart. Logan knows he's not what I want anymore. It's written boldly across every conversation we have, but he also knows I'm in a bad place mentally. Trust me, right after I initiated the break, I felt like an ass, but as time passed, I realized that while I may have been the villain in our story, he was the reaper, collecting all my truths only to cut them down to fit his narrative. Like right now. He is trying to portray himself as a martyr, but we both know it's his way of guilting me. That's why he brought up our lack of intimacy. He is trying to draw attention to the fact that he is also sacrificing. The part he's missing is, I'm not asking him to.

"Damn it, Aria, are you even listening to a word I'm saying? You're doing that thing again where your eyes glaze over, and I know you're a million miles away." Out of annoyance, I set my fork down and push my bowl away.

"Shit, Aria." He's up and out of his chair in a heartbeat. "I'm not trying to upset you. I just want to talk. I don't know what to do. You laid some heavy shit on me, and I feel like by keeping this secret for you, all I'm doing is hurting you more. I don't want to walk away, but this—this isn't working."

I stay quiet because, for a minute, I think he's finally seeing what I've seen for months. We don't click anymore. Somewhere along the way, we got lost, and there's no going back. But just when I'm convinced he sees that for himself, he adds, "I think we need to tell your family, or at least go to the doctor. I'm not going to leave you, babe, but you're not letting me in, and you need help." *Shit.*

Getting up from my spot at the picnic table, I give him a murderous glare before turning on my heel and heading back toward the car. I hear him mumble out a barrage of curses as he quickly starts wrapping up all the food. When I get to the car, I open the door and climb in, slamming it behind me as I do. That's part of our problem. Logan and I have never been on the same page. When it comes down to fundamentals, we are always miles apart.

After I've settled into my seat, bound and determined not to speak to him, I watch him jog back to the car, food containers in hand, as two women blatantly check him out. Logan can get any girl he wants. Hell, he's already done it. So why he's determined to shackle himself to me and my problems is perplexing. It hits me then; I only need one question answered. He gets one word from me, and that's it.

Tossing the food into the backseat, he slides into the driver's seat and openly stares at me, but I don't give him my eyes. Instead, I keep them firmly planted on the picnic bench we just vacated, determined not to give him an ounce of attention. My problems are solely mine. It's not for him to tell me how to live my life, and his latest declarations have me on edge. He doesn't get a say in my choices. We aren't even together, and for me, he sealed his fate when he decided to stick his dick where it didn't belong.

When he finally averts his gaze out the front window and off the side of my head, I give him one word. One word that will put all this to rest, because I'm done. I've been done, but for some reason, I keep letting him back. So I ask, "Why?"

His hands grip the steering wheel with a force that has his knuckles turning white. He knows exactly what I'm asking, and I'm almost surprised that his immediate reaction wasn't to spit out a line of defensive bullshit like 'What do you mean? What are you talking about?' or 'Stop overreacting.' Instead, he's quiet, and that's when I start praying like hell he doesn't lie to both of us and say three little words we both know would be total bullshit. They would be nothing but his futile attempt to salvage whatever we have left between us. Which, from my perspective, isn't much.

"Don't make me answer that. I shouldn't have to answer that. It should be obvious."

I'm unsure whether he's insinuating those three little words are how he feels, or if he's simply saying he shouldn't have to tell me he cares about me. Either way, I don't need his words of affirmation. I don't give him anything. He did us both a favor by not saying things he didn't feel in his heart. At this point, I'm relieved, and now I just want him to take me back to work so I can get out of his car.

When he finally starts the car and switches on the radio, the sounds of Three Days Grace, "I Hate Everything About You," rings out. I know the song wasn't an intentional play and it just happened to come on, but I didn't miss how he turned up the volume when it did. If I'm lucky, I won't see him again, but if the last two months have proven anything, it's that he has a penchant for punishment.

When we finally get back to my office, he doesn't park the car. Instead, he pulls up outside the front doors and keeps the car idling while he runs around to open my door. Once I'm out, he reaches in, grabs the bag of food, and places it in my hands before dropping a chaste kiss on my forehead and saying, "I'm sorry."

A throat clearing to our right has him breaking away, and that's when my eyes lock with those of my enigmatic boss, Garrett Callahan. While he's the reason I have a job here, outside of the day we collided in a coffee shop, he's been cold and distant, offering nothing but studied glares that always leave me feeling unsettled for reasons I can never seem to pinpoint. Right now though his heavy contemplative stare is a welcomed reprieve.

Logan can't expect me to draw this out any further under the watchful eye of my boss. While Garrett may have entered the building, standing out here like this is unprofessional. Rolling his eyes, he rubs his jaw in annoyance before walking around the car, climbing in, and taking off without another word. *Good.*

Walking into the reception area, I fully planned to decompress from my stressful lunch, but it appears the world hates me today, because when I look up, I find Kris sitting in my chair. She must see the annoyance on my face because she defensively puts her hands up before I even say a word.

"Look, Aria, I just wanted to apologize for earlier. I know I put you in a shitty spot, and I'm truly sorry. I fully understand if you don't want to come to my party. You are off the hook. I don't want my inability to keep my big mouth shut to get in the way of our friendship."

It's clear she's sincere and, truth be told, I've already forgiven her. I know she wasn't coming from a bad place. She didn't drop my name because I'm the only single friend she has. Kris is one of those people who is instant friends with everyone. There is no doubt in my mind she has an endless list of single friends to set up on blind dates.

"Yeah, we're cool. I've already forgiven you," I say, putting the leftovers on the credenza behind my desk.

Kris eyes me suspiciously, asking, "So, why exactly aren't you with that fine specimen of a man that just dropped you off?"

Bringing my hand to my forehead, I rub the spot between my eyes and blow out a breath. I have no real good explanation, so I give her the truth and hope it's enough. "We clicked in the beginning, and it just stopped working for me somewhere along the line. It's nothing he did or didn't do, per se. I'm just not that into him." I don't mention the hookup because, honestly, it's irrelevant. I wasn't satisfied with our relationship prior to calling for a break.

"I get that. If he's not the one, he's not the one. That's all there is to it. Life's too short to spend it wasting your time with someone who doesn't light you up inside." My whole body deflates on a breath when I realize she really does get it. My best friends don't even seem to understand, so I sure as hell didn't expect Kris to. My two best girlfriends have been with their significant others since high school, and I feel like they view my relationships as slut behavior.

I just turned twenty-one, and I've had three boyfriends. They look at me like I'm the problem, and hell, maybe I am, but I'm not the type of person who stays in a relationship just to have someone. Perhaps my friends are truly happy, but I can't help but feel like some of the hate they give me comes from deep-seated jealousy. They don't want to be tied down either; they want to sample other goods and play the field, but they also don't want to lose what they have. Our relationships are changing because of it. I no longer have the energy to play mind games with catty women. I haven't seen much of Lauren and Kyla lately, and honestly, that's been fine.

I'm just taking my seat in the chair that Kris kindly vacated when she asks, "So are you still going to come?" I can't help but smile. While that apology was sincere, I know she doesn't want me to back out of her party, and I don't have any plans to.

"Yes, I'm still coming, but do you care if I bring a friend?" She quirks a brow at me in question, so I clarify. "A female friend. Don't take offense, but you live like an hour away, and I've never been to Rose Bud. So I'd feel more comfortable if I had someone with me. Plus, she's not a drinker, so I have a DD."

She taps her freshly manicured nails on the upper half of my two-tiered desk like she's mulling over my request. I know she doesn't care; I'm asking to be nice. It's not like we're going to someone's house. The plan is to go bar hopping.

"You know I don't give a shit, but you might regret that decision by the end of the night." I don't have a chance to respond because she starts to saunter away, effectively ending the conversation—which happens to be fine by me.

## 2

# DECISIONS

### ARIA

It's Tuesday night, and I just finished showering after a two-mile jog through the streets of my subdivision. I haven't had a spurt of energy to work out in a while. So when I felt restless after dinner, I laced up my running shoes and tried to clear my head. Running into Logan at lunch yesterday left my head a mess. What's fucked up is, I don't care if I hurt him. Some would say that makes me a cold-hearted bitch, but I say it just makes me done.

A knock on my bedroom door pulls me out of my thoughts. I don't have a chance to even say 'come in' before my brother, Spencer, comes barging in. "Aria, what the hell? Did you go for a jog without me? That's our time. Are you getting too cool to hang out with me?" He parks himself on the edge of my bed before stealing the ball I had been idly tossing in the air.

"Yeah, well, someone hasn't been home much lately, and the streets were calling my name."

"I know; it sucks. School is taking up all my spare time. I knew pursuing my dream to be a doctor would be a lot of work, but I didn't realize I would have little to no social life in the process. I swear, I think the guys believe I left the state. I never hang out with anyone anymore. But you know I still love you right?" He slaps my thigh before throwing the ball against the wall. "Have you figured out what to major in this fall?" If he were looking at me, he would have seen my eyes practically roll into the back of my head. Here I thought he genuinely wanted to talk to me. Now, I'm not so sure.

"Did Mom and Dad send you in here to give me a lecture? I don't understand why they are so worried about what I chose to do at school. It's not like they are paying for any of it." Catching the ball, he halts his assault on my wall, granting me a small reprieve from its annoying thud. I'm surprised Mom didn't come running in to make him stop.

"No, Aria. Mom and Dad didn't send me in here. I was honestly curious. We haven't talked in what feels like forever. You've flipped-flopped a lot over the past few months, and I wanted to know if you've finally landed on something. Teaching? Nursing? Or Legal Studies, now that you work at the law firm? I'm just trying to talk to my sister. We've always been close, and now that I've started my first year of med school, we haven't been able to connect."

Closing my eyes, I take a second to process his words because I know my reactions lately have been nothing short of misplaced, and I hate it.

"Aria, are you okay? What's going on? Why do you look like you're on the edge of a mental breakdown?" That earns him a chuckle out of me.

"Maybe I am. I don't know. It's like I woke up one day, and suddenly so many things were different." I stop there because the rest is too telling, and the last thing I need is for Spence to worry about me. I'll figure this out. His shoulders deflate with my admission as he reclaims his seat at the foot of my bed.

"Look, you are not alone in feeling lost. Just because I know what I want to do doesn't mean I don't feel lost. There are so many days when I feel defeated and think I made one of the biggest mistakes of my life in choosing my career. I'm buried with studying, and labs, and I feel like I'm losing parts of myself in the process. We all have bad days, Aria. You're not alone."

I know doubts are typical—a lot of college students flounder. What's not normal is all the extra shit I have going on. The secret I keep from my family. The one that haunts me and threatens to take all the parts of me I once loved. I don't understand how I let things come to this. I've never been an insecure person. These new parts of me, this sickness, it doesn't fit. How can I be so fully aware that I don't want this and not be able to stop it?

Closing my eyes, I take a deep breath and try to keep the floodgates at bay. But it's useless. My brother and I fought growing up, like most siblings do, but the older we got, the closer we got. While we may have fought and disagreed on almost everything, he always had my back, and apparently, he still does.

"Don't cry, Aria. Shit, what do you want me to do? How can I make it better? Do you want me to get some ice cream?" I stop my blubbering and give him a knowing smirk. In high school, whenever I was having a bad day, he'd grab the ice cream out of the freezer and two spoons, no bowls. Most of the time, he would just sit and listen, but he would share his drama every now and again. Spencer rarely had drama though. He was the hot shot in high school. Captain of the football team, student council president, and prom king his senior year. Every guy wanted to be him, and every girl wanted to date him. Nothing has really changed on that front. He might not have the social life he once had, but he's still handsome and smart as hell. Whoever ends up with him will be one lucky lady.

"No, Spence. I don't want ice cream. Thanks for checking in on me. I'll be fine. I've just been overly stressed lately. That's why I went for the jog earlier, to help clear my head. I was doing pretty well until you came in and started laying the heavy on me." He smirks and starts tossing the ball in the air again.

"Well, I'm on break next week. So pencil me in for some nighttime runs." He tosses the ball over his shoulder, and I catch it. He laughs. "Lucky; we both know you can't catch for shit."

"Just get out. I didn't ask you to come in here, make me cry, and then make fun of me." He throws his hands up in defense before bowing out gracefully.

"Fine, I'm leaving, but I'm just a wall away. Remember that." He closes the door, and I'm alone. Honestly, being alone feels good right now. When I'm alone, I can just be. I don't feel the weight of people's gazes upon me, and I don't feel the burden of having to impress. I just wish I could rewind the clock to a time when my mind felt less like a prison.

Once I'm alone and my mind is quiet, I remember I need to text Kyla and see if she can go with me this Friday to Kris's party. Kyla and I aren't very close. Lauren is the glue that keeps our trio together. Unfortunately, Lauren is out of town with her family on vacation, so it's Kyla or nothing. When I told Kris I planned on bringing a friend, I hadn't officially solidified those plans. I'm just hoping Kyla's "Free Friday Nights" is still a thing. Her boyfriend Nick works the Friday night graveyard shift as a mechanic at the manufacturing plant in town. Hopefully, she hasn't made other plans yet.

Aria: Do you have plans this Friday night?

Kyla: Sara invited me to tag along with her and Matt to the movies, but I haven't decided if I want to go.

Aria: Any chance you want to tag along to a party with me?

Kyla: Whose party?

Aria: A friend from work is turning twenty-one, and she really wants me to come, but I didn't want to go alone. It's in Rose Bud.

Kyla: Rose Bud isn't too close.

Aria: Yeah, I know. So do you want to come?

Kyla: Honestly, not really, but it sounds better than staying or home or going to the movies.

Aria: So is that a yes?

Kyla: Yeah, I'll go.

Aria: Awesome! See ya Friday.

She shoots me a thumbs-up emoji, and I'm sure that's the last I'll hear from her until Friday. I know I have problems, but I swear, sometimes I think Kyla is a walking depression ad. Maybe depression isn't the right word, but she just never shows any emotion one way or the other. Even when I think she finds something genuinely funny, her laugh is monotone. Kyla and I don't typically hang out one-on-one for that very reason. I'm never sure where I stand with her, even though we've been friends for almost three years now. It's just strange. Either way, I have a DD, and a scapegoat lined up for Friday in case I need to get out of there.

It's only 9 pm, but I'm tired—which is the new normal for me. Constantly tired and always cold. I'm just climbing under my comforter when it dawns on me to cyberstalk this Holden guy. If I'm going to be subjected to an awkward meetup, I want to get a look at what I'll be dealing with.

Once I'm situated nice and cozy under my thick comforter and plush throw cover, I fluff my pillows, pick up my phone, and click open social media. Kris and I are friends, so I immediately pull up her profile and search her friend lists, looking for Holden's name. It's only fitting that when I find him, his profile pic is a baseball team, and his settings are private. My thumb is hovering over the 'Add Friend' button, weighing the pros and cons. Pros: I'll get access to his profile, where I'll not only get a picture of him, but I can whip up a bunch of uninformed assumptions about what he's like based on the pictures he chooses to publish. Cons: Since Kris mentioned me, he could read into my friend request and get the impression that I'm interested.

This is my problem lately. I can't fucking make a decision to save my life, figuratively and literally. I'm making a mountain out of a molehill. *Who the hell cares what he thinks?* Not to mention, he's probably just as curious. Deciding not to waste another minute on this absurdity, I hit send.

It's 10 am Wednesday morning, and the day is dragging by at a snail's pace. All the partners are out of the office, traveling to Boston for some big meeting, which means the office is dead. There's me, three people in HR, and a handful of paralegals. Accounting is handled at the Boston location. A few years ago, Garrett's brother, Colton, started the Boston branch after landing a few high-profile politicians. He constantly had to fly to the East Coast to work around their hectic DC schedules, so they said screw it and expanded the firm. While that office is enormous and growing like crazy, I know the Callahan's are from this area, which is why this office will likely never close. It settles my mind a little knowing that I have job security as long as I keep myself valuable.

"Aria." My hand flies up to my chest as I just about jump out of my chair.

"Kris, I swear to god, if you keep sneaking up on me, this whole friendship thing we have going will end. I mean, what the fuck, who does that?" Of course, she laughs.

"Sorry, I didn't even think I snuck up on you. Did you not hear my heels clicking across the floor? Anyway, not important. Why didn't you tell me you texted Holden?"

My eyebrows shoot up to my hairline, and I remind myself to close my mouth because I know it's hanging wide open. "What the hell are you talking about? I didn't text Holden. I sent him a friend request. I wanted to see what he looks like."

"Oh, well, he said you guys messaged each other and that he can't wait to meet you."

"Huh, maybe he's got the wrong girl sliding into his DM's

because we did not text." Quickly, I reach for my phone so I can pull up the profile I sent an invite to last night, just to make sure we are talking about the same guy, but when the screen lights up, I see that I have two messages from Holden Hayes.

Hey, pretty girl.

I was wondering when you were going to reach out.

"Why are you smiling? Did he text you? What does it say?" I put my hand to my mouth and, sure enough, I am indeed smiling. *Shocker.*

"Okay, he did message me but not until an hour ago, and I'm just now seeing it, so that hardly qualifies as *we messaged each other*." I gesture with hand quotes. "I haven't replied. I only planned on cyberstalking him to see what mess you got me into."

She's quick to reply with, "A hot one. The exact kind of mess you should be in. Seriously, looks aside, you guys would be good together. Are you going to message him back?"

I roll my eyes. "Well, duh. I'm just unsure what I'm going to say, so stop pressuring me. I haven't even had a chance to see what he looks like, since he only just accepted my friend request."

"I'll tell you what he looks like. He looks like sex on a fucking stick." Her comment has the wheels in my brain already spinning with countless questions, but I only want the answer to one.

"Have the two of you ever dated?" Her immediate response is genuine.

"Psssh, no. We grew up together. Plus, I'm dating his best friend. I can appreciate how gorgeous Holden is, but we wouldn't fit. Not to mention, he was never really available. I mean, sure, he was single here and there before he and his ex got together, but he's always been a loner in a way when it comes to women."

"So what you're saying is he's a player and you're trying to cover for him?"

"Aria, no. That is not what I'm saying at all. Holden is not a man whore. I'm not going to lie and tell you that he hasn't slept around. What twenty-two-year-old hasn't? I'm saying that I don't think he dates just to date. I've only seen him in one serious relationship, and I've known him since elementary school."

I'm about to question her further when one of the paralegals walks in with a client. Kris picks up a few folders from my desk that actually did need to make their way back to HR and walks off, leaving me to stalk all things Holden Hayes in peace.

The afternoon blew by because I was busy cyberstalking Holden on social media. The only problem is, there wasn't much to see. Most of his pictures were faraway group shots with his team, and the others were blurry at best, which is baffling. Who's taking blurry pictures anymore? From what I could tell, he's clearly fit, because his social media page was nothing but baseball. He's obviously an athlete. In most of his pics, he's wearing a baseball cap, but I'm pretty sure he has blue eyes and brown hair. He doesn't look too bad. It could be worse.

I have yet to respond to his earlier messages. I'm not sure what to say. The fact that he mentioned me to Kris means he's likely interested, and I don't want to lead him on by texting him, but I'm also curious. Staring up at the ceiling as I lay in bed, I decide to text him back. I'm supposed to meet him Friday, so it wouldn't hurt to feel him out, since his profile gave away nothing.

Aria: What made you so sure I'd reach out?

I wait a few minutes, staring at my phone, waiting for bubbles to appear but getting nothing. That's when I decide I'm losing my damned mind. *Who lays in bed waiting for a guy they've never met to text them back?* Tossing my phone on the bed, I get up and head to my closet to pick out my outfit for work tomorrow. I'm not sure when it started, but I like to be prepared. I don't like surprises. If I plan an outfit in my head while lying in bed, only to wake up and discover said blouse is dirty and I have to replan my outfit on the drop of a dime, I get stressed out. But it hasn't always been that way. I remember rolling out of bed, rummaging through my closet, and scraping up an outfit to wear last minute almost every day in high school. As an adult, I haven't been able to do that. Too much time is wasted overanalyzing my appearance and second-guessing my choices in the morning. Now I hang my outfits on the back of my door every night. Doing so brings me peace and relieves my brain from the thoughts that now torment me.

Tomorrow's outfit is going to be easy. I've paired a high-waisted black pencil skirt with a long-sleeved white polka-dot blouse that has a mock neck, making it look extra fancy. Nice work clothes make me feel good. For some reason, formal business attire feels like a second skin to me. When I wear it, I feel pretty. It's probably because business casual for women means conservative, which is right up my aisle. I'm just about to pick out my shoes when my phone dings. My back goes stiff, and my stomach twists into knots. Why is this guy making me nervous? Seriously, I need to get a grip. I decide not to immediately rush over to my phone like some lovesick schoolgirl waiting around for her crush to text her back, and instead finish my nighttime routine.

Once my clothes are laid out and my face is washed, I pull back the covers on my full-size bed, fluff my pillows, and climb under the sheets. After I've situated myself, I draw in a deep breath, preparing for whatever I'll find on the screen. I can't help but chuckle and shake my head when I read it.

Holden: Took you long enough.

Aria: You seem so sure I would message you back.

Holden: Well, I know you've seen my pictures.

Well, that was short-lived. Who is that into themselves? Not my type.

Aria: Wow! Cocky much? I think I'll pass.
Goodnight.

I'm not sure what I expected from him, but it wasn't that. Logan was self-absorbed, and I've had about as much of that as I can handle for one lifetime. I toss my phone across the bed, feeling dispirited. I should be thrilled he showed me his cards this early, because it gets me off the hook for Friday. I never wanted to be set up anyway. My phone dings again as I turn to my side to get comfortable for bed. I contemplate ignoring it. In fact, I do for at least five minutes until it dings again. At this point, my curiosity has got the best of me, and I reach across the bed to retrieve my phone to see what the cocky bastard has to say.

Holden: Hey, I was just messing around, relax.

Holden: Are you still there, pretty girl?

What is it about this guy that has me feeling some type of way? He's pulling me in, and I don't even know how. Logan was not my first boyfriend, and I wouldn't say I'm easily wooed, but I'm not sure I've ever been wooed either. I knew every guy I dated before we officially became a couple. That could be what this is. The thrill of the unknown. What the hell? It's not like I have anything to lose, so I play along.

Aria: Still here.

Holden: Good.

I wait to see if he says anything more, but he doesn't, and I eventually fall asleep.

# 3

## HAUNTED

### HOLDEN

"Yo, Hayes! You ready for that game tomorrow night?" We're in the middle of warm-ups, and Kane, my catcher, loves to rile me up. He knows I hate to be distracted when I'm warming up. It doesn't matter whether it's practice or not when I'm in game mode. Yes, he's asking me about the game, which is standard locker room talk, but for me, it's different. The team knows to just let me be. I go through my own mental exercises before every practice or game, and today is no different.

Tomorrow is our last game of the season. There will be minor league scouts in attendance, and we all want to be on top of our game. The problem is, Kane is a senior; tomorrow is his last game, and he wasn't drafted. He'll tell you he never wanted that, but let's be honest, what guy playing college ball doesn't want to be drafted? I think that's just what you start saying when you know it's not going to happen for you.

"Fuck off, Kane." He shakes his head before resuming his seated calf stretches. "Life lesson number one, Hayes: don't take yourself too seriously. No one else is." I swear, he and I click on the field, but off field, we are total opposites. He doesn't get me, and I don't get him. I know the chances of making it big are slim. Ask any young boy what their dream is, and most will tell you the same thing: to be a professional athlete. That wasn't always the case for me, but it is now, and I'll be damned if I let some bitter senior get in my head. Because I know that's what he is doing, I don't bother giving him a response. Instead, I stand up and start my lap.

I'm running, trying to refocus my thoughts. I'm pissed that Kane tried to throw me off, and now I'm letting him succeed. Pitching is a mental game more than anything. I need to have my head in the game if I'm going to help my team win.

Four years ago, things were different. It all came so easy. Visualize the success, focus, eliminate outside noise, and don't let fear eat you alive. The problem is that when you start playing for someone else, the dynamic changes. I used to play for myself. That's no longer the only reason I play. This is my atonement for the things I cannot change.

A whistle blows and Coach calls everyone over to the dugout. Glancing down at my watch, I see it's 6:30 pm. We should still have another twenty minutes of warm-ups. *Great, another fucking disruption to my stride.*

Once we've all huddled up, Coach says, "Boys, we've had a great season. We are already number one in the division, and tomorrow's game won't change that. I know this will shock most of you, but I want you to listen to my words before any of you start bitchin'. As you all know, fourteen of you will not be returning next season, seeing as how you're seniors. Two of you are going on to major league teams, and I can't tell you enough how fucking proud I am. The rest of you, I know you're hungry. Scouts will be at the game tomorrow, which is nothing new. We've all played for scouts, but I don't think I need to remind any of you that our success this season can be attributed to our mental preparedness heading into each game. In my thirty-year career, I've never seen a team with the focus and clarity you boys bring. That being said, I want everyone to take the night off. I'm not saying go out and party. Go home, rest, and get your head in the game for tomorrow. There's no question this team is physically fit.

Our weakness tomorrow will be our headspace. For a lot of you, this is your last game. For others, this is your time to shine. We all want to take home a win. Go home, prepare, rest, quiet the noise, and visualize the win."

*Fuck.*

The last thing I expected to happen tonight was for Coach to let us off early. He never lets us skip practice, but he's not wrong. Our team was strong this year because we were all good at keeping our heads in the game. It's so easy to get defeated when the other team scores a run. Whether it causes you to fall behind or not, it pisses you off.

Over the years, I've played with so many guys who developed a defeatist attitude after one bad play. Every player takes it personally when they screw up a play. If you're playing outfield and a ground ball bounces unexpectedly, causing you to overcorrect and lose seconds off a play, you feel the eyes of your team and the crowd judging you, holding you accountable for the other team's gained run. Hell, going up to bat is as invigorating as it is nauseating. You're hungry as hell and want to crush the ball, but when you know the team needs it to get ahead, it carries another layer of stress—and don't even get me started on pitching.

As a pitcher, I feel the weight of the world on my shoulders every game. Win or lose, I spend hours after a game going over every detail. I analyze what worked and where I could have done better every time. My dad comes to every game and records so that I can watch the footage back. I know it's a bit OCD, but it's how I operate.

Pulling into the driveway, I notice both my parents are already home. My mother usually plays bingo at the VFW hall on Thursday nights while my dad hangs out in one of the neighbor's garages, drinking beer and watching whatever sporting event happens to be on. But tonight, they are both home. Great.

Since I am an only child, all eyes will be on me, and they will undoubtedly bring up tomorrow's game in ten roundabout ways instead of being direct. They always feel like they are bothering me by asking me point blank what is on their minds. It pisses me off because I know why they do it. My life is fucked up because I made it so. I set the tone.

The summer before college, everything changed. My life was turned upside down in the worst of ways. I emotionally shut down that year, and it's been my pattern ever since. While I may not be able to protect myself from pain, I can save others from me. If I don't let people in, I can't hurt them, and what's more, I can't lose them.

Walking through the doors, the house smells like my mom's homemade lasagna, and I'm starving. As much as I want to head straight for the shower, my desire to eat is greater. Dropping my bat bag in the front entry, I kick off my slides before heading straight to the kitchen. I fully expect to find my parents in the kitchen when I round the corner, but it's empty, and there's a note by the plate of lasagna.

"We went to Linda's for drinks and cards. Call if you need anything."

There is a god, after all. The last thing I wanted to do was play twenty questions with Mom and Dad. Now I can eat in peace before I shower. Opting to eat in my bedroom, I grab a plate and dish out a serving of lasagna before grabbing a Coke and heading to my room.

We live in a three-bedroom ranch on the outskirts of Rose Bud. Lived here my entire life. I never thought I wanted to leave the small-town life behind until recently. Lately, I've had an itch, and I don't know if it's all about baseball or something else, but I need more. Which reminds me, I need to text Aria. Shit. I can't believe I just thought that.

When Kristine asked me to show up for her birthday party tomorrow, my immediate response was no. Kristine is awesome, and she's dating one of my best friends, but her party is on the night of my last college game of the season. I'm either going to be on cloud nine or eating shit. Either way, it doesn't change my after-game ritual. For the last four years, after every game, win or lose, I go back home and watch the game, without fail.

I couldn't tell you why I changed my mind when Kristine mentioned there was someone she wanted me to meet. Before I knew her name or had a picture to look at, I said yes, which is entirely out of character. I don't like being set up, and I hate when friends try to set me up, especially when it's with someone they know, because then you have the added pressure of not offending them if it doesn't work out or—even worse—running into said bad date down the road. No, thank you.

So ask me again why I said yes, and the answer is still the same. No fucking clue, but I'm nothing if not superstitious. Show me an athlete who isn't. Because I said yes without question, which is completely not like me, I now feel like it's because I'm destined to meet this girl. As lame as that may sound, I can't shake it, and after I saw one picture, I fucking felt her in my bones.

As expected, when I found her through Kristine's social media page, her profile was set to private, so I only got one picture of three girls. Two blondes and a brunette sitting on a brick wall. Kristine didn't mention what she looked like, only gave me a name, but when I saw the picture, I knew precisely which girl she was. She was the brown-eyed blonde in the middle with the haunted eyes. Anyone else looking at the picture would have seen three hot girls, but I saw her ghosts, because I know what it's like to live with demons. Seeing her picture only solidified my faith in my superstitions. I am supposed to meet her.

Holden: Hey, pretty girl. One more day.

I hit send and start to dig into my dinner. After I saw that Aria sent me a friend request last night, I spent the remainder of the evening scrolling through her profile pics until I fell asleep. Aria is beautiful. She's petite, which I find extremely attractive.

People always assume that taller men would like taller women, but that's not the case for me. I've always liked short girls, and her being a blonde is just the icing on the cake. I can tell from her pictures she doesn't know how pretty she is. I'll verify tomorrow, but from the looks of it, she's got thick thighs and ass for days. Aria's got the kind of thighs you want wrapped around your waist when you're pounding into her against a wall. Fuck, it's been way too long since I got laid. I don't even know this girl and I'm fantasizing about fucking her, and that's a problem.

While I may not know her, I know she could never be a quick fuck. For starters, there's the speed at which she almost wrote me off last night for simply messing with her. She clearly doesn't take crap, which means she's one of those girls who makes you earn it. But more importantly, I don't think I could give her that if she wanted it. I don't think she's the girl you get out of your system in one night. There will be no one-night stand with Aria Montgomery.

My alarm goes off at 5:00 am, and I feel like I didn't even sleep last night—probably because I didn't. Once I was done looking at pictures of Aria for what felt like the millionth time, I started thinking about tonight's game. Tonight is the last game of the season before senior year, and I haven't received any offers. Coach has always told me out of all the pitchers he's coached over the last decade, he believes I have what it takes to actually get drafted straight to the big leagues. While that's nice to hear, it doesn't mean shit unless it happens.

I've had two serious recruits follow my career—one from the American League and one from the National League—which seems promising. But until I have an offer, I have nothing to gloat about. They're looking for something before they pull the trigger, and I haven't figured out just what that something is yet. That's partly why I watch all my videos right after games. Watching while the adrenaline of the game is still running through your veins, while you are still pumped by the win or angry from the loss, gives life to the playback reel in ways that watching the video two to three days later just can't.

Grabbing my phone, I silence the alarm, noting I have no missed messages from Aria. Honestly, it's probably for the best. The last thing I need is another distraction. Baseball may not have been my dream, but I'll be damned if I don't see it through now. I doubted that I would get to this level, that I could come this close to a draft, but now that I'm here, I'm consumed by it, and I'm drowning in my pursuit to live the dream. Hopefully, the dream is worth it and my ghosts can find peace.

Rolling out of bed, I head to the shower. A shower first thing in the morning always wakes me up, and because every evening is spent busting my ass at practice, I'm usually dead tired the following day. My tuition was covered with a scholarship, but because I'm not an idiot banking on being one of the select few who makes it into the big leagues, I've been working as an apprentice engineer at the chemical plant my dad works at. I'm currently studying electrical engineering at school. Again, something I didn't choose for myself but rather fell into.

My dad is an engineer and built a quality life for my mom and me, and because I hadn't really shown interest in anything outside of baseball, my dad pounced. "Be an engineer... Union shops are drying up, and there will always be a need for engineers... I can open doors for you..." These are the constant conversations on loop in my brain for as long as I can remember, and since I dedicated every spare moment I had to baseball from the time I turned eighteen, becoming an engineer was a no-brainer. I didn't have to put any thought into it. All I had to do was take the classes and show up.

My issue is, I'm about to burn out, and I haven't even started. Baseball hasn't been fun for me in a long time, and because I never wanted to be an engineer, I watch the hours pass by on the clock every day at work and feel like I'm trading my soul for the security of a 401k. I feel like I've just been surviving, and now it's not enough. I need to feel alive. Fuck, I wish I could just feel something because I'm tired of roaming. I wish I could figure out who I am, but I lost that privilege, and now I live for others.

Over an hour ago, we won the last game of the season, but I can't seem to pull myself off the floor of the locker room. Tonight's game brought back too many memories that I try to keep buried down deep. In the last inning, I felt my mental walls dissolving. Luckily, we were ahead by five runs, but sitting here, I'm playing back every mistake I made. Every time I let a player read my pitch, every time I allowed a heckle to penetrate, and every time I couldn't bring myself to read and lead because I couldn't focus. I let my demons get the best of me when a flash from the past appeared.

The opposing team's catcher broke his pinky finger in the bottom of the eighth, and the guy they brought in to replace him knocked the breath out of my lungs. I literally had to pinch myself because I thought I was seeing ghosts. The kid couldn't be much over eighteen and was a dead ringer for my best friend, Luke. I've never been as rocked as I was at that moment. I considered asking Coach to pull me out, but I also wanted to keep it together for Luke. He is my purpose, after all.

A pounding on the locker room door breaks me out of my trance. "Janitor. Anybody in there?" Shit. I need to get my act together. I can't keep letting ghosts from my past interfere with the present. "Yeah, I'll be out in just a minute."

Stuffing my uniform in my duffle bag, I quickly throw all the remaining things from my locker in as well. We were supposed to clean them out after tonight's game, but when I reach for my phone, I see ten missed calls and five texts.

Gabe: Where are you?

Connor: Everyone's here, including some new hot girls.

Gabe: If you don't want Trent hitting on your girl, you better get here.

Gabe: Bro? Are you ghosting us?

Connor: What the hell? The game was over an hour ago.

Damn it! I completely forgot about meeting Aria tonight. How the hell did I forget about that? I'm missing out on something I wanted for the same reason life is passing me by too quickly. When you're haunted by your past, it's hard to live for your future. It's only 9:00 pm. If I hurry up, I might still be able to catch her. I shoot off a quick text to Gabe.

Holden: Don't let her leave. I'm on my way and tell Trent back the fuck up.

Luckily, I hadn't forgotten about meeting up with everyone before the game, so my outfit isn't terrible. Most of the time, I'm wearing warm-up gear, but today I packed a pair of dark jeans, a white long-sleeve, cotton button-down, and a pair of all-white Vans. Quickly, I grab the pomade out of my bag and tousle my hair before spraying on my cologne. I'm not into my looks; my style comes second to comfort and necessity most of the time, but I know when I look good, and tonight I look good. Tossing my duffle bag over my shoulder, I look around the locker room again to ensure I got everything and head out.

Everyone is meeting down on Main Street in Rose Bud. The town is small, and while other bars in the area might be bigger and better, Main Street is ideal because you can bounce between four different bars instead of driving or calling an Uber. Of course, it doesn't hurt that Gabe lives a block over, so the after-party is close.

The campus is only about a twenty-minute drive from downtown, but it took me an hour to get here. When I pull up outside Landry's, I check my hair and grab a breath mint from the tin in the console. Landry's has windows across the entire front of the bar, so I wait a minute to see if I spot her. That's when I spot Connor walking out of the bar for a smoke. I decide I've stalled long enough and jump out of the truck. I drive a lifted red Ford F150. It's a total country boy cliché truck, but I don't give a shit. I love this truck.

Connor spots me as I close the door. "Yo, Hayes. I would have driven you from the game myself if I had known you'd take so long to get your ass over here. What the hell? We thought you were going to bail."

I come in for a pound hug, take the cigarette out of his hand, and throw it to the ground. "Life's short enough without these." I feel like nobody seems to get that anymore.

"Fuck, Hayes. What is with you tonight? Seriously, we just won our last game of the season, and now we're on break. Loosen up, bro!"

I shrug my shoulders and scan the windows once again to see if I can catch a glimpse of Aria. This time, however, Connor notices. "Why are you still outside when clearly you have a damn good reason to go in?"

I allow a half smile and let his words marinate before I respond. Truth is, I have no good reason to be stalling, but for some reason, I know the minute I walk through those doors, shit is going to change for me, and I haven't decided if that's something I can handle. If anything, the last few years have taught me I can't handle much. All I've managed to do is lose. I lost my best friend, myself, and maybe even more. Not sure if I need to bring anyone else into my orbit.

"Don't suppose I can't talk you into going inside and getting me a beer?"

He crosses his arms and turns up his nose at me, seemingly perplexed. "Fuck, man, are you serious?"

I place my back to the windows and prop myself against the cement ledge that runs the length of the building. "Yeah, bro, I think I am."

His eyebrows shoot up in surprise before he says, "If that's what you really want." He pauses for a second to see if I'm going to change my mind, and when I don't, he shrugs and heads toward the entrance.

I had every intention of meeting her tonight, but now that I'm here, it seems like the worst idea I've ever had. I'm the last thing that girl needs. Hell, I'm the last man any girl needs. My ex made that clear. I've only had one steady girlfriend, and I couldn't even manage to keep her happy. We were high school sweethearts. When college hit, we threw around the idea of taking a break. Whitney decided to go three hours south for school while I would stay home, since the University in the bordering town of Waterloo had a D1 baseball team. She insisted we could make it work. We would take turns coming to see each other, text every day, and call every night. That lasted about two weeks—hell, maybe not even that.

I'll never forget the day I drove to her campus to surprise her. She was having a bad week. It was roughly two weeks before classes were scheduled to start, and she had gone down three weeks earlier to find a job and an apartment. She said she missed me like crazy, and I bought it. The night before I decided to drive down, I had spent the evening listening to her cry on the phone, telling me that she wanted to come home and how she was going to drop out and go to school with me, but I knew SIUE was her dream. It was her parents' alma mater, and she wanted to make them proud.

I remember being excited to see her. It had only been maybe a month since we'd been apart, but that was the longest we had ever been separated. I'll never forget the moment I walked into Whitney's apartment carrying a box of flowers, chocolates, and Tai food, only to find her legs wrapped around another man's back as he pounded into her on the couch. I literally walked in while she was screaming his fucking name. Turns out those weren't tears of sorrow she called with. They were tears of regret.

When I slammed the box on the table to make my presence known, the guy whose name I had learned by hearing my girlfriend scream it through her orgasm proceeded to tell me Alyssa and Carrie, Whitney's new roommates, weren't home. The fucker had no idea who I was, which meant he had no idea Whitney had a boyfriend. This wasn't a one-time, weak moment fuck. No, this was her guy. As I stood there, frozen to the spot, furious, hurt, and wrecked, he tucked himself back into his pants and said, "Baby, why don't we take this to the other room."

Looking back, I think I was supposed to punch him. But the damage had already been done. There was no point. The trust was gone, so there was nothing left for me. We were done. I didn't need closure, I didn't need a fight, and I didn't want her back. What's messed up is, she didn't even run after me. There were no texts, no calls—nothing. I was nothing.

My breakup with Whitney hit me hard for a long time. Not so much because of how it ended, but how it made me feel. She was my first kiss, my first fuck, and what I thought was my first love, but looking back, it wasn't love. We were slaves to our raging hormones, addicted to fucking, and too dumb to know the difference. I was done with letting people too close. Close equaled feelings, and feelings were a weakness that could be exploited.

Before I have any more time to walk down memory lane and remind myself of all the reasons I'm not stepping foot in that bar, my logic is shattered. I'm still leaning against the front of the building when Kristine comes waltzing out the front door, arm slung around Aria's shoulder, laughing as she pulls her down the street, probably in pursuit of Hagerty's Pub.

Of course, they would be walking in the opposite direction, giving me a perfect view of Aria's apple-bottom-jean-clad ass. While her legs are toned, that ass is the perfect combination of muscle and yum. Don't even get me started on the fact that she's wearing black fuck-me stilettos with a tight long-sleeve black lace top that looks more like lingerie than a shirt. Shit. I haven't even seen her face, and I'm obsessed. I catch a side view of her face as she whips her blonde hair over her shoulder to look back at everyone following them out of the bar to Hagerty's, my mind is made.

# 4

## NOT RUNNING

ARIA

We've been here for about two hours, and there's still no sign of Holden. I'm starting to wonder if he's going to show. I'd be lying if I said my stomach hasn't been in knots all night at the prospect of meeting him. I don't even know the guy, but he seems nice and genuine from the few messages we've shared. Sure, he is a little cocky, but I've yet to meet a man who isn't. Of course, none of that seems to matter now because it appears he's going to be a no-show. Honestly, it's probably for the best. I have too much baggage right now as it is.

"Aria, come to the bathroom with me." Kris is already getting wasted, as she should. You only turn twenty-one once, but I can tell Kyla is about done with this scene. When I glance in her direction to ensure she's cool hanging back while I run to the restroom, she gives me an eyeroll, which I take to mean whatever. Hopping off the bar stool I've taken up residence on since we arrived, I follow Kris back to the ladies' room.

"So what do you think about Gabe? Isn't he freaking hot? I love him. I haven't told him that, but I do. I know it's only been two months, but I know we're going to get married." Luckily, she is in a stall peeing as she tells me all this, so she misses the smirk and head shake that automatically occurs without thought at her young, naive heart. I'm only a few months older than her, but she must have led a very sheltered life to be so careless with her heart. Doesn't everyone know a young heart is raw and exposed? It hasn't even learned to protect itself, so it is pointless to pursue love. Clearly, I don't express this. I'm not trying to be a killjoy, so I ignore the last half of her word vomit.

"He seems super nice, and as far as hot goes, I'd rather not step into that steaming pile of dog shit. That's your man, not mine." If I told her the truth, I would be an asshole. Gabe does indeed seem super nice, but as for the rest, I'd pass. He reminds me of the popular athlete in high school who got all the girls and was too focused on partying and having a good time to set any real-life goals for himself. Now, he's meandering through life with no direction, taking odd jobs here and there, working for friends because he never went to college or tried to apply himself to anything. Gabe is your typical always-up-for-a-good-time guy, forever on the hunt for the next party. Since Kris has a similar personality, I see why she's drawn to him. She loves having a good time, but that would eventually get old for me. Gabe is definitely not my type.

Kris stumbles out of the stall on her wedges, and I catch her by the waist before she falls. Helping her over to the sink, I try to snap her out of the drunken haze threatening to take root sooner than she's ready for.

"How about you splash some water on your arms and chest? It will help clear the fog." She looks at me quizzically before doing exactly as I suggest.

"You know, you obviously haven't had enough to drink if you're giving me tips on how to sober up. This means you owe me a round of shots when we head back out."

"Oh, well, then I take it back. Don't splash water on your chest. I freaking hate shots."

Her index finger flies into my chest as she says, "Too late. Maybe you should have thought about that before you started acting like my grandma."

The next thing I know, she's pulling me out of the bathroom and to the bar, where she orders a round of Alabama shooters. I have no idea what the hell I'm about to drink, but it's red and full of bad decisions. If there's one thing I am not, that is a shot taker. I am a lightweight through and through, and this shot is a promised horrible decision.

After throwing back my shot, Kyla steps up behind me and thrusts a bottle of water into my hand. "Drink this. Now." Wow, I think I would have been better off coming alone. I had no idea she would be this much of a buzzkill. However, I don't want to cut out on Kris, so I appease Kyla and down the water bottle in one go while Kris has her back to me. When she snaps back around, I hold the empty bottle behind my back to hide the evidence and, surprisingly, Kyla does me a solid and takes it.

Looping her arm through mine, Kris calls out, "Hagerty's!" before winding us through the crowd, toward the exit. I guess we're heading to our second stop of the night.

As we make our way down the cobblestone street, I immediately regret my choice of footwear. I've never been to downtown Rose Bud, but it has that old-town riverside vibe. It reminds me that while I feel far away from home, I'm not. Cobblestone streets can be found throughout old historic towns in and around St. Louis. At one point, Kris wobbles on her wedges yet again, and I grab her hips to steady her. I may have downed a bottle of water, but I'm starting to feel the shot. My body is beginning to tingle, and my mind is letting go, and it feels so good.

When we walk through the doors of Hagerty's I'm shocked to find it's a pool hall. From the outside, it looked like your standard pub, but when you walk in, there are two rows of pool tables, four to a row, with pub tables surrounding the perimeter. The bar is in the rear. Each pool table is inlaid cherry wood and lined with green felt. A three-light stained-glass chandelier accompanies every table, casting a soft glow over each one, giving the player the illusion they're in their own private space. The entire place has a speakeasy feel to it.

Making our way through the dimly lit space and toward the bar, I get a better feel of the expanse of the place. It opens up the farther back you walk. What I thought were walls are thick, red floor-to-ceiling velvet curtains that serve as room dividers. The rear of the place is lined with tufted high-back crushed red velvet booths, and the ceilings are made of what looks like aluminum tiles, which reflect the light of the gold chandeliers, which only serve to dress up the theme of the place further.

Completely enthralled with the bar's aesthetic, I hadn't even noticed that I walked over to an empty booth and sat down, only to run my hands over the alluring, crushed red velvet. It isn't until I feel the bench dip beside me that I realize what I've done. When I look up to see who's joined me, the most dazzling, pale blue eyes I've ever seen burn into my soul. I will never forget this moment for the rest of my life. Those eyes on that face are hypnotic. I have never thought a man to be beautiful, but that's precisely what the specimen sitting before me is. He is painfully beautiful, and when he says, "Hey, pretty girl," in a deep, smooth timbre, I swear my heart almost beats out of my chest.

There is no way the guy sitting before me is Holden Hayes because I thoroughly cyberstalked that guy, and he and the man before me can't possibly be the same. The man online wore nothing but athleisure, played baseball, drove a red truck, and enjoyed hunting. A country boy through and through. The guy sitting before me isn't a boy at all. He is all man, with a perfectly chiseled jaw, broad, muscular shoulders that stretch the fabric of his cotton shirt, and hands that any woman would love wrapped around her throat. I'm not even into being choked but fuck if I wouldn't let him try.

When I don't say anything back, he raises an eyebrow at me in question while simultaneously biting the corner of his bottom lip. You'd think I'd take a hint and get a grip, but I don't. There is no way in hell I could ever keep this man's attention. He could have his pick of anyone in this bar—man or woman—so there is no reason for me to play this game. We both did our part. Kris wanted us to meet, and we did. We can now check that off the list and carry on with our nights separately.

Finally breaking our stare-off, I shake my head and drop my gaze to the tabletop before me, clearing my throat and saying, "Well, Holden, as fun as this has been, I think my friend is ready to leave. Kristine can't be mad. She wanted us to meet, we met, now, if you'll excuse me—"

Grabbing my wrist, he stops me from exiting the booth, and I swear it feels like a jolt of electricity runs up my arm and through my veins. My eyes immediately zero in on his hand atop my arm, and for a second, I believe he felt it too because his eyes are trained on the same spot before they briefly crash back into mine, stealing my ability to move.

"Don't do that. Let me talk to your friend. She's the tall blonde by the bar talking to Trent, right?" He must notice how my brow has furrowed at his ability to pick out the friend I brought with me tonight. I don't even need to question how he knows her because, in the next breath, he's adding, "It's a small town; newbies stick out." As he slides out, he bites that deliciously plump bottom lip again before saying, "And I may or may not have spent the last three days stalking your profile." Flashing a panty-dropping grin, he throws me a wink and heads to the bar. *Damn it.*

This is so not good. I've never experienced this type of attraction to someone in my life. Sure, I've heard it exists, but for the most part, I thought it was something Hollywood made up to sell movies. Who doesn't swoon all over a hot guy who seductively fawns all over the leading lady the first time he meets her? This is absolutely absurd, and I know it. The problem is, I'm not good at stopping crashes before they happen. I'm really good at watching though. With my head literally in my hands, I massage my temples before looking back up to find Holden with his arm slung over Kyla's shoulder. Great, he's even able to schmooze over the girl that hates everything.

At least with his back to me, I can study his profile without his eyes setting me on fire. I know he's an athlete, but fucking hell, the man has to do more than just train. He has a perfect bubble butt, trim waist, and what I'm sure is one of the sexiest backs you have ever seen, judging by how his cotton shirt hugs every muscle and every dip. All these feelings are so new to me. While I've had boyfriends and I'm not a virgin, I don't think I've ever been this attracted to someone I've dated. I'm sitting here fantasizing about running my hands up his back and around his front, when he looks over his shoulder and catches me openly gawking. *Damn it.* He smiles as if pleased that he caught me looking before grabbing two beers off the bar and heading my way.

I expect him to taunt me for checking him out, but he doesn't. Instead, he slides back into the booth and places a light beer in front of me.

Taking the beer, I spin it in my hands before picking at the label and trying to tamp down my ugly, misplaced thoughts.

"Damn, I should have asked if you liked beer. What do you want? I'll change it out."

The sincerity in his voice should be enough, but it doesn't stop my stupid mouth from asking, "Is there a reason you bought me a light beer?" I regretted the words before they even left my lips.

Without pause, he shakes his head before saying, "Honestly, it's been a minute since I bought a girl a drink, and I was hoping my favorite might be yours too." He spins his bottle so that the label is facing me and, sure enough, we have the same beer.

When his brilliant blue eyes land on mine, my heart stumbles and my breath hitches, stealing my ability to recall whatever absurdity I was letting consume me seconds ago. The attraction I have for this man is certifiable. His penetrating gaze has me nervously biting my lip, and when I do, his eyes dart to my mouth before he leans in and asks, "What are the chances I can get you to take a walk with me?"

I hold his gaze for a beat, somehow feeling incredibly exposed. I can't tell if he knows the effect he's having on me or if I just feel like an open book because of how insanely nervous I am. Unsure and not wanting to come off as desperate or overly interested, I sidestep and don't give him a response. "Is there something wrong with this booth?"

"You're not going to make this easy, are you?" That snaps me out of my lust-induced coma and back to reality. I was right. He thought I was going to be an easy hookup.

"No, I'm going to make it extremely easy." I grab my beer and slide out before he has time to register my movement. "Have a good night, Holden."

The minute I'm out of the booth, I make my way over to where Kyla is standing with Trent but am intercepted by Kris before I ever make it there. Linking her arm through mine, she says, "To the bathroom." This time, we're accompanied by two of Kris's other friends who I haven't met.

"Okay, spill. So how's it going? Do you like him? Isn't he hot?" My eyes practically bug out at the number of questions she hits me with all at once.

"Is he hot as hell? Girl, yes, I'm not blind. Do I like him? Doesn't matter. I'm not the girl he's looking for tonight." I gesture with my hand toward her friends before adding, "So if any of you want to take your shot, be my guest." I'm expecting them to start with fifty questions, but instead, they all just stand there looking at me. That's when I realize they're not looking at me but past me. When I turn my head to see what's so amusing, I find Holden propped up in the doorway with a shit-eating grin on his face.

"So you think I'm hot as hell? I can work with that."

*Great.* Now I'm completely mortified. I let out a huff of frustration before storming out of the bathroom, where I need to duck under Holden's arm to exit. This time, I don't even bother finding Kyla. I just head toward the front. I need to get out of here. I need air.

When I burst through the front doors and onto the sidewalk, the cool night air immediately pimples my skin. This could be one of the last cool nights of the year before summer hits full force. Needing to put more distance between myself and the bar, I slip off my heels and jog across the street to an empty bench. I need to collect myself. The thought of how transparent I felt prior to Holden hearing my verbal confirmations is just embarrassing.

I'm not sure what I expected going into tonight, but it sure as hell wasn't the man who showed up. I didn't know how to act within that booth. It was like all my insecurities were on full display. I needed to get away, take a breath, and refocus. My sickness is good at stealing all the better parts of me, and that's precisely what it was doing inside with Holden. It was picking me apart, and in doing so, I felt like Holden could see all the parts of me I hid from the world. Every guy I've dated has been part of my past. There was security in that. I felt I could hide behind the old me and pretend because they knew me before I was tormented. I don't think I could hide from Holden. His gaze is to knowing.

Sitting on the bench, I draw up my legs and hug them before taking a deep breath and looking up at the night sky. You can see all the stars in Rose Bud, and it's breathtaking. Sometimes, Mother Nature has a way of grounding you and putting things into perspective by reminding you how small you really are in this world. I am one tiny dot on the map in the grand scheme of things, and tonight is but one small blemish on the story of my life. It doesn't make any of tonight less embarrassing, but it does help me pull in the strength not to let it get worse. I'm in control here. I can't let my crazy get the best of me.

The sound of the front doors opening across the street brings my gaze out of the clouds and to the bar, where they collide with the stormy blue abyss in the eyes of the most gorgeous man I've ever seen. This man is going to wreck me. I feel it in my bones. It won't matter if I give him one night or ten. He's the man you never get over. The one who, if you don't marry him, will forever be in the back of your mind as *the one that got away*, your *what if*.

I fully expected him to walk across the street to join me, but instead, he takes a seat on the curb across from me. Silently staring. Communicating with his lack of action rather than with words. He's not going to chase me, but he's interested and letting me make the call. I can hold my ground and not give an inch, and this will end here—or I can give in and let the hurricane that is Holden Hayes take me out to sea.

Mind made up, I pick up my shoes from the bench, opting to keep them off. I'm not drunk by any means but buzzed enough, and I don't care to faceplant from walking on the cobblestone streets in heels. When I stand, I don't bother glancing back at Holden. He'll either pick up on my invitation or he won't. He is the one who asked for a walk. I start making my way up the street, destination unknown, when I hear the heavy footsteps of Holden jogging up behind me.

"You know, when I asked if you'd take a walk with me earlier, I saw it playing out a lot differently in my head."

I can't help but smirk at his antics. I'm not an idiot. Clearly, he's trying to make light of my dramatics, and it's working, but he's not the guy you show all your cards to.

"Hey, you should just be glad you're getting it."

He feigns offense, throwing his hand over his heart. "Look, I wasn't trying to infer that you were easy back there. I was only trying to get out of the spotlight. Every guy there wanted to see me fail so they could swoop in and steal the hottest girl at the bar while every chick was waiting for a proposal."

That last part makes me laugh out loud. He is not wrong about every girl wanting to see a declaration of love. They pounced the minute I showed up at the bar. He bumps into my shoulder and says, "If I'm making you laugh, I can't be that bad." When I glance over at him, he's biting his lip again. At this point, I believe he's doing it to tease me.

I don't give him any words because he already heard my confessions in the bathroom. He knows what I think. We walk in silence for a few minutes before I stop and look around to see how far I've strayed from the bar. When I look behind me, we've walked maybe two blocks, and because the entire downtown

Main Street is only roughly five blocks, we are now just standing on the corner. We'll be heading into a small park if I cross the street. If I turn around and head back toward the bar, I'm giving up whatever alone time this is right now. While it may be drenched in silence, it's some of the best silence I've ever had.

Holden's energy flows off him in waves, and when I don't let my mind twist the narrative, I can't help but feel like it matches my own. He's just as entranced as I am. It's a connection I never could have imagined were I not living it right here, right now. I was meant to meet him. Yes, I am unequivocally attracted to this man, but I also feel like he is mine. *Does it count as crazy if I know I'm fucking crazy?*

With indecision clearly written all over my face, I risk a glance at Holden, knowing his beautiful eyes will consume me the moment I do and any small grasp I might have held on the reality of this situation will dissipate. When I look up, his hands are loosely pushed into the front pockets of his jeans, suggesting he's relaxed, but his face is pensive as he intently studies me.

The sound of tires squealing down the street draws our attention toward the bar. A group of people has piled into the back of a truck bed, now heading our way. As the truck nears, I can see it's Kris and her friends, and fucking Kyla is driving. When she sees me standing on the corner with Holden, she glares at me, and, like usual, I can't tell if she's pissed or happy for me. Either way, I jog over to the truck. There are no other cars on the street, so it's not like I'm making my way into a busy intersection. It's a four-way stop in the middle of a backroads country town in Illinois.

"Hey, I'm driving these guys up to Gabe's. Apparently, he only lives right around the corner." She motions up the street, but if she says anything else, I don't catch it because my body is suddenly aware of the man at my back. I'm caged in as Holden leans into the truck window to catch Gabe's ear.

"Bro, meet us at my place," is all I hear before my mind stops functioning as Holden's hand rests on my hip. It's not meant to be seductive, but my body breaks out in a shiver all the same—

and damn it if I don't want to lean in for more. He says something back to Gabe as I stand rooted in place, my head slightly turned, examining his side profile. Seriously, the man's jaw looks like it's been chiseled out of stone. It's perfectly square and strong, only accentuating his high cheekbones.

Again, he catches me staring, but this time when he gives me that sexy-as-hell smile, he squeezes my hip, sending delicious tendrils of heat throughout my core. I suck in a nervous breath before he pounds his hand on the truck door, simultaneously drawing me out of my trance and signaling for Kyla to take off. His eyes briefly search my face before the hand he has on my hip slides around to my lower back, and he guides me out of the street. When we reach the sidewalk, he drops his hand from my back, and I know he doesn't miss the way my eyes follow his arm's decent back to his side.

"Pretty girl, you're going to have to stop looking at me like that."

Drawing my head back in confusion, I ask, "How am I looking at you?" This is my lame attempt at trying to play it cool. I know I'm looking at him like a lovesick fool.

"You're looking at me like you don't hate me as much as you've led me to believe."

My eyes widen, and I start stammering, "I...What? I never said that."

He knowingly smirks before nodding his head toward the bar. "Come on, let's go get my truck, and we'll meet up with everyone back at the house."

I look down at my feet and decide I'm probably sobered up enough that I can manage to put my heels back on and walk without falling. Setting my shoes on the ground, I'm just about to step in when Holden steals them. "Hey, what are you doing? I was just going to put those back on."

"As much as I love seeing you in these heels, I'd rather give you a ride." And with one sentence, my mind goes straight into the gutter. Maybe that's because any words that ever come out of that mouth couldn't be anything less than sexy. My face heats from his word choice, and he notices.

"That's a dirty mind you have there, but that's not the kind of ride I'm talking about." Bending down, he says, "Climb on." He wants me to get on his back.

"Holden, that is not necessary. I can walk. I'm fine."

Looking up, he thins his lips, holding back a smile before saying, "I'm sure you can, but maybe I want another excuse to touch you." I think my heart managed to do literal flips in my chest at that.

"Come on, Aria. I'm not going to take no for an answer." My brow lifts at the use of my actual name. I was wondering if maybe he had forgotten what it was. "And don't even start with any girly crap about being too heavy. I'm twice your size; I think I can handle it."

"Fine, have it your way." He smiles like he just won a prize as I walk around him to climb on. Fuck me. The man is solid muscle. That back I was checking out in the bar is not disappointing. I can feel every defined peak and valley, and his narrow waist has me salivating. With my legs wrapped around his middle, I can tell he has those well-defined hip bones that most likely lead to the distinct, delicious V that I find incredibly sexy on a man.

When he stands with ease, I don't miss how he hikes me up higher onto his back and squeezes my thighs a little tighter than necessary. *Damn it.* I'm so turned on. That's when a whiff of his cologne hits me, and I'm a goner. The man smells salty fresh. His cologne has hints of what I know are bergamot and patchouli because they remind me of the beach. The few times we've taken a summer vacation to the beach, the hippie shops were always burning something similar to these scents, and it does nothing but incite happy memories for me.

"Are you smelling me, pretty girl?" His face is suddenly next to mine, and it takes me a minute to calculate how that happened. Oh my god. I was so entranced in his smell that I leaned into his neck to get a better whiff. Lightning, please come down and strike me dead now.

Quickly, I pull back before saying, "Pfft, no. Why would I do that?"

That earns me a chuckle before he says, "Too bad. I kind of liked your face nestled into my neck." Yeah, me too.

Before I have time to process that admission, we're at his truck, where he's setting me down and handing me my shoes. I make sure to give him zero eye contact in the process. This night has me entirely out of sorts, and I need to stop embarrassing myself. Setting my shoes on the ground, I step into them, resting one hand on the front of his truck to steady myself as I do.

Once my shoes are on, I do my best not to meet his eyes. I begin looking around as if I'm searching for my car, knowing damn well it's five spots down, before adding, "Well, thanks for the ride. My car is right over there." I awkwardly hike my thumb over my shoulder while looking past him as if there is something behind him that has my attention. But, of course, he notices. Glancing over his shoulder, he looks to see what has me thoroughly captivated, only to find nothing; his returning expression is nothing short of amused.

"Man, my ego is really starting to take a hit tonight. I don't think I've ever had a girl try as hard to sidestep me as you have in the last hour. Tell me, Aria, what does a guy have to do to get your undivided attention?"

When my eyes meet his, I see the sincerity in his words, and damn it if I don't want to give him my undivided attention.

"Fine. You win. I don't have my keys anyway, Kyla does." I waltz over to the passenger's side door of his lifted red Ford truck and let myself in. Once inside, I examine the interior. It's surprisingly clean for a guy, and smells like his earthy cologne, which is fucking intoxicating. A cross hangs from his rearview mirror, a can of mints sits in one of his cup holders, and his baseball bag is at my feet.

Upon climbing in, he says, "So tell me, Aria, what were you able to learn from thoroughly examining my truck?"

I can't help but roll my eyes. This guy barely knows me, yet somehow, he knows exactly what makes me tick. "You like fresh breath."

He barks out a laugh before saying, "Really, that's it?"

"Okay, I'll play. Your truck is too clean to indicate that you have much of a social life." Kicking the bag at my feet, I add, "Probably because you spend all your time playing ball, going to class, and, I assume, working. The cross tells me you have something you don't want to forget." I won't elaborate on what I think that something might be, but from my experience, wearing a cross, displaying a cross, or even tattooing a cross on your person, typically means there is a more profound purpose behind the display than faith alone. Sometimes faith, and faith alone, is the sole driver, but more often than not, it's because a person has experienced pain, tragedy, or deep loss that has touched the depths of their soul in a way that can only be represented by a symbol meant to reference something not of this world. My analysis must have held some grain of truth because he's quiet as he stares out the front windshield.

This is typical Aria form, inserting my foot in my mouth to a stranger. While I know I can be very forward, it's never my intent to offend. My delivery is what screws me every time. Reaching across the console, I lay my hand on top of his before saying, "Hey, I'm sorry. I didn't mean to overstep, make assumptions, or judge. I just—"

He cuts me off, finishing the sentence for me. "Don't apologize for understanding; not many do." He drops his gaze to where my hand sits on top of his before flipping his own over only to interlace our fingers. The move is incredibly intimate, and I can't help the goosebumps that trail up my arm from his touch. Luckily, I'm wearing long sleeves, or I would be revealing more than I'm ready to admit to myself.

With his left hand, he pushes the ignition button and fires up his truck. I move to pull my hand away so he can drive, but instead of letting me retreat, he gently squeezes it, silently communicating that he doesn't want to let me go. That simple move has me feeling like a schoolgirl with her first crush, because —aside from my first crush—a man has never made me feel this way, and I'm hooked.

We drive in silence the short distance it takes us to get to Gabe's place. The quiet doesn't bother me like it does some people. You can tell when someone feels incredibly uncomfortable with silence, but with Holden, it almost feels natural. We don't even know one another, yet we aren't rushing to ask the other twenty questions just to fill an imaginary void most people feel obligated to when someone isn't speaking. Or at least that's how I feel, and if I don't let my sick mind get carried away, that's how I should leave it—but I'm nothing if not a glutton for punishment.

This has been one of the fundamental problems in all my relationships, romantically or otherwise. I presume to know what the other person must be thinking based on how I'm feeling. Right now, I'm telling myself there is no way the hot-as-sin man sitting across from me feels a morsel of the attraction or connection that I do. I'm turning this man who doesn't want to let go of my hand while driving into the bad guy simply by overanalyzing our shared silence.

When the car comes to a stop, and Holden cuts the engine, I immediately hop out. I'm not running; really, I'm not. I just need air.

## 5

# ALL OR NOTHING

HOLDEN

We've all done it: spent too much time focusing on all the things that could go wrong, all the *what ifs,* and typically, we let all those possibilities talk us out of doing what's imprinted on our hearts. That inner dialogue can be a gift or a curse. Mine has been the bane of my existence for the past four years. I try to take it in stride because at least I'm here and not buried six feet in the ground. The problem is, I no longer feel like just existing is worth it. I want more. I need more. And tonight, I'm taking something for myself.

When Connor came strolling out of the bar with two beers in hand, just as I started heading toward Hagerty's, he asked, "Have you changed your mind, bro? Let me guess; you didn't miss that ass when she came out, did you?"

His comment was innocent enough—no big deal—but the salty taste it left in my mouth by the insinuation that Aria was just a hot piece of ass gave me pause. I wanted to say, *Don't fucking talk about my girl like that*, but I didn't, because one, she's not my girl, and two, I don't know if I want her to be. I'm not the guy she needs. So I kept my reply short, "Yeah, something like that."

However, the more he talked, the more possessive I became. "Gabe and I had to keep Trent and Jeremy off her all night. You're lucky she's not already wrapped around one of them." The visual then and now still has me clenching my fists. While I'm not ready to claim Aria, I also know I wouldn't be able to handle seeing another guy touch her.

When I entered the pool hall, I didn't immediately see Aria. Still, the second I spotted her sitting on the red velvet booth, utterly oblivious to anyone or anything else, I swear my feet moved of their own accord. The next thing I knew, I was sitting in the booth with the most captivating woman I've ever laid eyes on. I hadn't even seen her face or those haunted eyes yet, but I was already inexplicably enamored.

The second her big brown eyes snapped to mine, my heart stumbled. I already knew Aria was beautiful, but those haunted eyes... those eyes shook me to my core and stole a piece of my fucking soul. I could get lost in those eyes for hours, trying to take the pain and replace it with everything I guarantee she doesn't see in herself. Something tells me she is nothing if not unaware of just how striking she is. I know from her social media profile that she's four years younger than me, putting her right at twenty-one. She hasn't experienced enough of the real world to find her value, but I'll be damned if I don't want to give her every second of my time, showing her just how perfect she is.

I wouldn't consider myself a cocky motherfucker, but I know I'm attractive. I've never met a girl I couldn't have. That's not always a good thing; most of the time, I'm judged for it. People assume, based on how I look, that I can't possibly be the settling down type, the relationship type, because I'm too busy being a man whore. Half the reason I always wear athleisure is so I don't come off like a preppy, pretentious prick. Most of the women I attract are fake—the type of women who are superficial and only give a shit about my looks and a quick fuck.

Aria is my type to a tee, from looks to personality. From the texts we've exchanged, I know she doesn't take shit, and from the way her eyes locked on mine like I would be her worst fucking mistake, I knew I had to have her. I wanted nothing more than to close the mere inches between us and suck the flavor of her candy-pink lip gloss right off her perfect mouth. I wanted to be her mistake as much as she would be every bit of mine.

As much as my superstition wants to believe that fate landed me here because I was meant to meet Aria, my track record tells me to run for the hills because she doesn't deserve the world of hurt that I would inevitably bring her. But at what point have I served my penance? Maybe she's the pain meant to change me because not seeing this through feels like a regret I couldn't live with.

I've just pulled up outside Gabe's when Aria bolts out of the truck. *Perfect.* She's running again. I felt her eyes on me the entire way over here. The thing is, I couldn't look at her. For as much as I don't want to let her go, I don't know that I can be anything she needs, and if I let those haunted eyes peer into my soul while her hand was in mine, I would be wrecked. *Why can't I ever just take something that I want? Why do I always have to feel so damned burdened?*

Pocketing my keys, I fully expect her to be in the house by the time I round the truck, but, surprisingly enough, she's only a few feet ahead on the sidewalk. She's hung back and is clearly waiting for me. I can tell by how she's rubbing her arms and shifting her weight that she's nervous. Aria didn't hate that I was holding her hand, but if I had to guess, she was not convinced she liked it either. Now her jumping out of my car is starting to make sense. As much as it pissed me off, I get it. She has reservations, and so do I—which is why I should be indifferent to anything in her orbit, but damn if I don't want to be caught up in everything that is Aria Montgomery.

I'm just about to catch up to her when Kristine and Mallory come charging out the front door, making a beeline straight for Aria. *Fucking hell.* Why do women have to be so catty? I have no doubt they're trying to get all the details about the two of us. Aria flashes me an apologetic glance before the girls whisk her into the house. I consider getting back in my truck and taking off, but the thought and my actions are at odds. Before I can consciously decide, my feet start heading toward the house. While I know leaving would be best, a bigger part of me wants to stay.

As soon as I enter Gabe's place, I do a quick scan for Aria and come up empty. Gabe's house isn't very big. It's a two-bedroom bungalow that he currently shares with his friend Trent. The house is the epitome of a bachelor pad. I know Gabe has been saying that Kristine has been dropping hints that she wants to move in, and while I understand not wanting to shack up with your girlfriend of two months right away, the house could benefit from a woman's touch.

The living room has a huge, big-screen TV, a state-of-the-art sound system, and a shit brown couch. They clearly blew their budget on the entertainment system and forgot about the rest of the space, because behind the couch is a ping-pong table and dartboard. The dartboard isn't even hung on a wall. It's hung on the back of the front door, which is super-inconvenient, considering anytime someone is coming or going, it jacks up the game. Trent insists that's the point. I don't fucking get it, but I don't have to. I'm not the one living here. Making my way toward the hallway that leads to the kitchen, downstairs bedroom, and bathroom, I still don't find Aria.

The kitchen is just as plain as the living room. This place probably hasn't been updated since the late 90s. It's an L-shaped design with fake granite Formica countertops. All the appliances are old-school, off-white, and dead center in the middle of the kitchen is a six-person patio set that they use as their kitchen table. Currently, everyone is gathered around playing poker and smoking blunts. Heading toward the fridge, I'm on a mission to grab a beer. I have no plans on getting wasted tonight by any means, but I'd love to catch a buzz and get out of my head.

"Hayes, so what's good, bro? You tapping that ass tonight or what?" With my beer in hand, I turn toward Trent and take a long pull, holding his eyes as I do. I'm not going to disrespect him in his own house, but I also need to make sure he understands I'm not fucking around. Sometimes words aren't required, but I also don't know him well enough to judge his character. Gabe met him through one of his side jobs. He's new in town, a drifter of sorts, and from the few interactions we've had, I don't care for him.

I think he gets the hint, but then he fucks up. "It's cool, man. I just needed to know if I should join her in my bedroom or not." I'm across the kitchen in no time, ready to pound his face in when Gabe pops up out of his seat and stops me before I make contact.

"Fuck, Holden, what's your problem? He's just messing with you. Dude, take a hit or something. You need to calm down." That's always been Gabe's personality flaw. He's too trusting. I haven't taken my eyes off Trent, and all I see is a slimy motherfucker I wouldn't trust around any woman.

"Come on, Holden, don't make me throw you out, bro." Gabe's still holding onto the front of my shirt when I realize I haven't backed off. I knock his hands off my shirt just as Kris and Mallory come down from upstairs. The only room up there is Trent's bedroom with an attached half bath. Immediately, I notice Aria isn't with them just as Trent steps around them to head up.

"Kristine, where's Aria? I thought she was with you."

Shrugging, she says, "She was, but we had to pee and do some things, and she didn't want to join."

That's when I realize I haven't seen Kyla either. I'm about to head upstairs and see if there is any merit to Trent's threat when I hear female laughter coming from the living room right before the base to Gorilla Zoe's "Juice Box" fills the entire house, drowning out any other noise. Grabbing my beer off the counter, I make my way to the living room. Blonde hair immediately catches my eye from the couch, but the color is all wrong. It's Kyla's and not Aria's. That's when the laughter hits my ears again, and I see Aria throwing her head back in a fit of hysteria as Connor pops his ass for her, acting like a complete idiot, doing his best Magic Mike impression. He's not too bad. I can see why Aria finds it amusing.

It isn't until he moves to put his hands on her hips that my feet take me across the room. Unlike Trent, I know Connor isn't going to try and make a move. He's a flirt, but that's about it. Connor doesn't have any issues landing girls. Same as me, he sticks to one-night stands. I've never asked why, and I don't need to. Usually, when people keep others at arm's length, there's a reason. I haven't decided if his reason is as dark as mine. Either way, when he moves to put his hands on her, I see red. I'm two steps away when he sees me and throws his hands in the air saying, "I'm out, Ari, baby. Catch you later."

I can't help how my brows pinch together or how my lips thin at the friendly exchange. It shouldn't bother me that they are getting along, but it does. It agitates me because that should be us right now. I should be calling her Ari, baby, and mine. *Shit.* Rubbing my jaw, I try to get a grip, but when she steps into me and rubs her thumb between my eyes saying, "Don't get me wrong, those moves were sexy, but I'd rather see them from you," she's smiling, trying hard to stifle a laugh I know she wants to let out as she delivers the message.

Nothing about her comment is meant to be seductive. My pretty girl is messing with me, and I'll be damned if I'm not a sucker for it. The way I can feel my heartbeat pounding in my ears and my blood rushing through my veins just from her touch tells me I want everything. I want her tears when she's sad, her smiles when she's happy, and that pretty mouth when she's feeling feisty. I want it all. Reaching out, I place my hands on her hips and pull her against me. I'm not messing around anymore. I want her.

The move catches her off guard, and her eyes widen in surprise, her gaze locked on mine. I almost lose it when she subtly bites the corner of her bottom lip. She is so fucking sexy.

Every guy in the room notices her, and she has no idea. I know she's unsure about me. Most likely, she has reservations. I have no doubt she feels the same way I do. I wasn't in her plans.

Hell, she tried to brush me off before we ever met, but she can't deny the chemistry we share. It's hypnotizing.

I'm just about to lean in to ask her to go outside with me when a ping-pong ball bounces off my shoulder. This time, she doesn't try to silence her laugh. Her laugh his fucking contagious. It's the only time those haunted eyes show me there's more. Jeremy comes over to collect the ball and grips my shoulder. "Sorry, man, that one kind of got away from me." He swats my ass with the paddle hard right as Aria steals my beer from my hand and takes a long pull. *Damn, that's sexy.* I want to let her keep it, but I also want to take it back just so I can taste her. I'm getting hard just thinking about it. *Shit.*

"Let's go, Hayes! Doubles, best out of seven." Jeremy shouts over the beat of the base. Before I have time to grab my beer back, Aria has already started making her way across the room to where Kyla is posted up on the couch, looking like she's ready to bounce.

"Yeah, yeah, let's go. Let's make this quick, boys. I got shit to do."

Connor chimes in. "You wish. Not only is there a major cock block sitting on the couch, but Aria isn't one of your groupies. Hate to break it to you, bro, but my chances of—"

I serve the ball hard, effectively cutting him off. "I wouldn't finish that fucking sentence if I were you."

After collecting the ball, he returns to add, "I'm just saying, that's girlfriend material, and you are not the boyfriend type."

This time, he serves the ball back with as much force as I gave him the first time, but I don't fucking miss. "How about you let me worry about what type of material I am." I can't help but grind my teeth in irritation at his remarks, because they aren't without merit. I haven't had a girlfriend since high school.

We're one point away from winning the game when I see Aria stand up from the couch to stretch. When Kyla stands to join her, the phone in her lap drops to the ground. Without hesitation, Aria bends at the waist to retrieve it, and I'm instantly hard and a million miles away when Connor nails me in the chest with the game ball. *Shit.*

Of course, the entire table turns to see what the fuck absorbed all my attention. Every fucking guy at the table is now staring at Aria's perfect heart-shaped ass. She's got one of those asses that is toned enough to have definition but also plump enough to give it that juicy weight that makes you want to lift and squeeze. A woman with a nice ass and thick thighs is heaven to me. I've never been a boob man, but a pair of thick thighs and a bubble butt have always been a weakness of mine. Maybe it's because I feel like they can take it when I go hard. A picture of Aria on all fours with that ass in the air for me as I pound into her from behind has me adjusting myself and stepping out the front door for a breath of fresh air.

I'm not the guy that looks at women like a piece of meat. Women are the sexiest creatures God created. There's not a part on their body I don't want to worship. I have sex because I enjoy it. Period. But looking at Aria like that has me feeling some type of way, and I think it's because I know I couldn't have her just once. Running my hands through my hair, I make my way toward the maple tree in the center of the yard and lean up against it to collect my thoughts.

Unfortunately, I can't catch a break, which seems to be the theme of the night. Kyla is barging out the front door with Aria hot on her heels. "I'm tired, and Nick wouldn't like me being out this late, so it's time to go."

"Yeah, that's cool. I don't need to say bye to Kris. She's plastered enough not to miss me—or, at least, enough not to care if she notices. I'll text her tomorrow."

The two of them start walking down the sidewalk, completely oblivious to me standing only about ten feet away from them. It is dark, but there's enough light from a distant streetlamp that I don't look like some spying creeper, should they notice me. That's when Aria slaps her forehead.

"Shit. My car is still down the street. Guess we'll have to walk down."

I could stay out of sight and let her walk away. In fact, it's probably what I should do, but I don't. Instead, clearing my throat in hopes of announcing my presence without scaring them, I kick off the tree and head their way. Aria does a double take before stopping in her tracks.

"So you were just going to leave without saying goodbye." She shrugs and thins her lips, a little caught off guard by my sudden appearance. Clearly, she wasn't planning on having to explain herself face to face. I probably would have received some half-ass message with a bunch of bullshit excuses as to why she ghosted.

"I guess you heard that, then?" Kyla huffs out an exasperated sigh before saying, "Just stay here. I'll grab the car, but when I pull up, we are out. Got it?"

I watch as Aria's eyebrows shoot up at her brashness, but she takes it in stride. "Yeah, cool. Thanks for doing that."

Aria watches Kyla as she walks away. I glance in her direction briefly, ensuring she's more than an ear's shot away before saying, "Is there a reason you brought Miss Personality tonight?" Which earns me a "Pfft."

"Easy. I've only just met Kris, and I wasn't about to drive to the middle of nowhere alone."

"Oh, good. I'm relieved it's Kristine and not me." She gives me a smirk as I step closer to her. I can't take my eyes off those plump lips painted in that pink lip gloss. She rubs her arms as if she's cold before turning her gaze away from me. That's when I grab her chin and pull it back to me. When her eyes meet mine, I see it. She wants me just as much as I want her, but she doesn't want to—she's torn.

"Tell me something, Aria." Her breath hitches as I slide my hand from her chin down the base of her neck, where I leave it. When she squeezes her eyes shut, I feel like I've just crossed some invisible line for her, and I can't tell if that's a good thing or not.

"Can I see you tomorrow?" When her eyes snap open, they immediately find mine, and she relaxes as the air leaves her lungs.

"I'll think about it." She bites that plump bottom lip, teasing me before attempting to step away from my touch. But I clasp at the front of her lace shirt to keep her near. "Hey, what—" she starts, but her words quickly fall away when I lean in. With our lips only a hairsbreadth apart, I steal her breath while I struggle to find my own. When her eyes dart to my mouth, I know she's expecting me to kiss her and fuck if every ounce of my being doesn't want to, but I don't.

Instead, I kiss the corner of her mouth before placing my face in the crook of her neck, trying to rein in my desire for so much more. She brings her hands up to rest on my hips, sending a trail of heat straight to my cock. We both pull in strangled, ragged breaths of stifled desire. With my palm against her chest, I can feel her heart pounding. *Thank fuck.* That hammering in her chest lets me know she has the same intense reaction to me as I have to her.

"Holden, I'm sorry—"

I bring my finger to her mouth before pulling back. "Whatever you're about to say, just don't. I don't want your excuses about how you're not looking for a relationship, or how we could never fit, and I sure as hell don't want you to apologize for what just happened because, no, you didn't read this wrong."

She looks to the ground before asking, "So you were about to kiss me?" And fuck me if the unease and disappointment in her voice don't cut me open.

Grabbing her face in my hands, I make sure her eyes are on me when I say, "You have no idea how badly I want to kiss you. I want to do a lot of things to you right now."

Of course, because fate is a fickle bitch, Kyla pulls up, honking the horn twice. Aria brings her hands up to my wrists, still gripping her face, and asks, "Then why didn't you?" Her right hand just barely trembles, letting me know her nerves are getting the better of her. She thinks I'm letting her down easy.

I take a step in, closing the distance between our bodies before wrapping one arm around her waist and pinning her to my front so she can feel every inch of my arousal. "Just so we're crystal clear, I fucking want you." Her eyes go wide when she feels my erection against her stomach, and she bites that damn pouty lip again. "Stop teasing me, pretty girl. I'm not going to kiss you tonight."

Kyla lays on the horn one more time. *Fucking cock block. Can't she see we're having a moment? I mean, for fuck's sake.* Resting my forehead against hers, I say, "I don't think you're ready for your last first kiss, pretty girl." I place a chaste kiss on her forehead before I let her go.

As she stands there, eyes locked on mine, I can't tell what she's thinking. "Holden—" I start walking backward, effectively cutting off her response. I'm either going to see her tomorrow or I won't. She either feels me running through her veins the same way I feel her, or she doesn't. It's as simple as that. I put my cards on the table, and I'm playing for keeps.

Aria Montgomery will be my everything, or she will be nothing.

# 6

## TEASE

ARIA

"What the hell, Aria? Aren't you still dating Logan? What the fuck was all that about? Seriously, that's really shitty of you."

Buckling my seat belt, I can't help but regret my decision to bring Kyla as my ride-along. Not that Lauren would have been any better these days, but she's at least a little more fake. Rather than be direct, she would sweetly call me a slut in a roundabout way.

"Kyla, we've been over this. Logan and I stopped dating almost three months ago. Hell, he even slept with another girl—not once, but twice."

When I look over, she rolls her eyes exaggeratedly. "Yeah, well, what did you expect? You told him you wanted a break. Was he supposed to sit around and wait for you?" *Is she fucking kidding me right now?*

Now, I'm pissed. I'm so tired of men getting free passes just because they have a dick. That doesn't give them the right to sleep around, be unfaithful, have one-night stands, and god knows what else. If a woman simply has multiple boyfriends or sexual partners in a short period of time, she's a slut. It's such a double standard and one I don't subscribe to.

"Actually, yeah, if he liked me as much as he claimed to I would expect him to wait, but the fact that he didn't solidified what I already knew. He's not the guy for me. If he were, he wouldn't have felt the need to go stick it in another hole while I figured my shit out." I can't help the ire in my voice. There's no containing it. I'm so tired of feeling judged by the people who are supposed to be my friends.

"Whatever, Aria. You don't have to get so defensive. I'm just saying you shouldn't lead him on. If you're done, be done." To that, I don't even respond. She knows damn well I'm not leading him on. The man refuses to leave me alone. I've said I was done ten different ways, but he refuses to listen. If it's not his ego keeping him around, it has to be because he feels like he needs to pay a penance for sleeping around while we were on a break. Either way, I'm over it. I've been over it.

We're about ten minutes from my house when Kyla decides to speak to me again. "I will say Holden is hot as hell. I would have been all over him if I wasn't with Nick. He's a fucking lady-killer." Just the mention of his name gives me butterflies. Those piercing blue eyes are burned into my memory. I'll never forget those eyes—they were ethereal.

"Hello, Earth to Aria. Are you even listening?" I pinch the bridge of my nose, immensely perturbed with Kyla beyond measure. I've known her for three years, and I think we've hung out one-on-one maybe twice, and now I remember why. She is a grade-A bitch.

"Yeah, I heard you. You think he's hot." She glances over and gives me a once-over with a petty smile before twisting the knife.

"You know, I wasn't trying to be mean earlier. It's just you're more suited for a guy like Logan. I don't want to see you get hurt." Wow, and there it is. The truth bomb. She doesn't think I could land a guy like Holden, or if I did, I couldn't keep his attention. Her eyes said what her mouth didn't: I'm not pretty enough. Such a fucking bitch. I know I'm not a ten, but damn. At least one thing is going my way tonight. Kyla pulls into my driveway, making what I'm about to say all the more convenient. I know I should bite my tongue, but I don't.

"Kyla, look. I know we've never been best friends, but that was just cruel. I'm unsure if you're intentionally being a bitch, or just that dense and you didn't think I'd pick up on your snide undertones. Either way, while I'm in the season of taking inventory of the people I care to keep around in my life, unfortunately, you didn't make the cut."

She snaps her head back as if she can't believe I just said that. I grab my keys out of her hand and exit the car. I don't care to sit out here and have it out with her. It's not like I'm losing anything by cutting ties with Kyla. If anything, I'm doing myself a favor. I'm already my own worst enemy without hateful comments from so-called friends.

I'm walking up the pathway that winds through the yard to my parent's house when I look over my shoulder and find Kyla exiting my car. At least I don't have to worry about her messing my shit up. I don't think she's that kind of girl, but who the hell knows? Actually, I was surprised she didn't want to get into a verbal sparring match with me. Regardless, I give zero fucks, and I won't be apologizing ever.

Walking through the front door, I notice a light on in the dining room. It's 11:00 pm, and I assume my parents forgot to shut it off. Slipping my heels off, I leave them in the entryway before crossing the living room. We live in an open-concept, ranch-style home with vaulted ceilings. I love our quaint suburban home. My parents work hard for what we have, and while it's not a lot, I know there are people with a lot less.

Making my way across the room, I'm just about to hit the switch on the wall when I notice Spencer lying on the floor, papers spread out all around him. Immediately, I rush to his side and put my hand on his chest to see if he's breathing. When I feel his heart beating, I'm relieved, but I shake him awake nonetheless. "Spence, Spence, wake up. Spencer, wake up."

When his brown eyes slowly blink open, my entire body

floods with relief. "What happened? Why are you lying on the floor?" Slowly, he sits up and takes inventory of his surroundings before shoving a hand into his hair and gently tugging.

"Shit. Aria, this isn't what it looks like. I didn't have a fall or anything. I ran out of table space and then sat on the floor to spread out more work. I guess I dozed off." He runs his hand down his face, and I can see that he is clearly exhausted. That's why I worry about him. Spencer is perfectly healthy, but I fear he'll literally work himself to death. "What time is it?"

"It's a little after eleven o'clock." I stand as he raises his knees to rest his forearms on them.

"Why are you getting home so late?"

"A friend from work had a birthday party tonight—and since when is 11:00 pm on a Friday night at twenty-one late? I'm fucking pathetic, is what I am." I start walking into the kitchen to grab a water out of the fridge. Spencer decides to get off the floor and follow me in.

"Yeah, I guess you're right. Okay, then, why are you home so early?"

Opening the fridge, I notice Mom has a bowl of watermelon cut up. *Perfect*. A low-calorie snack. That's a rarity in this house. I grab it and set it on the counter before hopping up to take a seat. "Let's just say I took the wrong DD. The night wasn't a complete waste though. I have one less friend to please." I pop a piece of watermelon in my mouth and watch as he purses his lips and furrows his brow, clearly concerned at my flippant dismissal of a friend.

"Are you going to elaborate on that or..." I can't help but smile at his predictability. Honestly, for as much shit as we gave each other over the years, now that we're older, I feel like he's one of my best friends. Or at least, when he's around.

"Kyla was my DD. I think you've met her a time or two."

He rubs his jaw, trying to think through the list of friends he knows, which isn't very long. "Tall, blonde, zero personality." He snaps his fingers. "You gave ole flower the boot."

I nearly shoot watermelon out of my nose when he says that. "Ole, what? Did you just call her flower? Why the hell would you call her that?"

"She was here on your birthday before we went to the Grove. Mike and Alex came up with that nickname for her that night. When she wasn't talking, she had hardcore resting bitchface, and when she did talk, it was worse. Alex called her a wallflower, but you know how I am with accuracy. I had to explain to him how that title didn't fit, yada-yada-yada, so we shortened it to flower. Pretty to look at, and that's it."

I stuff another piece of watermelon in my mouth and talk around it. "Yeah, well, *flower* was a real bitch, and she didn't make the cut."

Opening the fridge, he grabs a water bottle and adds, "Kind of like Logan."

*Great.* Here we go. "Don't tell me you are suddenly a Logan fan. I never saw you chumming it up with him whenever the two of you would see each other."

He gives me a knowing look before saying, "I'm just giving you shit. You know I wasn't a Logan fan. He seemed nice enough, but I knew he would be short lived."

"Great, thanks for standing by and letting me date a bunch of losers."

Coming toward where I sit, he grabs a piece of watermelon. "Okay, are you saying if I told you I didn't like a guy, you wouldn't date him?"

"Good point. But you—" My phone pings in my pocket from a text. I pull it out to make sure it's not Kyla. The number is unknown, but I know precisely who it is from the preview.

Unknown: Hey, pretty girl

*How did he get my number?* We've only messaged each other back and forth through our socials. My heart does a little flip in my chest regardless.

"What the hell has you smiling like that?"

I hadn't even realized I was smiling. *Damn, I have it bad.* "Oh, it's no one." I try to play it off, but my brother's not an idiot. However, I don't want to talk about it. I'm not even sure I have anything to talk about. I hop off the counter to put the fruit back in the fridge.

"That's cool you don't want to talk about it, but whoever put that smile on your face is probably a keeper, because I can't tell you the last time I've seen you smile like that."

I close my eyes and take a deep breath, letting his words sink in. He's right. I haven't been myself, but I'm aware of it and trying to do better. Closing the fridge, I retrieve my water bottle from the counter. I know he means well, but I also don't want to get into an in-depth conversation about it. What I really want to do is get back to my room so I can read my text message from Holden.

Changing the subject to one I know will steal his attention, I say, "Do you need me to help you pick up those papers before I head to bed?"

Turning his head, he does a double take. "Shit. No, I got it." He starts heading back toward the dining room, and I'm heading down the hall when I hear him call out, "Don't think I didn't catch what you did there." I let out a small laugh because I knew he would. *Predictable.*

Once I get into my room, I close the door and start stripping out of my jeans and lace bodysuit. Making my way over to my dresser, I snap off my bra and grab an old t-shirt before pulling back my covers and climbing into bed. Opening my nightstand, I pull out a makeup remover wipe and start toweling off my face. I hate falling asleep with eye makeup on. My lashes are always stuck together in the morning. After my face is fresh, I fluff my pillows and cozy into my sheets.

Unknown: I want to see you tomorrow, pretty girl. Tell me I can.

Why do I love it so much when he calls me that? I'm lying down, and this man makes me weak in the knees. I wish I hadn't had to leave tonight. I wanted to stay so bad. As I see it now, I have two options: ignore this text, knowing nothing good can come out of going down this road with Holden, or jump in, dive in headfirst, eyes wide open, and pray that I'm wrong. Any type of relationship is the last thing I need on my plate right now. I feel like my entire life is in limbo, and I'm at some monumental crossroads that I can't seem to navigate my way out of.

My head is a complete mess, and I don't need the added anxiety and pressure of trying to please someone else added to the mix. The problem is, I want him. I'm already fucked up. I already feel broken and utterly lost. How much more damage can he cause when all that's there to work with are pieces? That settles it. I quickly program his number into my phone. He'll either accept the parts of me I have to offer and be willing to board this crazy train, or he won't. Either way, I will still be sick. I'm not foolish enough to think a guy can fix me.

Aria: I don't think you know what you're asking.

Holden: Don't mess with me, Aria. Are you saying yes?

Aria: Yes, I'll meet you. What time?

Holden: Depends. In ten minutes, it's already tomorrow. Come back?

*Damn it.* A big part of me wants to climb out of bed and do just that. This guy has me crushing hard. I want to do whatever he asks of me. It's so messed up. Rolling over, I groan into my pillow and wrangle in my voice of reason. It's almost midnight, I'm already in bed, and that would look extremely desperate and show way too many cards. I have to play hard to get to some extent. He doesn't need to know he's the hottest guy that has ever laid eyes on me—not to mention, I'm no idiot; Holden Hayes is entirely out of my league. He's the guy girls like me wish they could land but never do. But hey, I'll take a romp in the sheets. Who knows? Maybe he could be my first orgasm. Wouldn't that be the icing on the cake? First 'O' from a guy I know I'll never keep.

Holden: Does your lag in response mean you're focused on driving back to me?

Aria: No, I'm already in bed for the night.

Holden: Fucking tease. You know I'll come climb through that window, right?

Biting my lip, I look at my window and imagine him doing just that. I want him to do so many delicious things to me, but I'm going to have to call his bluff on this one.

Aria: You talk a big game for someone who wouldn't even kiss me earlier.

Holden: Pretty girl, you're playing with fire. I'll crawl through that window right now and show you just how many things I can do to that sexy body that don't require my lips on yours.

Damn, that's hot, but I'd be lying if I said I didn't want his mouth. I want every delicious piece. There's no point in wearing these panties anymore. They're fucking soaked. I've never been so turned on by a guy in my life. Just picturing him gets me wet. It's pathetic. I'm just sliding my panties off when another text comes through.

Holden: I have a rec game tomorrow 4 pm, Waterloo. Come.

Oh, I'd very much like to come. If you only knew. I've never had an orgasm. Don't get me wrong, I get extremely turned on, and I get to the precipice where you think you'll explode—but then, nothing. It's like it just goes away. The guys I've dated have been attractive. Heck, every woman thinks Logan is hot as hell. But while he's attractive, he's not my type. I mean, we all have that dream catch in our heads of what our perfect guy would look like, and mine would not be Logan. None of the guys have been it, and maybe that's the problem. Perhaps I can't get off because I need more. That, or I'm fucking broken in that area, which is something I don't want to think about. Who wants to die never having had an orgasm?

Exiting my text screen, I put Waterloo into my GPS. I have a general idea of where it's at, but I want to ensure I'm right before I commit and drive hours to the middle of nowhere. Of course, another text comes through.

Holden: Your silence is killing me.

Aria: If you'd stop texting me, I could look at the maps app to see if your request is too absurd.

To my surprise, he doesn't say anything back. No snide remarks. That's the thing I'm starting to like about him. It's like he presses all my buttons just enough to stoke the fire, only to jump in and douse it with his sexy, sweet talk. He's a fucking tease.

Aria: I'll be there. Just text me the park and field number tomorrow.

Holden: Are you sure I can't change your mind about tonight?

Aria: Goodnight, Holden.

Setting my phone down on the nightstand, I readjust my pillows and fluff them back up again. I'm very particular about getting into a made bed with a fluffy pillow. Sleep is the one thing in life that I look forward to. I'm able to get comfortable, shut off reality, and recharge. Picking up my phone, I switch it to silent mode. It's Friday night, and I don't want anyone disturbing me at 2:00 am with drunk texts. I've just set my phone back down on the nightstand when it lights up. The last thing I read before my head hits the pillow is:

Holden: Sweet dreams, pretty girl.

After my head hit the pillow last night, I didn't wake up until 9:00 am today. I feel freaking amazing, aside from the anxious knot in my stomach over seeing Holden in an hour.

I've just finished straightening my hair and applying lip gloss and mascara when I head to my closet to pick out an outfit for the day. Weekends are my only exception to my rule of laying clothes out in advance. After all, I have time to scrutinize. Luckily, it's still nice spring weather and not too hot. I think the high today will only be around eighty degrees Fahrenheit, which isn't bad if there is no humidity. Growing up with an older brother who played every sport, I'm no stranger to a baseball field. I actually enjoy going to ball games, and I'm sure watching Holden's fine ass run around the bases won't be a disappointment.

All morning, I've gone back and forth on my outfit. Look cute in case we do something after the game or just rock some athleisure? As much as I want to dress up and look good, I want to be comfortable and not look like I'm trying too hard. That's it; mind made up, I grab a white t-shirt, my black joggers, and a pair of white Converse. I'm not sure what these fields will be like, so I grab my baseball cap and sunglasses, along with my fanny pack, because those are coming back and I love them. My style is very laid-back when I'm not at the office. While I love my nice wardrobe for work, I am most comfortable in precisely what I'm wearing.

I'm just heading out the front door to my car when my phone chimes. Pulling my pack around, I grab my phone and see it's from Logan.

Logan: Hey, I'll be at your place in ten minutes.

*Crap.*

See, this is what I hate about Logan. It's like he never thinks about me and what I want. You can't just show up out of nowhere and expect someone to drop everything or rearrange their plans because you decided you wanted to hang out. This isn't a new thing for him either. He's always been this way. Initially, it felt cute, like a surprise gesture, but as time passed, I realized it was never intended to be that way. He showed up when it was convenient for him or when he didn't have better plans. So over time, his surprise visits were just one more thing for me to add to the list of reasons he wasn't the guy for me.

Aria: I'm not home.

Quickly, I jog over to my car and make sure that's true before we end up passing each other out of the subdivision. That would be just my luck. Regardless of whether or not anything happens between Holden and me, I know I don't ever want to be intimately involved with Logan again. While I've told him in so many ways I was done, he just won't let me go for some reason.

Logan: When are you going to be home? I can wait.

*Shit. Why didn't I see that coming?*

Aria: I just left. I won't be home until late. Sorry.

Logan: Why do I feel like you're avoiding me?

This is precisely what I'm talking about. It's always about him. It couldn't be that he hasn't texted or called me since Monday when he left my office. Then he decides to show up out of nowhere unannounced, and now I'm the one avoiding him. I need to focus on driving, and honestly, this needs to stop.

Aria: I'm not avoiding you, but there is no us anymore. Just let me go.

No sooner do I get on the highway than my phone rings. It's Logan. I need my phone on for the GPS, but I also don't want Logan blowing me up nonstop until I answer. Quickly, I make a rash decision to turn it off. Hopefully, if he hears it going to voicemail, that will deter him. I vaguely know where I am going for at least another thirty minutes. I'll wait until then to turn my phone back on.

After driving for half an hour, I see the sign that says Waterloo next exit. Turning my phone back on, I ignore the missed calls and texts. There is no point in reading them. Logan couldn't say anything that would make me change my mind. It's been set since the day I asked for the break.

Pulling into the parking lot, I immediately spot Holden's lifted red truck. Unfortunately, there is nowhere to park near his truck, and I end up on the opposite side of the parking lot. Scanning the park, I notice there are very few trees for shade. We are definitely in southern Illinois. Nothing but flat farmland for miles with a baseball field plunked down in the middle. Reaching for my hat, I pull it on before getting out of my car and heading toward his truck. I'm assuming field six must be over there.

This morning, when I woke, I had a message from him

waiting that read, "Good morning, pretty girl. Krauss Athletic Association. Field 6." I never said anything back. I debated it all day, but I'm sure he saw I read it, and if he understands me the way I think he does, then he knows I'll show. If the way he makes me feel goes both ways, even in the slightest, there's no way I wouldn't. I'm hooked.

The minute I breach the car line and find field six, my eyes immediately find Holden. He's running through the outfield to catch a pop fly, which he doesn't miss, before throwing the ball into second base for an out. Damn, he looks hot in a uniform. The way his white pants stretch across his strong thighs should be a sin. No one should look that good. When he turns to run back to his outfield position and I get a view of that ass, I stop dead in my tracks. Sure, last night he was fine as wine, but today he's a god. That ass. That's the type of ass you sink your fucking nails into while he's pounding you into tomorrow. *Shit.* I need to get my act together. I'm about to head for the bathroom when someone calls out my name.

Spinning around, I find Connor jogging up to meet me where I stand, looking like a deer caught in headlights. I don't know if I look as awkward as I feel, but I feel incredibly out of place for some reason. That could be because I just had pornographic visions of Holden flipping through my head, or it's just my sickness getting the best of me, telling me I'm lame, I'm a nobody, and I sure as hell can't keep the attention of that gorgeous man out there.

"Hey, Aria, Holden said you might show up. Why are you standing over here? Come join Trent and me on the bleachers. I have an ice-cold beer with your name all over it." Connor is seriously so sweet. He's the kind of guy I should go for. He's got that typical boy-next-door vibe going on. The one where he's going to be your best friend, the one you sneak out your window at night to hang out with and literally do nothing else. Then, before you know it, he sneaks up on you and steals your heart.

Connor has that hair that's long on top and perfectly styled before it starts to curl from being on the verge of too long. His eyes are deep brown and highlighted by brows that make it look like he is always one hundred percent invested in what you are saying. Don't even get me started on his sexy little dimple. He's a catch. Not to mention, he's funny. I was dying last night when he started busting a move on me. When he catches me staring, he gives me the sexiest, knowing smile like he just read my mind before grabbing my hand and pulling me toward the bleachers.

I look up and scan the field for Holden. When I find him, his eyes are pinned on me as he pounds his hand into his glove, readying himself for a catch, but when he cracks his neck and subtly shakes his head, I know he's pissed, and when I look down, I realize why. Connor didn't just grab my hand; our fingers are laced, and we look way too comfortable. We look like a couple.

I don't want to be rude, so I choose not to pull my hand away. It's not like Holden and I are dating, and Connor did mention that Holden told him he was expecting me. Connor is just being a good friend and making sure I don't feel like a loner. When we reach the bench, Trent nods hello to me before pulling a beer out of the cooler and thrusting it into my hand.

"How much did I miss? Are they winning?"

Trent decides to use his words this time. "You missed one inning. Neither team has scored." I take a seat on the bench behind Trent. Interacting with Connor has already put me in an awkward situation, and I'd rather not earn any more disapproving glares. Instead, I try to strike up a conversation and distract myself from the instant drama that I feel my presence has brought.

"How long have you guys known Holden?"

Connor has yet to take a seat. Instead, he opts to stand next to where I sit on the end of the bleachers with his arm rested atop one of the higher seats.

"I've been playing college ball with Holden for three years now. He's a quiet guy. Keeps to himself for the most part, but I'm trying to get him to break out of his shell. Life is too short to be wasted holed up in your house watching game playbacks. But I will say, if one of us ever does go pro, I don't know how it couldn't be him. He lives and breathes baseball."

I don't know Holden well enough to draw a finite conclusion from what he's said, but I know from experience when people hyperfocus on some area of their life, it's usually for a reason. Hell, I'm living that nightmare every day. The problem is, if I could shut it off, I would. I wonder if that truth rings true for Holden?

"How come you're not out there then?"

He shrugs before saying, "Honestly, I wanted a break after this season. We have one more year. After that, we'll either get drafted or we won't, and all this will either become a career or a hobby. I needed to pull back to gain perspective and refocus. There's a lot of pressure at this level. I just needed a break. Don't get me wrong, I fucking love playing, and standing here instead of sitting on that bench is hard, but it's only a month until practice starts up again. This..." he gestures toward the field, "And this..." he gestures toward the benches, "is helping me put things in perspective. So I'm prepared for what's ahead. Good or bad."

"Okay, Callahan, what are you, the Dalai Lama now? She asked why you weren't playing, not for a speech about life."

I narrow my eyes at the back of Trent's head. What an ass. I want to reach out and slap him upside his head for being such a douche. But before I can let my irritation rise, another thought occurs to me. Turning to Connor, I say, "Wait a minute. Your last name is Callahan. Do you happen to be related to Garrett and Colton Callahan?"

"I might be. Why are you asking?" He throws me a coy smile and a head nod, and I can't help but shake my head at his antics.

"Well, I work for a law firm, Callahan Brothers & Associates, based out of Chesterfield."

Making a fist, he brings it to his mouth, smiles, and says, "No shit, small world. Yeah, Colton and Garrett are my uncles."

I furrow my brow before saying, "Oh, I didn't realize they had another brother."

"For the most part, my dad isn't involved in their dealings. They are corporate lawyers, while my dad is a family lawyer. I need to know though, how did you land a job with Garrett? His corporate law branch is highly coveted. Law students would kill to intern there, let alone work there for the experience."

That makes me cringe. I've always known I lucked into the job, but hearing someone else confirm it makes me feel worse for not loving it. "Well, actually, that's a funny story. I was grabbing my morning coffee at the local shop close to campus and was next in line to give my order. That's when Garrett spun around; he dumped his coffee all down my clothes. He was mortified, offered to pay for my clothes, give me money, and buy my coffee for a year. When I refused everything, he said, *Aren't you a college student? I bet you could use a job. Why don't you come work for me?* The rest is history."

Connor has his chin resting on his fist as he stares through me and asks, "Was the coffee hot?"

My eyes go wide as I'm taken aback by his question. After all that, he wants to know if the coffee was hot. Running the memory back in my mind, I think I was too stunned that morning to even think about the temperature of the coffee, but now that I recall it, the coffee was lukewarm at best. "Umm, actually, it wasn't." *Shouldn't it have been hot if he had just ordered the coffee?*

Before I have more time to think about this crazy coincidence or Connor's strange question, he slaps the bench next to me, drawing me out of my thoughts. "Hey, walk with me to grab a hot dog?"

"Yeah, sure, I'll walk with you."

As I stand and jump down off the bleachers, whistling and hollering rings out from the dugout. Holden's team just got off the field, and they are all staring in our direction. Immediately, I look behind me, expecting to find one of the guys' girlfriends in short shorts, but come up with nothing. Which means I'm getting catcalled. I'm sure my cheeks are probably the deepest shade of crimson a face can get. I don't even bother looking back at the dugout. As much as I would love to feel flattered by the reaction, I don't know how to process it. For reasons I can't explain, a group of men catcalling me has me on edge, and I need air.

I don't bother waiting for Connor. Instead, I take off toward the concession stands. He'll either follow, or he won't. At this point, it's probably better that he doesn't.

"Aria, wait up. Why the hell did you take off so fast?" I glance over my shoulder and give him a knowing look. He's not an idiot. Then, grabbing my arm, he stops me. "Hey, wait, the guys are just fucking around. Did that offend you? You're fresh meat. They didn't mean anything by it."

Crossing my arms over my chest, I shift my weight to one leg and give him the sweetest smile I can muster before saying, "Thanks, good to know they didn't genuinely find me attractive."

His head rears back, and his mouth drops open. "What, no, that's not what I was saying. Aria, are you serious right now? Half the team wants to bone you, guaranteed. Me included." Connor slaps a hand over his mouth, and this time I can't help but smile. He slipped, and he knows it.

"So which is it, Connor? I'm not worth a catcall, or they want to fuck my brains out?"

He shakes his finger at me. "You're a brat, you know that right? I was going to buy you a hot dog, but that's not happening now." This time, he leaves me standing in the dust. I really didn't mean to draw that confession out of him. Clearly, he's attracted to me, and I'd be lying if I said I didn't find him swoon-worthy in his own right, but I'm not here for him, and I'm not a shameless flirt. He took my insecurity for something it's not, and now I feel like an ass.

I do a little jog to catch up. When I find him, he's already in line. Strolling up beside him, I give a subtle hip bump before saying, "Look, I'm sorry. I really wasn't trying to corner you into anything back there. You had it right. I wouldn't say I was offended, just uncomfortable. I let my insecurities cloud my better judgment, and I bolted. You're a good guy, Connor."

He just rubs his chin like he's deep in thought, and hell, maybe he is, but the silence is making me nervous. "What if I buy you a hot dog to compensate for being a brat?"

This time, I stand up on my tippy toes, lace my fingers together, and rest my chin atop them with a big smile plastered across my face. Connor gives me those pretty-boy brown eyes and says, "I'm only forgiving you because you're buying me the hot dog, and you better not tell Holden. Just because I find you sexy as hell doesn't mean I would break bro code." *Damn it. Why did he have to say that?*

Immediately, I face forward in line so he doesn't see my face turn beet red yet again, and luckily, someone he knows spots him and calls out his name, gesturing for him to come over. I feel him squeeze my shoulder before he says, "Don't forget the mustard," and walks off.

All the food smells fantastic, and since I haven't eaten since breakfast, I should get something, but I don't want to feel bloated. Instead, I order a light beer, a granola bar, and two hot dogs. While Connor didn't ask for two, something tells me he'd eat two, and if not, I'll offer it to Trent.

Gathering up all the food, I start making my way back to the field, unsure of where Connor went until I spot him talking to some brunette standing beside a blue Mustang. She's stunning. I'm unsure what type of girl I would have pegged for him, but I wouldn't have picked her. While she's beautiful, she's the stuck-up kind of pretty, and Connor seems too down-to-earth to get caught up in that kind of drama. Either way, I want nothing to do with whatever they've got going on. From the looks of it, they're not getting along.

As I approach the bleachers, I notice Holden's team is back in the dugout, meaning I missed another inning. Hopefully, he's not one of those guys who gets mad if I miss half of his plays. Setting the food down, I risk glancing over at the dugout. Those crystal-blue orbs lock on mine when I do, sending a shiver straight down my spine. For a split second, I see fury that makes me want to disappear, but as I take my next unsteady breath, he jumps over the dugout wall and jogs up to me. When he reaches me, the spikes on his cleats have him towering over me even more than he already does, and I have to remind myself to breathe. The fact that Holden left the dugout to come over and speak to me is an attention grabber. If I thought the catcalling sucked, this feeling is monumentally worse.

His move has garnered the attention of his entire bench and a few people in the bleachers. "Eyes on me, pretty girl."

When I turn my attention back to him, his expression is mixed. "Holden, everyone's staring—"

He cuts me off. "Yeah, that's kind of the point. Apparently, everyone needed a reminder about what's mine." I don't miss how his eyes narrow on me or how his jaw clenches, like saying those words aloud pains him. But that can't be right. Why say them at all if that was the case?

Stepping into me, he places his hand around my neck before pulling me into him. His lips brush against my ear, and I swear my entire body feels like it's about to go up in flames. There is no way to hide the goosebumps that break out down my neck and arms from his mouth being so close. "I would love it if you'd sit down and watch my game now." His lips graze the corner of my mouth before his eyes search mine. He's telling me without saying the words that he doesn't like me hanging out with Connor. Because I can barely breathe with him this close to me, all I manage is a nod of agreement. He runs his thumb across my bottom lip before one of his teammates yells, "Hayes, field."

I'm just taking my seat on the bench when Connor shows up. "Was that Holden I just saw over here a second ago?" Pressing my lips together, I ignore the question. This is turning into one big mess, and I'm starting to feel like I shouldn't have come. Connor is super nice, and I don't want to be mean.

Luckily, I don't have to. "Yeah, dumbass, he came over here to ensure everyone knew she was here to watch him and not ride your cock."

Connor walks to the front of the bleachers where Trent sits and says, "Who the fuck do you think you're talking to? We went to get a hot dog."

"Speaking of hot dogs," I stand up, one in each hand, "I grabbed you one." Both of them turn to look at me simultaneously and give me a look that says, *sit the fuck down*. So I do. When I look to the outfield, I find Holden's gaze set directly on me and the show taking place right before his eyes. *Seriously?* I've never had this much drama in my entire life. This guy is probably regretting ever inviting me to the game.

I told Holden I would watch the game, but all I want to do now is leave. Looking around, I consider sitting on the other team's bleachers, but after Trent and Connor finish doing their macho, bullshit guy thing, they separate. Connor heads to the parking lot, no doubt to leave—or at least, a small part of me hopes for that so I don't have to be put in any more awkward situations. On the other hand, Trent takes his seat like nothing ever happened.

As agreed, I sit and watch the rest of the game with zero interruptions. Connor never comes back, and Trent and I don't speak, but in the bottom of the ninth, I have to pee after drinking two beers. I plan to hurry and be back before Holden ever notices, but I have no such luck. Returning to the bleachers, I see he's packing his bag in the dugout. A few of his teammates are doing the same thing, so I hang back. I don't want to impose and subject him to introductions. I'm sure, after tonight's drama, the last thing he wants to do is introduce me to his friends.

Slinging his bag over his shoulder, he exits the dugout and looks up to catch me watching him. Shaking his head, his lips quirk up to one side, ever so slightly, before he starts walking my way. Approaching me, he snatches the ball cap off my head and drops his bag before saying, "I knew you were going to be a problem." Placing his hands on my hips, he pulls me flat against his chest and bends down to whisper in my ear. "Tell me, pretty girl, have you thought about me as much as I've thought about you?" His lips once again skim the shell of my ear, sending delicious tendrils of heat straight to my core. *Shit.*

Pulling in a shaky breath, I find my words, determined not to let him see how much he affects me, and tease him right back. "Well, you didn't give me much to think about, so I can't say I have."

Pulling back, his eyes search mine, looking for a tell and finding none. "Is that all you want then? You just want to ride my cock and be on your way?"

I think my eyes practically bug out of my head as my eyebrows meet my hairline. "Jesus, Holden." I snatch my hat out of his hand and move to step around him. I'm not some prude who can't handle a dirty mouth, but I've had enough men insinuate that I want to ride their cocks for one day. Not to mention, I don't know what the hell he's playing at.

Throwing his arm out, he stops me. "Aria, you don't get to do that. You don't get to walk away from me. I'm the one who should be pissed, not you. I basically had to watch you flirt with Connor the entire game. The whole team thought you were his girl. Then you missed two innings to run off with him. Don't even get me started on Trent."

I throw my hands up in the air on that one. "I didn't even talk to Trent. I said maybe one sentence."

He puts his hands on his hips, and his jaw visibly clenches. "Yeah, that's one sentence too many. Just do me a favor. Stay away from Trent." I'm sure he doesn't miss my shocked expression at his bold request because he adds, "Please." Then, turning around, he picks up his bat bag and says, "Walk with me." I don't say anything. Instead, I wordlessly follow him over to his truck.

Opening the driver's side door, he throws his bat bag into the back of the cab before taking his hat off and tossing it on the dash. His hair is damp with sweat, and with his hat gone, I can now see the perspiration on the back of his neck and fuck me if I don't want to lick it off. That's just wrong. Closing my eyes, I squeeze them shut and take a deep breath, trying to calm my raging libido. A hand finds my chin, and Holden is there when I open them. His expression is soft and curious.

"What are you thinking, Aria?"

I don't know why the following words come out of my stupid mouth, but they do, consequences be damned. "I was thinking about how I want to lick the sweat off your neck." Surprisingly, my admission doesn't make me blush. I don't feel stupid or embarrassed, and maybe that's because the man staring back at me is biting his lip and closing his eyes with a groan before pressing his body against mine, pinning me to the truck. He wants me just as much as I want him.

With his sweaty forehead against mine, he says, "Let me take you somewhere."

And because I'm a glutton for punishment and can't keep my mouth shut, I say, "You want to take me somewhere, but you still won't kiss me."

He smiles, his lips so close to mine I feel like I can taste the mint of his gum. "Pretty girl, I want nothing more than to spread those delicious thighs and take a trip to heaven, but I had something else in mind."

Pulling away, he smacks the lid on my hat and says, "Get your head out of the gutter and get in."

## 7

# THE FALL

HOLDEN

Last night, after Aria left, she was all I could think about. She has consumed every waking thought since I laid eyes on her. A relationship is the last thing I need or want, but I can't walk away from her. I purposefully didn't text her all day, and it killed me. I wanted to hear her sass. Hell, part of me craved it. She is so easy to wind up, and I love it. Most girls I've been with do whatever I want and go along with anything and everything. While that has its perks sometimes, I don't want a fucking puppet. I want Aria.

My eyes immediately found her when she showed up at the game today. I didn't think she could get any hotter than she was last night in that black lace bodysuit, but seeing her dressed down in leggings and a white tee has had me partially hard all afternoon. Don't even get me started on the hat. There's nothing sexier than a chick that can rock a baseball cap. I've wanted to rip it off her head all afternoon for teasing me, and I did, but fuck me if that didn't backfire the minute her brown eyes met mine. I swear those eyes could get me to do anything.

Snatching her hat, I was trying to be a dick. When I asked her to come to the game, I'm not sure what I expected, but it wasn't for her to sit on the bench and get cozy with Connor all afternoon. I nearly lost my shit when the guys started whistling as she jumped off the bleachers. While I know Connor wouldn't break bro code, the insane jealousy I felt knowing the guys didn't realize she was my girl was telling. I knew then that this was more—she was more—and I wanted it all.

There's a reason the entire bench and small audience in the bleachers watched in awe as I walked over to Aria. When I play, I'm all in. There is no halfway, not even out here, playing beer tournaments. This is off-season rec ball. It's not that serious, but that's never stopped me from treating it like any other game. She managed to do what's never been done. Aria didn't just steal my focus. She smashed it to pieces by just existing. I left the dugout and the game for her to ensure everyone, including her, knew she was mine. The fact that she showed up said as much. Whether she knows it yet or not is a different story.

I quickly kick off my cleats and switch them out for slides before getting in my truck. Watching her climb into my truck all hot and bothered has me rock hard, and since I'm still wearing a cup, it's borderline painful. When she settles in and finds me staring, her cheeks heat, tinging them the cutest shade of pink. Add in that blonde hair framing her face, and she looks like she's glowing. Fuck, I want to see what she looks like, flushed with ecstasy as my cock is buried deep inside her.

"Are you going to sit there and stare at me all night, or are we going to drive somewhere?"

There's my girl. I let out a chuckle before starting the truck and answering. "Yes, I plan on staring at you all night, but I guess I should feed you first." To that, she's quiet, but I don't miss how she thins her lips while twisting her fingers together in her lap. Most of the girls I've messed around with never care to eat in front of me, and if they do, it's usually salad, but I don't want Aria to do that with me. I want her to be herself, and I'm hoping what I have up my sleeve will be perfect.

We've been driving for about ten minutes when I finally break the silence. "What did Connor have to say that had you so thoroughly captivated that you missed half of my game?"

She briefly presses her lips together before giving me that sass. "I can't tell if you're jealous or genuinely curious."

I throw her my best no-nonsense, pleading glare, hoping that she bites. Aria doesn't owe me any explanation, but I'm hoping she's invested enough in our connection to appease me and help put my demons to rest. I've known Con for roughly three years, and he's about as close as I've let anyone come since I started my self-imposed isolation, and not by choice. The guy doesn't relent. It doesn't matter how many times I've blown him off. He still shows up the next day like it's no big deal, ready to try again. My glower must have worked because she softens and lets me in.

"Well, Trent happened to call him by his last name, which coincidentally is the same as my boss. I asked if he happened to be related to Garret and Colton Callahan, and it turns out he is. Isn't that crazy? I work for his uncles."

My hands grip the steering wheel a little tighter, and my jaw sets from her revelation. I can't help it. Aria has gotten under my skin. I feel her in my bones, and I hate feeling like Connor already has an in with her that I don't.

She must sense my discomfort because she clears her throat and attempts to cut the tension by adding, "How I landed the job was unusual. That's what we were discussing. Garrett spilled his coffee all down the front of me one day at the local shop right off my campus and offered me a job after I had rejected all his other attempts to reimburse me for his mishap. I always thought it was crazy how it all played out, but it doesn't seem as far-fetched as it once did after meeting Connor."

Her loaded retelling of how she landed her job is revealing. The Callahans don't do anything by chance. They are well-known in the community for their work and charity. Recently, I've been hearing things that lead me to believe not everything is as it seems with them. But Aria's last words have me abandoning any other thoughts on the matter.

"How has meeting Connor changed things?" I try hard to keep the irritation out of my voice.

Shrugging, she says, "He seems nice. Garrett is a very intimidating man. I don't speak to him often so it's hard to say if he likes me, but his move in offering me a job so flippantly seems like something Connor would do... I don't know."

I'm incredibly perturbed, but I don't want to waste my time with Aria talking about Connor. We must be on the same page because she changes the subject and asks, "Is this the part of the night where you take me into the middle of some random field and leave me for dead?"

Glancing over, I catch her eye and smile. "No, pretty girl, we're almost there. Have you never been out this way?"

"No. I grew up pretty close to St. Louis. Definitely not a country girl. Not that I couldn't be, I guess. Boots are cute."

I can't help but burst out laughing. "So that's what you think country life is, boots? And let me guess, hay bales and tractors?"

"Ha-ha, very funny," she jests.

"Fine, country life is all that, but there's so much more. We're here." We're drenched in darkness when I put the truck in park and cut the engine. I hear her pull in a breath and catch the whites of her eyes as they look around. Once I know her eyes have adjusted to the moonlight and I haven't scared her to death, I hop out of the truck and put the tailgate down. Climbing up, I pull out the cooler I packed earlier, blankets, and extra clothes from my storage box. I've just started stripping out of my uniform, cup included, when I hear her open the door and hop out.

"Okay, Holden, I'm not going to lie. This might be a little too creepy for me."

Jumping down, shirt in hand, I pull her into me before saying, "I promise I'll make it worth it."

"Does that mean you're going to kiss me?"

I'm silent as I stand there, holding her around the waist. I want my mouth on hers more than I want my next breath, but I know it will change everything. I will change. It's been so long since I stopped living for myself and putting my wants ahead of obligation that I don't know who I am anymore, but I want to know who I am with her, so I ask, "Is that what you want?"

Her next move shouldn't surprise me, but it does. She smacks me on the chest and says, "Maybe," before breaking out of my hold to walk back to the truck. For a second, I think she's going back because she wants to leave, but then she pulls out her phone and turns the flashlight on. "Where exactly are we?"

Walking over, I snatch the phone from her hand. "One rule: no lights."

"Is there a reason you are opposed to me seeing?"

"Just give it a few minutes. Your eyes will adjust, and you'll be able to see everything. To answer your other question, this is the back side of my uncle's property. He owns about a hundred acres, but this spot is my favorite. I've hunted all over this land, but nothing compares to sitting at the edge of this old farm pond, listening to the frogs and the crickets."

She hops up on the tailgate before saying, "Oh, there's a pond? I wouldn't know. I can't see."

"Are you going to be a smartass all night, or just until I feed you? I feel like maybe you're a little hangry." My eyes haven't fully adjusted, but I can see her well enough to know she didn't like that comment. I kick my slides off and move to stand between her legs. "There's a reason I want to feed you, Aria."

At this proximity, I can see her face, and her brow is furrowed. "Oh yeah? And why is that?"

I slowly trail my hands up her outer thighs until I reach her plump ass. God, it feels better than I imagined. Squeezing hard with both hands, I pull her into me, making her gasp. I can feel the heat from her pussy against my chest, and my cock twitches in appreciation. Placing a kiss on the exposed skin of her chest, I say, "Because I made it."

I watch as her pretty pink lips turn up into a breathtaking smile. "You can cook?"

I squeeze her ass again. "Are you making fun of me?"

Shaking her head no, her smile starts to fade, and her eyes zero in on my mouth. I can't take it anymore. Since the moment our eyes met, I've seen it. This woman wants me just as much as I want her, but I'm still not convinced she's ready. Before she can object, I slide her off the tailgate, forcing her to wrap her arms around my neck and her legs around my waist. My entire body is humming as her soft curves mold around me. Turning, I walk toward the pond only a few feet behind us.

"Holden, what are you doing? Where are you taking me?" I don't answer and in the next second, my feet hit the water, making her squeal. "Holden put me down right now. I swear to god, you better not take me into the water." Instead of trying to get free, she tries her best to climb up my chest and keep out of the water, but her efforts are for nothing. I let my legs give out, submerging us both into the cold water. "You better not let me go." The seriousness in her voice instantly makes me feel like shit.

"Aria, I didn't even think. I'm so sorry. It didn't even occur to me that you might be unable to swim."

"Holden, I can swim, but I don't like being in water that I can't see in. It creeps me out. This entire scene is somewhat chilling." Her arms and legs are rigid, and I feel a slight tremble run up her spine. I run my fingers up her back slowly, trying to relax her, but I feel terrible when her teeth start to chatter.

"Aria, look at me." When her eyes find mine, I can see her anxiety, but what's more, I see her ghosts. That haunted look has never been more pronounced than it is right now, and all I want to do is make it go away because it's killing me knowing I put it there. "Do you trust me?"

"Enough." I'm unsure what I expected her to say, but I can work with *enough*.

When I got the idea to drag her into this pond, it was because I was hot and sweaty, hoping to kill two birds with one stone and douse my desire to be inside her while simultaneously cooling off. But now that I have her wrapped around me, giving me her trust when it clearly doesn't come easy, I'm rock hard. Cold water be damned. Leaning in, I pull her long blonde hair over her shoulder, exposing the curve of her neck and placing my mouth on the sensitive skin at the base. Her thighs immediately tighten around my waist as her hand slides into my hair, holding me in place.

I nip, lick, and suck my way up her neck to the base of her ear, where I graze it with my teeth before saying, "You're so damn beautiful Aria." Peppering kisses along her jaw, I stop when I reach her mouth. Her chest is heaving, and she wants it. She wants me to kiss her, but I know that there's no going back once I do, and I need to know more. I tease my lips over hers before nipping at her plump bottom lip and pulling back to walk us out of the pond.

"Tell me, Holden. Explain it to me because I'm really starting to feel self-conscious here."

Setting her on the tailgate, I take her hand and place it on my rock-hard cock, and she gasps. Then, bringing my eyes to hers, I ensure I have her attention before I say, "This is all because of you, pretty girl, so don't do that. Don't for a second think that you are not what I want. I want you so bad it hurts."

Grabbing one of the blankets, I wrap it around her before reaching for my joggers and stepping around the side to take my game pants off. I know what she's asking, and I know she heard me when I told her, *I'm playing for keeps,* before I walked off last night. What I don't know is if she's ready for that, and I can't just have parts of her when I need all of her.

I hadn't planned on swimming tonight or getting Aria all wet, so instead of putting my shirt on, I offer it to her. "Here, I'm sure you don't want to sit in your wet clothes."

She raises an eyebrow at me. "This was your plan all along, wasn't it? Take me to a farm pond, soak my clothes, and get me naked."

I can't help but laugh out loud, a deep belly laugh. "No. I wish I could say that was my plan, but I think we both know if I wanted you wet and wrapped around me, I wouldn't have to trick you into it."

To that, she retorts, "Okay, someone is full of themselves."

I hop into the back of the truck and start pulling dinner out of the cooler. "I'm not the one who admitted to wanting to lick the sweat off my neck earlier."

She hesitates before hopping down and saying, "You're an ass."

Then, because I can't resist messing with her, I add, "One that you find sexy as hell. Your words, not mine."

I've just finished laying out the shredded chicken wraps, hummus, and pita when she hops back up on the tailgate. I can't help the groan that escapes my throat at the sight of her thick thighs bared to me. My shirt barely comes mid-thigh on her. As soon as she notices my eyes on her, she wraps the blanket around herself before clearing her throat and asking, "Where did you learn to cook?"

"Well, I'm an only child. I played every sport growing up. My dad was constantly taking me to game after game. Soccer, baseball, football, basketball—you name it, I played it. While my mom would come to all my games, the older I got, the more I felt like I wanted to give her something. My parents tried having more children, but it didn't happen. I knew she wanted to have a daughter more than anything. My mom has always been a baker and loves to mess around in the kitchen, so around age seventeen, I started making an effort to hang out with her in her happy place at least once a month. It turns out that hanging with your mom while she cooks isn't so bad; it has benefits. One was the smile I was able to put on your face by telling you I made dinner. That was priceless." She fidgets with the fringe of the blanket, breaking our eye contact, which tells me I hit a nerve. But I think it's a good one. I pass her a chicken wrap and ask, "What about you? Do you have siblings?"

She eyes the wrap suspiciously before answering. "Yes, I have an older brother, Spencer."

I take a bite of my wrap, waiting for her to continue, but she doesn't. She's still staring at the plate. "I promise it's not poisoned."

Her head snaps up, and she asks, "Why lettuce?"

Shrugging my shoulders, I say, "I like 'em better that way. You can't knock it until you try it."

I watch as she stares at the wrap, unconvinced she wants to eat it, so I tease. "Do you want me to feed it to you?"

"Do you want to feed it to me?" I'm wrecked when she looks up and those big brown eyes land on mine.

"Pretty girl, I want anything that involves you and that mouth."

Her eyebrows raise in surprise, and she bites her plump bottom lip before she mocks, "Yeah, that's yet to be seen." I'm just about to make good on my threat when she pushes her hair behind her ear and picks up the wrap to take a big bite. I'm not going to lie, I expected her to take a bird bite just to be nice and appease me, but the fact that she didn't is hot. Covering her mouth with one hand, she replies, "It's delicious." I know her remarks are genuine because she takes another huge bite.

Once we've finished eating our wraps, I'm filled with contentment. Feeding her makes me happier than it should. I want to take care of her, and I love that I made her something she liked.

"Any chance you want to bring that blanket over here?"

When her eyes meet mine, they lock, and I know I'm pushing some boundary for her. I'm just unsure how. I'm starting to think her smart mouth and moxie are her shield for whatever pain lurks beneath the surface. Her spirit is swayed too easily from one second to the next for that not to be true. Regardless, she crawls over and joins me anyway. I only wish I didn't feel like I was part of the problem. Pulling a beer out of the cooler, I pop the top and hand it to her. After getting my own, I throw my arm around her shoulder and pull her to my side. We sit there in the dark with the sounds of the crickets and tree frogs, nothing but a blanket of stars in front of us. It's the most contentment and peace I've had in years, and I don't want this night to end. I want to feel like this all the time.

"Tell me, pretty girl. Why don't you have a boyfriend?"

She takes a long drink from her beer before saying, "That's what you want to talk about right now? The other men in my life."

"Are you saying there are other men in your life?"

Pulling out of my arm, she sits up straight and starts tearing at the label on her beer bottle. "Honestly, Holden, my life is complicated as hell right now. I am beyond lost. I broke up with my ex three months ago. We weren't together long, but he won't let go."

Knowing another man is vying for her attention fills me with rage. I hate the thought of another guy touching her. Taking another drink of my beer, I wrestle with what to say next. I want to ask for his address and tell him to stay the fuck away, but I also need to know if that's what she wants. A fresh wave of anxiety rolls over me at the potential that she might want him back, before another thought hits me: is he the one that put that haunted look in her eyes?

"Aria..." I stop talking when she looks over her shoulder and softly smiles.

"I already know what you're thinking, but no, Holden, I don't want him back. There's a reason I told him I wanted a break, and he proved me right. While my confidence might be crap, I know I'm worth more than a guy who can't be apart for more than a week without sleeping with someone else. I was done before I learned about that, but screwing another girl sealed his fate. The trust was gone."

Before I realize it, I grab her waist and pull her into me, placing kisses on her neck. She said the exact words I didn't know I needed to hear. Any doubts I may have had about her wanting to reconnect are silenced. She described how I felt when I caught Whitney fucking another guy. There was no point in fighting. No closure was needed. It was simply the end because we could never go back. The trust was gone.

I'm sucking the skin behind her ear when she reaches her hand up around my neck and says, "Will you please tell me why you won't kiss me?"

I kiss my way along her jaw as best I can before reaching around her waist and pulling her toward me. When she turns into me slightly, I grab her thigh and pull her onto my lap so she's straddling me. "My god, you're so fucking sexy." I take my hands and frame her face before saying, "I thought I made it clear last night." I rub my thumb over her bottom lip before adding, "I want more than just a kiss." My eyes briefly search hers for permission, and I know I have it when she bites that bottom lip. With one hand around the back of her neck, I move the other to her waist, sealing our bodies together. Our eyes are locked when I brush my lips over hers in a slow, tantalizing dance meant to tease and draw this moment out. I want to crush my mouth to hers, but there's only one first kiss, and I want this one to last. Slipping my tongue out, I slowly trace her bottom lip before pulling it into my mouth. When she rocks her clit against my throbbing cock, my resolve is gone. *Screw it*. I plunge my tongue into her mouth.

We both let out a slow moan as our tongues collide, both reaching for depth and connection that can't come from a kiss alone. I feel her soul in my veins. And her mouth... fuck, her mouth is pure bliss. Gently tugging her hair, I break our kiss, "Pretty girl, you taste like forever." Her eyes briefly search mine, and for a second, I believe she sees my truth. Before any doubt can register, her mouth is back on mine.

Sliding my hand down her back, I grip her ass, and when I do, her bare cheek is in my hand. Another agonized groan escapes my throat before I pull back and ensure there is no mistake about how I feel. "You're mine now, Aria. Do you get that?" She nods before bringing her swollen lips back to mine and thrusting her tongue into my mouth. I still have one hand twisted in her hair while the other is kneading her ass. I'm fucking rock hard and my cock is dripping, as she rocks against my erection, seeking her own relief.

Untangling my other hand from her hair, I drag it down her back until I reach her ass. With a cheek now in each hand, I squeeze hard before firmly pressing her into my cock, ensuring there's no mistake that I want her. "Do you see what you do to me, pretty girl? This is everything. You are all I want." I need to see her. I want to pop one of her perfect tits into my mouth. Slowly, I glide my hands up her back, lifting my shirt off her as I go, when suddenly, her hands dart out to stop me. Her entire body goes rigid. "Aria, what is it? Tell me." She shakes her head and tries to move to get off me. Wrapping my arms around her waist, I ensure she can't and say, "Talk to me, pretty girl. What did I do?"

Again, she shakes her head and looks away, her long blonde hair cascading over her face, shielding me from whatever emotion might be there. I want her to feel comfortable around me. I need her to, because somehow, over the last twenty-four hours, she's become my everything. Pulling her hair away from her face, I tuck it behind her ear before kissing her shoulder, collarbone, neck, jaw, and lips. When she kisses me back, I feel her relax, but I can't leave it alone. "I need to know what I did, baby. Please let me in."

Her eyes search my face before she averts her gaze and timidly says, "I just want to leave my shirt on."

I try to school my reaction and not look surprised by her confession, but I am. What the hell reason could she possibly have for wanting to leave it on? Lifting her chin, I find her eyes. "Aria, I want all of you, not parts of you. There is nothing under this shirt that will change that for me. You're the most beautiful woman I've ever laid eyes on. Let me worship you, pretty girl."

Just when I think I've eased any reservations, she says, "Maybe we should just stop. This is all moving too fast." I still have her pinned to me, and when she tries to wiggle free, I hold her tighter.

"Is that what you really want?" When she hesitates, I know it's not. I lean in and start placing open-mouthed kisses on her neck to get her to relax, and just as I thought it was beginning to work, she places a hand on my chest.

"Holden, please. Just stop. This was a bad idea. This isn't going to work. Can you take me to my car?" Now I'm mad. Not because I'm not going to get laid, but because she's running from me, and she doesn't get to do that. *She's mine.*

"Aria, what part about me saying that you are mine did you not understand? There are no takebacks. I'm not letting you go. If you want to take things slow, that's fine. I'm not trying to force myself on you, for fuck's sake. I'm just trying to understand."

Closing her eyes, she releases a frustrated sigh. "Holden, you can have any girl you want. You can have perfection. That is something I can never be. You think you want me, but that's only because you haven't seen me."

"Why do you think you get to tell me what I want? You think I don't know you have ghosts? It's written all over that pretty face. I never know what eyes I will get from one minute to the next. They're either full of life or dead on the inside, and don't for one second think I'm passing judgment, because I'm not. I simply notice my own reflection in them. So don't think I'll let you give me some bullshit excuse about how you don't want me when we both know that's not true. You're scared."

When she finally brings her eyes back to mine, I see anger and fear, and because I've refused to let her go, I feel her heart pounding in her chest, confirming I'm right. The issue is Aria will walk away regardless. After all, that's why we're haunted in the first place. We don't know how to choose what's good for us. In the end, I know my rightness means nothing, but I'm hoping my truth does. Putting my forehead to hers, I say, "I know this because I'm just as fucking scared. I feel it, Aria. It's all or nothing with us, baby, and I can feel you falling. Let me catch you."

We sit there, foreheads pressed together and wrapped around each other in silence. Our shared breaths mingle as our lips are only a hairsbreadth apart, beckoning for another taste. When enough time has passed without her trying to run, I risk asking her to tell me what she's thinking.

"Ari—" I don't even get to finish her name before her

mouth is on mine. This time, her kiss is slow and sensual, not demanding and loaded with lust. She wants me to feel what's on her mind and in her heart, and damn it if it doesn't tear me up. Her mouth seductively presses into mine before she parts her lips and slowly dips her tongue into my mouth. When I brush my tongue against hers, only giving her a taste, she dives in, demanding that I give her what she seeks. And because I could never refuse her, I let her take it. This kiss is us. Insane chemistry, timid minds, and crazy hearts, because only a fool could fall this hard so fast. She and I know it, but neither of us cares to stop it.

I slowly slide my hands back down, trying to be mindful of her discomfort, but I can't help but get a little carried away when I discover she doesn't have a thong on. Groaning loudly, I run my hand down her crack before breaking our kiss. "Aria, you're killing me." I thrust my cock against her clit to drive home my point and feel her wetness through my pants.

"Pretty girl, you're so fucking wet, you're making a mess on my pants. I love it." I drag my tongue along her neck before sliding my hand up her shirt and across her soft belly until I reach her perky tit. Rubbing my thumb over her nipple, I ensure it's sufficiently stimulated before tweaking it and earning the sexiest moan I've ever heard. Immediately, I bring my mouth to hers, wanting to devour every sound I create. She's letting me touch her underneath my shirt. I love that she's wearing it, but I want to see what's underneath it. While I don't want to push, it gives me an idea.

"Baby, I want this tit in my mouth." I bring her breast to my mouth and swirl my tongue around her erect nipple through the shirt before biting it. She throws her head back as she continues to slowly rock against my cock. "Damn, you're so beautiful." I thought teasing her through the shirt might give me the green light, but it didn't. Resting my hands on her thighs, I squeeze and let her take what she wants. I'm not sure what I did earlier that made her uncomfortable, and I don't want to fuck this up. Not to mention, I can dig a show that involves her naked pussy grinding on my dick.

She's not even looking at me when she says, "Holden, please, please don't stop."

Her head is up in the stars when I quickly sit up and pull her against my chest. "Tell me, baby, what do you want? Tell me, and I'll do it."

Bringing her eyes to mine, she leans in and says again, "Please just don't stop," before she takes my mouth, thrusting her tongue deep, the way I want to bury my cock in her soaked pussy. I can tell this is something more for her, and I hate that I'm not understanding, but I want to give her what she needs. I want to watch her writhe in ecstasy from the pleasure she takes from me. Throwing caution to the wind, I once again pull at the hem of my shirt, slowly dragging it up her torso until I reach the point where I need her help to let me pull it off. Pulling back, she thins her lips and squeezes her eyes closed, clearly pained by the act, before lifting her arms for me to continue. She's sitting on my lap, wearing absolutely nothing as she straddles my cock, and I can literally feel it weeping. I let out a slow, "Fuuuck." She's perfect, which again leaves me dumbfounded. *What could she possibly not want me to see?*

Grabbing a perfect handful of breast, I suck her nipple into my mouth and mumble, "So fucking good."

She lets out a heady, "God, yes," as her rocking picks up. I trail kisses across her chest, making my way over to her other breast. "You have perfect tits, pretty girl. I want to watch them bounce while you ride my cock." My hand lazily squeezes the breast I don't have my mouth wrapped around before slowly descending toward heaven. When I reach her pubic bone, I pause briefly, waiting to see if she'll stop me, but I get my answer when she slightly lifts, giving me access to her pussy.

Wasting no time, I slide my fingers through her soaked folds. The second I make contact, we both let out passionate moans of pure ecstasy. Her lips find mine again, and when she dips her tongue into my mouth, I slip my finger into her soft center. "Fuck, baby, this pretty pussy is so tight." She whimpers into my mouth as I add another digit. She's full-on riding my fingers now. "That's it, baby, take it. Take what you need." Curling my fingers, I know I've hit her spot when I feel her walls starting to contract around me. "Pretty girl, I want this pussy wrapped around my cock so bad, you have no idea."

"Please don't stop. Fuck, Holden, please."

I kiss her lips, her jaw, her forehead. "Why would I stop, baby? I'm not going to stop. Fuck, I want to give it to you. I want you to soak my fingers."

She's panting hard, her lips are parted and her eyelids are heavy, as she once again murmurs, "Just please don't stop." She rests her head in the crook of my neck and bites my lobe, making my body break out in shivers. When I start rubbing my thumb over her clit she cries, "Yes, Holden, right there."

"My name coming out of that pretty mouth while my fingers are buried deep in your pussy is fucking intoxicating." I steal her mouth and meet no resistance as her orgasm takes root. Nipping her plump bottom lip, I say, "Give it to me, use me, baby." Her pussy starts to spasm and clench tight. "That's it, pretty girl. Look at me. I want to see your face when you come." I place my lips on hers for a slow, open-mouthed kiss. She's too lost in how I'm making her feel to give me more. My girl can barely hold her eyes open, and I'm hypnotized. I'd like to think other women I've been with weren't faking it, but seeing Aria's reaction to how I'm making her feel makes me question it. Her perfect nipples are erect, her chest is flushed, and her eyes are shrouded in sheer ecstasy. I grab her jaw with my free hand and murmur, "So damn perfect," against her lips, setting her off. Her pussy starts contracting, and I feel her juices flood my hand.

I keep pumping my fingers in and out of her at a slowed pace, drawing out her orgasm when her mouth collides with mine. Her tongue is plundering my mouth like she wants to crawl into my skin, when suddenly she pulls back, her eyes on mine, and says, "Fuck me, Holden."

"Damn, baby, I want that so bad, but we're not doing that tonight." I retake her mouth before saying, "Tonight was about you, pretty girl."

My fingers are still buried deep when she pushes down and says, "Please."

"Aria, fuck. Don't make this harder than it already is, baby. I didn't plan on this. I don't have a condom." I run my free hand through the hair at the base of her neck and gently pull her into me before whispering, "Trust me, this pussy will be wrapped around my cock soon enough. I'm yours, pretty girl."

I hear her suck in a breath before she lifts off my fingers and sits up. "Holden, you can't say stuff to me like that. You know this is crazy. We just met." She turns around to grab my shirt and pull it back on before adding, "This isn't some romantic fairytale. This is you, finger-banging me in the back of your truck. You're thinking with your dick and letting it cloud your better judgment—"

"Aria, stop. You don't get to tell me how I feel. I've meant every fucking word I've said. You're right; I'm extremely attracted to you, and I want nothing more than to bend you over right now and fuck the sass right out of you, but more than that, I never want to let you go."

Tugging at her hips, I pull her onto my lap before placing my hands on her face. "Look at me, Aria, and I mean *really* look at me. Hear my words. I'm not the one that broke you. I'm not someone you need to fear. I'm just a man who wants to be a part of your world."

Her eyes soften before she falls into me, laying her head on my chest. I grab the blanket and pull it over us. I have no doubt she can feel my heart racing with her head lying flat against my bare chest. This woman scares the shit out of me in the best of ways. I've never met someone and instantly fallen so hard. I know what I feel is real. She could be my forever—if I have one to give.

"Holden, I want that too. So much." I pull her closer, wrapping her in my arms, determined not to let this end. Right now, everything is perfect. I don't know how long we stay like that, but apparently it was long enough for her to nod off. Scanning the truck bed, I search for my phone but come up short. I have no idea how late it is or if she has a curfew. My sensible side is telling me to wake her and take her back to her car, but the selfish and apparently possessive side is telling me to lie down, relax, and doze off with her.

I've never once felt possessive or protective over any woman I've dated. Sure, I expect monogamy, but I never got jealous when Whitney talked to the guys. Hell, I've fucked a girl in the storage closet at school and watched her walk out to another man. I will admit I felt shitty about that, not because I was jealous, but because I've been the guy who got fucked over by a woman. Aria brings out a side of me I didn't know existed. And while I'm not convinced I'm anything she needs, I'll be damned if I don't want to die trying to be.

Mind made, I pull the blanket up to her chin and carefully slide us down so we lie flat. Her head still rests on my chest when she stretches out and wraps her leg over mine, getting comfortable in this new position. When she doesn't wake, I close my eyes and let the moment's contentment wash over me right before sleep takes me.

# 8

## GRENADE

ARIA

S*hit, it's cold*. When I open my eyes, I soon find out why. I'm lying in the middle of a barren cornfield in the back of Holden's truck. I'm just about to move to sit up when I look up at Holden and see him peacefully sleeping. He's so fucking gorgeous. Even when he sleeps, he's the hottest guy I've ever seen. One hand is tucked behind his head, while the other is wrapped around my back. The entire scene is utterly romantic. Too bad I don't let myself get carried away with fanciful things. I'd like to think I'm a realist, but really, I think it's my defense to avoid admitting I'm a pessimist.

I will admit I was surprised when he said he could see my demons. Even my closest friends don't see those. Holden was right; he didn't break me, but I know we could never be because he sees me as broken. Fixing me temporarily silences whatever it is that haunts him. His words, not mine: "I notice my own reflection." He wants to tame my demons because he can't escape his own. The issue is, he doesn't see what I already know. I'm not the answer. I can never be his solution.

Squeezing my eyes shut, I push down the hurt I feel in my chest at the thought of losing him and slowly move to sit up when his arm tightens around my waist. Looking up, I find his magnetic, pale blue eyes piercing my soul, sending a shiver straight down my spine. It's like he's been sitting there watching me and silently reading my mind. I can't help but feel like he knows, verbatim, everything that just ran through my head.

"You thinking about running, pretty girl?" *Is he serious right now?* I take a deep breath and remind myself people can't actually read minds. Then, placing my hand on his stomach, I again try to sit up and brush off his comment's eeriness and the soul-crushing truth of how things must be.

"What would make you think that?" I act as if his question has no merit when I know damn well it most certainly does.

"Oh, I don't know. First, you tried to brush off meeting me in general, then, when I finally found you at the bar, you ran out, and let's not forget how you were about to ghost me when you left Gabe's house. Forgive me for having little confidence based on your track record."

Rolling my eyes, I keep my response superficial. "Well..." I look around dramatically, "there's not really any place for me to run off to right now, is there?"

He smirks before pulling at the arm I had propped against his stomach to get up, effectively crushing me to his front. "I can't say that was intentional, but I'm not mad about it." Placing a kiss on my forehead, he runs his fingers through my hair, tucking it behind my ear before adding, "Spend the day with me."

I want nothing more than to spend the day wrapped up in his arms, but that will only make the ending that much harder—because this *will* come to an end. He must notice my hesitation because he says, "Stop overthinking this, Aria."

Those eyes make me want to stay. They make me want to say yes, but I don't. Instead, I say, "Okay."

My agreement catches him off guard, and his eyes widen with surprise. "Yeah?" That is all he manages in response.

Five minutes ago, I was set on running, but when his eyes locked on mine and pleaded with me to stay, I couldn't refuse. I wanted to be the girl he sees. I wanted to be her so bad. And maybe if I stay and give him my time, I'll find her. I try to contain my smile before saying, "I need to get back to my house, shower, change, and check in." *Shit.*

"Crap, Holden, I need to get back to my car." This time, I jump up, leaving no room for him to pull me back under his spell. Jumping off the truck, I run around to the cab to grab my phone.

After I was done with the directions to the baseball field, I turned my phone off again so I wouldn't keep getting texts and calls from Logan. While I don't have a curfew, it's not like me to stay out all night. Chances are, if my parents haven't tried to check in, Spencer has. When I find my phone, it's officially dead. Holden opens the driver's side door and says, "Everything okay?"

I have no words. Holding up my phone, I say, "It's dead, and I need to go."

Luckily, he gets it, and I don't have to explain. "Let me just throw stuff in the back, and I'll take you back to your car."

Glancing out the front window, I spot my clothes that I had laid out to dry last night and hop out to grab my pants. They're still somewhat damp but good enough to throw back on. I don't need to show up to my house wearing no pants. That would be a disaster. After pulling them back on, I consider putting my top back on but instead, opt to keep Holden's shirt. This shirt is my new favorite. There is no way he's getting it back. Too many memories of a night I'll never forget.

Wrapping my bra and panties into my shirt, I climb back into the cab just as Holden finishes packing up. "You good?" I nod and close the door as he starts up the engine. "I'm sorry. I considered waking you up last night after you passed out, but I'd be lying if I said I wanted to take you home." Reaching across the center console, he grabs my hand and interlaces our fingers. My eyes immediately zero in on our connected hands. His hand all but swallows mine. Big, strong, tan fingers wrap around my small, petite hand, and my heart clenches. I want those hands wrapped around mine forever, but I'll settle for this car ride.

"I know it was dark last night, but I'm pretty sure you just made a wrong turn."

He taps his dashboard and says, "I need gas, but this is faster."

As we make our way down the gravel road, a shed appears, and I ask, "Are we still on your uncle's property?"

He smiles. "Yeah, this is my hunting shed, but I also keep my bike and a few toys here." My eyes widen in surprise when he says, bike.

"By bike, do you mean motorcycle?"

Parking the truck, he rolls his lips before giving me a half smile and saying, "That's exactly what I meant. Come on."

I quickly grab my shirt before joining him at the shed. When he opens the door, it has all kinds of stuff: four-wheelers, dirt bikes, razors, and a Harley. He tosses me a helmet before asking, "Have you ever been on a motorcycle?"

Nervously, I shake my head before answering. "No, but I'd be lying if I said I wasn't both scared and excited." I can't help the eager smile that takes over my face.

Holden pounces, wrapping his arms around my waist and pinning me to his front. "How do you expect me to let you go? Come back to my place. You can wear my clothes. After all, you look good in them." He nuzzles his face into my neck, simultaneously making my heart skip a beat and sending a shiver down my spine.

"I need to get home. My family is probably freaking out."

He kisses my neck before releasing me, saying, "Put that on, and let's go."

A thought occurs when I throw my leg over the bike and wrap my arms around his waist. "Were you really out of gas?"

Holden doesn't respond. Instead, he fires up the bike, making me squeeze him tighter, giving me the answer to my question without words. He wasn't out of gas. This is precisely what he wanted: me wrapped tightly around him. This is his payback.

He's not convinced I'm not running, and truth be told, neither am I.

Holden's hand rarely leaves my leg as we wind through the backroads on his bike. It slowly glides up and down my calf, occasionally squeezing it and making my heart clench every time—stupid, stupid heart. I can't help but hold him a little tighter each time he does it. The baseball fields come into view faster than I want them to, and I know it's because I don't want this moment to end.

The fields are empty. My car is the only one still in the lot, which makes sense because it's 6:30 am Sunday morning. Holden pulls right up beside my car and cuts the engine. He's slow to get off the bike, no doubt not thrilled about losing our connection. If I've learned anything about Holden in the last forty-eight hours, it's that his love language is physical touch. The piggyback ride, handholding, his constant need to pull me into him, and now this drive. I'd be lying if I said it bothered me; I love it. I've never felt more cherished, which makes all this even more challenging. I'm the first to climb off, but before my feet fully settle on the ground, he pulls me into him and holds me.

"Call me as soon as you get home. I'm going back to my house to shower and change, and then I'm coming to you, pretty girl." I swallow hard and squeeze my eyes shut tight as I pull him in closer, eliminating any space between us, before nodding in agreement against his shoulder.

We hold each other longer, neither wanting to let go, before I finally pull out of his embrace. He takes my face in his hands and makes sure my eyes are on his when he says, "No playing games, Aria. I want to see you."

"Okay," is all I manage to get out. Holding my driver's side door open, he adds, "Two hours, Aria. I want to see you in two hours."

"I'll text you as soon as I get home." He bends down and kisses my forehead, for which I'm thankful because I'd hate for him to remember me by my morning breath. As I start the car and buckle up, I can see out of my peripheral that he still hasn't moved. Holden watches my car leave the parking lot like he knows it's the last time he will see me.

The drive home sucks. All I can do is replay every intimate detail of last night. He gave me my first orgasm, and it was perfect. I wanted to jump on his cock so bad. Fuck, I'm clenching just thinking about it. He's also the first guy to ever suck on my breast, and it was heaven. I've always been too insecure to let my boyfriends fuck me without a shirt on. Last night was no different. I was so close to running and calling it all off when he tried to take my top off, but it was so dark, I was confident he wouldn't see much, plus, a small part of me believed his words. That I was sexy, beautiful, and his. Then add in all that dirty talk. I'm getting wet just thinking about it.

Pulling into my driveway, I see Logan's vintage Camaro and cringe because on the other side is a fucking cop car. This can't be happening. *Did he really contact my parents and the police?* I park on the street since the driveway is blocked. As soon as I exit the car, the front door opens, and Spencer comes storming out, running through the front yard. He throws his arms around me in a giant bear hug when he reaches me.

"Aria, what the hell? Where have you been?" He's still holding me tight when my parents, Logan, and two cops come trailing out after him.

"Spencer, what's going on? Why are the cops here?"

Pulling back, he grips my shoulders and says, "Logan showed up worried when you wouldn't answer your phone. He was convinced you might hurt yourself, so he came here."

Closing my eyes, I take deep breaths, trying to let the hate, pain, and anger settle. He did the one thing I asked him not to do because he's selfish and couldn't handle the rejection. This was his fucking payback. Logan doesn't give two shits about me. He wanted to hurt me.

When I open my eyes, Spencer's are pinned to mine. "So it's true then?" Without words, I know he sees it. He knows I'm sick, and now I have the added stress of letting my family down to add to the crippling anxiety I already feel whenever I'm alone with my thoughts.

I pull out of his embrace, not wanting to discuss this at all, but definitely not on my front lawn for the entire neighborhood to see. As I step around him, he grabs my hand and says, "We're in this together, Aria. I got you. Whatever you need, I'm here."

That should comfort me. The fact that my brother wants to help me should mean the world to me, and I'm hopeful the fact that I recognize that means I'm not too far gone. But all I can feel right now is anger. I'm going to kill Logan.

As I walk toward the front of the house, Logan's eyes slowly drag up my body until he reaches my face, and when he gets there, I know he sees it. *Good.* Obviously, I was out all night, but I'm hoping the slap in the face is that I'm wearing another man's shirt. I don't give a shit that my parents and two police officers are witnessing my walk of shame because all I care about is making sure Logan feels even a sliver of the hurt he has now caused me. He just threw a fucking grenade into my life, and I'll be damned if I don't want to wound him right back.

When our eyes meet, I see remorse briefly, but it's quickly replaced by rage when the scene starts to click into place for him. I watch as his fists clench and his jaw sets. It only takes a minute for him to make up his mind. Elbowing past the officer, he makes his way to his car. I'd like to say I feel bad that this is how things finally ended between us, but I don't. At least now, I think he knows I'm fucking done. Before anyone can comment on his abrupt departure, his tires screech as he pulls out of the driveway and takes off down the street.

One of the officers tips his hat and says, "Well, now that you're home, I don't think we are needed any longer. Make sure to keep your phone charged, young lady. Your family was worried sick." My dad shakes their hands as my mom follows behind with hugs before they head to the patroller parked in the driveway. We all watch them pull out, seemingly entranced by the entire situation, before my dad clears his throat and says, "I think we need to have a family talk inside right now." Spencer squeezes my hand, reassuring me I'm not alone as we follow our parents into the house.

~

Staring up at my ceiling, I'm a ball of mixed emotions. I'm angry, sad, hurt, and disappointed that I let this happen. As much as I'd like to pin this on Logan, I can't. He was the catalyst for today's trauma, but he wasn't the cause. Hell, I don't even know when I became this way. I feel like I went to bed happy one day, and when my eyes opened the next, I was suddenly changed. Out of nowhere, I was someone I didn't want to be. I want to get back to the girl I used to be. I miss her so much.

Growing up, I spent full summers living it up with my best friend, Olivia. We were inseparable from the day we met. My family had just moved out of an apartment and into our current house when an ice cream truck rolled down our new street. Olivia ran up, and we both ordered a pink bubblegum swirl bomb pop. There was only one left, and she looked at me and said, "You can have it." We were six years old then, and I still remember that day vividly, like it was just yesterday.

Olivia and I did everything together. She was, and is, truly my best friend. The only problem is that I don't see her much anymore. Her family relocated to California when we were sixteen. We do make a point of getting together at least once a year, and it doesn't hurt that she still has family out here, so she comes back most holidays, but it's not the same. I wish she were here now. I could use my best friend right now. That's when I remember I need to turn my phone on.

Getting off the bed, I head over to my dresser and pull it off the charger. Sitting back down, I realize that as much as I want to call her, I can't. I don't care to rehash all this again. I just want it to go away. My fingers turn the phone on regardless because I can't hide forever.

Surprisingly, when I switch it on, I have zero missed calls from Holden and only one text. I left him at 7:00 am this morning, and we said two hours. He wanted to go home, shower, and change. Then we would meet up. His text came through at noon.

Holden: Please don't do this.

That was it. Nothing more. I debate texting him back and think better of it. Texting him back would give him hope that there was a chance I would see him again. Not texting him back leads him to believe I'm running, which was the plan anyway. He doesn't need to know why I never replied to his text. What would I say? "Sorry, when I got home, my ex had called the police and told my parents I was sick, so I spent the remainder of my day discussing my condition with my parents and pre-med brother. Endless questions about why I am the way I am and how they can fix me." No, this needs to end now. Even if my physical scars weren't enough for him to leave, my mental ones would be. This afternoon's events only confirmed what I felt when I woke up in his arms. We are not endgame. There is no point in drawing this out.

Due to today's events, I now have two therapy sessions and one medical evaluation set up for the week. At least it's summer break, and I don't have to schedule the appointments around work and school. I'm going to the sessions to appease my family. They don't understand that, for what plagues me, you can't just go to the doctor, get medicine, and be all fixed up. That's what they believe is going to happen. In fact, it's what they explicitly told me would happen. So, I'll go and hope like hell it helps.

This week went by super-fast. First came my initial therapy session, which was highly focused on my past. My therapist was trying to help me dig deep and figure out why I was consciously hurting myself, even though it's something I know is wrong. Apparently, she has worked with a few cases of dissociative amnesia, where people experience pain or trauma in their youth that their brain has decided to block from their memory. She said while it's rare, it's not uncommon. Of course, I assured her that I had a good life and that was most likely not the cause of my problem. Like any therapist, she nodded as if to appease me and wrote notes in her journal, which made me think she hadn't ruled it out. I left the appointment on edge, but when I showed up Thursday, she didn't bring up my past or any further discussions about potential amnesia.

I thought about discussing her line of questioning with my family but ultimately thought better of it. All of this is already more than stressful for them. The last thing I want is to make them believe they are responsible for any of this.

The eval I had on Wednesday didn't go well. Again, I have no plans to share those details with my family. I am severely dehydrated, which is causing electrolyte imbalances. The doctor seems to think that is the root cause of my lightheadedness, lethargy, overall weakness, and heart palpitations. My takeaway was to drink more water, and I'll be good. But my heart sank when the doctor explained that my irregular cycles and almost nonexistent periods meant I could be causing irreversible damage to my reproductive health. I haven't put much thought into having kids but knowing it might not even be an option when I'm ready made me sick.

The doctor explained the most critical part of my journey would be therapy. Knowing I have a problem and actively doing the right thing will make the difference. He prescribed some antidepressants. While I explained I wasn't depressed, he told me the medicine would help my brain let go of the worry and confines I had set up for myself. I now have a standing appointment every two weeks until he believes my overall health is improving. Apparently, I was borderline admittable based on my blood pressure, heart rate, and size of my veins, so I did what any person would do: I sweet-talked and lied my way out of his office. At the end of the day, I'm only hurting myself. These problems are mine. I don't have a death wish. Things won't get that far.

It's been a long week. I had to face my demons head-on and take count of how this misplaced sickness had dug its claws into my back and turned me into a woman I barely recognized. After my therapy session ended last night, I decided to treat myself. I deserve it.

For the past month, I've had my eye on a white bodysuit hanging in a boutique window down the street from my office. The shop isn't cheap, but I knew it would make a fantastic addition to my wardrobe. I typically like to stick to black and gray because they are more slimming, but this suit has a corseted front that will easily hide the softness of my belly, which makes me self-conscious. So that's my reward today: my hot new top paired with dark-washed skinny jeans and black espadrille wedges.

On the last Friday of each month, we are allowed to wear jeans, and that's today. Running my curling wand through my hair to give it a little extra flirty volume, I spritz my finishing spray and apply my lip gloss before grabbing my work purse and heading out the door. When I reach the living room, I hear Spencer clear his throat and sit up on the couch.

"Aria, I have a granola bar, orange juice, and a banana on the counter. Take it." When I look up to meet Spencer's gaze, his expression is briefly pinched before it softens. While I know he's trying to help, it hurts my heart that he feels he has to. I know he has a lot on his plate as it is, and by the way he's made a point of being present before I leave for work—and every night when I get home—I know he's stretching himself thin. Usually, he would go to the library or study group, but he skipped those things to ensure he could monitor me. After I don't immediately move, he stands up, crosses the room, and gets breakfast.

"If I need to drive you to work every morning to ensure you're taking care of yourself, I will. I'll do whatever it takes." I pull him in for a hug and try not to cry. He's been the only one in the family who seems to have empathy for me. I've always been close to my dad, but he's mad, and my mom is indifferent. I don't think she means to be, I just don't think she understands, or if she does, she doesn't know how to help me.

Before I release him, I say, "I'll be okay. Don't worry about me."

He squeezes my shoulder and says, "I'll see you tonight. I'm going to fire up the grill with Dad and have some beers. It'll be chicken." His eyes search mine as if he's asking if that's okay, and I nod, assuring him that it's fine, and head out.

The office has been quiet all week. I haven't even run into Kris because she went to Boston with her mom and the partners for training. Apparently, she needed to help her mom set up and run the training, but today, everyone returns. I'm just getting my computer set up when Garrett walks in. But rather than walk by as usual, he stops at my desk.

"Good morning, Aria. How did everything go this week? I assume you kept everyone in line and on track." It takes a great deal of focus to keep my expression neutral and not let the surprise of this moment take over. Garrett rarely talks to me. Most of our communication is done via email and is strictly professional. When he raises an eyebrow at me, I realize he has asked a question I have yet to answer.

"Yes; it was a very quiet week, and since most everyone was in Boston, my job wasn't too difficult." I smile sweetly and mindlessly start moving things around my desk. Garrett is a handsome, intelligent man who oozes confidence. I've always felt nervous under his gaze. It's like he's observing me. Even now, I can feel his eyes on me, but it's not sexual. It's as if he's trying to piece something together.

I'm waiting for him to head to his office when he says, "I'd like you to set up an appointment to see me at 3:00 pm today. I want to discuss some potential growth opportunities with you."

I quickly school my expression to ensure the shock I feel isn't registering on my face before saying, "That would be great. I'll make sure there are no schedule conflicts. Is there anything else you need?"

He taps his knuckles on the granite top of my desk before saying, "No, that's all." His eyes linger on mine for a beat too long before Kris and her mom, Catherine, enter the lobby. When I turn my attention to them, Garrett heads toward his office.

Catherine greets me as usual as she heads toward her office. "Good morning, Aria." Today, she adds, "Love that shirt," before continuing. She never stops, she only greets me in passing, which is fine. Catherine is either really busy or good at looking busy. The woman is constantly stomping off somewhere with a fire under her ass that would suggest she's in high demand.

Kris, on the other hand, stops as expected. "Hey, I can't do lunch today, but can we do happy hour after work? My mom has me filing and catching up on everything we missed after being in Boston all week." My eyes go wide, shocked that she didn't mention Holden. For as much as I'm grateful that she didn't, I can't say that I'm not disappointed.

"Yeah, I can do a quick happy hour. What did you have in mind?"

She smiles. "Well, actually, it's this place in the Grove—Llewelyn's. They have live music tonight at 7:00 pm."

Inwardly I cringe, because I thought I would stop by for a quick drink, not multiple drinks until a live band starts up, not to mention I told Spence I'd be home for dinner. Before I can back out, she adds, "That top needs to be seen. You're going. I'm not taking no for an answer."

I roll my eyes and say, "Fine, I'll go and stay for two songs, but then I have to head out."

She smiles sweetly before saying, "Deal," and heading to her office.

I take a minute to text Spence and let him know I'm going to happy hour with a friend and won't be home until later. If I don't immediately text him, I will get sidetracked and no doubt forget. After the week of sacrifice I know he's put in to be present for me, he is the last person I want to blow off.

Spence: I'll make you a plate for when you get home. Please don't turn your phone off.

Aria: Promise.

Honestly, my meeting with Garrett is a welcome distraction. It keeps me from thinking about Holden and how much I miss him. My heart skips a beat whenever I think about him, and my stomach instantly knots. Logan did me a favor; I should be thanking his sorry ass. I'm a hot mess over Holden, and he's not even in my life anymore. Imagine the lovesick fool I'd be if I had let him stick around on Sunday.

~

My stomach has been in knots all day over this meeting, and now that I'm walking in, I feel like I might be sick. When I get to his door, I pull in a deep breath before lightly knocking. "Come in, Aria." Luckily, when I enter, his attention is focused on his computer, not me.

As he continues typing away on whatever he was working on before my arrival, I consider bringing up Connor. My thought is that I could use him as an icebreaker. The tension I feel right now is suffocating, but I think better of it and don't. The chances of seeing Connor again are slim since I ended things with Holden. I don't want to look like I'm trying to suck up or leverage any opportunities he might offer me based on loose family ties. I want whatever this might be, to be earned on my merit and nothing else.

After what feels like a small eternity, he leans back in his chair, untucks his tie, and laces his hands together in his lap. He doesn't immediately say anything. Instead, he brings his joined hands to his mouth, running his index fingers across his bottom lip before asking, "Have you declared a major for the fall?"

It's not the question I was expecting, but I'll bite. I give him a short, clipped response. "No, I'm still undecided."

Again, he nods and takes an unusually long pause before adding. "While I was in Boston, it was brought to my attention that, not only are we underpaying you for your work, but you more than excel at it. You are not just a receptionist, Aria. You are a legal secretary who also moonlights as a records clerk when required. As such, you have become a fundamental part of this team and an asset to the company. Therefore, Colton and I would like to pay for all your tuition costs should you agree to pursue a law degree."

I'm sure whatever expression I have on my face is one of shock. Mentally, I'm stumbling to find a response. While getting a law degree and being debt-free sounds fantastic, I can't shake the feeling that I would somehow be indebted to the firm. This is a highly sought-after law firm. While I know I am intelligent and excel at my job, Garrett could easily hire a qualified law student or graduate looking to get their foot in the door. I'd be lying if I said his offer didn't seem a little misplaced.

"Can I have some time to think about it?" He thins his lips and rubs his jaw, seemingly somewhat perturbed by my response. If I had to guess, he suspected I'd jump all over the opportunity. "Look, Garrett, I love working here, but I'm just not sure—"

Standing up from his chair, he holds his hand up for me to stop. "Colton will be in the office next Wednesday. Let's have lunch and discuss the details. You're smart for not saying yes right away, which is another reason I know you're meant for this, Aria.

You're brilliant on top of being a knockout. Half of my job is throwing people off their game and making them sweat. You accomplish that with your looks alone. Throw in that brain, and you're an ace. I know all of this is absurdly forward to say, but you're worth the risk."

Wow! That took a turn. I have no doubt I'm somehow being worked over, but I'll worry about ulterior motives later. My boss, an intimidating heartthrob himself, admitted that he found me attractive. He also told me I was smart, but I already knew that about myself. I don't know if it's the antidepressants finally kicking in, but for some reason, I'm choosing to believe his words, and it feels good.

Walking over to the paneled wall of shelves across the room, he pulls out a bottle of whiskey and two glasses before returning to his desk. "It's Friday, and I've had a long week." I watch as he pours two fingers into each glass. He passes a glass to me and says, "Next Wednesday. Lunch with Colton and me. I expect an answer." I nod in agreement. As I move to pick up the glass, he raises his. "Salute," and we tip back our drinks. I fully expected to wince and gag, but that must be some expensive shit because it went down smooth as hell, leaving a spicy taste on my tongue.

As I exit the room, Garrett says, "Be bold, Aria. You already pack a punch." His words only put a little extra pep in my step as I exit his office. This week sucked bad, but right now, I feel good. I can already feel my body starting to loosen from the double shot of whiskey I just took, and my outlook on happy hour tonight is looking up. I need a stiff drink and a good time. When I return to my desk, the workday is finally over. Thank god. Happy hour never sounded better.

~

Walking into Llewelyn's, I fully expected to beat Kris here, but I hear her before I see her. She's standing over at a dartboard, surrounded by a group of older men, probably in their mid-thirties, doing a round of shots. Don't get me wrong, mid-thirties isn't old, but it is when the two of us are only twenty-one.

I begin to make my way over, and she screeches excitedly when she sees me. "Eeek, Aria, it's about time. Meet my new friends. This is Chris, Jake, and Ryan."

All three of the guys stick their hands out at the same time, making me stifle a laugh, but I shake their hands all the same. It seems like such an awkward older-guy move to make, but for some reason, I feel relaxed. Of course, these guys are probably just dumbfounded by the fact that Kris is talking to them.

After I greet all the guys, I hike my thumb over my shoulder and say, "I'm going to go grab a drink—"

That's when Ryan cuts me off. "I'll get it. What are you having?" I purse my lips and consider letting him buy me a drink after slowly giving him a once-over from head to toe. He looks like an older version of Zac Efron minus the blue eyes and long hair from the musical days. Not a bad guy to have on my arm tonight, especially when I'm trying to forget the only one I want.

Ryan catches me looking and gives me a knowing smirk before placing his hand at the base of my back and leading me toward the bar. That's when I add, "Hey, I was still undecided if I was going to waste your money."

He laughs. "Okay, well, how about you let me worry about my money?"

Something about how he says that hits deep, and my stomach instantly knots. I'm jolted back to Holden's words, "Why do you think you get to tell me what I want?" They remind me that this is what I do. I shut people down before I give them a chance. The cycle needs to stop somewhere, so I let him buy me a drink.

When we get to the bar, I order a round of shots. I need something to take the edge off. Ryan's brows shoot up, but he doesn't question it. As I grab the tray of tequila shots, Ryan picks up his beer and the Bloody Mary I ordered, and we head back to the group. Kris sees me approaching with the tray and immediately starts whooping it up.

"Hell yes, girl! That's what I'm talking about. Where was this bitch last Friday at my party?" She passes a shot to everyone, and we all bring it in for a "Cheers" before throwing them back. I quickly suck my lime and reach for my Bloody Mary to chase the burn.

I ordered the premium Bloody Mary because they come with olives, pearl onions, pepperoni, and a pretzel stick wrapped in bacon. Since I skipped lunch, I figured the V8 juice and tiny appetizer that comes on top would be good for me. I don't know if that's the alcohol talking or just me trying to let myself indulge, but I feel zero guilt after I've devoured all the snacks on top.

"Aria, have you played darts before?" Ryan asks from across the table we're all currently congregated around.

I briefly wrack my brain, trying to remember. "Actually, I haven't." The fact that I've never played darts sounds preposterous, but I honestly haven't.

His face breaks out into a massive smile before he comes around the table and again puts his hand at the base of my back before saying, "Let's fix that."

I don't miss how Kris rolls her eyes. She sees it too. Ryan is trying to put the moves on me. She and I smile knowingly before I head to the dartboard with Ryan. I'm doing this. I'm stepping out of my comfort zone. I watch as he steps up to the board, removing all the darts before returning to me. Once he's back, we take a long pull from our drinks before setting them on a nearby table and starting the game. He shows me how to angle my body, keep my back straight, and not lean in even though it's what feels natural. I watch as he throws his hand. It seems easy enough.

I'm just stepping up, preparing to throw my first dart, when I feel hands grip my hips, but before I can register any response, another voice sends my heart into my stomach. "I'm going to need you to take your hands off my girl before we have a problem." When I turn around and meet Holden's gaze, I see fury. He's pissed.

Ryan must take my silence and overall lack of reaction as

something it's not because he steps in and says, "Aria, do you know this guy? Are you okay?"

My eyes haven't left Holden's when he arches a brow in question. His jaw is set, and he's clearly holding himself back. I can tell it's taking him real effort not to lose it right now when I continue to stand there, shocked that he's here at all. He steps toward Ryan, ready to fight, and I quickly snap out of my daze.

"Yeah, I'm good, Ryan. Could you give us a minute?"

To which Holden smirks and rubs his jaw, clearly agitated. "Don't bother coming back. She's mine." Ryan gives me a once-over and shakes his head before turning on his heel and heading back to the group. I have no words as Holden stands there with a poignant and venomous glare that makes me question his reasons for coming. My heart feels like it's about to beat out of my chest. I have so many things I want to say but no words.

Then, finally, his eyes soften briefly before he says, "Careful, pretty girl. If you keep looking at me like that, I might think you missed me."

But I did miss him. I more than missed him. It took earnest effort not to think about the first man who made me feel everything. Holden may have given me my first orgasm, but more than that, he sees me. He sees parts of me that no one else does. He sees my pain, and he's here regardless.

Standing before me now, he looks like the past week pained him just as much, and I cave. Without another thought, I throw myself into his arms and hold him tight, determined to never let go. It takes less than a second for him to wrap his arms around me just as tightly. "Fuck, Aria. Let's go." I nod in agreement before reluctantly pulling out of his embrace and remembering I'm here with Kris. I look around, trying to locate her, when he says, "She knows, Aria. How do you think I knew to come here? Let's go."

Holden starts to pull me out of the crowded bar, and I let him. Once we're outside and the bar's noise is behind us, I ask, "Kris knew you were coming tonight? She didn't mention it to me." That's when it dawns on me she didn't mention Holden at all today, which, in all honesty, should have been a red flag. Kris is a gossip queen and the person who set us up. Holden's name should have been the first thing out of her mouth when I saw her this morning or, hell, even when I arrived at the bar tonight.

"Yeah, I asked her not to say anything. I didn't want you to run." I feel like we're racing toward his truck as he pulls me along.

"Holden, can we slow down? What's the rush?" Rather than answer my question, he stops dead in his tracks, picks me up, and throws me over his shoulder, catching me off guard and causing me to shriek. "Oh my god. Holden, you're making a scene."

He slaps my ass. "I know exactly what I'm doing. Making sure everyone knows who you fucking belong to."

When we reach his truck, he opens the passenger side door and deposits me into the seat. Before he can close the door, I kick my foot out. "Holden, wait. I can't leave with you."

He stands there with one arm holding the door and the other propped on the truck frame, caging me in. "Aria, I'm done playing games. I gave you a week. I'm not giving you any more time."

My eyes narrow on his, and then I ask. "What do you mean, you gave me a week?"

He shakes his head in annoyance. "Do you seriously think I didn't want to pick up my phone and call or text you? You were literally my every other thought."

"So why didn't you? Why did you wait until tonight?"

He drops his arms, dragging his gaze to the ground before he brings his hands up to rest on my knees. "Because I needed you to miss me so that when I came back, that pretty heart would know it's mine."

"Holden, I—" His eyes snap to mine, and I lose my words. Those eyes are like an abyss threatening to swallow me whole with all the promise of what could be. My hand flies up to cup his face, and he leans into it, making my heart clench. He wants me. He wants me just as much as I want him. Slowly, he glides his hands up my thighs before winding his arms around my waist and pulling me into his chest. Holding him tight to my front, I lazily run my fingers through his hair, lost in the completeness I feel with him wrapped around me until my phone buzzes in my wristlet.

Reluctantly, I release him and move to check my message, but when Holden pulls out of our embrace, the expression on his face is a mix of anger and hurt. I grab his wrist before he has a chance to step away. "Wait, Holden, it's not what you think. We need to talk, but I have to go home."

His eyes search mine and find my truth. Motioning toward my phone, he asks, "Is that why you said you couldn't leave with me?"

I nod. "Yes. It's a lot to explain, and I don't know where to start, but if you don't think it's too soon to meet the family, you can follow me home."

My voice breaks with nerves at the end. Clearly, Holden likes me a lot, but meeting the family is boyfriend-girlfriend level, and we're not there. *Are we?*

But in the next breath, I'm reminded of why I'm so infatuated with this man. "I thought you'd never ask, pretty girl." It's like he senses my internal conflict and counteracts it.

I smile with what I'm sure is the goofiest-looking grin ever, before asking, "Really?"

This time, he pulls me out of the truck, clutching me to his body as he drops me to the ground. "Pretty girl, I'll follow you anywhere."

He places a kiss on my forehead and closes the door. "Where are you parked?"

Looking around, I get my bearings before spotting my car two rows over. "Just over there." I point in the direction of my vehicle.

"Come on. I'll walk you." He grabs my hand and interlaces our fingers like a legit couple would do, and my brain goes blank. Great. I'm a mindless idiot now that I've decided to pursue something with Holden.

He opens my door for me to climb in and says, "Aria, I want

the address before I walk back to my truck." My head snaps back in surprise before realizing he's seen this play out before and thinks I'm going to run. "Holden, I'm not running. I promise. Look, Sunday—"

He holds out his hand to stop me. "It's fine. If you're not running, giving me the address shouldn't be an issue."

I shake my head, somewhat perturbed that he doesn't believe me. Can't he feel my truth? Sticking my hand out, I say, "Fine. Give me your phone. But for the record, I wasn't running."

After handing me his phone, he adds, "And whatever you were about to say, I want to hear it when we get to your house." I put the address in his Maps app and hand it back with some extra sass as I shove it into his hand. His other hand quickly clamps down, holding mine in place. "Don't tease me, pretty girl. I like it rough."

I'm so screwed.

# 9

## ONLY HER

### HOLDEN

This week sucked hardcore. What's fucked up is I feel like I let it happen. I knew the moment Aria woke up in my arms on Sunday she was going to run, and I didn't do shit to stop her. I sat there and let her feed me half-truths. I knew there would be no convincing her that my feelings were real, that they weren't fabricated to get in her pants, because I know she thinks we don't fit. The night at the bar in the bathroom, she said, "I'm not what he's looking for." She was right about the not looking part. I wasn't looking for anyone, but I couldn't un-find her. She's a runner for a reason. I knew I had to let her go if I had any chance of keeping her.

This entire week, I put a lot of faith into the connection I felt with her. The minute her eyes latched onto mine that first night at the bar, I knew in my gut she was meant to be mine. Her eyes awaken deadened parts of my soul. Parts I never thought I'd get back. I felt her in my bones, and as much as it scared me, it made me feel alive. I've been empty on the inside for far too long, just going through the motions. I'm tired of watching this life pass me by. I don't want to be a slave to my past anymore. I need to let go.

Tonight, I took a risk coming after Aria. We all have something that eats away at our sanity and threatens to choke out the people we strive to be. Aria doesn't want to let me in because she doesn't want me to see her. She doesn't want me to peel back the layers and discover her ugly. The problem is, I'm not going anywhere. She is my light in the dark, and I'm not letting her go.

Pulling up to her house, I park on the street and triple check the address to ensure I'm at the right place. I don't think she put a bogus address in my phone because I caught her off guard, but I hauled ass to beat her here on the off chance she did and I would have to hunt her down.

Our conversation about how she landed her job crosses my mind. Garrett's random job offer strikes a chord with me, making me question if her demons aren't abuse-related. Just because he was a stranger to her doesn't mean the same was true for him. I can't help but feel whatever her demons might be, they placed her on his radar.

While Connor's family is known for their charity work for victims of sexual, physical, and domestic abuse, the rumors I've heard lately suggest it's a cover.

If the Callahan's aren't operating their business above board, I don't get the impression that Connor knows anything about it. However, those are the ones you usually need to watch out for. The people you least expect to have dark secrets can be the most sinister. Until now, I haven't had reason to dig, but knowing Aria might be mixed up in their world gives me cause.

My assumptions of potential past abuse are making my stomach churn. It's a possibility. She didn't want me to take her shirt off the other night. Once it was off, however, it wasn't like anything was wrong. She's gorgeous. But something triggered that reaction. Bile starts rising in my throat at the direction my thoughts are taking me. Luckily, her car pulling down the street catches my attention, and I hop out of my truck to meet her.

When she climbs out of her little Crossover SUV, I'm greeted with a perfect view of her perky tits before she stands up. Fuck, what I wouldn't do to have one in my mouth right now. Unable to resist touching her, I pull her into me and nuzzle my face into her neck, making her skin prickle. "Did I tell you how amazing this top looks on you?" Her hands rest on my hips, briefly sending shivers down my spine. I can't help but lick my way up her neck, needing to taste her. Those small hands make their way up my back, where she fists my shirt in her hands.

"Holden—" My name out of her mouth, all breathless and bothered, has me rock hard. I press my erection into her stomach as I pin her to the car, ensuring she doesn't miss how my body responds to her. She lets out a long "Mmm" before adding, "You probably don't want to meet my parents and brother with a boner. They're all home and very aware I have company." *Shit.* That sobers me up real quick.

Releasing her, I take a deep breath before running my hands through my hair to try and rein in my raging libido. When I turn to walk away, she grabs my hand, and when my eyes land on hers, I know what she wants. I pull her into my chest and run my hand through her hair as I tuck it behind her ear. With our faces mere inches apart, she says, "You aren't going to kiss me, are you?" I can't help but smirk.

Leaning down, I place a chaste kiss on the corner of her mouth before saying, "Not yet. At the bar, you were going to let another man touch what's mine, and I'm not over it."

Her eyes narrow on mine before she attempts to call my bluff. "So what was that a minute ago?"

Reaching behind her, I grab her ass hard enough to make her gasp before saying, "Payback for making me miss a week of this."

I slide her hand in mine and close her car door before walking toward the front of her house. Aria takes a deep breath, bringing back that feeling of unease that settled over me right before she showed up. "Aria, is there anything I should know before I go in?"

Her brow furrows and her eyes narrow at my question before she says, "Probably, but it's a little late for that now."

Before I can even respond to that, the front door swings wide open to an older man with salt-and-pepper hair, tan skin, and hands that look like they swing a hammer all day. His eyes zero in on me before he looks to Aria and asks, "Is he the reason the cops were at my house last weekend?"

My eyes go wide as I turn to Aria in disbelief. She closes her eyes and mutters a drawn-out, *"Dad,"* in unison with someone else in the house.

Releasing my hand, she walks into the house and past her father as I stay glued to the spot on the front porch, unsure what I just walked into. "Well, are you going to come in, son, or not?" Now I know where Aria gets her moments of complete bluntness. There are times when she seems so shy and introverted, and others when she's assertive and confident as fuck. I never know which one I will get, and honestly, I like it. Maybe I'm attracted to crazy.

I move to walk in and offer my hand to her father in greeting. "Hi, I'm Holden. It's nice to meet you, sir."

He takes my hand. "John, I'll let you know when I can return the sentiment."

"Dad, seriously. Give the guy a break," comes from another male voice behind me. Turning around, the guy I assume to be Aria's brother greets me. "Hey, man. I'm Spencer. Ignore my dad."

Spencer is close to my height, probably about "six, one, with brown eyes and blond hair that matches Aria's, and I can tell from his build, he's an athlete. "You said your name is Holden, right? Do you happen to be Holden Hayes?"

My brow furrows as I confirm. "Yeah, do I know you?"

Aria's father pipes up. "Good, now I have a full name to give the police next time they show up at my house." My eyes dart to Aria where she's standing across the living room, shaking her head and thinning her lips as she removes her wedges. What the hell happened last weekend? I can't help but wonder if it's the reason she ghosted me completely.

While I knew she was running, I expected her to at least give me a bullshit excuse as to why she didn't want to meet up. When the entire day had passed without explanation, I second-guessed everything. That simple act of not bullshitting me made me feel like I had her pegged all wrong. It's what made me doubt our connection. All week, I felt like maybe I'd missed something, but now I'm wondering if whatever her dad keeps referring to is the reason she wasn't around Sunday.

"Yeah, I stopped playing ball after my senior year of high school, but the summer of 2018, I still played select ball, and that year, your team versed mine in the Rose Bud tournament for first place. You were their ace." *Fuck.* This night is getting out of hand. I do not want to walk down memory lane with Aria's brother about the last game he ever played. We both remember that game for different reasons, and mine will forever haunt me. Seriously, what are the chances Aria's brother versed me on the night that forever changed the trajectory of my life? I try to play it cool and not let my nerves show.

Bringing my gaze back to Spencer instead of the floor, I say, "Wow, that's some memory you have. I remember the game, but I couldn't tell you shit about the other team." I shrug my shoulders, feeling somewhat bad.

He grips my shoulder before saying, "Don't sweat it. I probably wouldn't remember either, except it's hard to forget the last game you ever played."

"What are you talking about? You still play baseball," Aria chimes in from across the room.

He shrugs. "No, Aria, I play beer league softball for fun. It's not the same."

"He's going to school to be a doctor. Spencer could have played college ball if he wanted."

"Doctor? That's crazy. I don't think I could go to school that long."

Spencer runs his hand through his hair. "Yeah, it's a lot, but now more than ever, I think it's where I was always meant to be." He gives Aria a sidelong glance before walking off down the hall.

Aria approaches me and grasps my hand when I lean in and ask, "What happened last weekend that I don't know about?"

She gives me a timid smile before pulling me into the kitchen. "Mom, I'd like you to meet Holden. Holden, this is my mom, Cynthia."

"Oh my." She puts her hands on her cheeks. "Aria, you didn't mention how handsome he was."

She rolls her eyes before drawing out, "Mom."

Her mom swats her shoulder. "Hey, I'm old. I call it like I see it. No beating around the bush. Aria, I put plates for you and Holden on the back patio." Her mom holds Aria's eyes for a beat longer than necessary as Aria nods. There was some silent communication going on there. Over what, I'm not sure. Aria tugs at my hand and leads me through the sliding glass doors at the rear of the kitchen. "It was nice meeting you, Holden," her mom calls out just as we exit onto the patio.

The backyard isn't huge, but it is very private. One of her parents is a gardener. Hedging trees are strategically placed across shared fences to provide privacy between houses. Flowerbeds have been freshly mulched, and gold string lights are wrapped through the wooden trellis that covers the patio.

Aria releases my hand, snapping my attention from the serenity of the yard back to her. I follow her over to the table and sit in the chair opposite the one she is taking, where a plate has been laid out for me. "Do you like lemon water?" She motions with her hand to the pitcher in the center of the table. I nod, and she pours us each a glass. Once seated, she asks, "Where would you like me to start?"

This entire night has gone nothing like I thought it would, and if I thought I had questions before, it's nothing compared to what I have now. I know where I want her to start, but I also want her to tell me because she wants to share that part of herself with me—not because I demanded it, but because she feels the investment is worth it.

"Why don't you tell me what you want to tell me, pretty girl."

I can tell my words have caught her off guard because she stops pushing the food around her plate. I know then I made the right call because her expression says it all. She pulls in a deep breath before dropping her fork.

"I need to eat this dinner. Can we do that first?" She starts nervously fidgeting with the lace detail on her shirt, and that's how I know that statement alone meant something.

I answer, "Yeah, let's eat," trying to sound as casual as possible, given the immense stress I feel after walking into this house tonight. Looking at my plate, I notice the food is plain and simple, which doesn't fit her mom's personality. Sure, I just met Cynthia, but she strikes me as a woman who puts her whole heart into everything, including her cooking. The food I'm looking at screams clinical diet. It's even portioned out. I know what food portioning looks like, being an athlete. At my level, during the season, my plates look similar to this. Grilled chicken breast, plain, steamed broccoli, and what looks like zoodles with a tablespoon of red sauce.

I've just started slicing into my chicken breast when I look up and notice Aria has yet to touch her plate, and that's when I'm slapped with the realization of what this is. My girl has an eating disorder. The beer, the comments about not being what I want, her insecurity with her shirt, the wrap. The wrap was probably all she ate all day. *Fuck.* This hurts. I grab my plate and move to sit beside her instead of across from her.

"What are you doing?" She shuffles in her chair to move when I do.

"No, sit. I want to be closer to my girl."

"Holden—" she starts, but I hold my hand up to stop her.

"Can you do me a favor?" She narrows her eyes at me, trying to get a read on me, so I say, "I want you to sit on my lap."

She rolls her eyes. "I already told you, I need to eat dinner."

When she moves to pick up her fork, I take it from her hand. "Come here." I pat my lap before adding, "Now." This time, she doesn't argue and does as I ask. I can't make her feel better about the food. I know that much, but I'm hoping I can distract her and make her forget.

She sits her perfectly plump ass on my lap, and I can't help but groan at how luscious she feels on my thighs. I make a mental note for later to take her in this position, her riding my dick cowgirl style so I can watch this ass bounce. "Fuck, Aria. You have no idea what you do to me, pretty girl." I reach around and squeeze her breast. "Let's eat." She lets out a frustrated sigh, and I revel in it. I love knowing my touch gets her worked up.

"Want to play a game?" Turning her head, she eyes me suspiciously, and I can't help but smirk. "For every bite you take, I'll give you a reward."

She shakes her head no, preparing to argue. "Holden—" but her pleas die when my hand cups her pussy through her jeans. Once my intent is clear, she nods in agreement.

"Good girl."

Since she didn't cut up her chicken, I start feeding her from my plate. Sticking my fork into a piece, I bring it to her mouth and put my lips next to her ear before I say, "Take a bite for me, pretty girl." When she listens, I'm instantly hard for so many reasons. One: I fucking love that I'm helping her with something that hurts her. Two: she's following directions like she loves it, which is sexy as hell. And three: regardless of whether or not she knows it, Aria has a banging body. I run my tongue over the shell of her ear, pushing her hair aside before kissing my way down her shoulder.

Grabbing another bite, I bring it to her mouth again and smile when she waits. She wants me to ask her. "You're a fucking tease, you know that, baby? Wrap those pretty lips around that fork like it's my cock." Again, she listens, and fuck me if this little game isn't backfiring.

Quickly, I throw my head back toward the house to ensure we have privacy before pulling the front of her top down enough to let her tit out. I rub my thumb over her nipple before palming her breast. "I love these tits, baby. I want them in my mouth." She rests her head against my shoulder and lets out a throaty moan. I can feel a bead of pre-cum drip from my dick, and I have to force myself back to the task at hand. Dropping my hand from her breast, I say, "I'm going to need you to sit forward, pretty girl, if you want me to touch you." When she does, I have another bite waiting for her. This time, she takes it without prompt. "Is there something else you'd rather be doing?" She nods as I move her on my lap so she can feel my erection pressing against her ass.

"Tell me, Aria." I pull the other side of her top down so that both of her perfect tits are out and exposed. Both nipples are so fucking hard and pert. I palm both of her tits at once before tweaking those hardened peaks.

"Mmm, Holden. Please fuck me." The words haven't even finished leaving her mouth when the sliding door starts to open. Immediately, I fold my arm across her chest to make it look like I'm holding her.

"Hey, Mom wants to know if Holden wants dessert." Fuck, if he only knew.

Aria discretely pulls up her top before I release her. Her face is flushed, and I love it. I clear my throat, "No, man. I'm good. Aria was going to show me her room real quick, and I was going to hit the road. I still have a forty-five-minute drive home."

"Cool, I'll let her know. Maybe you can come out next weekend for my birthday. I bet a few of the guys remember that last game."

If he only knew how much I don't want to remember that last game. "Sounds good." I move to stand and follow him inside when I notice Aria isn't following. She's still thoroughly aroused, and I fucking love it. "You coming, pretty girl?" I can't help but smile at my not-so-subtle play on words. Her cheeks heat before she moves to follow us inside.

"So, where's your room?" She gives me a tense smile, and I can tell she's nervous about showing me her room. If I had to guess, she's probably wondering why I want to see it in the first place when I said I had to leave, but that's for me to know and for her to find out. As I follow her down the hall, she points out the bathroom, Spencer's room, and her parents' room. Her room shares a wall with Spencer's. I tuck that little piece of information away for later.

When she opens the door, I'm hit with her scent. The entire room smells like fresh strawberries. It smells like her. Everything is all white. There's a queen-sized bed with a white tufted headboard and a white puffy comforter with way too many white frilly pillows. A lamp and a picture of her with another girl sit on her nightstand. I walk over and pick it up. "Who is this?"

Smiling, she moves to sit on her bed. "That's my best friend, Olivia. She had to move to California with her family a couple of years ago, but we kept in touch. Actually, she'll be in town next weekend for Spencer's birthday. Strangely enough, they share the same birthday."

"Is she coming into town for him?"

Her eyebrows shoot up. "What? No, her family is from here, so she comes back a few times a year to visit."

I walk around to the other side of the bed and note how her eyes follow my every move. I pull open the white sheer curtain when I get to the window. "What are you doing?"

I shrug. "Just taking in the space my girl spends her time in." Spotting a CD on her dresser, I ask, "Hey, what CD is that?" I'm hoping she'll get up to see for herself, allowing me to make my move. When she does, I spin the lock on her window, unlatching it for later before heading to join her. As I approach her from behind, I wrap my arms around her and pull her tight against my front. "Incubus? I should have known."

"Why's that?"

"Because, Aria, I was meant to meet you, so it's only fitting that the only thing sitting out in my girlfriend's stark white room happens to be a CD from my all-time favorite band and the current one on deck in my truck."

Immediately, she spins around in my arms. "Girlfriend? That's mighty presumptuous of—"

Bending down, I crash my mouth to hers, silencing any further objections I know are bullshit. Honestly, the girlfriend part was a slip, but I don't fucking regret it. I dip my tongue into her mouth, and when hers brushes against mine, I'm in heaven. My entire body feels alive when she's kissing me. Briefly, I pull back. "Tell me I'm wrong." She answers by fusing our mouths back together. I can't resist grabbing her ass with both hands and pulling her against my front. Fuck, I need to be inside her, but I also need to walk out of this house without a boner.

Breathlessly, I pull back. "Aria, can I see you tomorrow?"

This time, there's no hesitation before she answers. "Yes. Will I be coming to another game?"

I kiss her lips one more time. "I'm not sure if that means you want to or..."

She places her hand on my chest and says, "Holden, I get it. It's your passion, and you're so close. I don't mind coming to your games. I like watching you play." I bite my lip to stifle the smile that wants to take over my mouth. She's my girl.

"Come on, walk me to the door."

~

Parking a block over from Aria's house, I sit in my truck for ten minutes before deciding enough time has passed, and it's time to surprise my girl.

*My girl.* I still can't believe those words are coming out of my mouth. Aria was not in the plan, but there is no way I could let her go. Looking back, I think she pierced my heart the moment her friend request came across my phone. Those eyes had me hooked from the moment I saw them. I'm almost positive that I'm right about her having an eating disorder. Of course, it doesn't change anything for me, but it pains me to know she's fighting demons only she can fix.

What's more, I can't decide if this revelation has anything to do with her job or if her run-in with Garrett Callahan is purely coincidental and not a charity case. I have difficulty swallowing the latter because if there's any merit to the nefarious rumors, she could have a target on her back. Connor's uncle, Colton Callahan, is somewhat of the celebrity in the family. He runs their Boston branch and has had several big-name cases for some well-known politicians. The scandalous part is that the female plaintiffs from two of his most recent wins were seen with Colton shortly after, only to turn around and disappear. I suppose since he won the cases for his clients, people assume the accusers accepted their loss and went about their business. Because Waterloo is a small town, I know gossip is typically overdramatized, but this past week, I did some digging, and this is anything but fabricated.

All these revelations have my head spinning. Hell, finding out her issues were related to some ex might have been an easier pill to swallow; at least then, I could do something.

I'm just approaching her window when I catch a glimpse of her walking through her room. Advancing, I watch as she goes through what I assume is her nightly routine, and I wait. Moving toward her dresser, she pulls out a shirt—but not just any shirt. My shirt. She pulls it out and brings it to her face before inhaling deeply. The move makes my heart do funny things, things I've never felt, and I can feel my cheeks ache from the massive smile taking over my face. My girl not only wants me; she misses me.

Aria has brushed me off so many times that I couldn't help but question if I was alone in my feelings for her. Maybe I didn't affect her the way she did me, but seeing that move just now only confirms what I feel deep down. She was just as scared as I was. If I had to guess, same as me, she's never felt this way. Setting the shirt on her bed, I watch as she unbuttons her jeans and shimmies them down. Her back is to me, giving me a perfect view of her plump peach of an ass. I bite my knuckle and stifle a groan. The corset top she's wearing is a body suit, and with her pants off, it now looks like fucking lingerie. She rests her ass against the bed before reaching between her legs to unsnap the clasps and pull her top over her head. My cock is now throbbing against the zipper of my jeans, aching to be inside her.

As I continue to stalk outside her window, I mentally remind myself to close my mouth as my jaw goes slack from seeing her in white lace panties and a matching bra. It sets off her creamy, slightly tanned skin perfectly. I watch as she walks to her bedroom door and looks at herself in the mirror. Standing there, she stares at herself before reaching behind her back to unclasp her bra. When her gorgeous tits fall out, she lifts her right arm and runs her fingers over the skin between her breast and underarm before repeating the move on the other side. When her eyes return to the mirror, she stares for long moments before running her hands along her lower abdomen and wincing.

God, I want to climb through this window right now, pull her into my arms, and tell her how perfect she is. I wish I could make her see what I see. I'm about to do just that when she drops her hands and walks back toward her bed, where she pulls my shirt on. *Why is it so fucking hot when a chick wears your shirt?*

Pulling back her comforter, she climbs into bed and checks her phone before placing it on her nightstand. I watch as she slides down between the sheets and fluffs her pillows. She looks like the epitome of the princess and the pea right now. Everything is perfectly in its place.

I slowly lift the screen from the window, careful to go undetected. Once it's off, I reach for the window but stop when I see she has her phone again. This time, she is smiling, and my jealousy rears its ugly head. I want to be the guy to put that smile on her face, not whoever's on the other end of that phone. However, the possessiveness I feel barely gets a chance to morph into anger because my phone vibrates in my pocket. When I pull it out, I see it's from her. *Dumbass.*

Aria: I promise I won't ghost you tomorrow.
Sorry about tonight.

My brows furrow as I read the last words. *What does she have to be sorry for?* Her bedroom light flicks off, and that's when I start to open the window. The window is old as shit, and there's no getting around the fact that I'm not going to enter all stealth-like as I had planned. The light flicks back on, and Aria jolts up in bed, bringing her comforter to her chin.

As I step through, I say, "Don't ever hide from me, pretty girl."

She whisper-yells. "What are you doing? You said you had to leave."

Closing the window, I head over to her door and ensure it's locked before kicking my shoes off and stripping down to my boxers. "That was just bullshit so I could come back and have you uninterrupted. I doubt Spencer or your dad would let me hang out with you undisturbed in any part of this house."

Her eyebrows rise as my words wash over her before she shrugs in agreement. Heading over to the bed, her eyes follow my every step, and I know she sees it. You can't fucking miss it. The scar I have as a daily reminder of my ugly past sits low on my stomach, right above my groin. It's unsightly, deep, and unmistakably tragic. Aria's eyes latch onto mine, but she doesn't ask, and I am reminded of why. She has her own demons. Aria knows what it's like to live with the dark, and she won't push. Reaching the bed, I pull back the covers on the opposite side and slide in. "Aria, these are some nice sheets."

She smiles. "I know. I take sleeping very seriously. It's one of the few things that makes me happy."

I run my fingers through her hair. "Oh yeah? Why is that?"

She hesitates, thinning her lips briefly before saying, "It's the only time my brain shuts off, and I can find peace." I'm quiet as I wait to see if she'll elaborate and tell me what I think I already know.

When she doesn't, I ask, "What were you sorry about?" Her eyes narrow before the text she sent registers.

"All of it. My dad, my brother, the never-ending blue balls." I can't help but laugh at that last part. "Holden, a lot of stuff has happened since we last saw each other, and it's heavy. So, if you want to renege on the boyfriend card and run for the hills, I get it."

"Unless you're pregnant with another man's baby, not much could make me run."

She swats my chest. "What? I'm not pregnant." Then, brushing her thumb over my chest, she asks, "What if I'm dying?"

I pull her chin up. "Are you?"

She shakes her head no before starting, "What if—"

I cut her off. "Stop deflecting and just talk to me, Aria. Trust that I'm not some superficial prick; trust that I want you just as much as you want me."

Pressing her finger to my lips, she says, "Wait, who said I want you?"

I pull her into me so her body is flat against mine. "Stop," I draw out.

Her eyes suddenly go wide, realization dawning on her face. "Hold up, how long were you outside my window?"

I roll my lips before answering truthfully. "Long enough to watch you sniff my shirt." Her eyes close, and I know it's because she knows I saw what she did in the mirror. I don't want her to feel pressured into discussing it, so I try to lighten the moment. "By the way, I'll be taking something with me tonight."

I slowly drag my hand up her thigh until I reach the hem on her panties, where I run my finger along the curve of her ass. Opening her eyes, she smiles. "You want my underwear?"

I move my mouth to her ear and say, "I want everything," before placing open-mouthed kisses all over her neck. I know she can feel I'm rock hard, considering my boxers are the only barrier between us when I press it against her stomach.

She slowly hums, "Mmm," from deep in her chest. Instantly, my mouth covers hers, wanting to consume all her delicious sounds.

Before I can deepen our kiss, she brings her hand to my chest and pushes me back. My eyes go wide, and for a moment, I consider that maybe I crossed some line again, but then she says, "Let me tell you about Sunday." As much as I want to do nothing more than what we are doing, I need to hear this story. Tucking my hands behind my head, I prepare to be all ears. She gives me a nervous smile before resting her head on my chest and starting.

"If I'm being honest, I did plan on texting you once I got home, but it wasn't going to be to hang out. I planned on telling you it wasn't going to work out, but for some reason, I think you already knew that." When her eyes snap to mine, I know she sees my truth. I did know.

"You never got the bullshit text because when I pulled up to my house, a police car was parked in my driveway, right next to my ex's Camaro." My heart rate kicks up a notch at the mention of her ex being here. Aria has her head propped up on one arm now while the other draws lazy circles on my chest, and I'm sure she doesn't miss the new pace in the rise and fall of my chest because she adds, "Holden, I came home wearing your shirt. I did the walk of shame up to my front door with two cops, my ex, and my family as witnesses. I don't think you need to get worked up."

I pull her onto me and kiss her lips, only to dip my tongue in briefly before saying, "You make me possessive, Aria. I don't want to hear about another man. You're mine."

She smacks my chest quietly before sitting up and straddling my hips. "I'm telling you the story. Anyway, he took off like a bat out of hell once he saw me, and I haven't heard from him since. He knew I'd been with someone else, and it felt good to revel in it because he dropped a bomb on my life that day." She looks to the window and stays silent for a minute. Whatever words are about to leave her mouth aren't easy.

"The cops were here because that Saturday I came to see you, Logan decided to pay me one of his surprise visits, but I texted him that there was no us and that he needed to let me go. He blew up my phone, so I shut it off, and it died. Logan came to my house and told my parents he thought I might be suicidal."

My eyes widen as my hands fly to her hips. "Baby..."

She puts her hand up to stop me. "I'm not suicidal. A month after I told Logan I wanted a break, he showed up on my doorstep, and I confided in him something I hadn't shared with anyone. I was sick. I am sick."

I sit up and pull her into my arms, but she stops me. She pushes me back down and says, "Just let me get this out." Blowing out a breath, she looks to the ceiling before continuing. "I'm trying really hard to get better. I've been trying for months, but it's so hard. I have good days, but the bad days are horrible, and I hurt myself on those days." I can't help but grab her hands.

"Aria, what do you mean you hurt yourself?"

When she closes her eyes, tears roll down each cheek. "I binge-eat, then get upset, then throw it up. Or I eat what I think is too much and work out until I pass out, or I starve myself. Which vice it is depends on the day." Her eyes find mine after the last word leaves her mouth.

I'm unsure what to say, but I'm not naïve enough to believe that telling her she's crazy to do that to herself would help. Hell, half the reason I suspected this was because I see it all the time being an athlete. There is so much pressure to be in the best shape to stay on top and win, even if it's detrimental to your physical health. It's obvious she knows there's an issue. So, I ask, "Did telling me make you feel better?"

"It does and doesn't all at the same time. It makes me accountable, but it also leaves me feeling very vulnerable. I don't want pity; I don't need a babysitter or someone to convince me I'm wrong. I know I'm wrong. But I have to figure it out myself."

This time, when I move to sit up, she lets me. I bring my thumbs to her face and wipe away her tears before kissing her forehead. "Aria, look at me." When her beautiful brown eyes find mine, I'm a goner. She trusted me with her demon, she exposed herself to me, and now I want to be her everything. "We all have a weakness, pretty girl. None of us are untouched by grief, pain, or loss. At the end of the day, some of ours are easier to identify than others. But I promise you are not alone. We have each other. You've uncovered all the better parts of me that I thought I'd lost. And I promise to help pull you back when it gets dark."

Her eyes briefly search my face for any doubt before she presses her mouth to mine in a searing kiss that feels more like a vow. When her tongue slides into my mouth and glides over mine, I can't help but groan in awareness that she wants me, that she's letting me in, that she's mine. For now, I have everything I never thought I would, and I want to live in it forever.

My hands run down her back and grip her plump ass. "Aria, you have the sexiest fucking ass I've ever seen." I squeeze it one more time before running my hands up her back and taking her shirt off as I do. This time, she lets me take it off without hesitation, and when she does, I see the marks that weren't visible in the dark the night before.

Immediately, my mouth seeks them out, and I kiss them before my eyes find hers. "Baby, these marks don't make me want you any less. These tits are perfect." Lowering my mouth, I find her nipple and suck hard. Her head flies back as she releases a moan that is borderline too loud. "Pretty girl, I don't want to stop, but you have to try and be quiet." She nods emphatically in agreement before I suck the other tit into my mouth.

When I look up, she's biting her lip. Releasing her nipple with a pop, I kiss my way over to the practically nonexistent marks that run along the side of her breast. She pulls in a breath and holds it, and I can tell they make her self-conscious, but I want her to be confident and comfortable with me. I'm pushing her because I need her to see what I see. Grabbing her breasts, I push them together, running my tongue over her erect nipples. "Fucking perfect." She grinds her pussy against my dick, and I can't take it anymore. I need to be inside her. Wrapping my hands around her waist, I flip her onto her back, catching her off guard and making her squeal.

"What did I say about being loud? I don't think your dad would like it if he knew the things I was doing to you in here."

Her cheeks heat, and she pulls a pillow over her face. I chuckle before kissing my way down her stomach, where I stop when I get to the white scars. Running my tongue along them, I feel her body tighten under my touch. Getting to my knees, I pull the pillow off her face and say, "Aria, do you think these beauty marks change anything for me?" I lower my boxers and stroke my cock from root to tip, producing a bead of cum. Then, rubbing my thumb around the crown, I say, "This is what your body does to me, pretty girl." Biting her lip, she slowly snakes her hand under her panties to relieve the ache building, but I stop her. "That pussy is mine."

I pull her panties off before sitting back on my haunches to take in the sight before me. Aria, completely bared to me on her all-white bed, looking like fucking heaven. "Spread your legs, baby." Her eyes widen, and she hesitates. I start stroking my cock before adding, "I don't have to touch you to get what I want." Her legs tremble slightly before she lets them fall wide. "Fuuuck." Now I'm the one struggling to be quiet when I see her pretty pink pussy slick with wetness. I don't waste another minute. My mouth is on it faster than she can blink, my tongue deep in her tight hole.

Her hiss becomes a moan of pure ecstasy when I slip a finger in. I groan against her clit, sucking it into my mouth before mumbling, "You taste so good." Thrusting my tongue inside her, I can't get deep enough. My god, I've never wanted a woman this much. Adding another digit, I curl my fingers to find that spot I know she likes and suck her clit back into my mouth.

"Fuck, Holden, right there." Her hand comes to the back of my head to keep me in place, and I feel her pussy clench.

"Yes, come on my face, pretty girl. Show me how much you like it."

She whimpers, "Don't stop," over and over. And I can't help but wonder if there's not more to those words.

When I say, "Show me what this pussy is going to do to my

cock," she goes off, and I lap up every drop, knowing I've discovered what makes my girl tick.

Before her pussy is done spasming, I bring my cock to her entrance and run it through her swollen lips. *That's hot.* "Holden, please."

I shake my head. "I need to get a condom." But, grabbing hold of my hand, she stops my retreat.

"Just the tip. I want to feel you."

Those big brown eyes are pleading with mine, and who the fuck says no? I repeat, "Just the tip," as I grip my cock at the base and run it through her folds one more time before slowly dipping it in. We both moan in unison at the feel of having no barrier between us. Pulling out, I smack my throbbing cock against her pussy before dragging my tip through her folds once more, but this time when I move to dip in, she pushes back, and my cock slips halfway in. My hands fly into my hair before my eyes dart to hers. "Aria?"

"I'm on birth control."

Leaning down, I cage myself around her before bringing my lips to her ear. "This is how you want me, pretty girl?"

She nods and adds, "Please, Holden, I want this."

The words haven't even finished leaving her mouth before I push in to the hilt. We're both silent as we take a minute to adjust to the feeling. I can feel my cock already starting to twitch with the need to come. "Fuck, Aria, do you feel what you do to me? I can't resist you." I slowly start to pump into her while kissing her neck. "You're fucking ruining me. Tell me, how am I supposed to ever have anyone else after having you like this?" Her hands slide up my back to my shoulders as her legs wrap around my waist. My jaw goes slack as I pick up the pace, and she bites my shoulder to keep from moaning too loud. I slam in hard as the sensation of her bite and the feeling of being bare threaten to push me over the edge. "Fuck, baby, this cock is yours. You take it so good."

She whimpers into my neck as her nails dig into my back, and she says, "Don't stop."

My jaw clenches for two reasons. One: she's a dirty freak and I love it, and two: I never want to fuck anyone else for the rest of my life. I feel it in the depths of my soul. "What do you want from me, baby?" I shove in hard. "You're the only one that's ever had me like this. Is that what you want to hear?" Her legs are still wrapped tightly around my back, nails digging hard enough to draw blood. When I hear her headboard hit the wall once, I pull back on my thrusts. "You want me to tell you you're the hottest fuck I'll ever have?" Her breaths are ragged, and I can feel her starting to clench. "What will it take to get this pussy to milk my cock?"

I feel the moment her orgasm hits, and she spirals over the edge, screaming. "Yes, yes, god, yes."

I quickly throw my hand over her mouth. "Fuck, Aria! What the hell, baby?" Her eyes roll back into her head as she releases me. When she falls against the pillows, her hands find her breasts, and I swear, when she tweaks her nipples, her pussy squeezes me. Her long blonde hair is splayed across her pillow, her cheeks are flushed, and when her eyes find mine, I'm a goner. I push in hard two more times and find my own release before falling on top of her.

Our chests are heaving as we come down from our shared release, then we hear a soft knock at the door. I throw my hand over her mouth, making sure she stays quiet, and she fucking licks it. My eyes go wide. Is she kidding me right now? The soft knock happens one more time, and we stay silent. After a minute passes and no more knocks occur, I roll off her and instantly miss the warmth of being buried inside her. Not wanting to let her go, I pull her with me, so she's partly covering my body.

"What was that? Are you crazy? We almost got caught."

She lays her head on my chest. "Sorry, I didn't realize I—"

My heart stumbles at the potential of what she might be saying. All her pleas for me not to stop suddenly come full circle. I know she's not a virgin, but... "Aria, tell me." I pull her chin up so that her eyes are on mine.

She closes her eyes to shut me out before saying, "I, um, I, um, well, that was only my third orgasm."

Now my heart feels like it's about to gallop right out of my chest—until she starts to pull away. I roll on top of her, pinning her down so she can't escape me. "Pretty girl, when was your first?" It had to have been in the back of my truck. My fingers were soaked, and I'd never had a girl respond to me the way she did.

"Holden, please."

I lean down and kiss her forehead, her cheeks, and her nose. "Tell me."

Those beautiful eyes land on mine before she says, "Saturday."

Fuck, that might be just as good as taking her virginity. Knowing I'm the only man who's ever pleasured her in that way wrecks me. "Tell me something. Am I the only man who's had you naked?"

I kiss her neck before trailing my lips up to the shell of her ear. As I make my way to her jaw, she lets out a breathy, "Yes."

I palm one of her perfect tits. "Has anyone ever had their mouth on these?" She shakes her head, and my mouth immediately finds hers. My tongue plunges into her mouth, wanting to take everything. I want all of her. I need all of her. She's my own personal heaven on Earth, and I don't want to let her go. I don't want to waste a moment. I've been so broken for so long, I forgot what it felt like to be alive. My tongue tangles with hers one more time before I pull back and lean my forehead against hers. "I'm forever yours, Aria."

Nodding, she closes her eyes as if what I've said is frivolous. "No, don't do that. Hear my words and believe them."

Then, bringing her hand up, she runs it through my hair and says, "Will you stay with me until I fall asleep?"

I hate how she's ignoring me, but I won't refuse her even as angry as I am. When you've been in the dark long enough, you start to embrace it. It's easier to hide your scars. But because I live there, I know she can't just accept my words as truth even if she wants to. It's part of our punishment. It's part of the hell we subject ourselves to. Or, in my case, what I deserve. Laying down, I pull her to my side and run my fingers through her hair. "Yeah, pretty girl. I'll stay." I'll hold onto her for as long as I can.

# 10

## OFF LIMITS

ARIA

It's been one week since Holden and I became official. I'm obsessed. I can't remember the last time I've been this happy. Don't get me wrong, I have a good life, I'm just lost. But with Holden, I feel parts of me I thought were gone coming back. I smile, I laugh, but most importantly, I feel. He makes me feel everything in the best of ways.

Somewhere along the line, things got incredibly dark for me, but Holden manages to pull me out of that. He pushes me outside of my comfort zone, outside the walls I've somehow boxed myself into. I was hesitant to share my secrets but telling him was also cathartic. Ever since we met, I've felt like he sees me, and not just the parts I want to show him, but the parts I hide away from the world. He's known from the beginning that I was haunted. All that's changed now is he knows why.

Now there is only one more person I care to tell, and she arrives today. I haven't seen Olivia since Christmas, and it's now June. It's one of the longest stretches we've ever gone without seeing each other. Her family usually travels back in the spring for the Easter holiday, but this year, her dad got stuck in the office on some new project. He's a big-shot executive for a chain of rehabilitation centers that cater to Hollywood's elite. But today, she arrives, and I couldn't be more excited. I took off work to meet her at the airport and bring her back to my house.

Fridays are pretty slow around the office, and I just took Garrett and Colton up on their offer to pay for school. How could I not? Garrett's an intelligent man. I have no doubt that he knew exactly what he was doing, playing off my insecurities. While I do my best to hide them, his job is to smell a lie, and now his studied glares don't feel so misplaced. He saw something in me that he wanted, found what made me tick, and used it. I don't blame him for it. Honestly, I don't know what I want to do with my life, but having a boss in my corner doesn't seem like a bad start. Regardless of how I ended up with my job, as strange as it was, I feel like I've earned his offer, and that's a win.

I'd be lying if I said Connor's left-field question about the temperature of the coffee that Garrett spilled on me hadn't crossed my mind during my decision-making process. But looking back, I think I let my imagination get the best of me. Asking if the coffee was hot wasn't out of place. It's the fact that it wasn't that allowed the eeriness to set in. And while I still find that detail odd, it's not a deal breaker.

For now, things aren't so dark, and I'm trying to hold on to that. Last Saturday, when I woke up alone, I was sad, but only until I turned over and found a string of texts from Holden.

Holden: Good morning, pretty girl

Holden: The game is at noon. Field 3 – Waterloo AA

Holden: I miss you so fucking much.

Holden: You're mine all night.

We spent the entire weekend together. Every spare moment we had, we were wrapped around each other. After the game, he fucked me in the cab of his truck, and I finally got to taste that sexy sweat on his neck. When I came over to his parent's house on Sunday, we lay in his bed and watched replays of games all afternoon until the spooning wasn't enough. Holden pulled my tennis skirt to the side and fucked me long and slow with his bedroom door open while his parents were only feet away, watching TV in the other room. It was the hottest sex of my life.

He sent me daily pictures of the bite marks I left on his arm while holding back my moans. I've never been so thoroughly fucked. Holden is a giver, ensuring I enjoy every second when he's inside me. I came twice before he ever found his own release. There's nothing sexier than a man with his arms wrapped tightly around you while he ruts into you from behind, sucking on your neck and whispering dirty obscenities in your ear.

I haven't seen him since Sunday, but we text on and off every day, and he calls me before bed every night. We both work full-time jobs, and while it is summer break, he has clinics and doesn't exactly live close. I'm glad I decided to take a chance on him and let myself have something because, while I might still be incredibly self-conscious, he makes me feel beautiful. The part I haven't figured out is why. Why is he different? I've had other men before him. So why am I giving this one so much?

Deep down, I know exactly why. Because, in my mind, he's the one. I want him to be my forever, but that thought scares the hell out of me. Those are not feelings I should have after knowing someone for a week. The problem is, Holden Hayes is making sure that he is an exception to all rules. He doesn't take no for an answer. I think he's convinced we are endgame, and I can tell he doesn't like it when I brush it off.

"Ari, I can't believe you've been dating a guy for an entire week, and this is the first I'm hearing about it. We tell each other everything." Olivia and I just got back from the airport, and she is currently unpacking her suitcase and hanging clothes in my closet. She could stay at her family's spare house while in town, but we'd be together anyway, so she's crashing here.

Sitting on my bed, I'm biting my nailbeds—not a habit I typically have, but I also don't know where to start this conversation. It's been a crazy ass week.

"Oli, I don't even know where to start. Holden is everything. He is the epitome of the perfect guy that every girl thinks doesn't exist, and for the time, he's mine. I ask myself daily how a guy like him could ever want a girl like me."

She swings around, hanger in hand, pointing it at me. "Ari, what the hell are you talking about? You're a fucking smokehouse, babe." I roll my eyes at her flippant remark, and she doesn't miss it. "When and why did you start putting yourself down? I've noticed it lately and don't understand where it's coming from."

"Let's be real, Oli. I am not the girl guys flock to at parties. That's your role—and don't get me wrong, I'm not mad at you for that. I came to terms with it years ago and learned to accept that I'm the girl that's just a little too thick."

Slamming the hanger down on my dresser, she asks, "Do you think I'm fat?"

Olivia is beautiful. She has long, dark brown hair with eyes to match, and a deep olive complexion from her Italian roots. Our body types are somewhat similar. We both have small boobs and big butts, but where mine is squishy, hers is toned and muscular. Not to mention, she can show off her body year-round. It's perfectly tanned, fit, and unmarked. "No, I don't think you're fat. Why would you ask me that?"

Then, throwing her hands into the air, she says, "Because we are the exact same size."

I shake my head adamantly in response. "No, Oli, I'm about two sizes bigger. My stomach is soft—" She starts unbuttoning her jeans and pulling them down. "What are you doing?"

"Apparently, something is wrong with your eyes, so we're doing this instead. Take your pants off and put these on." She's standing there in a thong, holding her jeans out on one finger for me to try on.

"You're serious?" I quirk an eyebrow at her.

"Do I look like I'm joking?"

I shrug before standing up and pulling my joggers off. "You better not laugh when they only come up to mid-thigh and my ass is hanging out."

"Whatever. Put them on."

I put both feet through the legs and pull them up, and they fit without the need to wiggle. I can even button them without sucking my stomach in. Walking over to the mirror, I stare at myself blankly but fully entranced. *How is it possible that I fit into Oli's pants?*

It's hard to explain how I feel on the inside. But putting on my best friend's pants—a woman I find incredibly gorgeous—strikes a chord with me. It has me questioning all my ugly thoughts. Where did this hate inside of me come from? I've spent countless hours trying to make myself better, not to be this person, but when I dig deep, all I feel is pain. A pain I don't understand. It's always felt so misplaced, like it's not part of me, but I haven't been able to shake it as hard as I try.

Olivia comes up behind me and asks. "Aria, what's wrong? You seem off."

I drop my eyes and take a deep breath before heading to my bed. While I was standing in the mirror trying to understand my body image issues, she threw on a pair of shorts. "I'm sick, Oli."

I'm unsure if my comment registers because she simply stands there staring at me until, finally, she waves her hand in prompt. "And...? That doesn't really tell me anything, Ari."

"A few years ago, things changed for me, and I don't know why, how, or exactly when, but shortly after high school, I started not liking myself or how I look. It became an obsession, and I wish I knew why. Then, one day I woke up and felt ugly, lost, and cynical." She sits on the bed as I turn to look out the window so I don't lose my train of thought.

"I started counting calories and watching what I ate, which was fine until it wasn't. When I started feeling like my dieting wasn't sufficiently yielding the results I wanted, like a thigh gap, I started jogging. I would eat no more than twelve hundred calories a day and work out hard. When I would go out with Kyla and Lauren, I would watch them eat and drink without a second thought. They were putting food and drinks in their mouths and weren't worried about gaining weight, but if I ate those same things, I would gain five pounds. So then, I decided that if I wanted to try some of their food or go out and have drinks, I wouldn't eat that day. I would save my calories for that one meal. Eventually, even that was too much, so a few months ago, I started making myself throw up when I felt like I had too many calories."

Olivia loudly gasps before throwing her hands over her mouth and shaking her head. "Ari, no. Please tell me you're not still hurting yourself. Do you know how bad this can get?" She now has my hands in hers. "We can get you help. You can go to one of my dad's facilities. We can beat this. I promise."

"Oli, I know I'm sick, and this past week, I've had to confront it head-on. Remember Logan? He was the only one who knew about my issues because he caught me with a surprise visit on a bad day, and I shared with him why I chose to take a break. My sickness was part of why I left him, but not the entire reason. He and I weren't a good fit, and I thought maybe if he knew I was damaged, he'd willingly leave me alone and maybe not take everything so personally. That did not happen. If anything, it fucking backfired."

I take a deep breath and try not to get too worked up over the events that transpired two weeks ago. "Logan was butthurt about me ending things officially," I use air quotes on that last word, "But technically, I never took him back. He wouldn't leave me alone. I think he hated that someone broke up with him instead of the other way around."

Olivia nods in agreement. "Honestly, I could see that. I understand why you started dating Logan. You guys were technically friends beforehand, and why not test out the goods? Logan is not hard to look at, but he's also a cocky motherfucker. That was always a dealbreaker for me. Not to mention, he always struck me as the kind of guy who, if you weren't around, wouldn't hesitate to flirt with another girl." Her words don't even sting a little. Before I can offer any rebuttal, she adds.

"And don't think I'm skimming over your earlier proclamations about guys not paying attention to you at parties. That's crap. We didn't even go to any parties. I think we went to a handful of bonfires, and the few times we did, you wanted to leave five minutes after we got there. Hell, I found you on your phone in the backseat of Spencer's car at the last one we went to. Guys were interested, Ari. You weren't. You've never dated anyone that you didn't already know. I'm shocked this Holden guy has made the cut."

She's not wrong about the bonfires. They always made me super anxious. It didn't matter who I attended them with. The woods, the shadows, it all thoroughly creeped me out. My first date with Holden did the same. When he pulled me into that farm pond in the dark, I was thoroughly petrified until he started kissing me and showering me with praise, making me forget my fear. But as far as the rest of it, I'm not sure.

Sitting on my bed, I run through my memories, trying to determine why my version of events differs from hers. Why is my perspective so negatively skewed?

Her expression is empathetic. She's not trying to hurt me. She's trying to understand. Resting her hand atop mine, she says, "Finish the story about Logan."

"To make a long story short, I shut off my phone and ghosted him. Then it died, and I hadn't come home. The next morning, when I arrived here, he had brought the cops to the house and told my parents he thought I was suicidal because of the sickness, which they knew nothing about. Needless to say, when I showed up wearing my new man's shirt and doing the walk of shame in front of him, my family, and the police, I was livid and so was he. I haven't heard from him since, but that week, Spencer and my parents made me go to a doctor and therapist. I'm now going to therapy twice a week and taking antidepressants." I give her a huge, sarcastic smile before saying, "See? All better."

"Fuck, Ari, this is all so messed up."

I roll my eyes before throwing myself back on the bed. "Don't I know it."

She lays next to me, and we stare at the ceiling for long minutes before she asks, "So, is it helping?"

I shrug. "I'm not sure. The pills help, but they also make me lose myself. I forget things, and things I know I usually care about suddenly don't matter. They make me feel like I'm losing parts of me, and I don't know, maybe that's good. Maybe I need to lose parts of me, especially the damaged ones, but sometimes it feels like those parts are still there, and then I'm back at square one."

Clutching my hand, she interlaces our fingers. "Don't leave me out of this. I know I don't live here, but I'm the press of a button away. I love you, Ari. You're my best friend. When the person you are today isn't the person you were yesterday, and you feel lost and alone, call me. We've been friends since we were six years old. I think I can help you find yourself." I squeeze her hand tight as a tear falls down my face. "None of that. Let's pick out our outfits for girls' night."

"Oh yeah, about tonight. It's just going to be Lauren and us. I kind of told Kyla to fuck off."

Olivia raises her brows. "It's about damn time. I thought you'd never tell her to get lost. Now, when are you going to tell Lauren to do the same?"

"What's wrong with Lauren? I know she can be catty occasionally, but that's part of having a vagina."

She puts a yellow sundress on the bed and puts her hand on her hip and says, "You're right, but there are two kinds of catty in my book. The barbed type where you're giving your friend shit in a funny, mocking manner, and then there's just the spiteful catty, where you're trying to cut someone down. She's the latter."

"Yeah, well, then I'll have zero friends."

She throws me a wicked smile. "Well, maybe that means you need to move out to California with me."

"Two weeks ago, maybe. But now that I have Holden, that will be a hard pass."

She strips out of her clothes to put on her yellow dress while asking, "So, when do I get to meet him?"

"He's going to meet us for Spencer's party tomorrow."

Once her dress is on, she adds. "He could always crash girls' night. It's not like the company is anything to be excited about."

I fake offense. "Thanks, I thought you missed me and wanted to catch up—" My phone pings, taking my attention away from Oli.

Holden: Incubus track 11. I've listened to it on repeat my entire drive home.

I fly across my room to grab my Incubus CD and find what song track eleven is. It's "I Miss You." My phone pings again. This time, it's a picture of him holding a notebook with the words "I miss you" written across the page.

Olivia peers over my shoulder. "Why the hell is the picture so blurry? Whose phone takes blurry pictures anymore?"

Because I know how beautiful he is in person, the blurriness barely registers. All I see is an enigmatic pale blue gaze piercing my soul. He has kept his own pain close to his heart, and while I wish he would open up and share that part of himself with me, I'll never push. The fact that he shared that some part of him was just as haunted as I am was probably more than he's shared with anyone. His eyes locked on mine when I saw his scar. He knew I saw it and didn't say one word, which told me he didn't want to talk about it. A scar like that isn't by accident, and I can't help but feel it's tied to whatever haunts him. If it wasn't, why wouldn't he tell me? Olivia smacks my back. "Well?"

"He's Spencer's age, so four years older than us, and his phone is from high school, easily making it six years out of date, which is a lot these days. I'm pretty sure it has sentimental value of some sort."

"You haven't asked him?"

I shoot her an *Are you serious?* glare before adding. "I don't think I need to. I've been to his house and met his parents. They live in a nice, upper-middle-class house with all the amenities and toys. Plus, Holden drives a suped-up truck, and I know he works. The phone isn't because he can't afford one."

"It's your relationship, but if I were you, I'd ask. If Holden doesn't share, okay, but what if he does?" She has a point. I've become so jaded and insecure from hiding my own sickness that I've failed to recognize what a normal conversation looks like. A black top is thrown at my face, followed by, "Get dressed."

Standing here in the bathroom stall at the bar, I'm letting my sickness win, not Lauren. Sure, finding out my so-called best friend sided with my ex and believes I'm doing all this for attention sucks, but honestly, I expected her betrayal. Our dynamic over the past year has changed, but I can't blame her for my weakness. She's not here telling me to stick my finger down my throat. No, she was just the catalyst. The rest is on me. I want to throw up.

I want to literally make myself throw up so that I can feel better. Every time I throw up, I'm instantly happier. All the noise fades away, and this feeling of unease that constantly weighs me down dissipates. I now know that my body releases endorphins when I do. It's part of the vicious cycle I need to break. But it grants me peace and a momentary reprieve from all the thoughts threatening to smother me.

My forefinger and middle have barely breached my lips when my phone vibrates in my back pocket—but not from a text, from a call. Snatching my phone, I see it's Holden.

I bang my head against the stall before answering. "Hello."

My voice is meek at best, even though I try to force normalcy into it.

"Pretty girl..." Holden's voice is instantly empathetic to my tone. There's a pause before he says, "Tell me, baby. Please talk to me." When I squeeze my eyes shut, the tears start falling. I'm fucking pathetic.

"Aria, let me bring you back, pretty girl. I envy the strength I see in you, your grit, that sass, and don't even get me started on that ass..." That makes me chuckle, and he hears it. "Why didn't you call me?"

I take a deep breath through my nose just as the bathroom door opens, and Olivia calls out, "Aria." She jacks open the door. "The witch is dead. I drowned her in that top-shelf margarita she was drinking, and she left screaming."

"Holden, I'm sorry I bothered you. I shouldn't have answered. I'm fine. I'll call you later."

"Aria, don't you dare—" I hang up the phone. He's pissed, and I know it. So I shoot a quick text.

Aria: I'm with Olivia. I'll be okay. I'm sorry.

"Did you just hang up on him?"

I nod. "Yeah, I did. I need to find my own strength. He asked why I didn't call, and that's the thing. For a second, I considered it, but I'm not his responsibility, and he's not always going to be around." My chest gets tight from the thought alone.

"Aria, call him back. It's okay to let people help you. If he makes you happy and makes you feel good, then that's not something you should push away."

She's not wrong. "Can you give me a minute? I'm just going to step out back real quick."

She nods. "Meet me at the bar when you're done."

When I look down at my phone, I see bubbles appear. Holden is getting ready to text me. Instead, I hit the call button. He answers on the first ring but stays silent. We stay like that for a few minutes as I consider what to say.

"This is new for me, Holden." I take a long pause before adding, "I've been dealing with this on my own for so long. I'm not trying to shut you out. That's part of the problem though, right? You think I'm doing something to you. No one ever understands that my selfishness isn't because I don't care about them. It never has anything to do with anyone but me. I don't think about who I might hurt in the process because I'm too consumed with me."

In the background, I hear someone yell, "Hayes, we're on." I know he had a doubleheader tonight, which is another reason I didn't want to text or call. Holden is dedicated to the sport and doesn't like distractions. All of this is a distraction. I try to shake off the self-doubt I feel creeping up.

I hear him let out a long breath before gently saying, "Aria...I gotta go, pretty girl." My heart feels like it cracks into a million pieces as I hit the end button on the call. I want to cry, but I'm done feeling sorry for myself. This is why I didn't want to get involved in the first place. I know I'm a lot to handle, and in my present state, I don't have the emotional stability to deal with it either. Fuck my life.

Making my way inside, I head to the bar and find Olivia. "How did it go?"

I give her a fake smile and a sarcastic, "Great!"

Neither of which goes unnoticed. "Perfect, let's get wasted."

~

My head is pounding, my mouth is dry, and I feel like I got hit by a bus. *What the hell?* When I finally peel my eyes open, the light from my window is blinding, and my room is empty. I know we both got fucked up last night. How Olivia even feels human enough to get out of bed is beyond me.

Rolling over, I reach for my cell phone on my nightstand. I

typically put it there every night before bed, but now my hand comes up empty. *Great.* Now I have to get out of bed. I lay on my stomach a little longer, trying to recall anything that happened last night, but coming up with nothing. The last thing I remember is feeling sad about how my call with Holden ended and then getting wasted to forget.

Closing my eyes, I remember I need to get up. It's Spencer and Olivia's birthday today, and we have planned an entire day of bar hopping.

"Knock, knock, room service." Spencer comes strolling in a little too chipperly with orange juice, eggs, and bacon. "First, take these and drink this." He hands me ibuprofen and orange juice. I sit up and take them immediately, praying for instant relief.

"Spencer, you realize you're my only sibling? You don't have to do all this. It's not like you're going to win any favorite brother awards. Why are you in such a good mood anyway? I know it's your birthday, but damn, this is extra." I gesture to my plate and room service.

"Don't get too excited. Mom made breakfast for everyone, not me. I just wanted you to eat before we leave in an hour."

Juice nearly comes flying out of my nose. "An hour? What the hell? Why did you guys let me sleep all day?"

He shrugs. "Olivia told me about last night with Lauren and the call with Holden. Figured it didn't hurt to sleep it off." He sits on the bed, letting me know this talk isn't over. "Eat, Aria." I roll my eyes and take a bite of my eggs. They melt in my mouth. Not every meal I eat comes with remorse. It depends on the day, and because today will be spent drinking, I know I need to eat. I waste no time devouring all of them. When he notices I haven't touched my bacon, he adds, "Mom made turkey bacon." I don't bother telling him that I wasn't avoiding the bacon. I eat it.

"Spence—" Olivia walks in, ready to go and dressed to kill. "What did I miss?" She plops down on the opposite side of the bed.

"Oh, nothing, just Spencer over here trying to win an Oscar for best supporting brother."

He throws his arms up in the air in mock surrender. "I'm out. Get ready. We leave at noon."

"Seriously though, Aria. He's really torn up about all this."

I give her a subtle nod of agreement. "I know, trust me. I'm grateful, but I try to make light of it because I know he's already under so much stress with school. I don't want him to worry."

She nods in understanding before throwing the covers off me. "Go shower. I'm picking out your outfit, and you will be wearing it. No questions asked."

I let out an irritated groan before scolding, "You know my hard limits."

She waves her hand, "Yeah, yeah, Go."

The outfit is laid out on my bed when I get out of the shower and return to my room. A black, cotton, long-sleeve, button-down, ripped light blue jean shorts, and a pair of black Doc Martens.

"Olivia, I'm not wearing those shorts."

She stops scrolling on her phone before asking, "Why not? You can fit my jeans. We are the same size. You're wearing shorts."

"You know shorts are a hard limit for me. My legs are too thick. They rub together."

She purses her lips and narrows her eyes. "Are you saying I have fat thighs?"

"What? No. Olivia, you know you're gorgeous."

She raises a brow at me before saying, "Our thighs are the same size. Humor me, and try the outfit on at least."

"Fine, I'll try it on."

She claps her hands together, adding, "I'm doing your hair and makeup."

We leave my bedroom at 12:10 pm after Spencer pounded on the door for the third time for us to come out. When we get to the living room, he does a double take when he sees me. His eyes go wide. "Seriously, that's what you're wearing to my party?" I already felt self-conscious about leaving the house in shorts. Now I want to go put my jeans on.

"Spencer!" Olivia scolds.

He mutters, "Shit, Aria, that's not what I meant. What I meant was all the guys will be drooling all over you." He waves his hands in front of me, motioning to my attire. "Since when do you wear booty shorts?" Immediately, my cheeks heat, and he must see my insecurity because he adds. "Aria, you look—"

He doesn't get to finish his sentence because Olivia cuts in with, "She looks like a fucking snack." Smacking my ass, she pushes me toward the front door before I can make a run for my room and change.

As we go outside, Spencer hands me my phone. "This was in the kitchen. I charged it for you. You might want to check it."

Once we enter the party bus, I check the messages.

Holden: 8:00 pm: You hung up on me again.

Holden: 10:30 pm: Goodnight, pretty girl. I miss you. I'm sorry.

Holden: 10:00 am: Aria?

What does he mean I hung up on him? He said he had to go. I thought that meant he was hanging up. Then I missed our goodnight text. We text or call each other before bed every night. Now, on top of everything else, I've also missed our morning text for the past two and a half hours. We were supposed to meet today, and now I'm sure he thinks I'm running.

"What's that face, Ari?"

I let out a sigh. "Oh, you know, just the standard me, fucking everything up. Apparently, I inadvertently hung up on him, seeing as I thought the conversation was over. Then I missed our nightly talk and his text this morning. Given how things started between us, I guarantee Holden thinks I'm blowing him off."

The bus stops outside Tony's house, and Spence hops off to get him. "Just text him your phone died, and you were hungover. No big deal." Olivia's right. I'm making it a big deal by not texting back.

> Aria: Sorry, my phone died, and I was hungover. I'm alive now.

It took us an hour to get here, but we finally landed at the Bike Bar to start our downtown pub crawl. I've never been on one of these, but they look fun. The bike looks similar to a trolly car and seats about six people per side on a seat with pedals. Everyone pedals while they drink, and it drives the bike. Ours has a keg of beer in the middle.

Once the tour operator explains everything, we head over and find our seats. Olivia sits on my right, while Tony sits on my left. Of course, it would have to be Tony. I had the biggest crush on Tony growing up. Hell, the man is still hot. All of Spencer's friends are hot, but Tony, he's your long-haired lover type. He's got the best hair I've ever seen. It's dark brown with a slight curl and barely brushes the tops of his shoulders. He has thick dark eyebrows and deep-set dark brown eyes, and don't even get me going on the five o'clock shadow that he seems to always have perfectly manicured. I swear the man owns nothing but black V-necks to tease women with a glimpse of his tattoo covering his right pec. I bet it's a conversation starter and pick-up line all in one.

Olivia is just passing me a beer when he bumps my elbow. "Are you going to be trouble tonight, Aria?"

"Pfft... Why would you say that?" I take a long pull from my beer, trying to act unaffected when, in all honesty, Tony will always make me nervous—boyfriend or not.

"Well, for one, you came out of the house looking like that." He rakes his eyes long and slow up my body before bringing them back to mine again. "And I don't think Spencer can keep us all back, not on top of the random guys that will no doubt hit on you tonight."

My brow furrows at his insinuation. "What do you mean keep the guys back?"

He takes another drink of his beer before saying, "Every guy in the school knew you were off-limits growing up. The problem is, you're all grown up now, and very much a woman."

I nod as if what he's saying is evident when, really, I'm stunned. For years, I thought all the guys viewed me as Spencer's little pain-in-the-ass sister. Not his hot sister who was off-limits. Taking a sip of my beer, I divert my stare across the bike, only to meet Spencer's tense gaze. His jaw is tight, and his breathing seems shallow, and I gather he just heard our entire conversation. Even Olivia notices, but she didn't hear my exchange with Tony.

Putting a hand on his shoulder, she squeezes it. "Spence, you okay? We're almost to the bar. You look like you need a shot." He gives her a tight smile before dropping his eyes to his beer. If I had to guess, he's feeling guilty about how his off-limits rule may have impacted my eating disorder.

When we reach Louie's, everyone heads straight for the bar. Olivia calls out, "First round of shots is on me, boys!" I'm following her back when a hand catches my wrist.

"Aria, can we talk for a minute?" Spencer's face has sadness written all over it, and that's the last thing I want to see on his birthday.

"Spence—"

Shaking his head, he says, "Aria, hear me out, okay? Guys have always found you hot. Hell, you're my sister, and I know you're hot. I was never trying to hurt you, Aria. I was trying to look out for you. There was so much more going on in high school than you realize. Shit was fucked up, Aria. Most guys at that age were after ass, but for others, it was more than that. Look, it doesn't matter now. I messed up, and I'm sorry. I was only ever trying to protect you." I feel like he just laid a lot of heavy on me. It's too much for my brain to compute after the few beers I've already had. There's more to what he's saying, I'm sure of it, but regardless, this isn't his fault. Sometimes, people are just sick. Period.

"You can't blame yourself for how I am, Spence. It is what it is. I'm going to get better." His face is pinched with regret. Spencer is not happy, which is a problem. It's his birthday. This is precisely why I never wanted anyone to know about my struggles. These demons I fight are mine and mine alone. They don't need to punish anyone else.

"Let's have fun. Please don't worry about me. It's your birthday." He pulls me in for a hug and says, "I love you. I won't overstep again. You're a grown woman, and you can date whomever you want. Just, maybe not Fisher."

That makes me laugh. "Fisher is the epitome of hit it and quit it. Not my style," I assure him.

"Now, let's go take that shot!" Slinging his arm over my shoulder, we walk over to the bar.

"Since you guys ditched, you both now have to do a double!" Olivia is ready to party. I'll take the double, but I'm ordering a giant glass of water. She's not getting me fucked up like last night.

After shooting my shot, I saddle up to the bar beside her. Louie's is pretty cool—it's what I would call your typical millennial spot—but it's not just a bar. They have an indoor/outdoor area with fire tables and pillowed loungers. There's a small restaurant area, but they have axe throwing toward the back. It's something I've never done, and I'm looking forward to it. Yet another reason I don't want to get wasted at the first bar I show up at.

Oli elbows me. "You guys all good?" She nods over to Spence.

"Yeah, we're good. You know how I've always had a crush on Tony?"

A huge smile breaks out over her face before she finds him

and eyes him herself. "Ahh, yeah, who doesn't have a crush on that man?" She kisses her fingertips and adds, "He's chef's kiss."

I smile and nod. "Well, on the bike, he basically told me I was hot and that the only reason guys never made a move on me is because Spencer ordered it, and Spence overheard the entire conversation."

Her eyebrows shoot up. "Well, that explains why you never dated a guy from school." After taking a drink of her Long Island Iced Tea, she adds, "Let me guess. He now feels responsible for your issue."

I shrug. "Basically, but I told him he can't blame himself for how I am. This is all me. No one did this to me. I've already tried to pinpoint the exact moment things changed for me, and I can't."

Nodding, she pushes me a Bloody Mary. "This conversation is getting too heavy. You know I love you, and I'm here for all this, but let's try to have fun tonight."

Standing up, I grab my drink from the bar and say, "Let's throw some shit."

She smacks my ass. "Hell yes! Let's go."

~

We've been throwing for about twenty minutes, and I think I've finally figured out how to throw the axe and make it stick instead of just banging off the board and falling to the floor. It's all in the feet and the wrist. I must plant my feet and keep my wrists taut when I throw. Bringing the axe above my head, I step forward, plant my feet, and release. When the axe hits the board, it sticks, and all the guys cheer, just as big arms wrap around my waist and salty notes of musk and cedar invade my senses.

"Holden…" His name is a breathy plea on my lips as I turn in his embrace and hug him back. God I missed him. "You came."

He buries his face in my neck, placing a kiss there before saying, "Where else would I be?"

I pull back and find his eyes. "I just, I thought..."

I'm stammering when he says, "Stop. I'm sorry. I'm so fucking sorry."

Before I can ask him what he could possibly be sorry for, Oli's tapping me on my shoulder. "Aria, what the fuck? You didn't mention your boyfriend was fine as hell." That's not true. I'm pretty positive I more than emphasized how sexy he was, but I don't correct her. Holden knows what he does to me.

I move to pull out of our embrace, but he tucks me under his arm and sticks out his hand. "Holden, and you must be Olivia." She places her hand in his, all dainty and shit, and he brings it to his mouth and kisses it before saying, "Nice to meet you. You don't mind if I steal Aria for a minute?" Oh, now I'm onto him. He's laying the charm on thick to get something, and that something is me.

He's already clearly won her over because she's placing her hand on her chest, clearly taken aback by the entire exchange. Shaking her head and furrowing her brows, she replies, "Of course; not a problem," before heading back to the guys.

His eyes find mine and soften as he takes my hand and pulls me toward the front of the restaurant. "Holden, I can't leave with you."

He throws over his shoulder, "I know." When we reach the outdoor patio, he pulls me over to an empty lounger and onto his lap. It's not meant to be sexual. I'm sitting across his lap like he's Santa Claus. The problem is, everything with this man is intense and sexy. He is a walking wet dream.

"Aria, last night I didn't say anything for reasons you don't understand. Yes, I was mad, but it's more than that. I wasn't mad at you, pretty girl. I don't think I could ever be mad at you." He pauses and takes a minute to interlace our fingers. "All I wanted was to jump through the phone and scoop you into my arms. I wanted to hold you until the pain went away. I wanted to kiss you from head to toe and tell you how much you mean to me. How perfect you are. No words would have been enough at that moment, and I was fucking pissed that I couldn't articulate that. Not much has ever made me want to leave the field." He pulls in a ragged breath before gently saying, "Until you."

Placing a kiss on my shoulder, he adds, "I only said I had to go because the game was starting. I wasn't going to hang up. You're important to me." I know what he is saying is true. I don't believe Holden would hang up on me. "Tell me you believe me."

I don't use words. Instead, I place a hand on his cheek and lightly rub my thumb across it before zeroing in on his mouth and taking his lips in mine. Our kiss is slow at first, both asking for forgiveness for letting our stupid hearts get the best of us, but the moment his tongue dips into my mouth and brushes against mine, I'm done with soft. I need him. All week, I craved him, and now I have him. He groans against my mouth when he feels how hungry I am. Pulling back, he bites my lip before saying, "Come to my truck."

I know exactly what he's asking, and I'll be damned if I don't want to take him up on it. "Holden, if I go to your truck, I won't want to come back."

He's slowly kissing me along my jaw and down to my neck when he says, "That works for me."

I swat his chest. "I can't do that. I can't ghost Olivia and my brother. It's both of their birthdays."

He groans in disapproval before conceding. "Okay, just make sure to walk in front of me for a few minutes." I laugh out loud before holding my hand out for him to take.

# 11

## MY EVERYTHING

### HOLDEN

We are at our fifth bar of the day, and it's only 8:00 pm. I've just ordered a charcuterie board. This bar is bougie as hell. I doubt we will be here long. It's a rooftop terrace with amazing views of the Arch and Mississippi River, but it's pricey, and the vibe doesn't seem to fit the group's mood. Olivia said she'd heard about this place in some magazine and insisted we stop by, and because she's the birthday girl and cute as hell, no one blinked an eye.

"Hayes, Spencer said you played for the Heat the summer of 2018. I knew a few guys on the team. I grew up just outside of Waterloo by Lake Kinkaid."

Before he can get another word out, I stand and act like I need another beer, even though mine is half full. This conversation needs to end here.

"Yeah, it was a long time ago. I don't keep in touch with any of those guys. College hit, and everyone moved away." I hold out my beer. "Need another one?" Narrowing his eyes, he holds my gaze for a second too long, and it irks me. I feel like he knows I'm trying to get out of this conversation. Aria returns from the bathroom just in the nick of time, offering me the guise of a distraction.

"Holden, I think we're all going to head over there." Aria points to a direction unknown because I don't bother following her line of sight. I'm too wrapped up in her to care about anything else. Instead, I pull her into me, inhaling deep, and letting her fruity scent wash over me and calm my nerves. She must sense my unease because even in her inebriated state, she allows me to hold her without question while she rakes her fingers up and down my back.

"Yo, Aria. Let's go." Spencer's walking over now.

Releasing her, I give him a nod before saying, "We'll meet you guys there. I just ordered a snack." I know he's aware of Aria's issue, and I can tell it bothers him.

"Okay, it's just a block over. I think it's Shannon's, but I can't make out the sign from here."

Again I nod, before giving him a pound hug and saying, "Yeah, we'll catch up."

Before he walks off, he asks Aria, "You good?"

Giving him her attention, she replies, "I'm fine. We'll be there after we eat." The guy who was asking about the team—I think his name was Tony—gives me a once-over before running his thumb over his lip. He looks offended or put off, but I realize it's more than that when I catch the way he looks at Aria before following Spencer out. Tony wants my girl. *Fuck that.*

I feel like I've been chasing my girl all night, and I need her. When I ordered the food, it wasn't just for her. Selfishly I knew I'd have a chance to get her alone, which I haven't had all night. Taking her hand, I pull her over to a corner booth on the edge of the rooftop terrace. It's semi-private and has an incredible view of the Arch.

When she moves to sit on the side opposite of me, I bite out. "I want my girl sitting next to me. I've had to watch you parade around in these short shorts all day while Spencer's friends check out my girlfriend's ass." As she scoots in next to me, she laughs, which pisses me off. I hate how she brushes off the seriousness of my comment. While I understand she has confidence issues, it doesn't mean the rest of the world doesn't see a hot piece of ass.

"You realize that Tony guy has a thing for you, right?" Again, she rejects my words as truth and shrugs her shoulders before drinking her water.

"I don't know if I would say that. Today is the first day he's looked at me as more than some little girl in over ten years."

Pulling her onto my lap, I teasingly run my finger up her thigh, and say, "Yeah, because you're hardly wearing any clothes tonight, pretty girl."

She scoffs before adding. "Holden, please, I'm wearing shorts, not lingerie."

Gripping her thigh hard, I say, "Baby, these sun-kissed thighs and that fine ass in these cut-offs more than qualify as lingerie. Every guy wants these sexy legs wrapped around his waist while he slides home, balls deep in that pretty pussy."

Her breath catches at the vulgarity of my words, but I know she likes it, so, I say, "Tell me, pretty girl, is that pussy wet for me?"

Her answering, "Mmm," has my cock dripping as I lean in and kiss her exposed collarbone. Dipping my finger into the low-cut front of her lacey top, I graze her nipple. Immediately she gasps. Her nipple is instantly erect and begging for more.

"Holden, stop. Someone's going to see us."

I run my tongue up her neck and say, "Then let them see." She lets out a sexy, frustrated moan before placing her hand over mine. I love getting her worked up. Aria makes the sexiest noises when she's turned on, and I'm a fiend, addicted to all of them. Kissing my way along her jaw, I pull her chin toward me and find her mouth, leaving her with a slow, open-mouthed kiss that I know has her wet.

"We're eating, and then we're fucking."

Her eyebrows shoot up. "What's gotten into you tonight?"

I know exactly what she's asking. I've been all over her since the moment I arrived. Squeezing her perfect ass and kissing her neck. Hell, I've been touching some part of her body all day, and while I know a big part of it has to do with the guys checking her out, another part has to do with the constant nervous energy I'm feeling being around Spencer's friends. I don't want to get cornered. I don't want any slips, and I sure as hell don't need any reminders. So I've been distracting myself with my sexy as fuck girlfriend, killing two birds with one stone. Being extra handsy with my girl ensures Spencer's friends know she's mine, and it serves as a way to forget the things I don't want to remember.

"If I wasn't in the picture, would you be into that Tony guy?" Her brow furrows, and she's about to speak right as our food is placed on the table.

Aria climbs off my lap, moving to sit next to me as she thanks the server. After the waiter walks away, I continue holding her eye, waiting for her response. Until the words left my mouth, I didn't realize how invested I would be in her answer. When she sees that my eyes are still zeroed in on her, she starts to fidget under my stare.

"Answer the question, Aria. Is that tall, dark, and handsome thing he's rocking your thing?"

She blows out a breath. "Fine. I had a crush on Tony for years, but it doesn't matter now because I have you. I'm not a cheater, Holden." I thin my lips, clearly perturbed by her confession. I don't want to hear that my girl had a thing for another guy, but at least she's not lying to me.

I nod to the food. "Let's eat." She hesitates, and I can't decide if it's because I made her nervous with my question or if it's the food. I quirk a brow and ask, "Do you need to sit on my lap, pretty girl?"

She reaches for a piece of cheese wrapped in meat and takes a slow bite, intentionally drawing my eyes to her mouth before asking, "Is that what you'd like?" And that's what I love about my girl. She's reserved, conservative, and somewhat timid, but there's also a confident, assured hellcat in there. You never know which one you're going to get.

"You think I won't play with that pretty pussy just because

we're in public?" Her face flushes and her chewing slows, but I also notice the subtle shift in her posture. She's clenching her thighs together, no doubt turned on by my dirty talk. Aria fucking loves it. Once she's finished her meat and cheese, I grab her by the waist, making her yelp in surprise as I set her on my lap.

"Hey, I was eating." I skim my hand up her front before grabbing a handful of breast and pulling her into me.

"I know, but I missed you. I can't stand not touching you. You drive me crazy, pretty girl." I nibble her neck, pulling her hair aside on my way to her back. The shirt she is wearing has a low dip in the front, showing off her perfect tits, and a subtle drop in the back. I trail kisses along her exposed skin, making her skin break out in goosebumps. "Do you like my mouth on you, Aria?"

"You know I do."

I pause momentarily to make sure she's still eating. "Do you remember the rules?"

I feel her pull in a deep, unsure breath. "Yes." *Fuck I love how she trusts me.*

I shrug out of the lightweight bomber jacket I wore tonight before placing my hands back on her waist. "Pass me your drink." She does so without question, and I take a long swallow of her glass, catching an ice cube between my teeth. Handing the glass back, she places it on the table and grabs another bite of food. When she brings it to her mouth, I rub the cube down the exposed part of her back. She jolts forward from the coolness until I wrap my arms around her front and pull her against my chest. Sucking the cube back in, I bring my mouth to her neck right below her ear, where I drag the ice down to her collarbone. The cube is quickly melting, dripping a slick trail down her chest and making it glisten.

Once she's lost to the cool sensation against her neck, I run my hand down her stomach until I reach the button on her shorts and quickly flick it open. "Holden—" her plea sounds more like a question than a true request for me to stop.

"Baby, I'm the first man you've trusted with this body. Do you trust me when I say no one will see what's mine?"

My forefinger runs along the hem of her underwear as a breathless, "Yes," escapes her lips. With my free hand, I pull my jacket over her lap.

"Do you want me to stop?" When she shakes her head no, I dip my hand underneath her thong, sliding my fingers to her clit. "Fuck, pretty girl, do you know how hot it is finding you soaked from my touch?"

"Mmm," she hums as I glide my fingers through her swollen lips. My cock is rock hard and begging for release. I slide a finger into her tight core when she takes another bite. Immediately she clenches around it, and we both groan.

"I'm going to need you to be quiet, or everyone will know I'm finger fucking my girl in the middle of the bar."

She shakes her head and says, "Please don't stop."

"Does this turn you on, baby? Do you like knowing we might get caught?"

I continue slowly pumping my finger into her when she says, "Yes, I like that we could get caught." Damn, my girl is a freak, and I don't think she even realizes it. She loves dirty talk, praise, and voyeurism. My mind goes blank. I'm so damn turned on that I don't even care if she eats anymore.

I add another digit and curl my fingers to hit the spot I know drives her crazy. "Give me that mouth, pretty girl."

When she turns her head, I crush my lips to hers. My tongue wars with hers for dominance as I feel her push back on my fingers. I can feel cum dripping from my dick, and all I can think about is ripping her shorts off and pounding into her. I know she's close. Her pussy is starting to strangle my fingers. Biting her bottom lip, I say, "Make my cock jealous, baby." Those words, coupled with the scene, set her off, and my mouth is more than happy to swallow every one of her delicious moans of ecstasy.

When her pussy stops spasming, I rest my forehead against hers and pull my fingers out. "So fucking pretty." I make quick work of buttoning her jeans before pulling her to her feet. When she sways on her feet, I toss money on the table and throw her over my shoulder.

"Holden, put me down. You're making a scene."

"Maybe you should have been more concerned about making a scene ten minutes ago when you decided to let me play with your pussy in public."

When the waiter sees me, I gesture with my free hand like she's had too much to drink, and he nods. Then, heading for the exit, I opt to take the open staircase down to the lower level instead of the elevator. Downtown here isn't very populated like most major cities, but since I know my girl doesn't mind getting caught, I'm not too worried about my next move.

On the third landing, I stop and set her on the open brick window ledge. I waste no time making my intentions known. Her top is already low cut, so it takes little effort on my part to have both of her breasts immediately exposed in one pull. "Holden—" her protests are halted the second I pop one of her perky breasts into my mouth. "Fuuuck," she draws out as she holds the back of my head to her breast. I suck and nip before making my way to the other, swirling my tongue around her nipple, teasing it to life while tweaking the other. My cock is straining so hard against my zipper it hurts.

While my mouth assaults her breasts, I unbutton her shorts. Once they're undone, I pull her into me and set her down. Hooking my thumbs under her waistband, I slowly start to lower her shorts and thong. "You going to let me fuck you right here?" Her hand flies to my jeans, where she unbuttons, unzips, and pulls me out before stroking me. "Mmm, that feels good, baby." Her thumb rubs the cum around the top of my swollen head before she strokes me again. I pump into her hand a few times before saying, "Turn around, pretty girl." Tonight, I'm going to take her the way I've dreamed about taking her since the moment I met her.

Without question, she turns, braces herself on the

windowsill, and sticks her ass up for me. "Do you know how hot you look with your pants around your ankles and this perfect ass in the air for me?" I trace my fingers down her crack until I reach her pussy, where I sink them inside. "You're always so ready for me." I slap her ass hard with my free hand, and she yelps. Then, pulling my fingers out, I grab my cock and bring it to her entrance, dipping it in slightly, only to pull back out and run it through her wet lips. "Is this what you want, Aria? You want my cock?"

"Holden, please, you know I want it." It's fucking hot how bad she wants me. I don't waste another second. Slamming in hard, I knock the breath from both of our lungs. Bringing my mouth to her neck, I suck and nip at her sensitive skin, giving us both a chance to acclimate before I pull out to the tip and slam back in again.

"Are you going to let me fuck you hard, pretty girl?"

She whimpers and rests her head on her arm before saying, "If that's what you want." *What? If that's what I want? What the fuck does that mean?* I don't let up; I keep up my pace, hitting hard, getting more pissed with every thrust—until it hits me, that's what this is.

"Is this what I am, Aria? The guy that makes you come? The guy you keep at an arm's length, the guy that only gets the pieces?"

She doesn't respond, and I realize I'm mad because this woman has all of my heart, and I can't take knowing I don't have a piece of hers. "Tell me, Aria. Tell me I'm not the guy, and that's why you won't let me in."

This time, her whimper sounds like a cry before she says, "Stop, Holden, stop. Don't touch me." *Fuck.*

I pull out and run my hands through my hair before turning her around and pulling her to my chest. I'm so scared of losing her. I can't control myself. "Aria, I'm so sorry, pretty girl. Look at me. Please look at me." She shakes her head and cries into my chest. I give her a second before pulling her chin up so her eyes are on mine. "Aria, I love you, pretty girl. I'm so fucking scared you are going to push me away. That you don't think this is real."

Her lips part, and her eyes dart back and forth between mine. "Holden, you can't just say stuff like that because you fucked up. You don't love me." Backing her against the wall, I cage her in my arms and force her to focus only on me.

"Why, Aria? Why can't I love you? Because society says we're too young? Or is it because we haven't been together long enough? Tell me, how long do I have to be with you before it's okay for me to love you?"

She shakes her head. "It's just...you don't..." she trails off.

"You've been real good at telling me how I should feel, baby, but I think you need to stop worrying that pretty head and just let me love you."

Her brow furrows before her eyes settle on my mouth and dart back to mine. "Holden—" she starts, but I stop her before she says something she doesn't mean.

"No, don't do that, Aria. Don't say it back because you feel obligated."

She puts her finger to my lips to silence me before saying, "I wouldn't be saying it out of obligation. I would be saying it because it's the only word that fits how I've felt about you since the first night we met. I've never been in love, Holden, but I can't imagine it's not this. You're all I think about. You're the last thought I have before I fall asleep and the first one I have when I wake, along with every other thought after that, but it fucking terrifies me."

I don't let any more words come out because my lips are on hers in an all-consuming, bruising kiss that I'll never forget. She feels the exact same way I do. From the moment we met, I knew she was different. We were different. Opening her mouth, she lets me in, but I soften my kiss. Hoping to convey how much I care, how sorry I am for doubting her, for hurting her.

Running her hand down my stomach, she grabs my cock and strokes it from root to tip, and I groan before stilling her hand.

"Aria, tell me, tell me you forgive me, tell me you know how sorry I am, baby."

Pressing a chaste kiss to my lips, she says, "Show me."

"I love you so much." Bending down, I grip her ass and lift. She wraps those luscious thighs around my waist, and I sink into her in one thrust. We both moan out our shared pleasure at the feel of this new position. With my forehead pressed against hers, I slowly start to pump into her. Her eyes never leave mine, and I know I'm not going to last because I know she meant every fucking word.

Her breathing becomes labored as she says, "You're so deep." With her back against the wall, I use it to help hold her in place and deepen the angle, raising her legs on my arms. "Yesss... right there."

"Fuck, baby, you love this cock, don't you?" Her pussy starts clenching, and I know it's from my words. "Choke it, baby." She throws her head back and starts letting out the sexiest little mewls. "Sing for me, pretty girl." That tips her over the edge, and with one more pump, I follow.

I hold her against the wall as we both catch our breath and come down from our release. I'm in heaven. My girl loves me.

Now, I just have to make sure I can keep her.

# 12

## GHOSTS

ARIA

**8 Weeks Later**

Yesterday I had my weekly Thursday night therapy session, and for the most part, I've felt like things have been going decent regarding my mental health. But last night, my therapist was intent on digging. Don't get me wrong, it's her job, and she basically does it every appointment, but this last meeting was reminiscent of our first, where she brought up the idea of potential delayed amnesia. While the word amnesia wasn't brought up, it was easy enough to deduce that her line of questioning was focused on trying to recover or awaken parts of my mind that she believed I might be holding captive.

She is well aware that I've been seeing Holden, and last night, she decided it was time to poke and prod, asking questions that had me thinking hard about when and why I developed these walls around my mind and how Holden is seemingly managing to get around them where others haven't been able to. Her questions were innocent enough, but I left feeling out of sorts and questioning things from my past that hadn't held much relevance until that session. It was a complete mind fuck that my brain still hasn't recovered from. For the past twenty-four hours, I've felt like so many things are right on the tip of my tongue, but they fade away before my brain can lock on.

To top it off, my doctor's appointment this afternoon didn't go as well as I hoped it would. I thought gaining two pounds would have earned me some points, but I had no such luck. All it earned me was another appointment next week. Apparently, my blood pressure is too low, and my regular low resting heart rate is up nearly fifteen beats per minute, so I need to go in next week for labs. But as I pull down Holden's street, all the stress of this past week becomes background noise.

Pulling up to Holden's, I'm just exiting my car when suddenly the door is flung open, and I'm pulled out. Holden lifts me, and I instantly wrap my legs around him. "I missed you so much, baby. He kisses my neck and holds me tight. Closing the door, he doesn't release me. Instead, he walks me up to the house.

"Holden, put me down. I don't want your parents to see me being carried into the house. That's inappropriate."

He bites my ear. "You think they don't know we're fucking?"

I pound his chest with my fists. "Holden, I'm serious."

"Relax, pretty girl, they're not home. I have you all to myself." The next thing I know, the front door is swung open and kicked closed as he walks me down the hall to his bedroom. I feel myself clenching from just the thought of what's coming. Placing me on the bed, he says, "I need to be inside you, Aria."

I can tell something's different about him tonight. Holden and I have a healthy appetite for sex, each of us is always more than willing, but there's a forced eagerness there tonight. He might want me, but he's also using me, and because I love him, I'll let him. I try to push away the hurt I feel from the pain I know lives inside him. The pain he refuses to share with me, but when he thrusts his tongue into my mouth, demanding I give him what he wants, a part of me feels like I'm taking it.

We only see each other three days a week, Friday through

Sunday, and we make sure to fuck every time. We can't get enough of each other. It's going on two months this weekend, and if I compare what I have with Holden to my past relationships by this time, I knew, I always knew by this time they weren't keepers. That's what scares me now. I want Holden more every time we're together.

Sucking my bottom lip into his mouth, he thrusts his hard cock against my clit before pulling back and saying, "Clothes off, baby. I want you fucking naked and spread out on my bed." If I'm being honest, Holden makes me feel beautiful, but it's hard not to be somewhat self-conscious. The man has the body of a god. Even the scar that mars his perfect stomach only makes him hotter. I asked him once how he got it, and his response was a short and clipped, "Not important." His tone said it all. While he may want me to believe it's not noteworthy, I know it's anything but, and I can't help but wonder if it's not part of his darkness. It's a deep scar. Whatever caused it had to be painful.

He's already stripped down to his boxers and I have yet to remove an article of clothing. "Aria." His voice is stern, leaving no room for argument. "Don't do this, baby. This body is mine. I fucking love every inch of it. Let me show you." Reaching for the hem of my shirt, he pulls it over my head and flings it across the room as I stand to pull off my shorts and underwear. My hesitance to remove my clothes wasn't from insecurity. It's because I can tell he's different tonight. When I sit on his bed, his tented briefs are right at eye level, and any concerns I may have had are silenced. I can't resist Holden like this, and I'll be damned if I didn't just have a day I want to forget. Bringing my hand up, I stroke his cock over his underwear before slowly pulling them down to free him. His eyes are on me when I look up, watching in pure adulation.

"You going to put my cock in that pretty mouth?" I've never actually given a blowjob. I didn't start having sex until I was eighteen, and that's when I started getting weird about what went in my mouth. But looking at Holden now, I want to give him that. I want to make him feel good. Darting my tongue out, I twirl it around his head before sucking the tip into my mouth. "Fuck, baby, that feels so good." I release him and run my tongue along the vein that runs root to tip, and he hisses. Cupping his balls, I lightly run my nails over them before taking his tip back into my mouth. I feel him bend down and release the clasp of my bra. "I want to see these tits while I watch you suck my dick."

Sitting back, I let my bra drop, but before I can bring my mouth back to his dick, he's cupping my breasts. "Aria, baby, these tits." He pulls one into his mouth, and it sends a pulse straight to my core that instantly makes me slick with need. God, I swear I could come just from him sucking my breasts. He kneads them in his hands as he sucks, swirls, and nips each one. "I swear, pretty girl, these tits are bigger." He pushes them together before adding. "Let me titty fuck you."

"What? Holden, I've never—"

I haven't even finished my objection before he pulls a bottle of lube out of his nightstand. Why am I not surprised this man has a bottle of lube next to his bed? He's a sex fiend. Sensing my hesitance, he says, "You pick, baby. Suck me off or let me titty fuck you."

I divert my gaze before saying, "Well, I've never done either, so..."

The next thing I know, he has me pushed back on the bed, devouring my mouth and running his thick cock through my soaked lips. "That's so fucking hot. Do you want to suck me?" He kisses the corner of my mouth, jaw, and neck before returning to give me his eyes. "I mean, is it because you don't want it in your mouth?" The fact that he thought about me in this moment means everything to me.

"Holden, I love you so much." I kiss him back with heat that would set us both on fire if it could. Then, pulling back, I say, "Let's do both."

A wicked smile stretches across his face, and he says, "You

have no idea what you've asked for." I squeeze my thighs together in anticipation because I know exactly what I've asked for. Holden Hayes is the best fuck of my life, and I have no doubt I'm about to have multiple orgasms.

"Naked in my bed and fucking perfect. Do you know how many things I've dreamed about doing to you in this bed?" Biting my lip, I watch as he reaches for my knees, pushing them back and spreading me wide before lowering himself between my thighs and spearing my pussy with his tongue.

"Fuck, Holden."

I swear I'm extra sensitive tonight. He spears my hole, and my entire body feels like it's humming. I'm already on the precipice of an orgasm. I squeeze my tits, and my pussy immediately spasms as Holden sucks my clit into his mouth, and just like that, I'm coming.

He laps up all my juices greedily before saying, "I love how you're always so ready for me, pretty girl."

Placing a kiss on either thigh, he crawls up my body and straddles my face. "Shouldn't I be sitting up for this?"

He looks down at me and smiles. "No, baby, I'm about to fuck that pretty mouth. Are you ready?" I nod, unsure of what I signed up for, but eager to please.

"Open up." As I do, he leans forward until his forearms are resting on the bed. Immediately, I realize he is literally going to fuck my mouth, but I'll be damned if I'm not down for it. As I open my mouth, he pushes in, and I suction my lips around his cock. My hands find his perfect ass, and I squeeze hard, digging my nails in and leaving my mark. He picks up the pace and pushes in a little deeper each time, but where I thought I'd enjoy making my man feel good, there's pain. With each thrust, my chest constricts and tightens. My mind goes dark as unease settles over me. With his next plunge, I choke. Immediately my hands fly to his thighs, and I start to push. He's quick to lift off.

"Aria, did I hurt you?" I haven't even processed his question before he's saying, "Damn it, Aria, you're trembling. Tell me, baby, help me understand this so I can fix it. Stay with me, pretty girl."

I have no words as he pulls me onto his lap. I'm momentarily stunned by what just happened because I don't understand what I'm feeling. All I know is that it hurt. Holden brings out a kinky side of me. Hell, I let him finger me in the middle of a crowded bar. I want to do everything with him. It makes me feel like the girl I used to be before I got sick. I was once spontaneous and fun, living for the moment. I feel alive when he pushes my boundaries. Why was this moment different?

"It was too much. I guess I'm not ready for that. I'm sorry." I don't bother trying to explain the crippling anxiety I felt. The last thing I want him thinking is that he hurt me.

"Aria, are you serious right now? You have nothing to be sorry for." He's kissing my forehead and gently stroking my back. "That was the best ten-second blow job of my life." I can't help but chuckle. That's one of the things I love about him. He normalizes my crazy. "Do you still want to do the other thing?"

That, I should be able to handle. "Yes, please." I nod emphatically. Reaching over to his nightstand, he grabs the lube. I'm still wrapped around him on his lap as he starts rubbing it all over my chest, kneading and tweaking my nipples as he does. Making my pussy drip with need. I can seriously feel my juices flowing. I'm so fucking turned on.

"You like this baby?"

I can barely keep my eyes open when I say, "You know I do. There's nothing you can do that I don't like."

"Is that so, pretty girl?" I feel his hard cock twitch against my clit. He loves rubbing my tits down with oil as much as I do. I press myself into his cock, ensuring he feels my heat and wetness.

"Fuck, you are so hot, Aria. Patience, baby. That pussy is going to strangle my cock soon enough." He gently pushes me back to lie on the bed before straddling my chest. Taking my hands, he places them on the sides of my breasts before pushing them together. "Hold them just like this, baby." As he straddles my chest, I take my time admiring his well-defined six-pack abs and the deep V that leads to his thick cock. Pushing my breasts together, I watch as he runs his dick up my sternum and between my breasts.

My eyes stay glued to his movements as the tip of his swollen dick pops through my breasts with each thrust. With each push, the head leaks a little more. When my eyes flick up to his face, I find him watching me, jaw slack, with hooded, lust-filled eyes. "You're mine, Aria. Do you see what you do to me, pretty girl? You like watching my cum drip out of my dick onto those perfect tits?" His dirty talk has me closing my eyes and clenching.

Pulling back, he climbs off me, stands at the edge of the bed, and pulls me to him, spreading my legs and spearing me with his dick in one move. "Yes," I cry out. He starts out slow with an unhurried, teasing pace, running his tip over the spot deep inside that drives me crazy—the place only he has ever found.

"Let me hear you, pretty girl. Show me how much you love my cock." My legs are wrapped around his neck as he starts to drive into me from the edge of the bed. "Fuck, baby, your tits are killing me tonight." When I look down, the entire scene is hot as hell. He's pounding into me, his cock glistening from my juices, and my tits are bouncing wildly with every thrust. "This is it, Aria; this is the only cock you're ever going to have—you hear me? This pussy is mine. You don't get to leave me."

That last line triggers me. It reminds me of the night he lost control at the bar and told me he loved me. "I'm not going anywhere, Holden." For a second, I see his darkness, the darkness that bleeds in from time to time. The darkness that he won't let me touch.

Dropping my legs, he comes down and cradles me. "Promise me. Promise me I can keep you. Don't leave me."

My heart clenches at the plea in his voice, and I wish he'd let me in. I pull his head to my neck and place my lips to his ear. "I'm not going anywhere. I love you too much."

He slows his pace, and before he brings his mouth to mine. "I love you more." My heart is hammering out of my chest as he deepens our kiss, trying to convey with his mouth and his thrusts how true those heavy words are. They send me spiraling. With one last thrust, he holds in deep, emptying himself inside of me. "You're everything to me, Aria."

"Aria, oh my god, aren't you so glad we have a three-day weekend? Work sucked this week. I felt like the week just dragged on." Kris has clearly already had a few drinks as she hangs all over me in her yellow bikini. We did arrive about two hours late, but it's only 8:00 pm. I've just walked through the door when she says, "Come on, let's get you a drink." Holden squeezes my hand before letting Kris pull me away.

Driving up, I knew this house was going to be nice. It's a sprawling brick colonial complete with a Juliette balcony above the double-door entry. Aside from Olivia's house, it's probably the nicest one I've ever been in. The living room is sunken, with solid oak wood floors that appear to run throughout the house. There are warm, brown leather couches that center around a brick fireplace, which serves as the room's focal point. When we enter the kitchen, oak beams run across the ceiling, but aside from those wood accents, the kitchen is stark white. White cabinets, white granite countertops, and high-end white appliances. I'm in love, and I never want to leave.

"What do you want? The Callahans have everything." I watch as she walks over to a butler's pantry and starts mixing a drink.

"I'll have whatever you're having."

She cheers. "Whoop, someone's getting fucked up tonight."

I'm just about to ask where Connor is when I hear him call-out, "Check it out. Look who's in my kitchen: my favorite groupie, in the flesh." Connor runs over and twirls me around. Just as Holden walks in.

"Connor, I'm only going to ask you once. Don't touch my girl."

His hands fly up in defense. "Chill, Hayes. I'm not trying to make a move."

Holden walks over to me, wrapping his arms around me from behind. He places a kiss on my temple and speaks softly in my ear. "Don't let my friends touch you, Aria. I don't like it." A chill runs down my spine from the graveness in his tone as the uneasiness I felt earlier returns.

"Holden, I—" He pulls my chin toward his mouth and kisses me. It's an open-mouthed, slow kiss where he only lets me have a small taste. Just enough to tease before pulling back, leaving me flushed, knowing we have an audience. When he releases me, Connor, Kris, and Gabe are all staring at us.

Holden clears his throat and says, "Are we doing shots?" He squeezes my hip before rounding the island and picking up the chilled vodka to pour shots.

Kris brings me my drink. "What is it?"

She smiles. "Take a sip, and I'll tell you."

It's in a colored glass, making guesses nearly impossible. I take a sip, and it's fizzy, fruity, and strong as hell. Hitting my chest, I cough and say, "Delicious. Really, it is good. I just wasn't expecting it to be so potent."

She laughs like it's funny. It's not funny. I will be shitfaced if I drink this entire glass. "It's orange juice, sprite, and cherry vodka." I'm surprised there's not more in it.

Kris bumps her hip into me and says, "Just throwing this out there: since I'm the one who hooked you two up, I fully expect to be the Maid of Honor at the wedding."

I slap her shoulder. "Kris, stop being ridiculous."

Shrugging like it's no big deal, she adds, "Seriously, Aria. That man looks at you like his whole world starts and stops with you. He's different with you. You must see that. I wish a man would look at me like that."

I know what she's saying. Holden bends for me. I get his

softer sides while everyone else gets the clipped, cold, fuck-off side he has mastered, but I know it's all a mask. Whatever secrets Holden hides haunt him. I see them from time to time, and that's how I know they aren't promises meant to be kept. Instead, they are locks to the gates of his own personal hell.

"Kris, are you kidding? Gabe loves you."

She shakes her head. "Could have fooled me. He has yet to say those words." Wow. I wasn't expecting her to say that. They have been dating for almost six months now. I just assumed, and now I feel like an ass.

"He's probably just nervous. You guys are attached at the hip. There is no way he doesn't love you."

When I look over at the guys, they're all throwing back a shot. Kris pulls my hand and says, "Let's go while they're distracted." She pulls me toward a doorway off the kitchen and we walk through what appears to be a library/office combo. The far wall is filled with floor-to-ceiling bookshelves while a huge, heavy oak desk sits in the center with wingback chairs at its front. It's very fancy and whimsical all at once. I wish I had more time to examine the books, but Kris pulls me into a backyard that looks like it could be at the Playboy mansion.

There's a blue lagoon pool surrounded by huge rocks that make it look like the pool is carved out of natural stone and has always been there. At the far end, there's a waterfall and what appears to be a grotto. I'm sure Connor has had a lot of fun there. Kris is still pulling me along when we reach the other side of the pool, but since I can see little steam tendrils in the night air, I know it's the hot tub. She wastes no time dropping in while I sit at the ledge and dangle my legs, grateful I went with the shorts.

"Didn't you bring a suit?"

I shake my head. "No, Holden didn't tell me I would need one." I don't bother mentioning that I wouldn't wear a suit in front of them anyway.

"You could always just strip down to your underwear."

I laugh out loud. "Yeah, let me do that. No way. I'm fine, seriously."

She shrugs. "Suit yourself." Then she laughs. "Oh my god, suit yourself. I didn't even mean to do that." I just shake my head and smile. The strength of her cocktail, combined with the hot tub's heat, amplifies her buzz quickly.

Laughter from the far side of the patio draws my attention, and I see Connor, Gabe, Holden, and two more guys from his team come out. Holden quickly scans the backyard before his eyes land on me. When he sees me, he gives me a come-hither motion with his finger, but I shake my head no. I'm not getting into any more trouble tonight. I can't control how a bunch of drunk boys react to me, and while Holden tried to play it off earlier, I didn't miss the anger in his voice. He was agitated, but Connor and I are just friends. Holden knows that. We've talked about how I like having Connor at the games. He tells me stories about them at school, stories about past games. Connor is just an ear to bend and pass the time while I watch my man. But something is different tonight. I feel it in my bones, and I don't like it.

"See, I told you Gabe doesn't love me."

I turn my attention back to Kris. "What the hell are you talking about? Why would you say that?"

She wades over to me and rests her elbows on the ledge while kicking her feet out. "What did Holden do the second he walked out that door?" I furrow my brow, confused at where she's going with this. "He looked for you. He cared where you were and what you were doing. Then, to top it off, he wanted you by his side. Gabe hasn't looked over here once."

I'm not sure what to tell her. Honestly, I wouldn't date Gabe to begin with, but I always hated when Kyla and Lauren would rag on my boyfriends, so instead I try to refocus the topic. "How long have you guys been here?"

"Are you trying to change the subject?"

"What? No, not at all. All I'm saying is you guys have both had a few drinks. Is he the lovey-dovey drunk, the angry drunk, or the I'm too fucked up to be either drunk?" I see her expression soften, and I think something I said must have registered.

"When he drinks, he's in his own world, but I know what you mean. Some people are angry drunks, and others are fun, like me. I guess I've never really thought about it like that."

"Yeah, Gabe strikes me as the guy who likes to be the life of the party and gets lost in the high."

She smiles. "That's one of the things I like about him." I stay silent because that is not the type of guy I am into. "I hate when people take themselves too seriously. That's probably one of the reasons Holden and I never clicked romantically. He's way too serious for me. Honestly, I haven't seen him this laid-back in years. You're good for him, Aria."

"You can say that again." Holden's deep voice startles both of us. We had our backs to the guys.

"Holden, how long have you been standing there?" Kris scolds. He smiles before taking a seat behind me and running his legs alongside mine to hang them in the hot tub.

"I caught that last bit where you said, 'you're good for him.'" I feel him shrug before he says, "Aria makes me believe I can have more, that I deserve more." I stay silent as I let those words wash over me. With Holden, I bite my tongue and let him reveal himself to me layer by layer. Every day, I feel like I get little pieces of whatever haunts him. Initially, he gave me nothing, but lately, I feel like part of him can't help but share. He wants me to see, but he's scared. So I don't push.

"Ugh, if you came over to be all sappy and shit, can you just go back to the guys and let us have girl time? Seriously, who am I supposed to talk to?"

He wraps his arms around my front and hugs me from behind before kissing my cheek. "Are you good, pretty girl?"

"Yeah, why wouldn't I be?"

He stands and says, "I don't know. I'm just checking. I feel like I'm always dragging you around to my stuff." He squeezes my shoulder. "Just want to make sure you are having a good time."

I furrow my brow, but I know he can't see. Why would he say something like that? Why would he think I don't want to be wherever he is? Does he not want me here? I bring my fingers to my forehead and rub the spot between my eyes, and chant: stop it, stop it, you're overthinking this, don't let the sickness win.

Luckily Kris responds for me. "She's fine. Go away. Geez, maybe I don't want Gabe fawning all over me. Always with the heavy," she says after he leaves. She nods at my cup. "Drink. It makes everything better." I take a long pull and immediately feel the alcohol warm my insides. As I lean back on my palms, I look up to the night sky and attempt to be present. I try to let out all the negative thoughts and focus on the good. Just as I'm starting to feel relaxed, Kris grabs my leg. "Time for a refill."

"I'll wait here."

Getting out, she grabs a towel from the rack off to the side and wraps it around her waist. "Okay, I'll bring back a special treat." She trots off, and I'm finally left alone with my thoughts, which, for once, seem to be nonexistent. Laying back on the cold stone with the hot tub heat lapping at my calves, I've found peace.

Hollering from the pool quickly drags me out of my blissful state. When I look over, a few of the guys have now jumped in the pool fully clothed. Holden is laughing, and I swear, it's intoxicating. Sure, I've heard him laugh, but he is full-on belly laughing right now. I've noticed that tonight he's letting himself drink as well, and I'm pretty sure I've seen him take a few hits off a joint. While he does have drinks when we go out, it's usually a few beers, nothing that gets him drunk. Tonight, he's done shots, and I know I've watched Connor make him mixed drinks, which I'm sure are every bit as potent as mine.

Deciding I need to pee, I sit up, but when I do, my gaze collides with a set of hazel eyes I'd know anywhere because I see them every day. Garrett Callahan is huddled around the back door with Connor and an older gentleman who I assume is Connor's dad. While they talk, Garrett's eyes remain locked on mine. His penetrating gaze gives nothing away. I never mentioned

Connor to him, not because I was hiding our relationship, but because I didn't want it to influence my position. You'd think seeing me in his nephew's backyard would at least warrant a look of surprise, and the fact that it doesn't is somewhat unnerving.

Breaking our blatant stare-off, he gives his attention back to Connor before wrapping up whatever conversation they were having and entering the house. *Great.* Connor joins the guys over at the pool, and I still need to pee, but now I'm hesitant to go inside. While I'm not scared of Garrett, the eeriness I felt creep up from our coffee incident has returned, and suddenly, things I thought were coincidences now feel purposeful. Shock or surprise didn't flow into his expression because he already knew I'd be here.

Standing, I make my way into the house, searching for a bathroom. I walk past the office and open a door that looks like it could be a half bath, and instead find a storage closet for a fully-decorated Christmas tree. *Who the fuck has a storage closet for just a tree?* The house is quiet, too quiet. I assumed I'd run into Garrett by now. As I make my way down the corridor, I spot a door ajar with a clear view of a toilet. *Bingo.*

After I'm done using the restroom, I take my time walking back outside. While Garrett may have been indifferent to seeing me here, I am anything but. I feel like I should at least say hi–I mean, he is my boss. My desire to find Garrett is momentarily paused as my attention is redirected toward the opulence of Connor's house. I've always loved going to people's houses for the first time. I'm a Nosey Nancy. I'm standing in the great room, taking it all in, when I finally hear murmurs down the hall. That must be Garrett. When I turn to search him out, I run smack dab into Connor's bare chest. *Shit.*

"Aria? Did you get lost?"

*Damn it.* Not only is he shirtless, he's only wearing a towel. I really hope he has pants on under that towel. His lack of clothes is distracting, especially when I'm trying to avoid being caught snooping.

"Umm, yeah, I just had to use the restroom. I was on my way back out."

He eyes me suspiciously. "Are you sure about that?"

His tone has no playfulness, making me feel like I just got caught doing something I shouldn't. This entire night has felt like one major mind fuck. Sliding my hands into my pockets, I say, "I thought I saw Garrett outside. Figured I'd try to catch him and say hi."

He reins in the intensity of his glare as his body slightly relaxes at my revelation, but it makes me feel like he has something to hide. Why would my standing in his living room make him anxious?

He nods and then says, "Yeah, that was him. He and my dad are going out for drinks. They just popped in to tell me not to let things get out of control. You know, normal parental BS. Are you hungry? I was coming in to see if the pizza guy was here. My app dinged."

Because Garrett's reaction to seeing me here still has me feeling uneasy, I ask, "Did you mention me to him?"

There's a subtle tick in his jaw. One that I'd have missed if I had blinked. Before he's able to give me a response, the doorbell rings. "That's the pizza."

When the door opens, the guy has about six pizza boxes and two bags. I join Connor at the door and help carry food back to the kitchen. We're just opening the boxes and bags, and I'm about to question him further on Garrett when Holden walks in. He, too, is shirtless. When he sees me standing next to Connor, he sets his jaw. "Aria, a word, please." He nods his head toward the office, and I follow.

"What's going on? Do you want to fuck my best friend? Is that it? You saw his big fancy house, and now you're moving on to the next guy? I can't believe you. I knew you'd do this."

My eyes literally bug out of my head in shock. I'm so taken aback that I'm speechless. I don't know what has gotten into him tonight. We seemed so good earlier, and now I feel like he's trying to find reasons to break up with me. I look down at the floor and close my eyes, willing the tears not to fall. Before deciding this is a fight I'm not going to have, I brush past him and make a beeline for the front door.

*Fuck this.* I'm out.

# 13

## DEMONS

HOLDEN

D*amn it. What the hell is my problem?* This entire day was fucked from the start. It's the same every year, and while Aria makes it better, she doesn't at the same time. Instead, she reminds me of all I don't deserve and everything I stand to lose.

"Aria, shit, wait." I run after her. She's walking so fast she may as well be jogging. "Aria, stop. I'm sorry, I didn't mean it." My words fall on deaf ears, because she does not stop. Finally, I jog and catch up to her halfway down the block. Grabbing her wrist, I attempt to stop her.

"Don't fucking touch me, Holden. Don't you dare."

*Ouch*. That hurts. I've never seen her mad, but the fact that she's taking that tone with me lets me know I really fucked up. What's messed up is, I knew the words were vile before I ever let them past my lips, and I said them anyway. I wanted to hurt her. Because my past and fear haunt me the most on this day, I let my jealousy get the best of me. First, Con touched her when we arrived, and then, when I saw them acting like a fucking happy couple laying out dinner, I lost it. I wanted to hurt her before she hurt me, because there is no way she'll ever keep me. I'm too fucked up. It's only a matter of time.

"Aria, please, if you love me." I drop my hands to my knees, fully winded from being drunk and high.

"No, Holden, you don't get to use that if you love me crap. That's bullshit. It works both ways, because if you loved me, you wouldn't have treated me like that back there. I know now those words mean nothing to you."

I don't care how fucking worn out I feel. Walking over, I wrap my arms around her and force her to submit. She hits me. "Holden, let me go." When I refuse to let up, she bites my bicep. Fuck, that's going to leave a mark.

"Aria, stop fighting me." She hits my chest one more time before breaking down into tears. *Shit.* "Please don't cry, pretty girl. I love you so damn much. I just wish you knew. I wish I could let you inside for one minute so you could see for yourself *the depth of my truth*."

"That's the problem, Holden. You don't let me in. Not really."

I know what she's saying, and I wince from the implication. I want to let her in, but I just can't. My hell is my own. Unlike her, I'm not trying to fight my demons. I deserve them. I'm only trying to live through them.

"Don't I make you happy? Can't you live with me the way I am? You make me feel, Aria. I've been dead inside for so long. I didn't think I was capable of loving anyone until you. Can't you be happy knowing you're the better part of me?"

When she brings her eyes up to meet mine, her face is streaked with mascara, and her bottom lip trembles. I can feel her entire body shaking from nerves, and it destroys me that I'm to blame. I did this to her, to us. "What happens when the pain inside of you wins, Holden? Is this it? I get hurt, I suffer?"

I drop to my knees in front of her. Fuck, this hurts. Leaning my head against her stomach, I hold her tight. "Please, baby, you need to know I'm so sorry. It won't win, not with you here. It only wins if you leave me. I'm dead inside without you. You made me believe I can have so much more, that there's a reason I'm still here."

Her body goes rigid in my arms, and I feel her hand slide into my hair. "Please don't tell me you want to hurt yourself, Holden. Please say that's not what you meant."

Squeezing my eyes shut, I try to find my words. How can I explain I've thought about suicide and contemplated it, but never had an impulse to act on it? Sometimes, when we are in a dark place, our thoughts wander and take us to places we didn't know existed within ourselves, but for whatever reason, that's all they'll ever be: thoughts. I shake my head and hope it's enough.

"Is it because your ex cheated on you that you believe I'll do the same?" Again, I shake my head. "Holden, please give me something."

Peering up at her, I find her beautiful brown eyes blurry with unshed tears. "I'm scared, Aria, so fucking scared. Everything we have scares the hell out of me. It all happened so fast, and now I feel like I'm waiting for the bottom to fall out. For all of this to blow up in my face. For fate to laugh at me and tell me this was all some sick joke."

I haven't even finished my thought when she starts nodding her head in agreement. "You're right. What we have doesn't exist. There's no way two people meet and instantly fall in love. Those are just punchlines Hollywood makes up to sell movies." Her hands find my arms and she unlocks them from her waist. "It's better this way. We just end this now on our terms before fate can get its hands on us. Because if it hurts this bad now, I don't want to know what another week might feel like."

What? That's not what I was saying. How do I say, fate's a fickle bitch who's already fucked me over more than once without giving her more? My pain is my cross to bear, not hers. She's already started walking away again when I jump to my feet.

"Aria, I'm not breaking up with you. That's not what I want." I let out a loud yell before raking my hands through my hair.

"How in the hell do you think the guy who just spent hours worshipping every inch of your body, the same one who made a point of ensuring everyone in that house knew you were my girl, wants to fucking break up? Damn it, Aria. You're mine!" I let out another furious growl of frustration. "Why is it always so easy for you to walk away from me?" Storming forward, I grab her wrist again. But she yanks it out of my grip.

"What part of my face is telling you this is easy, Holden?"

When I look at her, and I mean *really* look at her, I see her pain. Her eyes are swollen from crying, and black streaks run down her face as her chest heaves from the adrenaline coursing through her body. Catching her eyes, I say, "I know you love me. But can you forgive me?" When she drops her head and cries some more, I pull her against my chest, and she lets me. Why am I hurting her? I don't want to hurt her. She's my everything.

Pulling her chin up, I place my hands on either side of her face and whisper against her mouth. "I'm so sorry, pretty girl. You mean everything to me." I press a soft kiss against her lips, nose, forehead, and cheeks, before finally landing back on her mouth, where I try for more. When I slip my tongue out to slowly coax her lips apart, she lets me in, and I can't help but sigh in relief. As my tongue dips in, I taste the sweetness of the drink she's been sipping on all night. I'm instantly drunk on her. Dropping my hands from her face, I drag them down her arms until I can reach around and take an ample amount of ass cheek in each hand and squeeze. I can't help but get turned on. Her ass is fucking plump and perfect.

When she pulls out of our kiss, the first thing that comes to mind is I did something wrong, but then she says, "Truck. Now."

I instantly lift her up and throw her over my shoulder, slapping her ass and making her squeal. This may have been our first fight, but I'd lie if I said I wasn't excited about making up. Throwing open the door, I set her on the backseat of the cab. The windows are tinted, giving us some privacy. She immediately takes off her top and unbuttons her shorts, which are completely out of character for her, but I fully support. Aria has nothing to be ashamed of. She's perfect, beauty marks and all. No sooner have I've climbed up and shut the door than she's pulling my shorts down, freeing my cock, and straddling me.

"Fuck baby, do you know how hot this is? Please do not take this wrong—"

Before I can finish my sentence, she's sinking down onto my cock, throwing her head back with a moan and mumbling, "So good."

"Shit, you're so goddamn beautiful." I let my hands slide down her perfect hourglass waist and squeeze her hips. Her perfect tits are about to pop out of her bra, and I want them in my mouth. Reaching behind her I snap it off, and her full tits fall out with a weight that's new. I let her set the pace; right now, she's riding me slow and steady. My cock is hitting the spot deep inside that drives her crazy, and I already feel her starting to squeeze me. "Take it, baby. Ride me, pretty girl." I take a breast in my mouth and suck hard while kneading the other.

"Oh god, don't stop." Her hands find my shoulders, and she braces herself before she really starts to ride me. I groan against her breast, trying to stave off my orgasm because this is so fucking hot. Her pussy is so wet, it's dripping down my thighs. You can hear the sound of our arousal every time she slams down, and it's fucking hot. I can feel my balls tightening with the need to come.

Slapping her ass hard, I squeeze and slow her pace before I say, "Look at me, baby. Do you feel how deep inside you I am? This is where I belong. You are my home."

Her eyes search mine for truth, and I know she sees it. A breathy, "Yeah," leaves her mouth before her lips find mine, but because she's on the brink of orgasm, all she can manage are short pants. I love how she takes my dick. I've never seen a woman come so wholly undone.

I bite her lip and rasp out, "Baby, you were made for me," before wrapping my arms around her and pulling her tight to my chest, determined to keep her here with me forever.

"God, baby, fuck, you need to get there. I'm so turned on; I'm not going to last." I bring my thumb to her clit, and it instantly sets her off. Her head is resting in the crook of my neck as she comes undone and moans against the sensitive skin there, making my skin prickle in awareness that this woman owns me. She's slowly rocking against me, riding out the aftershocks of her orgasm when I shoot my seed deep. I pepper kisses along her neck and collarbone, pausing to tell her how perfect she is while letting my hands roam over every inch. The car smells like sex, the windows are fogged, and when she sits up to look at me, I swear I start to get hard again.

Her face is flushed, her eyes are wild, and those tits—I'm an ass man, always have been, but damn. She leans in and gives me a slow, open-mouthed kiss. "I want all of you, Holden. Not just the pieces." I groan, because fuck, those words are like a punch to the gut. They're the same ones I used on her.

"I want to give them to you. I just don't know how."

She kisses me again, this time dipping her tongue in to meet mine before pulling back to murmur, "I don't want to lose you."

Taking her face in my hands, I say, "You won't. I'm here. Just promise you won't stop fighting for me. I need you to *dig*. When I'm not the man I was yesterday, *dig*. DIG until you uncover the better parts of me, the parts that belong to you."

She nods before leaning in to kiss my lips and resting her head on my shoulder. We sit there in silence for a small eternity, neither of us wanting to lose the connection. My soul is tethered to this woman, and I don't know what will become of me if I ever lose her.

"Baby, do you think you can drive us back to my house? I don't want to go back inside, and I've had too much to drink." I have no desire to go back inside. All I want is sitting here in my truck.

The truth is that I only agreed to come here tonight for her. I wanted to see Connor's parents' house with fresh eyes. While I've been here a few times over the years, it wasn't until I meant Aria that I had reason to believe there was anything out of the ordinary going on here. Even though Con and I are friends, you can't ask someone, 'Hey, is your family keeping its business clean?' All that would get me is lies or half-truths. Over the past few weeks, I've listened with a renewed intensity, but if anything, it's felt like the rumors have dried up, and all I've found are my fears manifesting into my reality. That's what I've been doing with Con and Aria since the beginning—looking for reasons to push her away even though it's the last thing I want. It's my pattern, the reason I isolate. When I let the people I care about get close, I hurt them before they can hurt me because I don't deserve happiness.

"Can we have five more minutes?" I smile and hold her tighter. I'll give her the world, but for now, I'll start with five minutes.

"Yeah, pretty girl. Five minutes."

"Geez, do they not know what streetlights are out here? It's so dark. Holden, I don't like this. I hate driving in the dark."

I reach across and rest my hand on her thigh. "Baby, you're doing fine. Just go slow. We are not in a hurry, and no, they don't tend to line country roads with streetlights. You're almost to the main road that leads straight to my house, and then there will be more light."

I can tell she's nervous, and I hate that I'm not the one driving, especially tonight of all nights, but I'm trying to make good choices, to be the man she needs, to take care of her, and if I drove, I would have been putting her at risk. I'm just turning my head back to the front windshield when Aria slams on the brakes and screams. My brain doesn't even compute what's happening, because all I see are images flashing before my eyes: proposing, getting married, and watching her stomach grow with my babies.

All the beautiful things I want with her are taken from me right before my eyes. *Fuck.*

Yelling pulls me out of my fog. "Holden, I'm sorry, I didn't see it. I'm so sorry."

When I look over, Aria is jumping out of the truck. *Shit, she's okay.* We're okay, but we're not. This isn't okay. This is my sign. I can't have anything good. I don't deserve it. If it's not now, it will be later. I jump down and meet her around the front. There's a dent in my front bumper and a cracked headlight. The deer she hit is lying on the side of the road, dying. As if on autopilot, I walk around to the back of my truck, pull my hunting rifle out of my toolbox, and load a shell before heading back to the deer to put it out of its misery.

Standing over the deer, I watch it spasm and struggle. Its back legs are broken, and it's desperately trying to run off. Aiming my gun right for its head, I pull the trigger and end its suffering. Turning around, I see Aria standing in the beams of the headlights crying and shaking, and suddenly, I feel sick. I need to let her go. I'm nothing if not superstitious, and it's not a coincidence that this happened tonight of all fucking nights. No, this was fate saying fuck you, motherfucker. You don't get your happily ever after.

I want to walk over, hold her, comfort her, and tell her I don't give a shit about my truck, but I do none of those things. Instead, I walk back to my toolbox, put my gun away, lock the box, and return to the driver's side of the cab to climb in. Nothing like fate slapping you in the face to sober you up. When Aria sees that I've entered the truck, she comes around to the passenger side and gets in.

"Holden, I'm so sorry. That deer came out of nowhere. I didn't see it. I'll pay to fix your truck. I feel terrible."

Shaking my head, I hold my hand out to silence her. I give her no words. I can't. I can barely stomach being in the same car with her, let alone speaking to her. She was my everything, and now she has to be nothing. The drive back to my house is cloaked in silence. Aria's body was wracked with nerves the entire way home, and I'm sure my response has only made it worse. I'm a fucking dick, but I have to be. This has to be the end. There is no other way. It's better she thinks I'm pissed off that she crashed my truck. The truth is worse, and she'll figure it out, but not here, not in front of me.

When I pull into the driveway, I immediately hop out, walk around to her side, and open the door. She turns but doesn't jump down right away. When my eyes find her face, my heart shatters into a million pieces. Pieces I'll never get back because when she drives away tonight, she'll be taking all of them with her. Pulling her into my arms, I hold tight, breathing her in for the last time. Savoring how she feels pressed up against my body and committing every detail to memory, because this is the first and last woman I will ever love—and because I love her with all that I am, she has to go.

With her wrapped tightly around my body, I carry her over to her car. "Are you mad at me?" She sniffles against my neck.

"No, Aria. I could never be mad at you." Setting her down, she refuses to let me go, and I fucking hate it. It's tearing me apart inside. "It's been a long night," I say as I try to gently unhook her arms from my waist. Finally, she lets me go, and I know without even looking at her that those big brown eyes are peering up at me, wondering why I'm shutting her out again.

Opening her door, I say, "Drive safe, and text me when you get home." All things I don't want. I don't want her driving at all tonight. She should be with me where she belongs. When she ducks under my arm to get into her car without another word, I turn away and cough, trying to hold down the contents in my stomach that threaten to come up, knowing I'll never see her again. Then, pulling it together, I lean in and kiss her forehead before adding. "I love you, Aria. So damn much."

Her eyes search mine, but I turn away before she sees too much. I hear her say, "I love you too," right before I close the door and walk away.

I don't linger outside her car. I need her to go. I need her to drive away, so I start walking up the driveway toward the house. As soon as I hear her car start to pull down the street, I run to the edge of my yard, not wanting to miss the last glimpse I'll ever get. Standing in the middle of the road, I watch my heart drive out of my life and prepare to live in the hell I just made for myself.

## 14

# PIECES

ARIA

Numb. That's how I feel. There's no other way to describe the pain, emptiness, confusion, and loss that have settled upon me. Holden has pursued me since we met, never once taking no for an answer. His love was fast, fierce, and all-consuming, but it wasn't the everlasting type. What's fucked up is, I think I always knew that, and now, as I sit here and wallow in my own despair, I have no one else to blame but myself.

"Aria, can I come in? You've been in your room all day." Spencer jiggles the doorknob.

"Go away, Spencer. I already told you I don't feel good. I'm sick."

"It's the Fourth of July. I thought you were going to Holden's uncle's house or something."

Tears immediately start streaming down my face, but I hold back the sob and keep my voice steady. "I can't. I'm sick."

I hear him growl in annoyance like he's debating if he believes me or not. "Well, can I get you anything?"

"No, I'm fine. Go out and have fun. Don't worry about me."

I stay silent, waiting until I hear his footsteps clap against the wood floor as he walks off. Then I resume crying. Letting myself die inside so I don't ever have to feel again. It's now 7:00 pm, and I've turned off my phone so that I don't call or text him and make myself look any more pathetic than I already feel.

Last night, after the accident, he was different. He wasn't the Holden I've come to love. It's like he completely shut down. At first, I thought he was angry and didn't want to make it worse for me, but I knew it was something more when we got back to his house. I couldn't put my finger on it, but it was more. In my heart, his goodbye felt different, and I did nothing to stop it because this was how it was always going to be. I was never going to be his. That's why I fought him in the beginning. I just didn't know it would hurt this bad. It's never hurt this bad.

I texted after I got home, and he told me all the same things he always does: "Sleep tight, pretty girl. I love you." But after the night we shared, I'd hoped for more. I expected him to be so much more, but I'm not sure why, when all he's ever given me is pieces. Ultimately, I let myself fall asleep believing that our night was incredibly traumatic across the board. Our fight, the truth in our make-up sex, and the accident. We just needed to decompress —but it was confirmed when I woke up this morning. We were over.

> Holden: Aria, baseball starts up again in three days, and classes are in two weeks. We already only see each other three days a week, and you always come to me. I don't want to put you on the back burner. You deserve so much more. I think we both knew this was coming. Go find someone who can give you the world.

I read and reread that text a million times, wishing it away, and then confirming it was indisputable. That it existed and he actually texted me those words. For hours, I typed then untyped. I wanted to scream and fight. I fucking wanted to dig. I wanted to dig so I could find the man he was the day before, but this felt different. It felt so final, and in the end, I knew in my heart any text I sent would go unanswered, and I would be left with even more pain and hate.

I hate that I let myself fall so hard and fast when I knew better. He was the one. The one I wanted to spend the rest of my life with, but the hard truth is, those feelings only went one way. In the end, I was all I ever knew I'd be. A quick fuck until he got me out of his system. The girl he needed to conquer because she said no. A notch in his belt. Guys like him get perfect, and we both knew I was anything but. I made my bed, and now I must lie in it.

I've spent the last three days in bed. I locked myself in my room and refused to come out. Since it was a holiday, we were off Monday. I considered calling in today but decided against it. I'm stronger than this. I'm better than this. So what if I've lost two friends and a boyfriend over the last two months? I'm not defined by my friendships or the men I sleep with.

As I stand in the shower washing my hair, that strength I had five minutes ago to drag my ass in here suddenly vanishes. I'm tired, weak, malnourished, and a general hot mess. Turning off the shower, I don't know if I even managed to rinse all the soap out of my hair, but I know I need food because I'm about to pass out.

I've just pulled a towel around me when the worst pain I've ever felt in my entire life shoots through my abdomen, bringing me to my knees. I scream out in pain, and my mom rushes into the bathroom. Her face is the last thing I see before my world goes dark.

The feeling of ice shooting through my arm and murmurs of voices stirs me awake. When I finally find the strength to open my eyes, I see I'm in the hospital. *What the hell?* Closing my eyes, I run through my memories, trying to remember what happened that landed me here. The last thing I recall was climbing out of the shower and sharp pain shooting through my abdomen. I must have finally starved myself enough to cause serious damage.

"Aria, are you awake?"

*Damn.* I was hoping to stay still long enough to hear what everyone was saying instead of them telling me what they think I need to hear. Unlike Spencer, my mother avoids her feelings, and my father—the man who's been my rock my entire life—has all but ignored me ever since he found out I'm sick. I don't think he means to; I just think it hurts him too much, and he doesn't know what to do. I believe he feels helpless. I never wanted any of this. The pain I'm putting my family through is unforgivable. I'm disrupting their lives.

"Hey, Aria. Talk to me. How do you feel? Tell me what's wrong." If Spencer is this attentive and genuine with future patients, he will make a great doctor. I move my feet and sit up slightly in bed. Other than soreness in my abdomen, I don't feel too bad.

"I'm okay. My stomach hurts, but I suppose I did that to myself. Are Mom and Dad here?"

He runs his hand through his hair. "Yes, they went down to get coffee. I got here as soon as I could."

Looking around, I try to gauge what time it is. Unfortunately, it's raining outside, and the shade over the window is drawn so I can't tell.

"How long was I out?"

"A few hours." He walks around my bed, checking the bags on the intravenous pole and reading the papers from the machine hooked up to monitor my heart, blood pressure, and oxygen.

"So, doc, what's wrong with me?"

Spencer shoots me a serious look as he rubs his chin. "This isn't the time for jokes, Aria. Healthy people don't get admitted to the hospital. The labs haven't come back, but the attending D.O. said they should be back by 6:00 pm."

"Holy crap, it's 6:00 pm? I passed out for that long?" I bring my hands to my face and rub my eyes. This morning, I passed out getting ready for work, which means I've been out all day.

"Yeah, well, that will happen when you're dehydrated and malnourished from starving yourself for days. What the hell is going on, Aria?"

"Knock, knock. I see our girl is awake." A tall, older gentleman with white hair and thick-rimmed glasses walks in. He looks like he could double for Colonel Sanders in his early years. "I have the bloodwork back, dear, but first things first: how are you feeling? Any pain, discomfort?"

Spencer decides to speak up for me. "She said her stomach is bothering her, and I've noticed her heart rate keeps dropping and spiking, which could—"

The doctor holds up his hand. "Young man, I know you love her, but let's hear what she has to say, hmmm?"

"My stomach hurts, and my arm is killing me."

Walking around the bed to my right arm, he inspects it before saying, "Your IV looks to be functioning correctly. However, sometimes these hydration packs can cause discomfort. Once you're done with this bag, we can take a break."

As he drags on about the tests he ran and what they mean, I start finding it hard to focus because the pain in my abdomen is back with a vengeance. It's so sharp, I wince and close my eyes only to see stars. "Fudge, this hurts." I turn onto my side, and as I do, I feel a gush of fluid in my underwear. *Great, how embarrassing.* I haven't had a period in months, and now it decides to show up. That must be why the pain is so bad.

"Dear, is there any chance you could be pregnant?"

I shake my head. "I'm on the pill, and I don't have periods."

"I see. Well, I'll run a test just to be sure."

My parents are just walking through the door when I double over in blinding pain and start dry heaving. "It hurts, it hurts. Can you make it stop hurting? Please make it stop." I'm all-out sobbing now.

The nurses rush in from the hallway, either from the sounds of screams or the monitors, just as I hear the doctor say, "I think I know what's happening. That's too much blood." Blood? What the hell is he going on about?

"Let's roll her down to radiology? Can you please notify Dr. Roberts we might have an emergency D&C?"

I turn to Spencer, preparing to ask what all this means, but his face is pale white and solemn like I just got the worst news I could ever receive. "What's going on?" I ask to anyone who's listening.

"Aria, dear, I believe you're having a miscarriage."

"What..." I don't even know if the sounds that pass through my lips are audible because my heart is too busy shattering into a million tiny pieces that I'll never get back.

Spencer rushes to my side as I'm being wheeled down the hallway. "Do you want me to call Holden?"

"No, no, no. Do not call Holden. We broke up. I'm not his problem, and neither is this." I press my head back into the bed and fight back the tears as I breathe through more pain. "Spence, please don't tell Mom and Dad. Just let them think it's the sickness. Don't tell them this. Please."

I've been in the hospital for two weeks now. After being rushed in for an emergency D&C and kept for observation for twenty-four hours due to the other health issues involved that made my recovery nontypical, I agreed to check myself into the hospital's eating disorder recovery program.

The program has been good for me. They took away all communication with the outside world. No phones, iPads, or even music. My room has a TV, but it only has five channels. Apparently, songs and shows, everyday things we see and hear, can be triggers without us even realizing it. I was so annoyed in the beginning, but now that it's release day, everything has come full circle. I'm going to miss the solitude that the program afforded me.

Before I was admitted, I sent a message to work and told them I would need sick time for a personal matter. I put Spencer as my point of contact, knowing I wouldn't be available for two weeks. He spoke with HR, and I was able to use FMLA to keep my job. If I had shared with Garrett why I was in the hospital, I'm sure I could have kept my job regardless, but I don't want to share this struggle with everyone, at least not yet. Right now, everything I went through is still too raw. I lost something I didn't even know I wanted.

I'm young, still in school, and live with my parents. A baby is the last thing I needed, but having the choice to keep it ripped away broke me. The second the doctor told me I was most likely having a miscarriage, a part of me died. For days, I cried over the loss of another part of me and the last part of him. The doctor explained that while the cause of most miscarriages is unknown, stress, dehydration, and lack of food, coupled with my already diminished health from my eating disorder, most likely attributed to the loss.

Spencer has visited me every evening to hang out and just be present while doing his studies. The company has been a blessing I didn't know I needed. We've talked for hours about school, work, growing up, how I feel inside, and the baby I lost. During those conversations, Holden never came up, and for that I am grateful. For me to heal, I need to put him out of my mind. There's no going back. He made his choice, and it wasn't me, it wasn't us—and that's okay. Somewhere through all of this, I've found my worth. Maybe I had to break so I was forced to pick up the pieces and slowly put them back together one by one and examine all the parts of me I wanted to keep, all the parts of me that are strong, resilient, and fierce. The parts of me I used to love.

I've just finished getting dressed, and I'm waiting on my bed for my discharge papers when my door flies open. "Aria, oh my god, I can't believe you're coming home today!" Olivia enters like a bat out of hell with two smoothies and flowers. Setting everything down, she quickly rushes over to pull me into a hug. "I've been chomping at the bit to get in here, but they wouldn't let me. They said you weren't allowed to have any visitors."

"What? Spencer has been here every day."

She rolls her eyes. "Apparently, he convinced someone on the board who was a friend of a friend he played ball with a long time ago that he was a med student doing research or some crap; otherwise, he wouldn't have been allowed either."

"Figures. I assumed my parents weren't coming after what my dad said before I checked myself in." I shrug and try not to let the memory bother me.

She gives me a sympathetic smile before adding, "Aria, they don't know what to do. They feel helpless because you're battling something only you can fix in the end. You need to dig deep and find the strength within you to choose better, to want more, and to love yourself. Aria, growing up, I wanted to be you. You were always so strong and confident, not to mention witty as hell. You still are when you're not stuck in your head. Somewhere along the line, you veered off your path. You just need to find yourself again. We have our entire lives ahead of us. This is just a bump in the road, a tiny speck that you'll one day look back on and find didn't define you. It built you. It made you strong."

I can't help it. I'm bawling like a baby. Leaning in, she hugs me again. "Ari, don't cry. I wasn't trying to make you cry."

"I know. It's probably just the HCG still leaving my system." She tries to give me a surprised look. "Don't give me that look. If you're here, I have no doubt Spencer flapped his big lips and told you everything, which is fine. I would have told you anyway. But I'm not ready to talk about it. I just want to go home and try to start fresh."

Taking a seat at the foot of the bed, she flips her hair over her shoulder with a renewed sense of vigor and excitement. "I was hoping, after you're discharged, you'd catch a plane back to Cali with me."

I give her an *are you fucking serious?* look before saying, "Oli, I've already missed two weeks of work. I'll get fired if I miss any more days that aren't FMLA related." She starts shaking her head.

"No, I'm asking you to move back with me. Hear me out before you say anything. You just said yourself you wanted a fresh start. There's no better fresh start than a new state where you don't know anyone but me. You can remake yourself, be anyone you want to be, or simply take the time you need to find yourself without the added pressure of running into all the reminders of what you have lost, all the things that inadvertently made you sick to start with."

While that sounds amazing, I also can't afford it. I can barely afford my school, car, phone, and social life as it is. But, before I can tell her it's not feasible, she adds, "I've already talked it over with my family. You can stay as long as you like, rent free. You already know you're like a second child to my family, and Spencer and your parents think it could be good for you."

As if on cue, Spencer comes walking through the door. I don't miss the uneasy smile they both share before he walks around the bed to take a seat opposite Olivia.

"Clearly you were standing outside the door this entire time."

He shrugs his shoulders. "Well, yeah. I thought I'd give you two a minute before I busted in and tried to convince you to leave. I have your discharge papers, by the way." He hands them over and adds, "Aria, I want you to take her up on this offer. I'll miss you like crazy, but I think this will be good for you. I'll come and visit, and I know Mom and Dad will too. You need this, Aria."

I look between the two of them with my mind already made up. Choosing *me* is no longer going to be hard. "Okay."

They look back and forth between each other and then back to me before saying, "Okay," in unison, as if they're not convinced I'm agreeing.

With a massive smile, I jump out of bed and say, "Let's go!"

# 15

## MORE

ARIA

**5 Years Later**

"Babe, we're here. Aren't you excited to be home? I still can't believe you grew up here." Nate has been going on and on about this trip. He's a sports agent and has just landed one of his biggest accounts. That's why we're here. Saturday is signing day for this athlete whose identity remains a mystery. Technically, the guy has already been traded, but that announcement will come out this weekend at the party he's throwing. While he became a free agent at the end of last season, he's hired Nate to manage all his other contractual agreements.

"You won't be excited when we walk out those doors." It's the end of July in Missouri, which means it's hotter than balls and humid as fuck. I already miss California.

It hits him as we walk out the double doors to our waiting Uber. "Holy shit. How am I instantly sweating?" He rubs his forehead, mystified by the absurdity, and I can't help but laugh.

"And that would be the lovely humidity. I told you not to wear long sleeves."

He takes my suitcase and throws it in the trunk. I climb into the waiting Expedition just as he rounds the vehicle and comes back to my side. "Scoot in. There is a bus on the other side."

As the car pulls out, Nate asks, "Are you sure you want to stay at the hotel? I don't mind staying at your parents' house. Spence said I could take his room since he's out of town."

Of course he talked to Spencer. The two of them have become thick as thieves. Spencer being a sports med doctor doesn't hurt. They are constantly talking about athletes and sharing contacts.

"No, I'd rather stay at a hotel, but we are going there tonight for dinner, right?" Being back here already has me on edge. The last time I was in my room, I had my fucking heart ripped out. I don't particularly care to sleep with those memories. They already haunt my every waking moment. Sleep is my escape.

Picking up my hand, he kisses it. "Yes, Aria. I want to see where you grew up. I'm excited about this. I know this isn't easy for you, so I need you to tell me when you're uncomfortable. I don't want to upset you." I nod, and he leans in and kisses my cheek. "I'm going to check my emails while we drive to the hotel, and then I promise I'm all yours."

I smile and give him a knowing eyebrow raise. Nate's phone may as well be glued to his hand, but he's good to me. We're good together. We're both focused on our careers and building our portfolios. We know what we want and won't settle for anything less. It's perfect. It feels healthy and balanced. We're both upfront and honest about our expectations and five-year plans. Each of us has goals we want to reach before we settle down.

Turning on my phone, I see I have three missed calls. One's from my mom, probably checking to see if we've landed. The other is from Olivia, but since we are roommates and work together, it could be a friendly check-in or a work-related call. The last is from my patient, Maggie. Maggie is the reason Nate and I met.

Maggie Harrison is the wife of Tom Harrison, principal owner of San Diego's MLB team. After moving to California, Olivia got me a job as a receptionist in one of her dad's elite rehab facilities. They help celebrities with a range of addictions across the board. Mrs. Harrison's case hit home for me because I watched her struggle with bulimia for months. I imagine it's hard being a billionaire's wife in one of the most plastic cities in the world. Everyone is constantly getting implants, injections, or some new therapy that promises to be the fountain of youth and make them look younger. Watching her go through her recovery and seeing her relapses helped solidify what I wanted to do with my own life.

The following semester, I officially started attending school to become a licensed nutritionist. I wanted to share my journey, my stories, and what helped me come out on the other side. I don't believe our hardships are meant to be saved just for us. I think sometimes they are given to us because fate knew we were strong enough to conquer them. Those hardships never truly broke us; they built us. They forged us into the people we are today. I've never loved myself more than I do now. I'd be lying if I said there weren't times when I'm self-conscious or something triggers me, and I'm taken back to a dark place in my mind, but over the years, I've found strength in that darkness.

I press talk to ring Maggie and wait for her to pick up. "Aria, thanks for calling back so quickly. I was wondering if you and Nate will be back in town next Friday for a little social gathering Tom and I are having with a few friends." Before I can even ask for details, Nate shakes my arm and frantically gives me prayer hands, while mouthing 'yes, yes, yes.' "Sure, Maggie, we'll be there. Just text me the time and attire."

I hear her sigh in relief before she says, "Great, I'll text you as soon as we get off. Have a great trip."

After I hang up, I ask, "What was that? I thought you and Tom were close?"

Tom is the reason I met Nate, after all. Maggie and I do not have your typical doctor-patient relationship. While I'm her nutritionist, I'm also her friend, making weekly house calls when needed. During my visits, Nate and I would run into each other from time to time. Tom had hired Nate to handle a few accounts for some of the players on the San Diego's feeder team that were starting to gain more clout from fill-ins when guys were benched with injuries. Nate asked me to dinner one day, and the rest was history.

"Aria, we are close, but Tom didn't call and invite me. Tom has his hands in every aspect of the sports world. This will be a good networking opportunity for both of us." He's not wrong. However, I don't network the same way he does.

Nate is flashy, and to land big contracts, he needs to be, but I avoid the spotlight. I build my clientele through word of mouth, knowing that discretion is vital for the level of sensitivity most people have regarding their disorders. That's why I refuse to enter parties with him. I don't want to be seen on his arm and give people the wrong idea that I'm out here scamming people, landing high-profile clients because of who I'm dating. The only events I attend and allow myself to be photographed at are charity events where the proceeds support foundations that help with recovery. Typically, Oli is my date, not Nate. Nate and I work because he doesn't push. He lets me be.

"Well, we're going, so no need to fret. I'm pretty sure my invite was for moral support. This is Maggie's first event since she got out of rehab." Nate puts down his phone and gives me his full attention. That's one of the things that's always made me melt. He knows about my past, why I do this type of work, and how important it is to me. In some ways, it helps me stay on track. While I haven't stuck my finger down my throat or starved myself in over five years, the mental work to remain cognizant that I'm always recovering and never recovered is a constant.

"Are we still talking about Maggie?"

I furrow my brows, confused by his meaning. "Of course, Maggie hasn't had an event where she's had to entertain the who's who of San Diego's finest. I'm sure she's nervous, and then alcohol, food, and pretty women dressed in next to nothing could easily trigger her—"

He grabs my hand. "Okay, but how are you doing? This is your first time home since you left five years ago. Babe, I want you to tell me if you start feeling emotionally unstable. We'll be on the first flight back, Aria. I swear it."

I shake my head. "Nate, this will be good for me. While I'm not particularly thrilled to be here, I'm also not the same girl who left. It means a lot that you would do that for me though."

He scoots over and pulls me into him, placing a kiss atop my head. "I'd do anything for you."

While Nate hasn't said the words, I think he wants to. We've been dating for roughly a year, and I feel like the L-word is always on the tip of his tongue. But he hasn't said it, and for that, I'm grateful. One of the reasons we work so well is because he doesn't push for more, and it doesn't hurt that he's waiting until marriage for sex. Funny enough, that came up on the first date, and I think it's what sealed the second one for me. I immediately felt relaxed.

We had casually been talking about our past relationships and why we were single, and I told him it was the sex for me. After I slept with someone, I would end it. I never elaborated on the reasoning behind that statement, and he didn't ask. All he said was, "Well, no worries there. I'm waiting for marriage." I'd choked on my drink when he said that and felt incredibly rude. Nate is an attractive guy. However, he is not the guy who looks like he's saving himself for marriage. In the looks department, I haven't dated anyone who remotely resembles him. Nate is your clean-cut, business suit, penny loafers with no socks, and not a wrinkle to be seen pretty boy. He is the epitome of GQ, all the while rocking a man-bun.

The hair is the first thing I noticed about him. Everything about him is serious, except that hair. That hair is fucking wild and sexy as hell. One of the best parts of the day is when we cuddle in bed, and I run my hands through his blond locks when he lets them down. I swear, it's almost as thick as mine. He could be pulling all the ass he wanted.

I considered that maybe he had been joking about the whole

waiting until marriage for sex talk, but the more dates we went on, the more I was convinced he was being truthful. Never have I caught him even looking at another woman. I am his sole focus outside of his career when we are together. But I would never fault him for being driven or focused. Those are his dreams, desires, things he's wanted long before I ever came around. I would never want him to change for me.

"How long of a drive is it to the hotel we're staying at anyway?"

I link and unlink our fingers. It's a nervous tick I've developed. Whenever I think about more or want more intimately, I find myself doing it. Then, dragging myself out of my memories, I look out the window and see the dove sign right outside of West County Mall, and I know I'm home. "We'll be there in roughly ten minutes."

"Well, I'm getting in the shower immediately and changing. What time did you tell your mom we'll be over?"

"Crap, I need to text her back. What time do you want to head over?"

He pulls my chin up, forcing me to meet his smoldering brown gaze. I swear the man's eyes have one look, and it's always set to a seductive slow burn. Hell, maybe it's just me, and I need to get laid. Scratch that. I know I need to get laid, but I don't want to fuck it up. I don't want to lose him. We are so good together. Finally, his eyes find my mouth, and he says, "The timing is up to you, babe."

Leaning in, he lets his lips hover above mine. For a man who's waiting until marriage, he fucking loves to tease me. He's got the most perfectly suckable lips that I've ever kissed. "We could do other things for a little while." His lips gently graze mine as the hand that held my chin drops to my neck and starts to lazily drift over the exposed skin of my tank top. When my skin breaks out in goosebumps, he knows he has me and goes in for the kill, crushing his lips to mine.

The man knows how to use his mouth. While we may not

have sex, it doesn't mean that we don't do other things. As his tongue dominates mine, I submit. Lately, I've wanted more, and being here has amplified it. We keep things relatively PG-13 so that we don't cross the line. I've dry-humped his cock more times than I can count, and the man is a master with his hands, but it stops there. I feel like it has made our relationship stronger. He knows my boundaries, and I know his, and we respect them even when the other person can't find the will.

We were both so lost in each other that we didn't notice the car had stopped until the driver opened the rear door to let us out. Nate laughs and kisses my cheek. "Fucking tease."

As I step out, I throw back, "Fucking cockblock." It's our inside joke because we don't cross the line, but lately, everything has been feeling like so much more, and I can't help but feel like we might be approaching a point of no return, and it's fucking terrifying. I'm not ready to lose him.

"I'll grab the bags, babe. Go start getting us checked in." I throw my fanny pack over my shoulder and head into the lobby, checking the time as I do. It's 1:00 pm now, so I shoot my mom a quick text.

> Aria: Just got to the hotel. We'll be over at 5 pm. Love you.

Fuck this! I'm home, and I'm a changed woman. This woman takes what she wants, and right now, that's a hot shower with a sexy man and a good finger-banging.

Once I hear the shower turn on, I change out of my leggings, tank top, and Converse. Nate and I have never showered together before, and I'm hoping he won't turn me down. We've avoided being naked together thus far. If we're both fully nude, it's too easy to just let it slip, but I'm hoping he's been feeling the same level of tension I have. That he's ready for more intimacy, even if that doesn't mean sex. I don't think I'm prepared to go all the way, but I'm ready for more, and I'm hoping that he thinks we're strong enough to handle it without crossing the line.

When I enter the bathroom, the shower stall is already fogged up. I am stark naked, and the old me would have felt extremely self-conscious making this move, but the new me has learned to love her body. Sure, I have stretch marks. Who doesn't? But I'm also the healthiest I've ever been. I work out daily, nourishing my body with healthy foods that make me feel good, and I have a body I can be proud of. I'm heavier than I was five years ago, but I'm also more toned and defined. We are given one body in this life, and I'm learning to fuel mine and treat her like a temple. I've found my inner peace and self-love. I found me again.

As I pull open the shower door and step in behind Nate, I wrap my arms around his waist. "Aria!" He jumps from being startled, then turns and rakes his eyes up my body from head to toe. It's clear he likes what he sees because his cock is standing at attention and ready. "Babe..." He pulls me into him and kisses my neck while his hands roam down my back until they find my ass and squeeze. "What is this, babe?"

I run my hands up his chest before dropping a kiss on it and finding his eyes. "I want more with you, Nate. I know you're waiting, but I thought maybe we could try other stuff." Trailing my hand down his torso, I find his cock and stroke it from root to tip.

His eyes are on mine as they darken with desire. "Are you sure, Aria?"

I stroke him again. "Yes, Nate, I'm—"

Before I can even finish the sentence, his mouth is back on mine in a searing kiss that makes me clench with anticipation. He pumps his cock into my hand three more times before saying, "You're so fucking sexy. You're more than worth the wait." Trailing kisses down my neck and to my chest, he takes a nipple into his mouth and sucks hard. I swear I almost come on the spot.

"Mmm, that's so good, Nate." He bites my nipple before moving to the other, teasing it until it's pert and sufficiently ravished, just like the other.

Nate drops to his knees before questioning me one more time. "Are you sure?" Running my hands through his hair, I nod. He bites his lip and gives me a sexy sly smile before hiking one leg over his shoulder and saying, "I only have one request." I furrow my brow, not sure where he's going with this. "I want you to watch me feast."

Before his words even have a chance to compute, his tongue darts out and runs through my folds. "So good..." I draw out, throwing my head against the wall. When I don't feel him on me, I look down only to find him watching me. Once my eyes are back on his, he sucks my clit into his mouth, and I swear I see stars. Fuck, it's been too long. When I feel his finger tease my entrance, I whimper in anticipation. Nate adjusts my thigh over his shoulder, opening me up, spreading me wider, and I can't help but curse when I feel his tongue slide in. "Shit, yes..." I feel myself start to rock against his face. His eyes roll back in his head as a deep guttural moan escapes his mouth and vibrates throughout my core, sending tendrils of pleasure throughout every nerve ending in my body. When his finger finally slips in, I feel myself clench down tight, wishing it was something more.

"Nate, I need more." His eyes snap open to mine as he adds another digit. It feels so good, but it's not enough. Fuck. Why isn't it enough?

Just when I start thinking I've made a terrible mistake and ruined us, he takes his free hand and links our fingers together. That gesture, coupled with those emerald eyes boring into my soul, saying all the things I believe he wants to but is scared to say out loud for fear of rejection, sends me over the edge. My legs go weak, and my breathing becomes labored as I come down from one of the best orgasms I've had in over five years. "Shit, babe..."

Lifting me into his arms, he carries me into the bedroom and lays me on the bed. "Aria, look at me, babe." I don't open my eyes. I'm too scared. He just gave me what no other man has been able to since I left this place, and I don't know how I feel about that. "Aria, please, please look at me. I need you. Please don't shut me out." His body is pressed up against mine, and this isn't his fault. I wanted this, begged for it, and got it.

When I open my eyes, I run my hands through his hair and pull his mouth to mine. My tongue parts his lips and dips in, searching for more, wanting more, needing more, but still only scratching the surface. My eyes lock on his before I say, "I just needed more."

Swallowing hard, his hand nervously tucks a loose strand of hair behind my ear before he says, "I love you, Aria Montgomery. I've just been waiting for you to say when."

Those three little words should thaw my hardened heart, but they don't. They fucking terrify me.

"Nathan, I'm so glad you finally made it to our neck of the woods. We've heard so much about you. Spencer just won't stop raving about you. I'm sure once you get past the humidity, you'll like it enough to bring our Aria back for more visits."

I swat my mom's shoulder as I pass her in the kitchen. "Mom, you know Nate is not why I haven't been back. I've been busy with work." When I started out, I took referrals from doctors, but after garnering the attention of a few prominent patients who referred me to friends, all my work comes through word of mouth these days.

"I'll admit it's freaking hotter than crap here, but I'll follow Aria anywhere." Nate comes over and throws his arm around my shoulder, placing a kiss on my head before moving to the kitchen table.

"Mom, you act like you haven't already seen me twice this year."

She shrugs. "It's just different having you back home. I miss having you and Spencer around, and now that your dad started playing handball at the Y three days a week, I'm getting lonely. I didn't think you'd move away and never come back. When I had a daughter, I thought I had a best friend for life."

That pulls at my heartstrings. It really does, but I had to go. Mom never thought I'd stay gone, but neither did I. "You and Dad could always move out West."

To that, she rolls her eyes. "Sure, we'll move out West when we win the lottery. Unfortunately, we couldn't afford to move out there."

Clearing his throat, Nate chimes in. "Well, maybe we could buy a vacation house or something here and rent it out when we're not using it. Then we'd have a place to stay, and it would give us roots here."

My eyebrows shoot up in surprise, and I feel him move his hand to my thigh under the table. We don't live together as it is now. Buying property together seems like a huge jump. While we did just have a breakthrough in our relationship earlier, my heart is not in the same place as his, and it hurts my soul. Resting my hand on top of his, I smile and lie. "Yeah, that's something we can look into."

Changing the subject, I ask, "I thought Dad would be home by now. It's almost 7:00 pm. I can't believe he chose to play handball tonight instead of meeting us for dinner."

My mom jerks her head back. "Oh, he's not playing handball. He got stuck at work. The crews had to stay late to make up for rain delays on a big project. It was supposed to be ready for some big party tomorrow, and it's not. Dad's boss had everyone stay late to finish."

"That's crap. What asshole doesn't understand rain delays?"

My mom rolls her eyes in shared annoyance. "Speaking of big parties, is tomorrow still a secret, or did you finally cave and spill the beans?"

Nate smiles and finishes his pork chop before saying, "No, tomorrow is still a surprise. I still can't believe I landed this guy. If I gave any details away, Aria would know who he was right away, with all the sports talk she hears from work and being around me.

Let's just say this guy helps me reach one of my career goals in a big way." I feel him gently squeeze my thigh, and my heart drops into my stomach, the words 'five-year plan' and 'career goals' sinking like a rock into the pits. All that we shared earlier and crossing the lines we set start to come full circle. If he's achieving his goals and crossing things off his list sooner than later, that might mean he wants more sooner, and I'm not convinced I'm the one who can give it to him.

Standing up, I excuse myself. "I need to go to the bathroom. I'll be right back." I'm halfway down the hallway when I register that I don't need to go to the bathroom. I needed to get away from the pressure I now feel to give Nate more. The problem is, I asked for it. I practically begged for it.

Being back here is making me feel all types of things. However, it's not necessarily stress. I don't feel compelled to start up any of my old habits, but the minute I turn the knob on my bedroom door and see my old room for the first time in five years, the memories come rushing back in.

All this time, I've been telling myself that I was coming back here for Nate, but now that I'm here, I know it was a lie. In a way, running from this place freed me. Suddenly, things weren't so heavy, but now that I'm back, I can feel it in my bones and to the depths of my soul. I was always going to come back here. This is where I will heal.

Looking around my room, I see that my bed is made, but I know I wasn't the last one to make it. The morning I left this room, I was a complete mess—distraught, starved, and damaged. While I'm not that girl anymore, I feel her pain. I remember her heart. It's strange to look around at my things the way I left them and remember the girl I was and how she felt. I'm so much stronger now that my heart breaks for her. Running my fingers over my dresser, I click to open the top of my CD player and find Blue October on deck. I used to lay in bed and listen to this CD on repeat, and when I was really weak and hated myself, I'd turn up "Hate Me" and lose myself in the trashcan beside my bed.

I still don't know how I ever became so dark and tormented. All I know is, it felt like I was watching a car crash in slow motion, unable to swerve and avoid the coming head-on collision. Getting out of this place was the best thing I ever did for myself.

Since I started working with women and sharing my stories and my journey to recovery, I've only lost one. Recovery looks different for everyone. For me, hitting rock bottom was the miscarriage, but that wasn't the only thing. It was just the last straw. Like with any addiction, an addict typically knows they're fucked up, but they must find their reason. Mine was that I didn't want to be chained to my addiction. I was tired of my days being ruined by a weakness that threatened to choke out all the good in my life. I wanted more for myself. I had always been headstrong, until suddenly, I wasn't, which was utterly frustrating. How does a straight A, student council member, and varsity girls' soccer captain go from healthy to sick overnight?

"Babe, are you okay?" Hands wrap around my waist from behind as I stare at my bed. "You've been gone a little while, so I came to check on you." Nate places a kiss on my temple.

"Yeah, I'm good. I was just taking a walk down memory lane."

Squeezing me tighter, he asks, "Do you want to talk about it?"

"No, I think I'm good." I don't want to get into any in-depth conversations with him right now. I'm struggling with a lot of mixed emotions. Being back here definitely has my mind reeling.

Nate swings around to sit on my bed and pulls me into his lap. "So, this was your room growing up? Why all white?"

I laugh. "Have you not noticed my OCD tendencies? I'm very type A, and I have no doubt that's part of why I have had my issues with food for some time. It was my need to control. I think this may have been a precursor of what was to come. Everything white and pristine felt peaceful, calming, and clean when my head felt anything but. The all-white décor happened around age sixteen. That's when I started phasing out my leopard prints, posters, and mood lamps."

He's gently trailing his fingers up and down my arms in a manner meant to soothe when he says, "That's new, isn't it."

I furrow my brow, not following his train of thought. "What do you mean?"

"Well, whenever we've talked about your past and when everything started, you always say you woke up one day and just felt different, and it started shortly after graduation, but this," he gestures around the room, "started earlier."

I sit there quietly, letting his words sink in as I go over the implications in my mind. I'm a nutritionist, not a therapist, but when dealing with eating disorders, it's so much more than just food. People assume that you have an eating disorder because you have an issue with food, but it's usually deeper. Something typically manifests itself into that outlet. That's not to say it's true across the board, but generally, something influences a person's choices. I've wracked my brain for hours trying to think if I could have gone through some sort of trauma that my mind has decided was better I forget. I've never once felt triggered in such a way that stirs something inside of me to indicate that is the case.

Early in my therapy, I went through dissociative amnesia testing with a doctor at Gallo's in California. I figured it couldn't hurt, even though it wasn't the first time the idea had been brought up. But, ultimately, it didn't go anywhere because there has never been an event or moment that I can recall when things changed. The brain can hide memories from us, usually brought on by some type of stress, fear, or traumatic situation that threatens to cause profound emotional pain. Over time, those lost memories can morph into anxiety, depression, or even post-traumatic stress disorders like eating disorders. But, for as much as I wish I could find something, if only to feel validated in my pain, I never have. I've only ever felt like what was happening wasn't me, like I was trapped, unable to escape my mind and change the things that felt incredibly out of place. At some point, I stopped trying to find a reason and just accepted what was.

But now that I'm back and seeing things through a new lens, I can't help but feel like my acceptance was ignorance. I was too close to whatever caused my pain to see it as the source, but that's no longer the case.

"Aria, are you still with me?" Nate pulls me out of my thoughts, and it takes me a second to recall the question he asked.

"Maybe. I mean, you're not exactly wrong in your observation, but I don't know." I move to stand up and say, "Enough with the heavy. We should probably get back to my mom."

Grabbing my wrist, he pulls me back. "Are you trying to avoid me, Aria?" Those green eyes pierce my heart as he rubs his thumb over my knuckles. Damn it.

Closing my eyes, I say, "I'm not avoiding, just processing."

He wraps his arms around my waist and lays his head on my stomach before asking, "Can we process together?"

"What if I said I'm scared to share it with you?"

"What if I said I've never been more scared in my life than when I told you I loved you earlier?"

I pull in a ragged breath before saying, "What if those words might be a trigger for me?"

"What if I said I know, but I said them anyway?"

He's pushing. He never pushes. "Why are you pushing me?"

Then, releasing me from his grip, he pulls back and asks, "Why did you ask for more?" *Fuck.*

I start pacing the length of my room. "I don't know, Nate, because I do want more. I want so much more. Parts of me are still dead inside; parts of me are still dark, and I want the light back. We are good together. Aren't we good together? I mean, we both work a lot, sure, but we like to work. It drives us. We knew that about each other going in. And yeah, we haven't had sex, but that's okay. I feel more connected to you than any other man I've been with." I think. "Plus, we have our five-year plans. We promised neither would stand in the way nor tie the other down. We made these rules to break the cycle."

Standing, he comes over to me with a perplexed look on his face. "Aria, what rules?"

"Are you kidding me right now? That's what you want to talk about, the rules?"

He throws his hands up in the air. "Yes, I'd love to hear them because I don't recall making them."

I hold up my hand and walk past. "No, no, you are not going to make me feel crazy. You know exactly what I'm talking about. We made rules."

Rushing out of my room and down the hall, I grab my purse from the coffee table in the living room and head to the kitchen. "Mom, we're going to head out. We're both jet lagged, and Nate has a big day tomorrow." He's standing in the doorway looking mystified, which further aggravates me.

"Well, do you think you guys can swing by Sunday? I know your dad would love to see you."

I kiss her cheek. "Yeah, Mom, that shouldn't be a problem. We can do breakfast."

Nate walks over and gives her a hug. "It was good to finally meet you in person, Cynthia. Facetime did your looks no justice."

She waves him off. "Oh, stop it. You're too sweet. No wonder Aria keeps you around." He throws a cautious look my way, no doubt wondering if I am, in fact, going to keep him around.

"Okay, bye, Mom," I call out as I start heading toward the front door. "I'll text you about breakfast or brunch Sunday morning. Love you."

When the front door closes behind us, he says, "Start talking, Aria." I ignore him and keep walking to the car. Then, climbing into the passenger side, I shut the door just as he gets into the driver's seat. I watch him white knuckle the steering wheel before saying, "I don't want to fight, Aria. I'm just trying to understand."

"Then take me to the hotel. We have nothing more to discuss."

"Bullshit. Tomorrow is a big day for me, and I want you by my side. I don't want this, Aria. I need my girl. Fucking stop and talk to me."

"What if I make you a deal? You pull out of my parents' driveway, and I'll make you a list of the rules. A list that I will give you tomorrow."

He looks at me like I have two heads. "Why would you need to make a list and give it to me tomorrow? Why can't we have a conversation?"

"Because, Nate! I shouldn't have to give you an explanation, but since you're in the mood to push me tonight, I need to process. What if the roles were reversed, and you thought we had rules, and I said, 'what fucking rules?' I need to process, Nate!" I'm practically screaming by the time I'm finished.

He nods and says, "Okay." In a voice that is way too calm. I know he's fucking pissed. Hell, he's probably hurt. He told me he loved me tonight, and I didn't say it back, and now I'm refusing to have a conversation with him. This might be our first fight, and it sucks, but to me, it's not a coincidence. It's coming on the heels of me asking for more. I've only ever wanted more with one guy, and no one has ever been able to make me forget.

# 16

## SURPRISE

ARIA

"Aria, look, I'm sorry about last night—"

I shake my head. "Nate, you had every right to be mad at me, frustrated, or whatever that was. All your feelings were one hundred percent valid. Look, being back here is triggering me." I pause to fix his sport coat. "But not in the way you think. Nate, when I ran from here, it was for more reasons than one. You know the obvious one, but the others..."

"Babe, look at me."

I bring my eyes up to meet his, and he says, "If you think I don't know someone hurt you, you're wrong." I straighten the lapels on his jacket. They don't need straightening, but I need to calm my nerves. Being in this area is getting to me, and talking about this subject with Nate isn't helping.

"It's not even that. Young love is stupid. It doesn't know how to protect its heart. I don't blame the guy who broke it. At the time, I don't know that I truly had it to give. This is more than just that though. Something feels different, and I can't put my finger on it. I'm not ready to talk about it, but I wanted you to know."

He pulls me in and places a chaste kiss on my mouth before

saying, "Thank you for telling me, and I'm here when you're ready."

Sometimes, that's the problem with Nate. He's too sweet for his own good. I have more to say to him, but writing the rules helped me. It unlocked something in my mind, but this isn't the place, and now isn't the time to bring them up, even if I did slip them into his coat pocket without his knowledge. I'm honestly unnerved. It's crazy; I shouldn't be, but I am. This place is hitting too close to home for me. Stepping away from the car, he takes my hand. "Let's go, beautiful. You look so fucking hot today, babe." I tried to match my outfit to Nate's the best I could, given the description he gave me over the phone before we flew out.

This isn't an event with cameras or paparazzi by any means, but it's a signing day party for a major client who is a celebrity—but we're also in the Midwest. Nate always looks fantastic, no matter what. He's wearing light denim, a white button-down layered with a beige sport coat, navy pocket square, and light brown Italian leather oxfords. A walking billboard, like always. I went with a tight-fitting, belted, beige linen romper and paired it with a cute, braided, double-strapped, chunky heeled white sandal. My hair is down in loose curls, and my makeup is light.

I never like to stand out at these types of events. The limelight is not my thing. I don't mind it when it comes to my job, but that's because it's raising awareness, and I'm helping people. When I'm with Nate, it feels different, almost vain, and I've never been that way.

As we walk up to the enormous white Victorian-style house with wrap around porch, I'm drawn to a little girl on the far end playing with her dolls. She has blonde curls for days and a yellow sundress on. The girl can't be any older than four or five, and from where I'm standing, it looks like she's focusing really hard on something. Once we reach the top of the steps, I can see she's struggling to get the doll's clothes back on.

Squeezing Nate's hand, I nod in the little girl's direction and let him go. He knows these events aren't my thing, and he's already started talking with two guys on the steps anyway. As I walk away, he calls out, "Ten minutes, babe. He'll be here in ten." I nod and keep walking. I couldn't give two shits about whoever this guy is, but I'm excited for Nate.

"Hey, do you need some help getting her clothes back on?"

The little girl eyes me cautiously before saying, "I can't get her legs in. The pants are all tangled up." I laugh. Barbie clothes are the worst sometimes. When I grab the pants, one leg is inside out.

"My name is Aria. What's yours?"

She picks up another doll and says, "My name is Summer." Of course her name would be Summer. She looks like Summer.

"What a pretty name. How old are you, Summer?"

I finish putting the pants on the doll and hand it back. "I just turned five yesterday. We weren't able to celebrate because Daddy was preparing for the party with Uncle H, but they said tomorrow we could go to the Zoo and then the doll store, and I get to buy two dolls since I had to miss my party."

My heart starts beating rapidly in my chest from hearing her say Uncle H. I'd be lying if I said a small part of me hasn't thought that this new client could be Holden. We are in the Midwest, practically in his backyard, but the last time I heard anything about Holden, he was still playing for Arizona.

Before I can give it anymore thought, an all-too-familiar voice calls from behind me, "Summer, there you are." My stomach is instantly in knots. "I'm sorry, was she bothering you? I told her to stay in the library."

When I stand up and turn to face the voice from my past, it's like we haven't missed a step. "Aria Montgomery, are you fucking serious!?" He picks me up and spins me around. His eyes rake up my body from head to toe when he sets me down. "I swear to fuck, you got hotter, if that's even possible. Where have you been hiding? I can't believe you're here."

Summer stands up and pulls on his pantleg. "You know her, Daddy?"

He picks her up and says, "Yes, Aria's an old friend."

She looks between us and says, "Can we keep her? She's really good at Barbies." We both laugh.

"So, who are you here with?" Thinning my lips, I look around until I spot him.

"Over there. The guy with the man-bun."

Connor follows my line of sight and says, "No shit, you're here with Nathan Keller? This is fucking fate, Aria. Nate's my second cousin. Wait, so are you two dating?"

I give him an *are you fucking serious?* face. "Really, Connor? Why else would I be here with him? We've been together for almost a year now."

He sets his daughter down. "Hey, Summer, can you take these dolls into the house? I think it's their nap time."

Her little eyes go big. "Oh no, I can't believe I forgot about their naps. I'll tuck them in their beds, Daddy." She collects the dolls and takes off running into the house.

He's rubbing his chin and fidgeting when he brings his eyes back to mine. "Look, Aria, I had no idea Nate and you were a couple. This might get a little awkward—"

Our attention is pulled to the gravel road as a red Ford F150 rolls down the drive, kicking up dust in its tracks, with 38 Special's "Hold on Loosely" blaring from the speakers. The closer it gets, the sicker I become. I'd know that truck anywhere, and when it comes to a stop in front of the circle drive, and I see the dent in the front bumper from the last time I drove it, I grab onto Connor's hand to stabilize myself.

"Aria, are you okay?"

I give him the best fake smile I can muster and say, "Yeah, I'm good. I think I need some water. I'm not used to the heat anymore. Suppose I've lived in California too long."

"Come on. I'll fix you up."

Connor pulls me toward the front door just as I hear Nate call out, "Babe, come here."

I stop dead in my tracks and close my eyes to quickly give myself a pep talk. *You've got this. You've moved on. You're a badass bitch.* I focus on my breathing and put one foot in front of the other as I walk down the stairs so that I don't fall from the nervous energy coursing through my body.

"Hayes, how are you doing, brother?" I hear Nate say before the two go in for a pound hug and slap each other's backs.

Then that voice, the voice that haunts my dreams nightly, speaks. "I've been better, but it's nothing a good lay can't fix." Fuck, that hurts. *Why does it hurt? Damn it.*

When I look up, I see a skinny brunette wearing a tight, short black dress tucked under his arm. If she bent over in the slightest, her damn vagina would be hanging out. His comment doesn't even phase her. She rolls her eyes and says, "Baby, I'm going to get a drink." Before she walks away, he slaps her ass. He was always an ass man, but apparently, he likes tall, blue-eyed brunettes, because that's all he dates now.

Stepping up beside Nate, I slip my hand into his and steel my spine as I prepare to look into the eyes of the only man I've ever loved. When Holden's pale blue gaze lands on me, my entire body feels like it's been engulfed in flames. I'm hot, I'm nervous, and fuck me if those eyes don't still make me weak in the knees. I've always been a sucker for those eyes. From the first day I met him, they pierced my soul and etched a place into my heart.

His eyes blaze a trail from head to toe before making their way back up. I swear I see a muscle in his jaw tick when he sees where I have my hand linked through Nate's. Well, screw that. He's the one who broke up with me, not the other way around.

Clearing my throat, I hold out my hand. "I'm Aria. It's nice to meet you."

He quirks a brow at me and sticks his tongue in his cheek giving Nate his attention before saying, "I'll meet you inside, Nate." Without another look, he walks off in the direction of the house, avoiding anyone who tries to stop him.

"Well, that went well. I'm sorry. I probably shouldn't have come."

Nate rubs his hands up and down my arms. "Aria, I knew

Holden Hayes was an asshole before I took the contract. Don't let him bother you."

"Look, I should go. I'm going to call an Uber."

"What? No, I need you here, Aria. This is important to me. You're important to me. Please stay." He kisses my forehead and pulls me into him, wrapping his arms around me and calming my inner turmoil.

"Okay, but do we have to stay long?"

I feel him tense beneath my hold. "Well, the announcement doesn't come until 8:00 pm, and it's only 5:00 pm now."

I drop my arms from his waist and pout. "Great!"

I take in the surroundings as we make our way up the front steps and into the house. It doesn't feel like a house Holden would have built for himself. Every room is massive, with crown molding, wainscoting, and chandeliers. Most rooms have huge bay windows with crushed red velvet tufted pillow seats. Those pops of red are the only color in the otherwise stark white, empty house.

The place has clearly been set up very last minute for a party. "Did he just move in here?" I ask Nate as we make our way toward the back of the house in search of the kitchen.

"I don't know, babe. It looks like it."

Rounding the corner into the kitchen, Holden stands next to the island with his back to us, telling the crowd about his last game, where he struck out Jimmy Ramsey on his last at-bat before retirement. Jim has been the National League's number one hitter for the past five years and decided to retire while he was on top. I swear my skin prickles from just being in the same room with him. It doesn't matter how much I hate him. I can't deny his broad shoulders, narrow hips, and tight ass are what wet dreams are made of—especially mine, seeing as how I've ridden his cock many times. Fuck I need to stop thinking like that.

Dragging my eyes away, I focus on the man holding my hand. "Hey, can we get a drink?"

He smiles, leans in, and kisses my cheek. "Pinot?"

"Yes, please."

Grabbing my chin, he surprises me and gives me an open-mouthed kiss before squeezing my ass and heading to the bar across the kitchen. Holden's eyes are on me when I look up, and the hate I see there is palpable. The problem is, I know why I hate him; what I don't know is why he hates me.

"Aria, I still can't believe you are dating my cousin." Connor cuts in front of Holden's noticeable glare, unaware of the welcomed distraction he just brought me. "Where is he at anyway?" Beer in hand, he throws an arm over my shoulder, and we head to the bar. "Nate, you lucky bastard. When you mentioned you'd found the one, you should have said her name was Aria. Groupie and I go way back."

Nate spins around and hands me my wine before giving Connor a secret handshake. "You know my girl?" He reaches out and pulls me to his side.

"Well, yeah. She and I spent a summer watching Hayes play beer league." I try my best to subtly get his attention so that he stops talking before he tells Nate that I dated Holden, but he doesn't. "Yeah, Aria and Hay—" I pretend to choke on my wine and spit it all over him.

"Oh my god. Connor, I am so sorry. Here, let me help you." I start pushing him out of the kitchen and toward the hallway. "I feel terrible. Let's find a bathroom and get you cleaned up." Once we're out of sight, I slap him on the back of the head.

"What's your problem?"

I shove him into the first open door I find, which happens to be an unfinished office, again stark white. "Why would you tell him? You know what, never mind. Just forget it." I start pacing the room, massaging my temples as I mumble, "I'm so screwed."

"Aria, what the hell is going on? Are you telling me Nate has no idea the two of you dated?"

I stop pacing and shake my head. "Of course not. No one knows I dated Holden. Why would they? It was short-lived. Nothing to boast about."

He puts his hand to his chin, running his thumb across his bottom lip before saying, "Isn't that kind of something couples talk about? Who they've been with, especially when their boyfriend is a sports agent and his girlfriend used to fuck one of the National League's top ten pitchers?"

I groan out of frustration. "Look, Connor, I have reasons for not bringing up my past. It's already hard enough having tonight sprung on me. I had no clue I was coming to Holden's signing party. Nate was excited and kept me in the dark about who his new client was. I'm sure you know this is a big deal for him and his career. I don't want to fuck that up for him tonight."

Connor starts unbuttoning his shirt before hastily tearing it off. "Aria, you realize you have to tell him, right? You can't keep him in the dark, because I sure as hell know Holden won't."

"What's that supposed to mean?" He doesn't get a chance to answer because Nate comes walking in.

"What the hell are you guys doing in here?"

Connor and I both share a guilty glance before I say, "We couldn't find a bathroom. I shoved him in here to help him with his shirt, but it's a lost cause." I wave my hand up and down his body, where all the buttons have now been torn off his shirt. Nate narrows his eyes on me, and for a second, I think he's sensed my bullshit—and maybe he has—but he drops the issue all the same.

"Come on. I always carry an extra shirt." Connor looks between us before lowering his head and heading toward the door. "Aria, if you don't mind, I'd like it if you came with us." I nod and follow them out. *He knows.*

There is no doubt in my mind that Nate has figured it out. He is an intelligent man. Nate is constantly flipping the script for celebrities who fuck up, reading through their bullshit, and deciphering their lies. I messed up the second my eyes met Holden's. I lost my ability to reason and introduced myself, and now that Connor let the cat out of the bag about our past, Nate knows.

Nate knows he's the fucking guy.

Two hours later, and who knows how many glasses of wine —I stopped keeping track around the fourth glass—I make my way out to the back deck. I couldn't stand listening to Holden's voice or watching him paw all over his girlfriend. Every time I glanced over, he had his head in her neck, his hand on her ass, or his tongue down her throat. I couldn't take it anymore. I needed to get some air.

When I walk out the double doors to the back porch, the view before me is a punch to the gut, and suddenly, I wish I never came out here. Standing at the top of the steps, the vista before me is one that has been ingrained into my soul since the first time I saw it. Holden built his house on the lake he took me to on our first date.

Taking a seat on the step, I let the memories of my night here all those years ago wash over me. His words, his praise, his devotion. I was so young and naïve to believe any of it, but I wanted to so badly. I wanted it to be real with every fiber of my being.

He's the reason I stopped having sex. After a few guys couldn't satisfy me, I gave up. Truth be told, I compared everyone to him, and when they didn't measure up, I didn't call back. That's the problem I'm having with Nate now. He did what only Holden has ever been able to do. I fucking came, and I came hard, but it wasn't enough. It will never be enough, because he's not him.

The back door slides open in an angry woosh, and Holden comes stumbling out. He's piss drunk, and when his eyes land on me, if looks could kill, I'd be dead. "What the fuck are you doing here, Aria?"

Standing, I collect my glass before saying, "I was just leaving." There's nothing more to say. As I walk past, he grabs my wrist, and I swear my heart clenches. So many memories come rushing back in. So many tender moments that I locked away deep in my heart. "Please don't touch me."

His head snaps back like I've slapped him. Good. But he doesn't release me. Instead, he pulls me against his front, wrapping his free hand around my waist and pressing his erect cock into my stomach. Then, leaning down, he nuzzles his face into my neck, barely grazing my skin with his lips, and whispers, "You still take my breath away, pretty girl." He takes my hand and places it on his cock. "It's fucking yours." *Shit.*

My entire body breaks out in shivers as my core tightens from the memory of his cock buried so fucking deep. But reality is a spiteful bitch. He's done nothing but treat me like shit since the moment I arrived, mistaking my kindness for weakness and slapping me in the face with his skinny slut all night.

I run my hand up his length over his jeans and squeeze as he draws out a long, euphoric, "Fuuuck."

"Go find your girlfriend, Holden. It isn't me."

## 17

# THE TRAP

## HOLDEN

I let her walk back into the house. I keep my distance as I watch my heart walk away from me again. But I have no one to blame but myself. I did this to us. I chose this fate for us. There's not a day that goes by when I don't think about her. I've tried and failed countless times to push the memory of her aside and move on, but my own fate is worse than death. I get to live with the ghosts from my past as a constant reminder of why I'm alone.

When I watch her seek comfort in Nate's arms, I want nothing more than to walk over, punch him in the face, and carry her off over my shoulder, but I don't. Instead, I let the pain, hate, and anger spread throughout my body as I watch another man take her home. Once they're out of sight, I throw my fist through the wall, gaining the attention of everyone in the room.

"Party's over!" It's 10:00 pm. I signed with St. Louis, where I always wanted to be. I never wanted to leave home, but I did what I had to in order to keep my promise. Taking the stairs two at a time up to my room, I head toward the windows and watch as Nate opens the passenger side door to let Aria in. When Aria pulls on her seatbelt, my chest tightens, and I realize that for the first time since I pushed her away five years ago, I can feel again, and it fucking pisses me off because I know it's her. She is supposed to be mine.

"Holden, what the fuck was that downstairs?" I don't turn away from the window to acknowledge Connor's presence. This is all his fault anyway. I watch her car pull out down the driveway until the lights are no longer in view. I start to unbutton my Oxford before deciding I don't give a fuck and rip it off.

"How the fuck was she here, Con? How did you not know? He's your cousin, for fuck's sake."

"I didn't know. When I saw her on the porch talking to Summer, I thought I was seeing a fucking ghost, man. I couldn't believe it. Nate has never been photographed with her. How was I supposed to know? We're not that close. I haven't seen him in years. When we talk, it's never about women. Shit, man, I had no idea."

When I look up to glare at him in annoyance, I can't help but reel it in a little. Connor is seriously one of the most genuine people I've ever met. He wears his fucking heart on his sleeve, and when he says he didn't know, there's no doubt in my mind that he's telling the truth.

"Holden, this is so fucking crazy. If you need to back out of the contract, I'll understand. I know what she meant to you. I get it."

As I head into my master bathroom, I sarcastically call out over my shoulder, "Thanks for understanding that I don't want to work with the guy that's fucking my ex." I don't add in the 'love of my life' part.

He follows me in. "So, that's it then. You want me to call him? Tell him you want out?"

I strip down to my underwear and say, "No, I want you to invite them to golf tomorrow. Make sure Aria is there."

"Golf?" He questions with a puzzled look.

"Yes, 10:00 am. Now get out."

I lost my girl once but fuck me if I'm going to lose her twice. Aria Montgomery will be mine.

"Just so you're aware, I've been told Aria is not very happy. Apparently, your 10:00 am tee time interfered with breakfast with her dad."

I take a sip of my coffee as we wait on the golf cart for Nate and Aria to arrive, before asking, "The cousin you're not that close to told you all that." I'm sure he doesn't miss the sarcasm in my voice. He laughs.

"No, he didn't tell me shit. He called to ask why Aria needed to come golfing, and, in the background, I heard her borderline yell, 'Seriously? We're supposed to have breakfast with my dad today!'"

I gesture with my hand for him to continue, and when he doesn't, I ask, "And what was the reasoning you supplied for why she needed to attend?"

His mouth quirks up on one side when he says, "I told him that you felt terrible about being a dick to her last night and wanted to apologize in person, seeing as how you're working on improving your shit people skills."

"When did he witness me being a dick to her?"

He practically spits his coffee. "I don't think he missed that you snubbed her when she tried to shake your hand, not to mention you proceeded to throw daggers at her with your obvious glares the entire night."

"I didn't stare at her the entire night. If I recall correctly, I was wrapped around Payton most of the night." That's not an exaggeration. If Aria was going to hang on Nate, I was damn sure going to hit on Payton. Those fucking eyes, the ones I fell in love with, are different now. She's different. Aria looked like she hadn't thought about me once in five years and fuck me if that didn't piss me off and make me jealous. Of course I was going to openly flirt with my date. I wanted her to be just as envious as I was.

"Pfft. Seriously, who the hell do you think you're talking to? We both know you don't give two shits about Payton. I'm pretty sure Payton left with Jackson." He's not wrong. Payton's another clinger looking for her next meal ticket, but she fits the bill. Brown hair, blue eyes, and stick thin. Never blonde, never brown eyes, and definitely no curves.

When Nate's car finally pulls up, I check my watch and see that he's ten minutes late. He climbs out wearing gray pants, a white polo, and black golfing shoes with his hair in a bun, looking way too fancy for a course in Illinois. I don't take my eyes off him as I watch him round the car and open Aria's door. My lips thin of their own accord in annoyance when I see him hold out his hand for her and she takes it. When she stands up, he fixes her white hat and tucks her hair behind her ears before placing a chaste kiss on her forehead, and I practically see red.

"Stare a little harder, bro. Not fucking obvious at all. What's your plan with this anyway? You realize they live in California, right? They fly home tonight."

No, I hadn't thought about any of those things. I haven't thought past seeing her again. Brief panic sets in at the thought of her flying out tonight. Shit.

Connor punches my shoulder before hopping out of the cart and mumbling, "Get it together."

"Nate, you fuckers are late. What the hell?" He goes in for a pound hug with Nate before hugging Aria. Hell, even him touching her pisses me off. She's supposed to be mine.

"Yeah, sorry we're late. We didn't pack golf attire, so we had to stop and buy some on the way out here." Aria wraps herself around Nate's bicep, rubbing it gently in reassurance as if something's wrong. That's when it dawns on me. I'm flat-out staring, unamused by the entire exchange. I'm sure I have fuck off stamped across my face. I roll my eyes in frustration with the whole situation. What I really want to do is pull Aria aside and talk, but that will have to wait. Instead, I get to business.

"Nate, you're with me. Connor, you can drive Aria." Connor loops his arm through Aria's and walks her to their cart. Of course, she's wearing all white. It couldn't be any other color. It had to be all white. Just like the night I made her mine. Spread out before me atop her covers, surrounded by an endless cloud of white. *Fucking perfect.*

"I'm glad you called this outing today. I don't feel like we got to discuss much last night." Nate pulls me from my thoughts as he sits next to me on the cart.

"Yeah, last night was a little crazy. I started drinking too early. Signing with St. Louis has been a dream of mine since I was a kid."

"Yeah, I bet you are glad to be able to stay close to home for at least the next five years."

I nod in agreement. "Yes, putting down roots here is something I've always wanted to do. Of course, I live here in the off-season, but being here year-round is different."

"So, how did you and Aria meet?" His question catches me off guard because it's the very one I was going to try and subtly slip in later for him, and here he is, asking it right out of the gate. It's obvious she never mentioned that we dated. Otherwise, I'm sure he wouldn't have taken the contract. Who signs up to rep a guy who used to sleep with their girl? I'm surprised I didn't come up though, especially with what he does for a living, but the fact that I didn't says a lot. I'm not ready to show my hand, so I say, "It was a long time ago. I believe it was at a birthday party."

He nods, seemingly satisfied with my response, but as we drive to the first hole, I can tell his wheels are turning. Something isn't adding up for him. We get out of the cart to grab our clubs off the back, and he looks me dead in the eye and asks, "Did you date my girl, Hayes?"

Tongue in cheek, I rock back on my heels and fight back the urge to say, "Yeah, I more than dated her. I fucking loved her with every ounce of my being. I never fucking stopped." Instead, I say, "Don't you think that's something she would have mentioned if I had?" Reaching for my bag, I pull out my driver and head to the first hole. Connor and Aria clearly aren't going to golf. They're still sitting in their golf cart, laughing and talking about who knows what, just as they always used to do. It's like they never missed a beat, and it pisses me off.

As I take my first practice swing, he says, "I don't push Aria about her past, but I'm not an idiot. There's obviously bad blood between the two of you. You both acted like you didn't know each other when that's clearly not the case." His phone starts ringing in his pocket, and it's a call he doesn't want to miss. "Shit, I have to take this." He returns to the cart and sits as I take my first swing. I swing for the fucking fences like it's a baseball, not giving a fuck that the ball will land nowhere near the hole. We've only been out here ten minutes, and I'm already over pretending to be her nothing.

~

We're now on the eighth hole, and Nate has been on his phone since we teed off. I'm not complaining because it means I haven't had to answer any more of his questions, but I also haven't been able to pry myself—and to top it off, I've had to watch Connor paw all over Aria in that short-ass golf skirt. Aria was never fat, but I can tell she's into fitness now. Her legs are defined and sexy as hell. She still has her thick thighs and perfectly round ass, but you can tell it's all muscle now. Her arms are perfectly toned, and where her stomach used to be soft, it's now flat and solid. I felt that last night when I pulled her against me. She doesn't just look good; she looks fucking amazing.

I've ignored her and Connor all morning, trying to keep my distance and not give Nate more reasons to suspect that we used to date. While I honestly don't give two fucks if he finds out, I also don't want to provide Aria with another reason to hate me. But when I look over and see Connor helping her line up her swing, I've had enough.

"Seriously, Con, back off. I'm sure you can teach her how to swing without getting up on her ass." They both turn and look at me like I'm crazy. I shake my head in annoyance. "Is this what he always does? Makes plans and spends the day on the phone?" Connor's eyebrows shoot up while Aria just blankly stares at me.

"I'll go talk to him." Connor takes off toward the cart, and because I can't resist, I twist the knife.

"This is what you like? You like being back-burner girl, coming second to his work?"

She visibly flinches from my words, and once they're out, I realize they couldn't have been more wrong. "Damn it, Aria, I didn't mean it like that."

"Holden, just leave me alone. My relationship doesn't concern you. There's nothing wrong with having a career. He's damn good at his job, and you're lucky to have someone with that dedication at your back."

"Aria." Nate jogs up and places a kiss on her cheek. "It's Tom. I need to go to the car and get on my laptop." Then, turning around, he says, "I'm sorry. Finish your game, and we can do lunch after." Before I can even respond, he has his phone back up to his ear, and power-walks off to the golf cart, where he slides in, and Connor takes off.

"Great! That cart had my clubs on the back."

Aria snorts behind me. "That should be the least of your worries. Your ass can walk back." I watch as she storms toward the remaining golf cart, and I follow, hot on her heels. Fuck that. This is my chance alone with her, and I'm not messing it up.

Just as she sits in the driver's seat, I push in next to her, sliding her over. "I'll be driving."

"God, you're infuriating," she huffs.

"Fucking ditto," I retort before I pull off toward the next hole with no plans of golfing—but there's no way I'm taking her back. I know exactly where I'm taking her.

"Seriously, Holden. I'm not even golfing. Just take me back." I ignore her until I pull into a clearing of trees just off the tenth hole that provides coverage from onlooking golfers.

"Holden, take me back now. I'm not doing whatever this is."

When I turn the cart off, she climbs out. I dart out and grab her around the waist. "Aria, I just want to talk. If Nate's going to be my agent, don't you think we should at least be cordial to each other?" There is no way Nate will be staying on as my agent, but she doesn't need to know that.

She relents, but adds, "Fine, just let me go. Don't touch me."

I gesture with my arm to head back to the golf cart, and she goes. Thank god, because I'm tired of wasting our alone time fighting. Once we're back in the cart, I have so many things I want to say, but I mostly want to kiss her. I feel like if I could kiss her once, all this madness would end.

"Are you just going to stare at me, or do you plan to start talking?" I bite my lip. There's that feistiness I always loved. I loved when she'd give me her confident, sassy side, putting me in my place and making me work for it.

"Why didn't you tell him about us?"

"Seriously, this is what you want to talk about? You want to talk about why I didn't tell my boyfriend about my ex?" I shrug in response, and she says, "Fine. I didn't tell him because there's nothing to tell. We spent a summer fucking. Do you tell all your girlfriends about the girl you fucked five years ago?" She has me turned on and pissed off all at once. I want to pull her onto my lap, push her panties to the side, and hit the spot deep inside that drives her crazy, but I'm pissed that she's referring to that summer as just a quick fuck.

Gripping the wheel, I say, "So, that's all it was? Fucking?"

She mutters, "Unbelievable," before climbing out of the cart and pacing. Throwing her hands into the air, she yells, "This is ridiculous, Holden. I owe you nothing. You have no right to ask me any of this. You left me, not the other way around. I was your back-burner girl, remember, the one that would never be more. Is any of this ringing a bell for you?"

Once she's done laying into me, pointing out every detail and bullshit excuse I fed her to push her away, she huffs out her frustration at my lack of empathy and decides to bolt again. This time when she glances back and sees I'm following, she takes off running. Shit.

"Don't run from me, Aria," I call out as she breaks for the trees. What the hell? She's fast.

"Aria, stop running."

She calls out over her shoulder, "Stop chasing me." Her pace hasn't slowed, and we're getting deeper into the woods.

"Aria, you're going to get lost." She doesn't respond; instead, she picks up her pace, ducking in and out of trees to try and lose me, and she almost does until she decides to stop. It's suddenly quiet, and the density of the canopy above us has made it hard to see, but because she's a beacon wearing all white, I catch a glimpse of her dress poking out from behind a tree in front of me. I'm more than familiar with the woods. When I'm not playing baseball, I hunt; right now, she's my prey.

Once I'm close enough to make my move, I sneak around and pin her against the tree. "Crap, Holden. You scared the shit out of me." I have her caged in. She can't escape and fuck me if this entire chase didn't turn me on. Leaning down, I place my face in the crook of her neck as I try to calm my racing heart.

"Don't fucking run from me." I place a kiss on the side of her throat and feel her skin prickle beneath my lips.

"Don't. Holden, please don't." Her words might tell me to stop, but her body tells me a different story. The goosebumps from my mouth, her heaving chest, and erect nipples tell me she likes it. I may not get another chance, so I shoot my shot and drag my tongue up her neck to the spot behind her ear and suck.

Her hands find my hip bones, sending delicious tendrils of heat straight to my cock, only further spurring me on. There is no doubt in my mind she remembers how much I loved it when she touched me there. I trail kisses across her jaw until I reach her mouth, where I pause and find her eyes before I seal my lips over hers. Our kiss is slow and unsure as our eyes stay pinned on one another, but when I part her lips with my tongue, seeking entrance, and she grants it, I can't help but close them and get lost in her. Her taste, her smell, her feel, everything comes rushing back. I feel everything, and I never want to lose it ever again.

My hands slide down her hips as her body molds against mine, and I grab a handful of ass in each hand and squeeze before lifting her up. When she wraps her legs around my back, I press her into the tree to find my balance, drunk on the fact that the woman I've spent the last five years regretting is now once again wrapped around me where she's always belonged.

"Pretty girl, you drive me crazy."

I press my erection against her clit, and when she moans, I cover her mouth with my own and swallow it down. I want my mouth everywhere, but I also don't want her to think. If she thinks, I lose this. She'll remember we aren't together, I'm not her boyfriend, and then I'll lose her. My cock is rock hard, and I can feel her heat through the thin lining of my golf shorts. When I grind against her clit again, she breaks our kiss to say, "More." Cum drips from my dick at the possibility of what more means.

"You want my cock, baby?" Using my weight, I keep her pinned between myself and the tree as I bring one hand around and trail it up her thigh before reaching her center. I'm toying with her panties while her eyes are locked on mine. I'm waiting for her to tell me to stop, but when she doesn't, I pull them to the side and run my middle finger through her wet lips.

"God, yes," she draws out, her hooded eyes locked on mine.

"My god, you're beautiful," I say before I dip my finger into her tight hole. Her pussy immediately clenches, and my dick throbs. Crushing my mouth to hers, I reluctantly pull my fingers out and make quick work of freeing my dick. "Pretty girl, you're going to take my fucking cock."

She sucks the side of my neck, and that's all the confirmation I need to line up and sink in. I can't help but hiss out, "Oh, fuck," as I push in; she's tight as fuck. I have to pull back and work myself in deeper a few times before I'm able to fully seat myself. *Shit.* She feels even better than I remember. Once I'm fully sheathed, I stay still, giving her a chance to acclimate to my size while taking a second to stave off my need to come. It's been way too long since I've fucked, and I don't want to blow my load in two pumps.

"Pretty girl, I need your mouth." I need to know this is real and that I have my girl back. This isn't just some random girl, a quick fuck, but she's here and wrapped around me, letting me have her. Bringing her face out of the crook of my neck, her mouth lands on mine. When her tongue plunges in deep, it makes me think she's missed me as much as I've missed her. I push in hard and hit that spot deep inside, making her whimper. "Fuck, Aria, you always did take me so good."

Her legs are wrapped tightly around my hips, her back is to the tree, and my hands are palming her plump ass. When I look down and watch my cock disappear inside her pretty pussy, my heart clenches. This is mine. I'm not letting her go. Picking up my pace, I push in fast and hard, incredibly turned on by the scene in front of me until I hear her cry out. *Fuck.* When I bring my eyes to her face, she's thrashing her head from side to side, and tears are streaming down her face. Holding her tight to my front, I say, "Baby, did I hurt you? Aria, talk to me."

She continues shaking her head and says, "Don't stop." *What the hell?* When I don't resume, she opens her eyes, and I see it. They're fucking haunted, and I'm sick from the thought that I've done this to her. Smacking my chest, she cries, "Don't you dare fucking stop now. Finish it, and make it fucking hurt. I need it to fucking hurt." She squeezes her thighs around my waist, pushing her heels into my ass, further seating herself on my cock. *Shit.* I don't know what this is, but I want to hurt her. I want her to feel me for days and remember how she let me have her, how she begged for my cock. I need her to miss me the way I've missed her every day for the last five years.

Grabbing her ass, I reposition myself to go hard. "You want it to hurt? I can make it hurt." I slam in, knocking the breath out of her and making her cry out. Her eyes are squeezed shut tight when I do it again. She takes it repeatedly until finally, her eyes snap open and land on mine. That's when I say, "You want it to hurt, baby. I can give you pain. I'll give you all the pain I've lived with every day since you walked out of my life."

She doesn't say a word; instead, she bites her lip and keeps her haunted, empty eyes on mine as I continue to pound into her. I don't know if it's the scene, fucking her bareback against a tree in the woods after five years of missing her, or the way her eyes focus on mine as she squeezes my shoulders, pleading with me not to stop, but I come undone, and thank fuck, so does she. I was her first orgasm, and I'll be damned if I don't deliver now.

Pinned to the tree, I hold her in place as my cock pulses deep inside her as we come down from our shared release. That was incredibly hot, and for more reasons than one. A loud buzzing has her pulling back.

She pulls a phone out of her pocket, and the name Nathan Keller appears on the screen. I'm instantly livid. "Are you really going to answer your boyfriend's call while my dick is buried deep inside you?"

Her eyes narrow on mine, and she hits my arm. "No, you're going to put me down first. Then I'll answer his call." Fuck, that sass makes me want to go again. I give her a second to reconsider, holding her eyes, and when she doesn't, I set her down.

Tucking myself back in, I watch as she adjusts her skirt and picks up her hat. I'm furious that there's another man in the picture, but I did this to us, and I know Aria will run if I don't play my cards right. But because I can't help myself and I want to remind her whose dick she just came all over, I say, "Do you want me to answer that and tell your boyfriend I just fucked his girl?" She shoots me a warning glare that I only heed because her pussy was just wrapped around my cock, not his.

"Aria, where are you guys?" I hear him ask before she walks away for privacy. While I'm pissed that he's her man, I'm confident it won't stay that way. She is mine, and there is no way in fuck I'm letting her go back to him.

"Let's go, Holden," she calls out as she starts walking back.

The walk back to the cart was silent. Aria seemed perfectly content with not talking about what happened, which only served to further piss me off. Something happened back there. That was more than just sex. I messed up, but I don't believe those tears were all mine. I know I broke through her walls, built her up, and earned her love, only to turn around and tear her down. I don't deserve another chance, but I'm not letting this go. Fate brought her back to me. She's meant to be mine. I feel it in the depths of my soul, but there is one thing I need to know before we get back to the clubhouse, so I ask, "Do you love him?"

Without missing a beat, she says, "You don't get to ask me that." I should have seen that coming.

"Please don't get on that plane tonight."

This time, she turns and glares at me. "You can't be fucking serious right now."

"Have dinner with me tonight?" She takes her hat off and runs her hand through her hair.

"You have seriously lost your damn mind. There is nothing that could make me agree to that."

"That's bullshit. Are we really going to act like we didn't just fuck? You want me, Aria. You may not want to, but you do. I'm asking for a conversation, Aria. You have no idea what losing you did to me. I've regretted it every day for the last five years. There's not a day that goes by that I don't think about you and what I did." I stop the cart before we reach the clubhouse, in an attempt to stall.

"Yeah, I saw how much you missed me last night. What happened back there was a mistake, Holden. Let it go. We've both moved on. You can have any girl you want. Go find one who makes you happy."

"First of all, that back there was no fucking mistake. My cock was made for that pussy, and I won't be looking for any girl when the only one I've ever wanted is sitting right next to me. Every day I was with you was the best day of my life."

She gives me a sad smile before saying, "If that were true, you wouldn't have let me go." Stepping out of the cart, she starts walking back on foot. I drive up alongside her.

"You're having dinner with me tonight."

She doesn't even look my way when she says, "No, Holden, I'm not."

"You will. I expect you to be at my house at 6:00 pm, don't be late."

Stopping in her tracks, she looks at me deadpan and says, "It's not happening, Holden. You can fuck off. I'm not the same girl I was back then. You don't get to call the shots. I'm not suddenly yours because you say it's so. I did it your way last time and look where that got us."

She's not wrong. I messed up. The only reason she isn't still mine is because I made it so, but I'll be damned if I'm going to let her walk away again. There is no way in hell I'm making the same mistake twice.

"The way I see it, Aria, I'm the one who holds all the cards right now. You have a boyfriend who's completely in the dark about our relationship, not to mention I can fire him." She doesn't need to know that I'll fire him anyway. There's no way in hell he can be my agent when he's slept with my girl. Nathan Keller is only useful to me now because he is my connection to her for the moment. The second that usefulness ends, he will be gone.

Aria stomps her foot and yells, and I can't help but smirk. I have her right where I want her.

"Holden, I have a life back home. Clients I need to be home for. Stop being selfish. That was always your problem. You never thought about anyone but yourself. Good to know nothing has changed."

"If I recall correctly, I kept you more than satiated."

She groans and harrumphs, but it doesn't go unnoticed that

she never mentioned him in her rage. None of her reasons for not wanting to meet me for dinner were because of him. "What do you expect me to tell everyone?"

Suddenly, my phone starts pinging in my pocket. It must have just started getting signal again. I pull it out and see that my sports drink campaign meeting just got pulled up to tomorrow, and they're flying here. Apparently, signing with St. Louis was the leverage I needed to seal the deal. "I'll handle it."

"What does that mean?"

I give her my best smile and say, "That means I expect you at my house tonight for dinner." This time when she walks off, I don't stop her. Instead, I pass her on the cart and say, "Oh, and Aria, don't even think about running."

# 18

## PUSH

ARIA

On the way to our golfing outing this morning, Nate called me out. I'm actually surprised he waited this long. There's no doubt in my mind that he put everything together last night, but he didn't say a word. That's the thing about our relationship. Neither one of us has ever pushed the other; we were content to let things be.

Nate told me he found the note I snuck into his pocket last night. None of the rules I listed had ever been discussed, but I already knew that. Sitting there, writing that list, I knew it was my way of coping instead of healing. It was my way of protecting my emotional stability. Nate did say he was waiting for marriage, but we both know that was more of an icebreaker. He knew I would run for the hills, and for some reason, he stuck around anyway, knowing he wouldn't be getting laid.

I'm not a fucking idiot. I know Nate is not your typical guy. He has his own past and set of issues, and I've never pried. It's worked for us, and what sucks is, I have no doubt that there was a morsel of truth in his confession that he loved me. I fucking felt it. What hurts is that I love him back, but it's not enough. It could never be enough.

Before we got to the course, he asked, "He's the guy, isn't he?

The one who fucked you up." I stayed silent, unsure how to answer his question without hurting him. I've never wanted to hurt Nate.

"Nate, it's more than—"

He cut me off and said, "Don't lie to me, Aria." So, I didn't. I told him Holden and I dated and that he broke my heart. I didn't have a good reason when he asked why it never came up. I stayed silent because I hadn't breathed Holden's name out loud since I left this place. It's how I coped with the pain.

When we pulled into our spot at the golf course, before he got out, he said, "I still love you, but it can never be me, because it will always be him." My eyes held his for what felt like the longest second of my life until he climbed out and came around to open my door. He kissed my forehead and said, "Just give me this." I know what he was asking. He wanted me to play the part, and because Nate doesn't ask for anything, I did. Until I couldn't.

Being alone with Holden, in the woods, with no one around to witness our indiscretions, was intoxicating. When I ran from Holden, my intent was not to let him fuck me against a tree. My purpose was to clear my head. I wasn't about to sit there and let him tell me that he had regrets, but the further I ran, the more I didn't want to. I was done with running. I'm a grown-ass woman, and I've wanted that moment.

Coming home, part of me hoped Holden was the guy Nate landed. It was too coincidental not to be, but I hated feeling that way after so many years. Regardless, it didn't stop me from thinking I needed to see him one more time to find closure and move on. Of course, nowhere in that did I expect to fall even harder, and I sure as hell wasn't banking on him giving two shits about me. In fact, I was counting on the exact opposite so that I'd be forced to accept the hand he had dealt me all those years ago.

"Aria, are we going to talk about this afternoon, or will you just continue to sit there and stare out the window acting like nothing is going on?" Dragging my eyes off the parking lot below and back to Nate, standing in the middle of our hotel room with a towel wrapped around his waist, looking sexy as hell. I know I need to leave. I'm not leaving because of Holden or for Holden. I'm going for Nate. He deserves so much better.

"Nate, look, I'm sorry. I never wanted to hurt you, and—"

He crosses the room in two strides, pulling me into his arms. "Aria, stop. You are not doing this. Don't run from me. After everything, I think we can at least have a conversation."

I rest my head against his chest and breathe him in. He is so good, and I wish so much that he was mine, but he's not, and I need to let him go. Putting my hands on his chest, I press back for him to let me go, and that's when he sees it. My suitcase is in the corner, packed and ready to leave. This needs to be goodbye.

"Aria, while I know I'm not the guy you want, it doesn't change the fact that I still want to be."

Those words are meant to strike a different chord. He wants to hurt me, and, for that, I can't be mad. Nate knows I care about him, he knows this isn't easy for me. The man spent the past year putting time into me, into us, and in twenty-four hours, I've managed to undo all of it. I've never seen a vengeful side to Nate, but he's hurt, and I'm done playing games.

"Why, Nate? Tell me why."

He puts his hands on his hips, dead serious. "Are you really asking me that? You're asking me why I want you, why I love you? Here's a better question: why don't you love me?"

"That's not fair, and you know it. You don't say I love you to someone and expect them to say it back. You say it because you mean it and hope it's true for the person who holds your heart. You don't love me. You're in love with the idea of me."

It's true; I know it is. We've never gone beneath the surface in our relationship. We were both more than comfortable with keeping things at arm's length, especially regarding our pasts. Honestly, if Nate had asked me, I probably would have shared more, but he never did. It was as if knowing it existed was enough. He didn't need the details, and I wasn't going to just offer up things I cared to forget.

Watching him pace, I can't decide what this is. I can't get a read on him. While I know his contract with Holden would be great for his influence and social status, I know he doesn't need the money. Nate's family is loaded. He does what he does because he likes it. I'm certain he'll probably find a way out of his contract after today if Holden doesn't do it first, which is why this moment is perplexing. That's when it hits me. This isn't about me, this is his past haunting him, and I can't help but ask, "Why did you stay with me?"

*Bingo.* He stops, and I see it when his eyes flick to mine. Something or someone fucked him up. It's like Holden once said: "Dark calls to dark."

"I have my own issues, Aria, but I'm pretty sure you weren't too self-absorbed to at least notice that much."

His comment makes me feel like a complete ass. I know I have been more than selfish, but sometimes, it's necessary. Focusing on me instead of the world around me gave me strength and confidence. I had to turn off the noise, block out everyone, and lose everything around me to find myself. At the end of the day, I may have been self-centered, but he never had to stay. He chose to stay.

When he moves to his bag to find a shirt and pants, I ask, "Are you going to tell me?"

He meets my gaze with a condescending smirk and half smile and says, "Same way you told me?"

Turning, I grab my bag and start heading for the door. "I'm going to my parents'."

Before I can step out of the room, he says, "Just tell me one thing, Aria. Are you throwing us away for him?"

"No, Nate. I'm not leaving you for him, but it is because of him." I can't give Nate my heart because it doesn't even belong to me. The future is unclear, but, hand over heart, this time, I'm choosing me.

This afternoon, I took an Uber back to my parents' house. I didn't want to break up with Nate and leave him stranded; he technically still has work. I'm not sure what he'll decide with Holden. I've been going back and forth on whether or not I would say anything to Holden about it at dinner, but I know I won't. As much as I want to be upfront and honest, I don't. I don't need Holden thinking I broke up with Nate for him, and after I let him fuck me this afternoon, that's precisely what it would look like. How fucking desperate does that look? Plus, I didn't. I broke up with Nate for his own good.

I wasn't lying when I said I wanted more. From the moment we touched down, I felt it deep in my soul. A part of me is begging to come out. I've spent so many years trying to live through the moments that caused me agony and stress, and now I just want to let it all go. Returning to this place has released parts of my mind that I didn't know I was holding hostage.

I've been subconsciously fabricating parts of my life that didn't fit, and I think it took leaving my home and coming back for that to click. I spent years hyper-focusing on my eating to the point that it made me sick because my mind was coping. Walking into my childhood room brought back all the memories of him that I've tried to forget, but that room also reminded me of the girl I used to be before him.

Running through the woods today, I did something for myself, and I can't tell you the last time that I didn't think about the consequences of my actions. I fucking did what I wanted, and I reveled in it. For the past decade, that's all I've done: overanalyze, compartmentalize, and work through the moments.

Who cares if Holden wanted a quick fuck? So did I. I've missed him something fierce, and as I let him fuck me, something inside of me broke. I felt this immense pain from a place I didn't recognize. It was dark, I was restrained, and I was scared. I saw shadows that terrified me, but with every thrust, I felt Holden taking my pain and replacing it with power. It felt as if I was straddling this thin veil between a dream and reality, letting go of the things I've let haunt me and embracing the strong, confident woman I've always wanted to be.

The pain can only win when I give it the ability to dictate my behavior. I ran from what I wanted before. I didn't fight then, but not anymore. I know what I want, and I'm taking it back.

Spencer is still in Connecticut, finishing his residency, so I borrowed his car tonight. Pulling down the gravel driveway to Holden's house, the land resonates deep within my soul and brings me back to the first time I ever saw it, when I woke up in his arms. Looking at it now, I don't know how I missed it before. Probably because I was so nervous about being this close to old memories, memories that I'd tried hard to bury deep down. But sometimes, the memories we want to forget are the same ones that give us strength. I've been trying to run from the girl I left behind five years ago because I thought forgetting would be easier. But all it has done is stunt my growth.

As I pull into the circle drive and climb out of Spencer's blue Mustang, Holden has already started descending the front steps, and fuck me, I don't think he's ever looked hotter. His light blue, worn jeans stretch over his muscular thighs in all the right places, and when he lifts his white tee to wipe the sweat off his glistening forehead, I catch a glimpse of that perfectly chiseled stomach, his scar playing peekaboo right above his delicious deep V. *Shit.*

He fucked me so good earlier I can still feel him, and I'd be lying if I said I didn't want to take another ride. I never could get enough of him. Holden catches me looking and gives me a devilish grin that I know promises endless hours of orgasms if I let him.

I tear my gaze away from him and act like I need to check my phone, and when I do, I immediately regret it.

Nathan: I'm leaving after my meeting tomorrow. Just wanted to let you know.

Before I even have a chance to process his words, Holden's at my front. "Why do you look like someone just pissed in your Cheerios?"

I stick my phone in the back pocket of my jeans and say, "Ha-ha, very funny. Can we just get this over with, please?"

He runs his thumb across his bottom lip, clearly unpleased by my attitude, but I don't give a shit. Today sucked. I hurt someone I truly care about, even if I know he's not the guy for me, and the man standing before me is nothing if not a vault full of secrets. Holden came out here intent on teasing me. Obviously, he remembered how turned on I would get seeing him hot and sweaty in his uniform, but that scar reminded me of why we couldn't work back then, and why we can't work now. He refused to let me in.

Holden nods back toward the house. "Come on... I want to show you something." I don't move. It's like my feet decided to grow roots and force me to choose myself.

"Holden, I'm not coming with you." He furrows his brow in question, probably confused at why I would even show up if I wasn't going to come in, but until I was here, I didn't realize what I needed, and it's a dealbreaker.

"Aria, we had an agreement—or did you forget?"

"I didn't forget. I just don't care." He comes over faster than I can blink and throws me over his shoulder. I start pounding his back, and I bite hard into his side when he doesn't release me.

"Fuck, Aria." He slaps my ass hard, and it stings even through my jeans.

"Put me down, or I'll do it again."

"Fine." He sets me on the top of the steps before lifting his shirt to see the damage. The spot where I bit him is already purple. Before he can pull his shirt back down, I touch his scar, which just so happens to be in a very sexy, sensitive spot. He hisses from my touch, pulling me into him. "You want it, pretty girl? You can fucking have it."

I shake my head. "No, Holden, I want what you couldn't give me five years ago, and if it's not on the table, I have a plane to catch."

Those eyes that captured my heart all those years ago bore into mine, and for a split second, I think he's going to let me walk, but then he shocks me and says, "That's why I asked you here tonight, Aria. I'm tired of not living. I'm done with being only half a man. I want my heart back." He leans in and kisses the corner of my mouth. "Let me show you something."

Wrapping his hand around mine, he leads me through the house, which now has couches in the living room surrounding the fireplace, along with side tables. The formal dining room is still empty, but as we enter the kitchen, the island is filled with meats, cheeses, and a bucket of iced light beer. We continue down the hall and out the back doors that lead to the pond. When he pulls me down the steps and starts heading toward the water, I yank my hand out of his grip. The puzzled look on his face from my abrupt stop doesn't go unanswered.

"Oh, no you don't. You're not pulling me into that water again."

He laughs. "I'm not going to pull you into the water." Then, quirking an eyebrow, he adds, "But it's tempting." He looks down at his clothes. It is clear he's been working on something. "I'm hot as fuck." Holding out his hand, he says, "Come on. Do you trust me?" I roll my eyes at his absurdity, but the fact that he asked me that exact question five years ago in this very spot is not lost on me. "Okay, maybe not, but please."

"Ha, Holden Hayes begging. Now that's something I could get used to."

Stepping up, he grabs my hand. "Funny. Come on." We're following a footpath around the tall grass surrounding the lake when a dock suddenly appears. "Ta-da," he announces like it is some big surprise I'm supposed to be stoked about.

"You built a dock? That's great. Good job."

"My god, woman, can't you just humor me?" I thin my lips and try to fight back the smile threatening to take over my face. He's clearly really proud of this dock, which is adorable.

"Will you come out here with me?" I walk out and join him on the dock. It's actually pretty great. You can be on the water without getting in. If you put some Adirondack chairs out here, it'd be a perfect coffee spot in the morning, and an ideal location for a glass of wine in the evening.

He's watching me intently, like he expects me to say more. "What is it, Holden? Spit it out."

"Do you like it?" he asks sheepishly.

"Not that it matters, but yeah; it's nice. It's a perfect location to watch the sunset through that break in the trees out there." I point out over the horizon.

His face breaks out in a big goofy smile, and then he's on me, hands around my waist, lips at my ear. "Good, because I built it for you." My skin instantly pebbles from his proximity as my heart skips a beat from his words.

"Sure, you did. I know this deck wasn't built in a day, and I've only been back in town for two, so you can stop with the bullshit. I'm not buying it."

He kisses my cheek and walks to the edge, pulling his shirt over his head and tossing it to the ground before stripping his jeans off. Then, throwing his hands in the air, he says, "Look around, Aria. This entire fucking house is a shrine to you. This is the spot where we had our first date, the first time I ever held you in my arms, the spot where I kissed you for the first time and told you that you were mine. When I pulled you into the water that night, you told me you didn't like water you couldn't see in. This dock is so that you could be on the water and not in it. It's always been you, pretty girl. It will only ever be you." Then he turns around and dives into the lake, leaving me speechless.

He's not wrong. All the things he said were true, and he remembered them to a tee, but I haven't forgotten that this was his uncle's property—property that he grew up on. It wouldn't be the first time Holden has whispered meaningless sweet nothings in my ear. This time, I know better than to just fall for his words.

Before he can even come back up for air, I start walking back toward the house. If he thought trying to convince me that he built a house for me was what I meant when I said I wanted what he couldn't give me five years ago, there is nothing here for me.

I'm halfway through the yard when he jogs up behind me. "Aria, what the hell?"

I turn and look him dead in the eye. "Holden, you must think I'm an idiot. I know this was your uncle's property. This property held sentimental value to you long before I came along. I haven't seen you in five years. You didn't build this house for me. Go fucking tell your fairytale bullshit to some groupie who would be more than happy to live in this big house and spend your money."

"Are you trying to drive me mad? Are you trying to pick a fight?" His chest is heaving, his hair is dripping water down his smooth, sculpted chest, and there is no imagination needed as his boxers cling to every crevice. Fuck.

"Stop looking at my cock unless you're planning on riding it." His comment wasn't sexy in the least. He's pissed. Grabbing my wrist, he hurriedly pulls me toward the house. I almost trip as he pulls me up the steps. "You can do better than that, Aria. You ran from me like a track star earlier."

"Fuck off, Holden."

"Not until you see."

Entering the living area, he comes to a dead stop, and I run into his back. "A warning would have been nice."

"Look around, Aria, and I mean really look. What do you see?" I've already seen this room. It is stark white, which is no different from the other parts of the house I've seen.

"It's white." I shrug, not understanding what he wants me to see. Blowing out a breath of frustration, he turns me around to face what I assume will be the formal dining room. Again, all white, apart from the red cushions that adorn the window seat.

"The night we met, you were sitting in a booth at Hagerty's, completely enthralled with the feel of the crushed red velvet booth, entirely unaware that every man in that bar wanted you. Before I even sat down, I knew you would be mine."

He spins me back around to the living room. "All white couches, white walls, sheer white curtains—the night I made love to you for the first time."

Placing his hand on my lower back, he walks me to the window and pulls back the curtain. "The truck you climbed up in, the windows we fogged up, and nights on the tailgate I could never forget. I never let it go even though it's a daily reminder of the night I lost you." The front bumper was never fixed. The dent from the night I hit the deer is still intact.

"Pfft, coincidence." I'm trying my hardest to play it cool and not fucking melt when all I want to do is throw myself into his arms, but damn it, he broke me. He deserves to squirm and work for it.

"Seriously!" he exclaims, wholly peeved.

Leading me down the hall, he walks me into the office that Connor and I stumbled into last night, but at that time it was covered in drop cloths from construction. The bookshelves that were colorless last night are now stained in a deep oak color, and the furniture draped in drop cloths is now uncovered, and I see it. It's a mirror image of the office at Connor's house. "The room that caused our first fight and the best make-up sex of my life."

My hand flies up to my mouth in shock. "Why are you doing this, Holden? What was your plan?"

Running his hand through his hair, he says, "I battled against going after you for years, Aria. Talking myself out of it every time, convincing myself you were better off without me. I was destined to fuck us up, just like I did before. You drive me crazy, pretty girl. You always fucking have. I did this to us, and if I couldn't have you, I would live with your memories. I deserved this. I let the best thing I ever had walk away. But, Aria, I never wanted to be the bad guy in your story. You need to know that."

As I stand there looking around, my mind is blank. This is the last thing I ever expected out of tonight. Holden was always romantic, but after he broke my heart, I told myself it was all part of the game. I was just another notch in his belt. "Say something."

When my eyes find his, I see his vulnerability. He's telling me the truth. "I don't know what to say."

He walks over to me and reaches for my hand. "Stay." I still don't have what I came here for, and the way he has me feeling right now, coupled with the fact that he's only in his underwear, is not a good mix.

"I'll stay if you put some pants on."

He thins his lips to fight back a smile but says, "Seriously? You're not going to run out the door the minute I go grab pants?"

I chuckle. "No, Holden, I won't run."

Taking my hand, he leads me to the kitchen. "Eat, make a drink. I'll be right back." He lingers for a second, probably not convinced I'll stay, before he finally walks down the hall.

What am I doing? I want to believe him. In fact, I do believe him, and that hard truth scares the hell out of me. I've spent the past five years trying to move on from him. But during that time, I never stopped wanting him back, wishing that things had ended differently and that he was still mine. I still want him. What sounds like a dryer door slams, and I hear his footsteps approaching on the hardwood floors.

When he enters the kitchen, our eyes meet. We both take a visible deep breath before he walks over to the island to grab a beer. Cracking open the top, he hands it to me. "Thanks," I say before taking a long drink, eager to calm my nerves.

He pulls out his own and says, "Figured you would have already started after everything I just laid on you." I nod my head in agreement but add nothing.

His new attire may as well be his underwear. He's wearing gray joggers and a black tank that hugs his body like a glove. I squeeze the bridge of my nose and try to refocus my thoughts. I'm just about to demand that he get on with it before I turn into a hoe again and accomplish zero of what I committed to getting, which is answers. But, thankfully, the gods grant me mercy, and he asks, "Can we sit?" The earnest tone in his voice tells me he's ready to talk.

"Yeah, let's sit." I pull one of the stools out from under the island, and he does the same.

We both drink before he says, "Aria, this memory hurts. It hurts so fucking bad for so many reasons." Suddenly, he stands and walks over to the freezer, pulling out a bottle of vodka and two frozen shot glasses.

After he takes his seat, he pours two shots and passes one to me. We clink glasses and throw them back before he pours himself one more. "It was our last game of the summer before we all left for college. The last time we would all play together. That game was like saying goodbye to an era, and we went out on top. I pitched a near-perfect game with my best friend and longtime catcher, Luke. We were an unstoppable pair. Both of us landed full-ride scholarships at the local D1 college two towns over. Luke and I were convinced we would make it. We were going to break the mold and beat the odds, be the guys from the small town who made it big."

He pauses to pour yet another shot. After he throws it back, his eyes linger on me, and I see his pain. This story haunts him. This story is what ended ours. I stand, walk around the island, and hop up on the counter to sit next to him. He slides me over and wraps his arms around my waist. "I'm so sorry, Aria. I need you to believe me."

I run my hand through his hair and say, "Finish the story, Holden."

"That night, one of the guys from the team was having a huge bonfire on his dad's property. A bunch of the guys headed over straight after the game, but I rode with my dad that night, so I had to go home first and get my truck, but by the time I got home, I wasn't into it anymore. I wanted to shower and go to bed, but Luke was adamant that I had to come. He was blowing up my phone with texts, and two hours later, he showed up at my house, clearly drunk, talking about how he had a gift for me."

He stops and buries his head in my lap, squeezing my hips so hard I yelp. "What was the gift, Holden?"

"It doesn't even matter. We never got there. That night, I wrapped his Challenger around a tree. That's how I got the scar that I carry with me every day. We were both airlifted to a hospital in St. Louis. He didn't make it. I killed him, Aria. I took his life." My heart breaks for him. I can't imagine the burden he carries from being the survivor of a car crash where he was the driver, and his passenger and best friend didn't get to walk away. I'm sure he's lived with crippling guilt every day, but we all have sad stories. It doesn't add up.

Pulling his head off my stomach, his tear-filled eyes find mine. "The night you drove us home and ran into the deer was the same day I took his life four years earlier. I saw our entire future flash before my eyes, Aria. All I saw was you being taken away from me, and I couldn't bear the thought of losing you, so I ended it. I pushed you away so you wouldn't be cursed by my fate."

The tears fall down his face, and I immediately kiss them away. I kiss his tear-soaked cheeks, his eyes, and finally, his mouth. Our kiss is slow, unhurried, and laced with all the apologies, regrets, and years of anguish that we've endured. He pulls me into his lap and deepens the kiss, exploring my mouth with a renewed spirit after revealing his demons.

Pulling out of our kiss, he says, "I fucking love you, Aria Montgomery. I've never stopped."

I nod and place a chaste kiss on his lips before saying, "Okay."

His eyebrows briefly shoot up, and his face contorts into sadness. "What do you mean, okay? This changes things. I want you back. You have to come back." I move to climb off his lap, which I'm currently straddling, but he holds me in place.

"Holden, real life doesn't work that way. You don't get to just demand that I come back. I have an entire life in California."

His hands move to my face to focus my eyes on his. "But you want me too. I know you do."

"It doesn't matter, Holden. I thought maybe if I knew your pain and why you left me, it would somehow give me the answers I've been looking for, like it would forgive everything, but it didn't. In the end, the fact is, you left me. You loved me so much, but you still left. What's changed? How do I know you won't do it again? You broke me, Holden. You have no idea how much I lost."

He sits me on the counter and stands up, pissed, knocking his stool back. "No, Aria; that's bullshit. You don't get to blame this all on me. I might have pushed, but you didn't even try to get me back. I texted you that it was over, and you never said anything back. You didn't even try to keep us together. You just accepted it like it was no fucking big deal."

I hop off the counter. No big deal, my ass. "What the hell was I supposed to do, Holden? I crashed your truck, and you turned into a fucking zombie. When I needed you, you shut me out and told me it was over. I didn't realize I was supposed to give up all my self-respect and dignity and grovel at your feet."

"No, Aria, you were supposed to *dig*! You were supposed to uncover the better parts of me, and you didn't even try. It was like the man I was every other day before that day didn't even matter. He wasn't worth fighting for, right?"

Over the years, his request for me to dig has been the bane of my existence. I thought about digging at the time, but I wasn't strong enough back then. As more time passed, I told myself it was meaningless talk, just like everything else he had ever told me, but now I know those were all fucking excuses. I let him down just as much as he let me down, but we were both so young and clearly disturbed.

"Would it have made a difference?"

"Is that question even relevant? We can't undo what's already been done." My eyes narrow on him in question before my phone vibrates in my back pocket, stealing my focus. Pulling it out, I see it's from Oli.

Olivia: How is it going back home? How come you haven't told me who the big reveal is?

"Is that him?" Holden all but bites out. Leaning against the counter, I shake my head no. He visibly relaxes before coming over and caging me in with an arm on either side. "Give me a week." I scrunch up my face in confusion. In answer, he kisses my neck. "A week to show that, while fate tore us apart," he kisses behind my ear, sending chills down my spine and heat to my core, "fate also brought us back together." He kisses my jaw before adding, "And you're meant to be mine." His mouth covers my own, and I let him take it because I want him. I've always wanted him, and I want to believe in us.

I rest my hands on his hips—Holden always loved when I touched him there—and he takes the move as an invitation to do the same. I don't stop him. His hands feel like they're burning my body as they trail up under my shirt and around my back. I copy his movements, making him smile against my mouth before he slowly starts testing the waters and toying with the hem of my shirt. When he starts to lift and meets no resistance, he deepens our kiss hungrily, plunging his tongue deep into my mouth right before briefly breaking it to take my t-shirt off.

"Aria." My name comes out as a breathy plea of warning. He's telling me not to tease and warning me that he will take what I'm offering. Then, with my eyes pinned on his, I answer by finding the hem of his tank and lifting it over his head.

Once his shirt is off, his mouth is on mine. His hand trails up my back as he snaps my bra open. Gently pulling it off, he drinks me in, standing before him topless in my jeans. "Damn, you're so beautiful. I've missed you so much."

Cupping a breast in each hand, he squeezes them once before

pinching my nipples, making my core coil with need. "Yes." It's a breathless cry of pleasure that escapes my lips.

"You always did love it when I played with these. Tell me, baby, did these tits miss my mouth?"

I almost come on the spot when he sucks a nipple into his mouth. Fuck, why does that turn me on so much? Pushing my tits together, he flicks his tongue over the buds of each before settling on one, swirling his tongue around its pert peak and gently tugging it between his teeth. "Stop teasing me," I pant. Releasing my nipple with a pop, he flashes me a devilish grin before starting his descent down my stomach, leaving a trail of wet kisses that make my skin prickle in their wake. Reaching my jeans, he undoes the button before peeling them off.

"So perfect." His hands glide up my thighs until he reaches my hips, where he lifts me to set me on the island. With one swift wave of his arm, he clears the food behind me before tearing my shoes and pants off. "Lay back," he orders, and I do as he says because I want it. I want everything he's about to give me. Sliding my underwear down my legs, he says, "Spread them." I can't help it. My cheeks heat, and I hesitate. I don't care who you are; that level of exposure isn't something that just comes naturally.

"Don't do that, baby. You're all I ever wanted then, and you're all I want now." He pulls me until my ass is on the edge of the counter, throws my legs over his shoulders, and dives the fuck in.

"Shit." I jolt back in surprise.

Placing a hand on my stomach, he holds me in place as he runs his tongue through my folds before sucking my clit into his mouth. Holden is a giver—he wants to pleasure me—but fuck me if he doesn't get just as much out of it. The way he's groaning against my pussy sounds like a starved man eating his last meal. When he adds a finger, I shamelessly rock against his face, seeking my own pleasure until he adds that second digit and curls it up to hit the spot he knows best, setting me off. His fingers pump me through my orgasm as his tongue laps up my juices. "So, fucking, good. I've missed this pussy," he mutters.

He pulls his sweats down and runs his thick tip through my folds. It isn't until he dips it in and says, "Fuck the week, Aria, there's no going back after this," that I come to my senses.

I'm still in my post-orgasm haze, but this can't happen again. "No, no, no," I shake my head and close my legs. "You can't, we can't. Not without a condom."

"Baby, I fucked you bare this afternoon. I'm clean." He spreads my legs and nudges my entrance again. Holding my eyes, he says, "You're the last woman I've been with."

I sit up and scoot back like I have a fire under my ass. "Wait, what?"

He pulls me forward, wrapping my legs around his waist, and kisses my neck. "You're the last woman I ever slept with. If I couldn't be with you, I didn't want anybody else. No one could be a replacement for what I had lost."

"You expect me to believe you haven't been with anyone else? Holden, you have a new girl on your arm every month."

His hand finds my breast. He tweaks my nipple and as his teeth graze my neck, he quips, "So you've been keeping tabs on me?"

"It's not hard when you're one of the top pitchers in the league and known for being a playboy."

His eyes find mine when he says, "I haven't touched one of them. They weren't you. They were distractions. I only said what I did to my date the other day because I was pissed I had to watch you hang all over another man who wasn't me." His forefinger runs between my breasts and down my stomach until he reaches my pussy. Dipping his finger in, he says, "Let me in, pretty girl."

My head lolls back as he starts to pump me again, and I get dizzy with desire. I'm so wet you can hear the evidence of my arousal as he plunges in and out. "God, yes. Don't stop, Holden."

"Fuck, baby, let me have you. I want to make you feel good." Withdrawing his fingers, he pushes me back and spreads my legs. I slam them shut.

"Get a condom."

He furrows his brow as he strokes himself. "I don't have a condom, and I don't need one. You're mine, Aria."

"How do you not have a condom?" I practically screech.

"I don't need condoms when I'm not fucking. Now open up."

"No. It's not up for debate." His frustration is evident, but I don't care. I'm not getting pregnant again.

"You're serious?" he questions.

"Deadly," I retort.

He quirks a brow and then adds, "Fine. Spread them anyway."

"Holden, please—"

"I want this, Aria. I'm not done making you feel good. I promise I won't fuck you unless you say so." I nod and let my legs fall open. "Damn, you have a pretty pussy." Bending down, he runs his tongue up my center. "So sweet." His tongue spears my hole. "So tight." Standing, he takes his cock and runs it through my lips teasingly and fuck me if it isn't the hottest thing ever to watch his jaw go slack as he rubs me back and forth. "Just the tip." He pleads as his eyes find mine, and I close them, allowing it, but knowing precisely what just the tip earned me the first time.

I got pregnant the first night we slept together. I was nine weeks pregnant when I miscarried.

The pinched expression on my face doesn't go unnoticed because he's on top of me a second later, kissing my forehead. "Hey, hey, I'll stop, baby. I'll stop. I'm sorry. I want you to enjoy this."

I can't help it. The memory and his words make me cry. I wanted to call him so many times. I needed him. I wanted to share my grief and pain with him because no one else but him could possibly understand my loss—but I didn't. I held it in then, and I'll hold it in now. There's no point. "Shit, don't cry, Aria. Tell me what to do. I swear, I'll do it."

"Just hold me." His arms instantly slide under my back as he lifts me up and pulls me forward. I wrap myself around him, breathe in his warm, salty scent, and revel in how his strong arms make me feel like I'm home. I want him to be my home, but I need to walk away. I need to think.

"Does this have to do with what happened this afternoon?" His hands are gently stroking my back when my body goes rigid from the memory. Pulling out of my embrace, his hands fly to my face, and his eyes search mine. "Tell me. Did I do that to you?"

"Maybe." I squeeze my eyes closed tight and replay the scene. Something about it made me anxious, and the memories that assaulted me couldn't have been mine. Because the recollections were not my own, even though they felt so real, the images that ran through my brain had to have represented how I felt living here. They had to have been my brain's way of letting go of the traumas I endured. Shadows that haunted my every waking moment, and ties that bound me to a pain I never understood. All of it always threatening to choke out my light. My fear was never getting free. My brain is slowly starting to heal. This afternoon, I was scared, but not of Holden. I've never once feared Holden. I was only ever scared of losing him. Today was different. It felt like I was remembering and letting go all at the same time. None of it made any sense.

When I open my eyes, I can see the defeat in his. "Today wasn't your fault. It happened because you make me feel, Holden. You always have."

Pulling out of his embrace, I say, "Holden, I need to go. It's getting late."

He sets his jaw, and his face gets serious. "You can't go back to him, Aria. Not after this. We'll figure this out. You're not going to go back to him."

I shake my head. "No, but I need to leave. I'll stay at my parents' house."

"Tell me; talk to me. What are you thinking?" He catches my chin between his thumb and forefinger, pulling my eyes to his.

"Holden, I never stopped loving you, but this is the last place I expected to be when I flew into town. I need a minute to process." I can tell my words aren't the ones he wanted to hear, but he respects them all the same, because he pulls up his sweats before grabbing my jeans off the floor and walking around to collect my shirt and bra.

"I'll wait. I've waited five years, and I'm not throwing in the towel now."

# 19

## MINE

HOLDEN

I've been in this Fuel Sports Drink meeting with Nathan Keller for the past two hours, and I haven't heard a word that's been spoken for that time. All I can focus on is the man sitting across from me. Last night, when Aria left my house, she said she wasn't going back to him, and I believed her then—or, at least, I wanted to—but now that I'm staring at him, I don't know what I believe.

Jealousy as I've never known it, has taken root, and the longer I sit here, the angrier I get. He's been kissing my girl, parading her around as his, and fucking her anytime he wants. That last thought is what sends me out of my chair.

The entire boardroom turns to look at me. Nate's brows shoot up in surprise, but then he asks, "Can we take ten?" Everyone nods in agreement and casually starts to head out of the office. Nate unbuttons his sport coat, leans back in his chair, and runs his hand over his jaw before asking, "Is there something you want to talk about?"

I don't respond. Instead, I continue to openly glare at him. If I lay into him and Aria finds out, it just gives her more reasons to walk away. She's spent the past year with this guy, and I'm not dumb enough to think he doesn't mean anything to her.

"I think we both know what, or better yet, who this is about. I'm just wondering when you'll be a man and admit that you used to fuck my girl."

Putting my fists on the table, I lean in. "Correction: my girl. Then, now, fucking always."

Running his thumb across his lip, his eyes narrow on mine before he says, "So she did go to your place last night?"

I narrow my eyes in question, positive that his comment was rhetorical, but unsure of his angle. I'd be livid if I thought my girlfriend was with another man. But fuck it, I'll play his game. "Are you even asking?"

Calmly and matter-of-factly, he leans back in his chair and steeples his fingers in an almost condescending manner that only gives me more reason to kick his ass. His lack of desire to do the same to me for stealing his girlfriend is perplexing until he adds, "No, I'm not. I have no doubt she ran to you after breaking up with me. But here's the thing, Hayes. You'll fuck it up just like you did before. I'm counting on it."

I don't give a fuck what he's counting on. I've heard all I need to hear, and I'm done with this meeting. Aria broke up with him and didn't tell me. I couldn't care less about getting this endorsement.

Micha, the representative for Fuel Drinks, walks back in. "Are we ready to start back up?" Reading the room, it's obvious Nate and I are at odds, so she asks, "Or should we take lunch?"

"No, I have to go. Nathan will finish up the negotiations." I don't even look at him before I head out of the room. Whatever he decides to do with the contract doesn't matter. It's in his best interest to get me the most money because it pays him more, but if he screws me over, that's fine too. I don't need the money. Either way, he and I will not be working together.

I'm done letting Aria call the shots. I'm getting my girl back.

"So, you just walked out of negotiations and left him there? He is going to screw you hard. I would," Connor says. He's been here since I got home, helping me prepare for tonight. I have friends coming over to see the place. While I still need tons of furniture, and the house is nowhere near show ready, I need a break. I've been working my ass off for the past five years, keeping myself busy to numb the pain and forget, but now that I'm home, I'm ready to accept whatever fate I'm due. I'm done running from my past. If my demons want me, they can fucking have me. I'd rather embrace the darkness than live one more day without her.

"I'm done, Con. I want my life back, and if I need to lose all this for her, I will. It's the choice I should have made five years ago."

"Did you tell her?" I know what he's asking. Con is the only one in my crew who knows the whole truth about the night of the crash, and I plan on keeping it that way.

"She knows enough." I take a pull off my beer and head to the kitchen.

"The caterers should be here any minute. I'm going to hit the shower." Tonight isn't anything significant, it's just a few friends from back in the day I haven't seen in forever. I tried to keep up with the occasional text on birthdays, but once I made it big, anyone and everyone started coming out of the woodwork. Even my ex, Whitney, tried to make an appearance, going so far as to stay at the same hotel I was at for an away game, sneaking into my room and waiting for my return.

That was a fun night. After I called security to get her out of my room, she tried to play the victim card. Luckily, everything was caught on camera. She showed up with her boyfriend, who happened to be the same guy I saw her fucking years ago. The plan was for us to fuck so she could trap me. Her purse had a box of condoms that all had holes poked into them. That was my first year of making it big. Needless to say, my self-inflicted celibacy was only solidified. I know it sounds warped, but I didn't want anyone else. The thought made me sick.

When I get out of the shower, I head to the closet and grab a pair of ripped black jeans, a crisp white tee, and all-white Air Force Ones. Heading to the window, I check to see that the catering truck is here as planned and notice Aria's car pulling down the drive. I had every intention of finding a way to get her over tonight, but I didn't have her number—so this is fucking perfect. I couldn't have timed her arrival better if I had planned it myself. Taking the steps two at a time, I rush out of the house to meet her when she pulls up.

Aria steps out of the car wearing a tight-fitting baby blue dress that makes her sun-kissed skin pop, and tan wedges that make her legs look like they go to heaven. I'm instantly hard. She hasn't even finished closing the door when I snatch her up in my arms. "You look amazing, pretty girl." I place my hand at the base of her back and press her against my front, ensuring she feels every inch of my arousal before asking, "When were you planning on telling me about Nate?"

She bites her plump bottom lip and quips, "There's nothing to tell."

Reaching around, I grab her ass. "Don't play with me, Aria."

Her hand snakes down to my dick, and she strokes it before saying, "It doesn't change anything." I don't even get a chance to argue because she fuses her mouth to mine.

This woman undoes me in every sense of the word, always has. Backing her against the car, I kiss her back with passion and hunger that rivals her own. She doesn't protest or resist at all, and I swear I feel my heart clench at the thought that this could be my reality, her coming home to me every day. Her tongue gives back just as much as it takes as we both lose ourselves in each other.

A throat clears behind us, breaking our moment. "I swear to fuck, Connor, whatever you have to say better be important." I'm so tired of him hogging my girl when he's around.

Aria smiles and pats my chest. "I'm here for him. Sorry, big boy." She clasps her hands together and says, "Where is she?"

Connor rocks back on his heels, giving me a wink before

replying, "In the living room, getting ready to take her Barbies downstairs to watch a movie."

"Perfect." Aria claps her hands before turning to take off toward the house.

Quickly, I steal her arm before she can trot off. "What's going on?"

"I'm watching Summer. Connor said you were having people over tonight, and his parents were out of town, so he didn't have a sitter."

"Wait a minute. How the hell does he have your number?"

She rolls her eyes at me like I just asked the dumbest question. "We exchanged numbers yesterday at golf." Throwing her thumb over her shoulder, she adds, "So, if we're done with twenty questions, I've got some Barbies to play with."

Before she makes it too far, I call out, "And, Aria, it changes everything." Her eyes hold mine for a beat, neither confirming nor denying my words, but I let it go for now. She's here, and that's more than I could have hoped for.

I'm fuming that Connor has her number, and I don't. "Connor, you better—"

"What you're about to say is, 'Connor thank you for getting my girl here.'" We start heading up the steps to the house when he says, "Summer asked if she could be her mommy."

I grind my teeth and grit back my response because Connor got dealt a shitty hand in that department. The summer I was with Aria, Connor knocked up some chick on a one-night stand. Turns out she was Trent's girlfriend, the asshole I never liked who moved in with Gabe. Trent and Holly were transients, bouncing through town, making quick cash and stealing credit cards. They got caught at the baseball fields.

Holly tried to lure the wrong guy. He was a cop in town for a tournament, and she was too stupid to realize it. He let it play out, and when she took him back to her place and tried to roofie his drink, he arrested her. The closet had ten stolen wallets and roughly fifty credit cards. Holly gave birth to Summer in jail, and when she was released, she ran off. Connor hasn't seen her since.

I squeeze his shoulder. "You know that's not going to happen, right?"

He smirks and says, "I don't know. We do get along. She loves my jokes, and having a cute little girl doesn't hurt." This time, I punch him in the arm hard.

"Fuck, you know I was messing around."

We enter the house just in time to watch Summer pull Aria down the hallway and toward the basement door. "We're going to the movie room, Daddy."

Aria pushes her long blonde hair over her shoulder. "Movie room?"

"Yeah, Uncle H built me my own movie room." Without another word, they head downstairs. I built the movie room to watch playback reels of my games, but she loved it so much when she saw it that I told her it was for her.

"So, when do you plan to fill me in on this plan of yours to get Aria back?"

I pinch the bridge of my nose and start heading toward the kitchen in search of a stiff drink. "There is no plan. She may have come for you, but she knew where she was going and still showed up. She's here, which means she's mine."

"Just like that?" he questions.

"Yeah, just like that. I'm not letting her go this time, Con. She was always meant to be mine."

It's been two hours since everyone got here, and while catching up has been nice, my thoughts are on the woman in my basement. I'm just about to sneak off and see her when Kristine comes strutting into the kitchen, heavily pregnant.

"Holden Hayes, how dare you not tell me Aria was here."

Setting my beer down, I laugh. "Kris, I'm surprised I didn't hear you coming down the driveway." I walk around and hug her. "When did you get here?"

"I've been here for ten minutes, and I ran into Connor, who casually said Summer was downstairs with Aria like it was no big deal. What the hell?" She throws her hands up in the air right as the basement door opens, and Summer comes up with a barefoot Aria behind her. The two of them have been making themselves at home, and I love it.

"Aria *fucking* Montgomery, how dare you come back in town and not text me!"

Aria squeals and runs over to hug her. "Oh my god, Kris. Look at you! I was going to text you, but things have been crazy. I thought I'd get a chance today but got stuck on the phone with a client."

Summer pulls on Aria's dress, and Aria bends down to listen. After Summer whispers something in her ear, they head toward the living room. "Kris, come join us."

The girls all follow out, and I'm left standing at the island with Con, Jeff, and Brandon. I walk over to the far end, where I can see the girls in the living room sitting on the couch. Aria is braiding Summer's hair while Kris clearly talks her ear off.

"Are you ready to be a dad?" Con asks Jeff. Jeff and Kris met over a year ago and eloped after being together for two months. It sounds crazy as hell, but sometimes when you know, you know.

"I think so. I'm nervous and don't really know what to expect, but I'm trying to enjoy these last few weeks of it just being us. Kris has had a pretty good pregnancy. I've talked to some guys who say their girls didn't want to be touched or they were fucking sick all the time. Kris wants to ride my dick nonstop, and her tits—I swear her tits grew overnight. She's super fucking sensitive too, and it's hot as hell. I'm not looking forward to that ending."

His words jolt me back to the last night I had with Aria. A night that has played on repeat in my head for the last five years. We fucked for hours before we ever left for Con's place. I had to pull myself away from her. She was so willing and wet, and her tits... I mean, she has great breasts, but that night they were more; she was more. Then her words from last night punch me in the gut. "You broke me, Holden. I lost more than you'll ever know." And she wouldn't let me fuck her without a condom. My heart skips a beat, and I feel like I'm going to be sick. Summer comes running into the kitchen, and when I look up, Aria's eyes find mine. It's then that I know I'm right. She was pregnant.

Marching into the living room, I stand behind the couch and say, "Aria, a word, please."

She furrows her brow but stands and follows me into the office. "What's up?"

"Were you ever going to tell me?"

Crossing her arms over her chest, she asks, "Tell you what, Holden?"

"Don't fucking play with me, Aria."

"Why don't you just say what you mean then, and stop playing head games."

"You were pregnant, Aria! You were pregnant with my baby and didn't think to tell me."

Her hand flies to her mouth as a cry escapes her lips. I watch tears fall down her pretty face as her body starts to tremble with nerves, and I still don't move. "You had no right not to tell me. I wanted that baby. I wanted that baby with you."

She steels her spine and wipes her eyes. "Fuck off, Holden. You have no idea what you're talking about." Then, heading toward the door, she says, "This was a mistake. It was a mistake then and now."

Coming up behind her, I slam the door just as she pulls it open, caging her in from behind. "No. No more running. You're going to tell me. Is that why you left?"

She doesn't turn around and acknowledge me at her back, which pisses me off. "You got rid of our baby and left?"

She spins around, her voice vexed when she says, "You don't know what you're talking about!"

"Then tell me." I pin her to the door, her arms above her head. "You're not leaving until you do."

"Let me go, Holden. Let me go, and I'll tell you."

"No, you'll tell me right here, just like this. I'm done doing things your way, Aria."

Closing her eyes, she throws her head against the door and says, "I didn't get rid of it. I didn't even know it was there until I lost it." Fuck.

I nuzzle my face into her neck, keeping her hands pinned. "Keep going."

A cry escapes her throat as she mumbles, "What?"

"Tell me. Tell me what I did to you. Tell me how this was my fault." She fights me to get loose, which only makes me double down. My fate is already fucked. What's another layer of darkness now? At least now, maybe I can take it from her. She's had to endure it alone for the last five years.

"The weekend you broke up with me, I locked myself in my room and didn't come out until I had to get ready for work. I was weak from not having consumed any food or water and collapsed on the bathroom floor in pain. My parents rushed me to the hospital. We all assumed my eating issues finally got the best of me, and they had. They took my baby."

"Fuck!" I slam my fist against the door.

She startles before weakly retorting, "This isn't your fault."

"The fuck if it isn't, Aria! I broke up with you. I ended us and caused you pain. That pain starved our baby."

She adamantly shakes her head. "Holden, please. Please let me go." I'm not going to hurt her any more than I already have. When I release her hands, they fly to my face.

"Look at me. I spent a good year blaming you because I wanted to hate you, but it was never your fault. Miscarriages happen for so many reasons. I wasn't healthy, Holden, you know this. Children may or may not be in my future because of how I treated my body. That's on me, not you."

Her big brown eyes hold mine, and I can see her sincerity. She doesn't blame me, but I have to know; I have to know if there's even a chance she'll stay when I've given her a lifetime of reasons to run.

"Why, pretty girl? Why are you here?"

"Because I never stopped loving you." My eyes search hers for a split second before I crash my mouth to hers. I don't deserve her. She never saw herself as enough, but she was always my everything. The girl with the haunted eyes that called to my soul, who shared my demons and understood without words that we all have weaknesses, but unlike mine, hers were always her strengths. Through her weakness, she found her power. It built her.

Pulling back, I say, "This stops here. You're mine. No more games."

She nods vehemently as I reach around and grab her plump ass hard. A slow, tantalizing moan escapes her lips before she asks, "Did you get condoms?"

I lift her and pin her against the door as she wraps her legs around my waist. "I don't need a condom, Aria. This pussy is mine." Trailing my hand up her thigh, I'm grateful she wore a dress, because all I have to do is pull her panties to the side and run my finger through her soaked folds. She lets out a delicious moan from the feel of me touching her there. When I dip my finger in, I say, "You're taking me bare, and I'm going to put another baby in you." My cock is so fucking hard from the thought of shooting my seed deep inside her that it hurts. I unbutton my jeans, pull the zipper down, and slowly start to let her sink down on me.

"Holden—" Her protest quickly dies as she feels me ease my way in.

"God, you feel good, pretty girl. So fucking tight." I kiss her neck, nipping and sucking my way up to her mouth. "Relax, baby. Let me in."

"Maybe it would help if you let me ride you."

"Damn, baby, are you serious?"

"Yes, now let me down." There's no way I'm letting her off

my dick. With her wrapped around me, I walk us over to my desk and prop my ass against the side before sliding on and leaning back. Once I've laid back, she pulls off me anyway, and I immediately miss her heat.

I groan in protest, but the reward far outweighs the loss. She grabs the hem of her sundress and pulls it up and over her head. Those perfect tits that I love fall out. "No bra?"

She shrugs, "It's a strapless dress." Because I don't want her getting up and I'm impatient, I tug at her thong and tear it in one go. "Holden! Now I don't have panties to leave the room." And I can't help but smile. *Good.*

"You don't need panties with me. Ride my dick, pretty girl." Taking my dick in her hand, she rubs it through her lips, back and forth until my cock is thoroughly covered in her juices. When the pre-cum starts dripping from the tip, she rubs her thumb around the crown, spreading it before bringing it to her lips and sucking. "Aria, I swear if you don't put my dick in that pussy right now, I'm going to come without it." Lining me up with her entrance, she slowly starts to push down. Grabbing her hips, I ask because it's killing me. "Did he make you come?"

She pulls up and eases down again. "I haven't slept with him, Holden."

"What?" My eyes are glued to her pussy as I watch myself disappear.

"Mmm, so good," she mumbles, tossing her head back.

"Aria, tell me." But as the last syllable leaves my lips, she fully seats herself, and I feel her flood my cock.

"Yes," she cries as she throws her head back and pinches her nipples. *Damn, that's hot.*

I sit up. "Tell me."

Her eyes search mine. "You're fucking me and want to talk about another man?" I know that's messed up, but I need to know this is ours. That I'm still the only one. She rocks into me, teasing me, distracting me. I take her lips and dip my tongue into her mouth, rubbing it against hers and finding my peace. She was always home. Pulling back, she says, "They were never you. The minute I would get intimate, all I could think about was you. I figured maybe if I stopped having sex, my relationship couldn't get ruined before it had time to start. Nate told me he was waiting until marriage. He heard a joke. I heard a reason to stay. I felt safe with him because he never pushed."

Just hearing his name makes me furious, but knowing he didn't sleep with my girl is a relief. But it doesn't change anything. I'm sure they did other shit; he's had his mouth on her, and he already told me he's waiting for her to come back. "He loves you," I point out, and she nods.

"I know."

I palm her breast and bring it to my mouth, running my tongue around her nub until it's hard. "Do you love him?" I take her other breast and do the same thing, making her pussy squeeze my cock.

"I do, but not like I love you."

"That doesn't work for me, Aria." Releasing her breast, I flip her over, line up my cock, and slam in, knocking the breath out of her. "I'm going to fuck any memory of him right out of you, Aria. This tight pussy is mine." I push in deep, making her moan. "These are mine." I palm her breasts before placing my lips over her heart and saying, "And this pretty heart is all mine."

I pump into her in long, deep, hard strokes, making her tits bounce. Pushing her legs up, I spread them wider, extending my reach.

"Fuck, Holden, you're so deep. Don't stop." Her euphoric moans are picking up.

"That's it, baby. Sing for me, so the whole house knows you're mine." The sound of our arousal fills the room. My balls are slapping against her plump ass, and I'm about to come when the door opens. Aria doesn't even notice because she's got her back toward the door and currently writhing beneath me in ecstasy on the brink of orgasm. Her pussy starts to choke my dick, and I don't stop as Nate stands there watching me fuck my girl. "Whose pussy is this, Aria?" I bring my thumb to her clit, and she starts to shatter. "Say it, Aria. Say the words, pretty girl."

"Yours, Holden, it's yours." I slam in one more time, and she strangles it.

"Milk me, baby." I shoot my seed deep, ensuring that I coat her womb.

Since Nate hasn't retreated and decided to give us an audience, I pull out and tuck myself back into my jeans instead of pumping her through the waves of her release.

"So this is why you ended it, Aria. Only his dick would suffice? You couldn't even wait twenty-four hours after breaking up with me to turn around and fuck him."

Aria bolts up and turns around. "Nate? What the hell?" She turns to me and says, "Did you know he was there?" I was cool with him watching me mark my territory, but he's not going to keep looking at her naked. I tear my shirt off over my head and pull it over hers.

"He was only here for the end. Why are you here?"

"What?" Aria protests, "You knew he was here, and you kept going?" She searches around for her dress, but I pull her into me.

"It doesn't change anything. You're mine."

She's mad, and I see Nate clenching his fists in anger when I look up. Releasing Aria, I step around the desk and ask, "Do we have a problem?"

He rubs his jaw. "No, we don't have a problem. You can't make someone love or respect you."

His eyes find Aria's, and that pisses me off. "Nate, you're not going to come in here and disrespect Aria in my house. I think it's time you go."

As I start walking toward him, he says, "No problem. I have no reason to stay." He throws the manilla envelope he was carrying onto one of the side tables. "This is the Fuel contract, and we're done."

Aria comes to my side and asks, "Why did you watch?"

He holds her eyes and says, "To make sure I have no reason to love you. This is the guy that broke you. This is the guy that haunted you for the past five years. Just remember that when your demons come back to visit."

I step forward, ready to lay into him just as Spencer, Con, and some guy I can't place come storming into the room. The minute Spencer's eyes meet mine, he crosses the room and punches me square in the jaw. Fuck, that hurt.

Nate chimes in with, "Oh yeah, and I brought your brother. He wanted to surprise you." Fucking asshole.

"What the hell are you thinking, Aria? Are you kidding me with this shit? After everything he put you through, you take him back?"

When Aria doesn't answer, I turn to her, ready to defend her, but her face has turned pale white, and her eyes are pinned on the guy who came in with Spencer. Spencer is pacing the room, going on about how I'm a piece of shit, and how she's making a huge mistake. Nate's eyes are pinned on hers with a mix of intrigue and concern that sparks a jealous rage inside of me, but before I can fan the flames, I notice the guy who looks eerily familiar slips out, and I nod to Con for him to follow. When Con follows, it only confirms what I've surmised for years. He's into some shady shit. It was like he was waiting for my cue–as if it was a silent validation of my suspicions.

Aria's gaze lands on Nate as she falls to her knees and screams, "You knew! You fucking knew, and you never told me. How could you? How could you hurt me like that?"

She's bawling and shaking when Nate comes over. "How could I know that, Aria? Are you serious?"

Shaking her head, she says, "You suspected. It's the same thing."

"That's not remotely the same thing, and I did say something."

Spencer comes over and pulls her into his arms, but she fights him and screams, "Don't touch me! Don't you dare! You all fucking knew."

I'm done watching other men try to comfort my girl. *She's mine.* Walking over, I drop down in front of her and pick up her hand before asking, "What did we know, Aria?"

When her eyes find mine, I have my answer without words, and the air all but leaves my lungs. Those haunted eyes are back, but now I know why they always called to me. She's the one. She's the one they tied up for me.

20

# TWISTED FATE

ARIA

"Tell us, Aria. Tell us what we know," Spencer says from beside me as Holden continues staring through me like he's seen a fucking ghost. His empty gaze reminds me of the night he left me the last time.

The door opens, and my cousin Rainer, who I haven't seen since I was thirteen, comes flying in with a bloody nose. "What the fuck," Spencer asks when he sees Rainer's face.

Connor swipes his lip with the back of his hand and says, "Trust me, he deserves so much fucking more. Tell the damn story, asshole." Connor punches him in the gut as Holden stands up and locks the door.

Rainer shakes his head, "I didn't do anything to her. I fucking swear." Spencer flinches from his words and looks at him, then back at me, and I see it. Spence doesn't know.

Holden rolls his office chair over and commands him to sit. "Sit, fucker, or I'll make you."

He sits as Holden takes the bungee cords from the scaffolding left in the corner with the painter's tools and straps him to the chair before saying, "We're only going to do to you what you did to her." Slapping his face, he adds, "That shouldn't be too bad, right?"

Spencer yells, "Somebody fill me in on what the fuck is going on here."

Nate points to Rainer. "He is the reason she was sick. He is her demon."

Spencer turns to me. "Aria?"

The memories of the night Rainer and I last saw each other come flooding back. Spencer had a baseball game that my parents attended, and Rainer was supposed to watch me. I didn't need a babysitter, but I remember my mom was paranoid because a girl a block over had been taken at the beginning of the summer. I had homework, so Rainer came over to sit with me. He planned on staying until Spencer got home to hang out, but that night, no homework was done.

Rainer was that cousin you loved to hang out with because he was so much fun—always pulling pranks, quick with hilarious comebacks, and crazy as fuck. I recall being excited when my mom said Rainer was coming over.

"This is bullshit, Hayes. You're just as much to blame, you fucking prick," Rainer all but spits out in anger.

Holden comes over and squats down in front of me. Pushing my hair behind my ear, he cups the side of my face and says, "Aria, I want you to tell me I'm wrong. I need you to tell me I'm wrong, because I can't take it back. I can't change it." I furrow my brow in confusion, not understanding what he's saying. "I love you, pretty girl, so damn much." And my heart breaks because it feels like he's leaving me all over again and I don't know why.

"Why do you keep leaving me every time I need you?"

He closes his eyes as if my words pain him and says, "Tell the story, baby, and if you still want me, I'll be right here." Standing, he walks over to his desk and grabs tape. Tossing it to Con, standing beside Rainer, he says, "We don't need any interruptions." Connor takes the duct tape and places it over Rainer's mouth.

"Talk, Aria," Spencer demands.

I nod and pull in a deep breath. "You had a baseball game, and it was a big deal for some reason. I can't remember why, but Mom and Dad both wanted to be there. It was around the time that the girl two blocks over from our house went missing. Rainer came over to watch me, but instead of staying home like we were supposed to, he took me to a bonfire in the middle of nowhere."

"I remember that night. It was my last game of the season, and a scout came to watch me play. It was the night I told Mom and Dad I didn't want to play ball in college." Of course, I don't remember those details, but I nod anyway.

"By the time we arrived, most of the guys had already been drinking. At first, it wasn't so bad. There was this guy there, I think his name was Lance or Landon. I can't remember, but I believe it started with an L." Connor shifts, catching my eye, and I watch as he exchanges a glance with Holden, but I keep going. "He was sort of flirting with me, but I didn't take him seriously. I was thirteen, and these guys were all about to start college. I sat on the back of a tailgate, watching them all get plastered for most of the night. I didn't have any service, so I couldn't text anyone. At some point, I jumped down to look for Rainer. There weren't any girls, so I thought he'd be ready to go, but when I found him, he was busy, and I was in trouble."

"What the fuck do you mean you were in trouble?" Spencer spits. I pull in a ragged breath because the next part hurts. I look around the room, not wanting to meet anyone's eye, especially Rainer's, who starts yelling through his tape.

When my eyes land on Nate's, he nods and says, "If you want to heal, you have to grow through the pain." His words hit deep because I think he's saying them for himself as much as he is me.

"Rainer was getting fucked in the ass while giving another guy a blow job. I quickly turned around to leave, but it was too late. The guy getting a blow job caught me. He grabbed me from behind and said, 'You're not going to say a word. Time to have some fun.'"

Holden lets out a growl of frustration before punching Rainer in the jaw and saying, "Are you fucking serious? You let her get hurt because you couldn't be a man and own your shit!" He lands another punch to his temple before Connor pulls him off.

"Finish the story, Aria," Connor says.

"The next thing I know, I was tied up to a tree, and the guy called out, 'Boys, it's time to have some fun.' A group of guys from the bonfire came over to see what was happening, including the one whose name I can't remember. He said, 'Fucking perfect. He'll be here any minute.' They started catcalling me, asking if I was a virgin. Some of them started saying I was too thick and that Hayes wouldn't want me anyway, and they should have some fun before he got there. Then, one of the guys said, 'Okay, we don't fuck her, but we can use her mouth. She's going to suck my dick before she gets Hayzed.'"

Wait, hold up, did I just say his name? When I look up, Holden is staring at me, jaw set, fists clenched, and suddenly I feel sick. "You're him. You're the guy I was tied to a tree for."

Closing my eyes, I let my pain seep in. The years I spent hating myself, the hurt I caused my family, and all I lost. I've always felt like I was searching for something to wash out all the darkness that threatened to choke out my light. It never added up until now. The pain of this memory brought me to my knees. But I've lived with the torment inflicted by these ghosts for so long they no longer have the power to hurt me. I had to go through hell to find the strength to stand in this moment and not break but heal. I hold it tight one last time and let it wrap around me, because this is the last time I will ever let this pain be my weakness. It no longer hurts me, because it's changed me.

Nate pulls me out of my daze and says, "Aria, let's go. It doesn't have to be me, but it can't be him."

Spencer holds out his arm to halt him and says, "Wait, so you don't remember Holden being there?"

Rising to my feet, I shake my head and say, "No. I bit the guy who tried to put his dick in my mouth, and he knocked me out. I don't remember anything after that."

"Let's go, Aria." Nate clasps his hand around mine and starts pulling me toward the door.

But I can't leave without knowing. "Did you know? Have you always known it was me?"

He grits his teeth. "I don't know. I can't answer that. Maybe."

"How is that even an answer, Holden? After everything we've been through, you owe me that much!"

"Just fucking go, Aria. Go, find your happily ever after. It was never going to be me anyway."

Snatching my hand out of Nate's, I storm across the room and slap him hard across the face. "No. You don't get to do that. Where's the man who said I was his, the man who wanted to make a baby with me, the man who loved me? You want me to dig, Holden? Here I am. I'm fucking digging. Are you going to come back to me?"

Connor chimes in, "Fuck, bro, if you don't tell her, I will. It's not your fault."

His nostrils flare, and he curses. "Damn it! Luke. His name was Luke, Aria. The guy I spent the last decade living for, keeping our shared dream alive because I took his ability to live away, was the same guy that helped hurt you. We crashed that night because he told me he had a surprise for me, and when I asked what it was, he said check your phone. When I opened the text, it was you. I was so fucking shocked by what I saw that the right tire went off the road. The next thing I know, I overcorrected and wrapped us around a tree."

Spencer flies across the room and tackles him to the ground. "You sick piece of shit. You knew my sister was tied up to a tree, and you never thought to tell me?" He doesn't even try to stop Spencer from landing the blows. Connor jumps in and pulls him off.

"He didn't know it was her. I saw the fucking picture. You can't tell it's her."

Holden sits up and rests his arms on his knees before dropping his head. "I tried to get there, Aria. I wouldn't have ever let that happen. I'm so fucking sorry. I never knew the other half of the story until you told it tonight. The ten guys there that night did a good job of fucking off. Half of them went away for college, and the other half I didn't know. Like that dick over there." He nods toward Rainer. "I think I remember seeing him at a house party that same summer, but I didn't know his name. There wasn't anything I could do. I never knew if I was being pranked or if it was real, but your eyes haunted me for the past twelve years, so when you asked me if I knew, maybe I did, because some part of me felt you in my bones, Aria. Your eyes captivated me from the moment I met you."

When Holden's pale blue gaze lands on mine, I see him, and I mean really see him. I see him stripped down, raw, and exposed. I see his pain and the anguish that has tormented him for years because his way of dealing with his demons was to bury them. He couldn't fight them because he felt like he deserved them. But this pain that has cursed him doesn't have to define him. Holden has paid his dues. He has lived with it long enough, and it's time for it to become his cure, his power, his strength.

Dropping to my knees in front of him, I say, "We can't change the past, Holden, but we can choose not to live in it. We can choose us. You always said there was a reason we met. Maybe it was to bring us both to this moment, where we let go of the things we cannot change and finally break free of the chains that bound us to our own personal hells."

His eyes search mine as he processes the meaning behind my words. To ensure there is no question about my intent, I add, "You said you'd be here if I want you. I haven't stopped wanting you."

Reaching out, he pulls me into his lap and holds me, but our moment is short-lived because Spencer says, "If you two are done with your kumbaya bullshit, what the hell are we going to do with this asshole?"

Holden moves to stand and offers me his hand to help me up

before saying, "Well, we could tie him to a tree and shove a dick down his throat, or—"

"The fuck if we are. *We* are not doing anything. I'm out." Nate looks me over one last time, thinning his lips, no doubt in disbelief over my choices, before making his way out the door.

That's when Spencer chimes in. "Connor, help me take him to the car."

My eyes go wide. "Spencer, don't do anything stupid. It's not worth it. He's not worth it."

"Aria, you don't get to tell me that. What happens to him is not your cross to bear."

Connor starts pushing the chair toward the French doors at the far end of the office, and I'm reminded that Holden's friends are still here. I begin to head after Spencer and Connor when Holden pulls me back. "Don't, Aria. He's your brother. You know his character. Trust that whatever happens is what he needs to heal." He hands me my dress and asks, "Can you put this on? As much as I love you in my shirt, I need to ask everyone to leave, and Summer's out there." I nod silently, taking my dress. I step into it and pull it up, ensuring I'm fully covered before taking Holden's shirt off and handing it back.

After my clothes are on, he says, "Come here." As I step around the paint cans piled in here for projects still in process, he closes the gap and pulls me into him. "Are you okay? Don't put on a show for me, pretty girl."

I step up onto my tippy toes and press a kiss to his lips. "I'm good. I promise."

He kisses me back before taking my face in his hands and running his thumbs across my cheeks. His eyes quickly dart around the room, and he walks over to the scaffolding and picks up a drop cloth. Returning, his expression is pinched and somewhat unsure when he says, "You're beautiful, pretty girl, you know that, but your makeup is smudged."

I laugh. I can't help but laugh at the absurdity. After everything we just went through, telling me my makeup is all over my face is hard for him? When he asks, "Why are you laughing?" I can't help but laugh harder. It's probably my nerves and the stress of the night catching up with me, but I finally feel free. All the mental barriers my mind built to protect me came crumbling down, and for the first time in so long, I feel like I am me. "Just go. I'll clean up."

He furrows his brow at me, probably not convinced I'm mentally stable after everything. Pushing him by the shoulder, I walk him toward the door. "Go. I'm fine. I'll be out in a minute."

I'm more than fine. I feel alive for the first time in a long time.

I've been curled up on the couch with Summer for half an hour when Holden comes in. "Baby, let me take her to bed." Bending down, he scoops sleeping Summer off my chest and into his arms.

"Is Connor not coming back tonight?" He gives me a look of warning that says, *Don't ask questions you don't want answers to.* "Holden, will you tell me?" Bringing his finger to his lips, he shushes me and starts to walk toward the steps, and I follow.

As we climb the steps, everything feels incredibly surreal. Summer may not be mine, but she could be. This entire scenario before me could have been. Holden carrying our baby upstairs to bed—I pause to collect myself. While Holden has told me time and time again that I'm what he wants, a small sliver inside of me wonders if that still holds true. I mean, our story is twisted and fucked up.

Clearly, he lets himself suffer when he thinks he deserves it. I don't want him to stay with me because I'm the girl he couldn't save and now he thinks he owes me. I'm standing in the middle of the staircase when he whisper-yells, "Aria," and jerks his head for me to follow.

The second floor is open to the first floor. A spindled rail runs its length, opening to the living room below. Holden walks down the hall, and I pick up my pace to catch up. When he opens the door to the room he plans on putting Summer in, my jaw drops. It's a pretty pink princess room. The man's house is still primarily unfinished, but this sweet little girl already has a room decorated just for her. I watch as he lays her in bed and turns on her pink nightlight that illuminates the ceiling with stars. He grabs a bear off the window ledge and lays it next to her before pulling the covers up to her chin.

Once the door is closed and we exit to the hallway, I ask, "Why does she have her own room here?"

Pressing his lips together, he rubs the back of his neck nervously before saying, "Connor and I became close over the years. I don't know when or how it happened, but the fucker got under my skin, and so did that little girl. If she asks for something, I'm a sucker and she gets it. Con's here all the time anyway." He shrugs like it's no big deal, and I can't help but smile. "Stop looking at me like that. It's not that big of a deal."

I lean in and press my lips to his, trying to communicate with my mouth the words he doesn't want to hear, but he pulls back and says, "Can we talk?" I draw in a deep breath and brace myself. Just because I'm okay doesn't mean he is. I'm a daily reminder of a past that's haunted him for far too long, and that might be more than he can handle.

Taking my hand, he pulls me down the hall and through double doors that open to a sitting area that leads into his master bedroom. Again, another room that's been fully finished. This room reminds me of his bedroom at his parents' house when we were younger. The room had dark furnishings and a gray bedspread. This room is all gray as well, just more sophisticated. Dark gray hardwood furnishings, light gray bedding and curtains, white and gray multi-toned pillows on the bed, and window seats. His eyes catch mine taking in the space, and he asks, "Do you like it?"

Because I'm done with the innuendos, and I'm tired, I say, "Does it matter?"

"Well yeah, it matters." He stalks across the room to a small table set beside a cozy chair in a bay window. "This is the chair you'll sit in and drink your morning coffee while you watch the blue heron stalk the shallow parts of the lake." He takes a few steps to his right and opens a door. "This is the closet you'll hang all your clothes in." Then, closing the door, he walks over to the bed. "And this is the bed you'll sleep in every night with me wrapped around you, poking you in the ass." The last part makes me smile, but I'm still unsettled.

"This is what you wanted to talk about, Holden?"

He reaches me in no time. "No, it's not, but I can tell you're tense, so I figured I'd try to break the ice and make sure you knew I still want everything. What are you think—"

Cutting him off, I wrap my arms around his middle and hold him tight, not wanting this moment to end. "I love you, Holden."

Pulling me over to the bed, he makes me sit before saying, "Tell me, Aria. What's worrying that pretty head?"

"I just thought maybe you wouldn't want a reminder of the day that fucked up your life. I'm not only the girl with the haunted eyes anymore, but the girl that caused you to crash and kill your best friend."

He clenches his jaw and narrows his eyes. "That's one way to look at it, I suppose, but I don't see it that way—at least not anymore. As fucked up as it sounds, Aria, we were always meant to be. Don't get me wrong, I wouldn't have laid a finger on you that night, but fate has brought you to me more than once for a reason, and I think that's because you were always meant to be mine." He leans in and takes my lips, gently coaxing them open and dipping his tongue in to tease me before pulling back to say, "I love you, pretty girl, more than you'll ever know."

# 21

# FREE

## HOLDEN

A phone buzzing stirs me awake, and it takes me a minute to realize where I am. The warm body I have tucked into my side quickly reminds me. I've only been in this house for a few weeks, and I can count on one hand the number of times I've slept in this bed. I hate beds. They're always a reminder of how alone I am, but with Aria wrapped around me, it will soon become the only place I want to be. Rubbing my eyes, I try to reach for my phone on the nightstand without waking her.

When I finally get to my phone, I realize it's my workout alarm. It's 5:00 am. This is when I usually get up and run trails through the woods, but today is also a game day, meaning I have to be at the stadium by noon. Looking down, I take in the sight before me. My girl is wrapped around me, her leg thrown over mine while her head rests on my chest. Her perfect tit is playing peekaboo with the sheet as it rises and falls with her breath.

I gently dust my thumb over the bite marks and beard-burn that still linger from last night. I fucked her long and hard for hours, reacquainting myself with every inch of her flawless body. The girl I knew five years ago grew out of her insecurities. She met me thrust for thrust. When I pounded into her from behind, she slammed herself back on my cock like she wanted to feel the pain.

I hadn't fucked in five years; I was starved, and as much as I tried to be soft, she demanded I make it hurt. At one point, she said, "The pain makes it real," and I'll be damned if I didn't feel the same way.

We've both been so numb for so long that feeling anything, even if it hurts, is everything. I've never known the details about the girl in the photo with the haunted eyes. She was always an enigma to me. I had so many questions, and no answers. The night everything happened, I knew Luke and the guys were trashed, but Luke was not the kind of guy who would tie a girl up to a tree, prank or not. We had been best friends since grade school. I spent the past decade trying to redeem not only myself for that night, but him. I didn't understand how or why he would be so reckless, so heartless, and maybe I never will.

My phone vibrates on the nightstand, and I grab it.

> Connor: Heads up, Spencer came back with me last night. Thanks for putting Summer to bed.

*Great.* I know Spencer is not my biggest fan, and I can't fucking blame him. If my sister got knocked up and then miscarried while the guy that fucked her over went on without a care in the world, I'd be pissed too. I will never blame Aria for anything that happened between us, but for as much as I made mistakes, she did too. She didn't believe in how much I loved her. She never once questioned my decision to break up, and then she sat in a hospital all alone, miscarrying our baby because she thought I wouldn't care.

While I may have given her reasons to believe that was true, I also asked her to dig. I fucking asked that of her the very night I broke up with her, and she didn't do it until last night. Last night, she fought for me, she fought for us, and now there's no going back. No matter how fucked up things might get, she is mine. If our hearts are destined to be black, they will be black together.

It's early, and I don't want to wake her, but I need to shower and get ready. I've almost entirely slid out of her bear hold when she mumbles, "Baby, where are you going?" My heart soars from that one word: baby. Aria has never called me anything but Holden.

Immediately, I slide back in and roll her over, so I'm on top of her. "Look at me, pretty girl."

She opens her eyes and throws her arm over her mouth before saying, "Morning breath. It's too early for this."

I laugh and poke her with the raging boner I've had since the moment I woke up with her draped over me. "I'm keeping you, Aria Montgomery, morning breath and all." I pull her arm away from her face and kiss her cheek. "Can you do me a favor?" Her brow furrows in question. "Ask me again." Still not understanding, I pepper her face with kisses, leaving the last one on her lips. "Ask me where I'm going?"

She smiles knowingly, "Baby, where are you going?"

I groan and press my cock against her clit, and she screws up her face in pain. "Are you sore, baby?"

"Maybe just a little."

I pull back the covers and sit on my haunches to see the damage. Her hips are bruised from where I gripped her while I slammed into her from behind, her thick thighs have bite marks that match her tits, and her pretty pussy is chaffed from my beard. Leaning down, I place kisses on all the spots that brought her pleasure last night before jumping up and heading to the bathroom. "Don't move," I call out as I start her a bath. But, of course, she doesn't listen and comes strolling in behind me, completely naked, without a care in the world. I fucking love this new, confident woman.

"I was making you a bath. I have a game today, so I needed to get up and shower anyway." She looks around, taking in the bathroom. I forget that she hasn't seen it yet. It feels like this is us, this is our place, and this is all hers. Hell, for me it is, but I'm reminded that it's only been a few days since she's returned. Heading over to the vanity, she opens the cabinet that splits the his and her sinks down the middle, and finds what she's looking for, mouthwash. Once she is done, she spins around and asks, "Do you have time to take a bath with me?"

I need to start my warm-up routine, but there's no way in hell I'm passing up a bath with my girl. She strolls over to the bathtub, her plump ass on display, and my cock twitches. "Yeah, pretty girl, I'll make time for a bath with you any day." As she steps in, I head over to the sink and throw back some mouthwash before climbing in with my girl.

"Scoot forward so I can get behind you." She does without question. Once I'm in, I pull her between my legs, where she rests her back against my front. We sit in silence as the hot water and bubbles rise to fill the tub. After coming to bed, we didn't talk much, and it's been killing me not to ask any more details about the night she was tied up. Last night, she mentioned one of the guys attempted to have her blow him while she was tied up but then he knocked her out. But I'm curious if that's all that happened or if there's more she just hasn't uncovered, which makes me sick to think about.

"Aria, can I ask you something about that night?" I cross my arm over her chest and place a kiss on her neck for comfort.

Taking my free hand into hers, she interlaces our fingers and says, "Holden, I don't want there to be any more secrets between us. If it's on your heart, I want to know." She has always been so much braver than me, and honestly, it intimidates the hell out of me. This woman will have me by the balls in this relationship, that is for sure.

"Do you think they raped you after you were knocked out?"

She's silent but squeezes my hand in reassurance. "No, I don't think so. I believe when I passed out, it freaked everyone out. I remember waking up the next day on the couch at home, still fully clothed, but I had a terrible headache and a knot on my head. It's so strange having memories come back that you didn't know ever existed." Of course, that doesn't convince me that foul play wasn't involved. But before I can press for more, she adds,

"Plus, at eighteen, when I slept with my first boyfriend, it was messy."

I squeeze her breast and growl against her neck, "This is mine. I don't want to hear about the men that had you before me. I just wanted to know if you were hurt more than you remembered."

"The scars I have are different. Now that I have all the pieces, I can see how that night influenced so much of who I became after. The obsession with my body and thinking I was too thick, hyper-focusing on how others saw me, watching everything I put into my mouth. Remember when I tried to give you a blowjob?"

"Is that even a question? I remember every time with you."

I pull her tighter to my chest before she continues. "When I think back now, I see a barrage of triggers. It's like my brain was constantly on the cusp of letting me see. You were the first guy I ever dated that I didn't know beforehand. A part of me wonders if that's not why you triggered me. Every time with you was new, and it forced my brain to accept situations that I wouldn't usually subject myself to. Our first date at the pond, the blowjob, even the other day at the tree. You always pushed."

"Baby, I'm so damn sorry. I never meant to hurt you. I was only trying to love you."

Turning her head so she can see my face, she says, "I know that. Pushing me outside of my comfort zone wasn't hurting me, Holden. It was healing me. The pain was there before you came along, but I had to leave this place to be able to harness it. I can see that now. Back then, I thought I was less than, not good enough, not pretty enough, not worthy, if that makes sense. I think that's why I didn't dig, Holden. It's not that I didn't believe your words. I didn't believe in myself."

"Aria, you are so damn strong, pretty girl," I murmur against her mouth before I seal my lips over hers. Coaxing her mouth open, I dip my tongue to find hers more than willing to receive.

Reaching her arm behind her back, she strokes my cock.

"The praise, Holden. You were the first to talk dirty to me, to tell me how good it was, the first to give and not take." I know what she's saying. I made her feel comfortable because I showered her with affirmations that she was perfect. After all, she was and is. Those words battled her demons, and I was the first to give her an orgasm. I suck the spot behind her ear before nipping at her lobe and sucking it into my mouth.

"I'm still the only one, huh?" She squeezes me harder, and I'm sure if we weren't in the tub, there would be cum on my dick.

Turning her head, she bites her lip and says, "Well, technically—"

"Don't you dare finish that sentence." I cover her mouth with mine and dive deep, taking what's mine. Sliding my hand down her stomach and between her thighs, I find her clit and start rubbing slow, teasing circles. She said she was sore, so I keep it light. Placing her hand over mine, she takes my fingers and moves them lower. "You want my fingers in that pretty pussy, baby?"

As I dip my fingers in, she lets out a slow, delicate moan into my mouth before saying, "No, I want your cock in my pussy."

"Fuck, baby. Do you know how hot it is when you talk dirty to me?" I steal her lips one more time, only breaking apart to say, "Ride me." Sitting forward, she rises to her knees to turn around, but when her perky ass peeks out of the water, dripping wet and covered in bubbles, I pounce. "Damn, I love this ass." I squeeze her cheeks and spread them before licking her straight up her center. Her entire back prickles with goosebumps. "Did you save this for me, baby?" She nods, and I slap her ass hard before saying, "Sit that pretty pussy on my cock before I do something you're not ready for."

Turning around, she straddles my legs, resting her hands on my shoulders as she lines herself up. When she sinks down onto my cock, we both let out delicious moans of rapture in tandem. Slowly, she starts to ride me with her head thrown back. Her perky tits subtly sway, and I can't help but squeeze one and pull her forward, bringing them to my mouth. As I suck and swirl my tongue around her nipple, her pussy pulses around my dick. I love how sensitive she is. "You still love getting these perfect tits sucked, baby. That pussy squeezes my cock so fucking good when these gorgeous tits are in my mouth."

When I move my mouth to the other breast, I suck harder, causing her to whimper, "Fuck, yes," before she picks up her pace. The water is now lapping out of the tub as she rides me hard.

"Baby, I thought you were sore," I rasp out, so turned on by this fiend. Aria and I always had great sex, but I had to give it to her. Now she fucking takes it. Last night, she put my hands where she wanted them and told me to suck her tits, and it was hot.

I know what my girl likes, but I love that she feels comfortable enough to demand it. I want to give her what she wants. She doubles down, sending the water out of the tub in waves. "That's it, baby, fucking take it." Biting her bottom lip, she tries to stifle the sexy noises she makes with my dick buried deep in her pussy. Reaching up, I pull her lip out of her teeth with my thumb. "Fuck that. Let me hear how much you missed me."

With her ass cheeks in my hands, I spread them, making room to run my finger over her puckered hole. When I dip inside, she cries, "Ah yes, that's so good." Her pussy really starts to clench my dick.

"Shit, baby, you're choking my cock. You need to get there." Once my finger is fully seated, she goes off. Hands in my hair, she tugs and pulls as she grinds her clit against my pubic bone.

"Holden, I love you so much, baby." As if the scene alone wasn't enough to undo me, those words from her mouth shatter me, and I explode. Both hands immediately fly to her waist as I hold her tight and shoot my seed deep, ensuring no drop is wasted. Her lips find mine and her tongue goes deep as she slowly rocks back and forth on me, coming down from her release.

In the other room, I hear my alarm sound again. *Shit.* That's my protein shake alarm. I always set the alarm to ensure I drink my shake precisely twenty minutes after my run. Pulling back from her kiss, I say, "Pretty girl, I want nothing more than to spend the day with you, but I seriously have to get going for my game." She pecks my lips, swings her leg off me to dismount, and lays against the tub's ledge, fully sated and bathed in that just-fucked afterglow.

"God, you're beautiful." I place a kiss on her cheek and climb out. Then, grabbing a towel, I say, "Take your time, baby. I'll meet you downstairs, but heads up, Connor and Spencer are here." Her eyes pop open real quick, and she splashes me.

"Hey!" I wipe the towel over my face.

"That would have been nice to know before you let me scream. The entire house probably heard me."

I throw her a wink, and because I can't help myself, I add, "I know."

Aria has never been a quiet fuck, and I love it. She loves every fucking inch I give her. Connor and Spencer hearing her intoxicating mewls was not my intent, but I won't apologize for it either. Exiting the bathroom, I head over to my phone and silence the alarm before getting ready.

~

I've just finished shaking up my protein drink when Spencer walks into the kitchen. From the look on his face, he's a mixture of pissed and sick. I want details on what happened last night, but I'll get them from Con, not him. I'm not dumb enough to think I'm in his good graces just because Aria has accepted me back into her life.

Spencer takes a seat at the island and doesn't say anything. Instead, he openly glares at me with enough hate and malice that this entire house would burn if it was tangible. Luckily, I'm saved from his malevolent ire when Connor rounds the corner with Summer in his arms.

"Uncle H!" she squeals in delight when she sees me. Connor sets her down, and she scurries around the counter for me to pick her up. "Did you know my ceiling glows with stars?"

I throw her up into the air and say, "Yeah, who do you think put them all the way up there?"

She smiles. "I knew it was you. You remembered when I said I wanted stars like my friend Lena has in her room."

I tap her nose. "Of course I remembered."

Connor has already popped waffles into the toaster for her and poured her a glass of milk, and because I didn't buy either of those things, I'm starting to think Connor is going to be here more often than not. But before I let that happen, we need to talk. Last night only confirmed what I've suspected for years. As happy-go-lucky as Connor appears on the outside, he has a lot of dark in him, just like me. The darkness isn't what bothers me. It's the fact that he felt he couldn't share his even after I revealed mine. But I'm grateful as much as I am mad at him. I think whatever secrets he's harboring aided him in taking care of our problem with Rainer last night.

"Yeah, I'll be on the next flight out. No, don't be sorry. You have nothing to apologize for. I'll see you tonight." Aria hangs up her phone as she pulls out a stool right next to Spencer.

Her face is clear of any makeup, her hair is tied up in a messy bun atop her head, and she's wearing one of my t-shirts and a pair of my compression tights, looking fucking perfect. But when Spencer says, "What do you mean you're flying out?" My jaw clenches in frustration. She said she would stay the week. I just got her back.

"One of my patients has an event on Friday, and the anxiety is getting to her. She's been in and out of treatment for months now, but her recent stint out has been her longest, and I'm hoping to get her over the hump this time around. Maggie holds a special place in my heart, so I go the extra mile for her."

Spencer gets up and walks over to my refrigerator, making himself at home as he searches through it before he finds what he wants. He pulls out yogurt and then proceeds to open all my drawers one by one until I pull out the one right next to me and say, "Spoon?" Scowling, his eyes narrow on mine in annoyance before he walks over, grabs one, and places it and the yogurt in front of Aria. Damn it. That should have been my move, but she's fine. Right?

Aria looks healthy, and her job is to help other people with their own eating therapy. When I hear him mumble, "Sorry, old habits," I feel my body noticeably deflate. She's fine.

Patting his back, she reassures him. "It's cool. I get it."

Summer decides to add in her two cents with a big bite of waffle in her mouth. "When will you be back to play Barbies?"

Licking her spoon, Aria replies, "Umm, I don't know, princess. I don't live here, so it might be a while."

I've been biting my tongue, but that's over. "What the hell are you talking about, Aria?"

Furrowing her brow, she looks at Summer and says, "Ears! Holden, what did you think was going to happen? I live in California, my job and my home are there."

I slam my bottle on the counter, thoroughly enraged. We haven't had time to discuss us or our future, but I thought I made it pretty damn clear last night that this was her home, and I was her man.

Running my hands through my hair, I start to pace. "Aria, I just got you back. You said you'd stay the week. How the hell am I supposed to go play a game now?"

Shrugging, she takes a bite of her yogurt as if completely unaffected by all this and says, "Same way you always have. Drown out the noise."

Placing my hands on my hips, I hold her eyes and say, "My motivation isn't the same, Aria. That's not going to work."

Spencer smirks and adds, "Oh, you mean because you're no longer dedicating your career to some dead guy who tied my sister to a tree, and you knew it and still memorialized him anyway?"

"Spencer!" Aria scolds.

"No, fuck that, Aria. He doesn't just get a free pass from me. He knew!"

"Summer, can you go upstairs and get your Barbies? We're going to head out." Connor sets Summer down off the stool, and she skips off down the hall. Then, reaching into his pocket, Connor pulls out an old flip phone. My fucking phone that I'm positive was in my safe. I should be pissed, but I bite my tongue when he sets it down in front of Aria. She deserves to see it. "Here, this is what he knew." Aria's eyes flash to mine. I know she recognizes that phone. She made fun of it countless times while we were dating; now, she knows why I kept it. It held his last text and the picture of those haunted eyes. Her eyes.

When Connor's gaze pops up to meet mine, I know he can read my expression without words. We will be having some discussions about his access to my house. Even in light of these new revelations, I trust Connor explicitly, but there should be boundaries.

Aria's eyes are pinned to the phone, and she's toying with opening it. Probably nervous about what she might find. Her gaze lands on mine one more time, and I see it. She wants to open it, but not if I don't want to share it. Putting her at ease, I say, "Do it, Aria. No more secrets."

When she flips the phone open, Spencer scoots in to see the picture for himself. The image is dark. Apart from shadows cut by firelight, you can't make out anything except those eyes that penetrate the darkness and pierce the soul. And as fucked up as it sounds, I would go through all of this again if it meant I got to keep her. I've spent most of my life hating the darkness surrounding my every waking moment, seeping over into all that I touched, but it also brought me to the most beautiful thing I've ever known. She is all the light to my dark, and stars can't shine without darkness.

Rising from her stool, she comes around the counter and throws her arms around my waist, holding me tight as I wrap my arms around her, determined to never let her go. "You couldn't have known. There's no way to tell that's me. I only know it's me because I lived it, and those shadows are ones I'll never forget." Her last comment catches me off guard, and I see Con and

Spencer share a glance, making my jaw clench in irritation. I want the details on what went down last night.

Summer comes running back into the kitchen. "I'm ready, Daddy."

Aria unwraps herself and heads over to her, and I'm immediately jealous. Bending down, she asks, "Hey, I was wondering. Do you have any mermaids at home?"

Summer nibbles her lip in thought before answering. "No, but that's because Daddy says mermaids aren't real."

She throws Connor a wink over her shoulder before saying, "Well, I happen to live by the ocean, and I saw one swimming in the bay the other week. What if I bring you back a mermaid?"

Summer's eyes go wide before she says, "Oh please, oh please, oh pretty please. That would be the best!" She jumps up and down and throws her arms around Aria, making me sick to my stomach. If Aria hadn't miscarried, that could be us. That could be her talking to our daughter. God, I don't want her to go.

Walking over, Connor swoops Summer up into his arms. "Okay, say bye. We have to go see Grandma so Daddy can get to work." Connor started working with his dad a few years ago. The fucker is smart as hell. Unlike me, he wanted to follow in his dad's footsteps. He always knew he'd get his law degree and work for his dad, which makes me wonder why he'd get involved with anything that could jeopardize that.

Spencer stands and says, "Hey, wait up. I'll walk you out."

Spencer's desire to walk Connor out only further serves to piss me off, because I know they're talking about shit I need to know. Not to mention, I hate how Connor so quickly cozies up to people, especially my girl, and now her brother, while I'm over here grasping at straws. Usually, I would demand they fucking say what they need to say in front of me, but I need to talk to my girl.

"Aria, I thought I made it clear last night that I want you here with me in this house."

She rolls her eyes before saying, "Yes, you made all that clear, but we haven't discussed anything. You can't expect me to drop everything and come running just because you said, let's date again. I love you, Holden, so damn much, and I don't want to be halfway across the country, but—"

"Then don't go. Stay."

"I'll fly out this weekend, or maybe you can come to see me?" She sheepishly shrugs. "Please don't make this any harder than it already is." Walking around the counter, I pull her into my arms and breathe her in as I let her words reassure me that this isn't goodbye.

Pulling back, I take her head between my hands and say, "Promise me you're not running."

She gives me a coy smile before answering. "If I am, will you chase me?"

I walk her back until her ass hits the island and say, "I'll chase you to the ends of the Earth," before kissing her long and slow. I feel her nipples pebble under my shirt, and I'm reminded she's not wearing a bra or panties. I groan into her mouth, drunk off the way this woman sets me on fire with one taste.

With one last kiss, I draw back and squeeze her ass before asking, "Do you think I put a baby in you last night?"

She kisses my lips softly before saying, "I hope not. I'm on the pill."

"What the fuck do you mean, you hope not?" Of course, Spencer chooses that moment to stroll back in.

"It means she's keeping her options open and deserves someone who wants to do more than just knock her up." Then, turning to Aria, he says, "Let's go. I'm coming with you to California."

Aria tries to push me back. I still have her pinned between myself and the island, but I bring my hands down around her, caging her in so she can't leave. Bringing my eyes to hers, I say, "You want a ring, baby? I'll give you a ring. I'll give you everything. Just say you're mine."

Bringing her hands to my hips, a move that she knows drives me crazy, she says, "You already know I'm yours. Always have been. But this time, I need more." Then, placing a light kiss on the corner of my mouth, she adds, "I loved you then, I love you now, I'll love you always."

This time, when she moves to step away, I let her, because I don't know what this is. There is no way she's running. This is something different. She knows I'll give her the world. I just all but told her I'd marry her, and I'm not convinced I didn't fucking knock her up. So, what is this? I'm still processing that thought when she walks out of the kitchen with Spencer.

When I look at the clock, it's almost noon, and I need to be at the stadium. Damn it.

# 22

## CHOICES

ARIA

"Now that we have boarded the plane, will you tell me why you insisted on coming back to California with me?" Spencer hasn't given me anything since we left Holden's place this morning. I've been given zero details about what happened last night or why he now needs to come home with me, but I'm done with the secrets.

"Do you remember the night of my twenty-fifth birthday when we went bar hopping, and Tony told you I wouldn't be able to keep the guys off you anymore?" I have no clue where he's going with this, but I bite.

"Yes, I remember. You felt like an ass because you thought guys not hitting on me contributed to the way I saw myself." I watch as he pinches the bridge of his nose before running his forefinger between his eyes.

"That comment was so much more than you understand, Aria. Tony legitimately is a good guy, but not all the guys in my crew were. You know I hung with anybody and everybody, but there was a reason for that. It was to protect you. That was always my goal—to protect you—and you still got hurt." His talking in circles is driving me nuts. I'm not some delicate flower who can't handle the truth.

"Stop talking in riddles, Spencer, and spit it the fuck out. I'm a grown-ass woman who can more than handle the truth."

He turns to me with a pinched expression before saying, "It's not that I don't think you can handle the truth, Aria. I was there last night. I know what you endured. It doesn't mean I'm ready to deal with everything." My heart sinks into my stomach as I contemplate what potentially went down last night.

In hushed tones, I ask, "Did you kill him?"

"Did you really just ask me that?" he queries in disbelief.

I shrug, throwing my hands up and adding. "Well, I don't know. You're being elusive, and it can't be that bad if you didn't kill him."

"You don't find it coincidental that Rainer left right after your incident, never to return until this weekend?"

This weekend held absolutely no significance apart from my reconnecting with Holden. I don't see how that is relevant to Rainer returning to town, so I say, "You're going to have to give me more, Spence. I'm not following you."

"He was sent back, Aria. That night you caught more than one guy doing things that certain people don't want getting out. You know Uncle Lewis has a seat in the House. I'd like to believe he'd support Rainer if he opened up about his proclivities regardless of his re-electability; however, the other two guys are a different story."

"Who are the other two guys, Spence?"

The flight attendant walks by to take our drink orders. Spence orders an orange juice, two vodkas, and a Bloody Mary for me. After our drinks are poured and we've both had a few sips, he finally says, "Only one matters: Tyler Marx. His dad is the current conservative frontrunner for the open Supreme Court seat. He was the guy you caught fucking Rainer in the ass."

I take another long swig of my drink. "I knew none of those guys. I only knew Rainer."

Opening his second bottle of vodka, he throws it back in one go before pulling his phone out and showing me a picture of Rainer with some guy and a girl in between them. Searching my face for a reaction, he says, "That's Tyler. His face isn't familiar to you?"

Scanning my memory bank, I say, "No, I don't recognize him." Rubbing his hand over his jaw, I can see that my response bothers him. "Are you going to tell me why that pisses you off?"

"This morning, you mentioned shadows you would never forget. Did those shadows have faces?"

"Spence, I meant that metaphorically. I was only thirteen. Hell, my mind chose to block out the entire night from me for years."

He slams his fist down on the armrest. "That's what's so fucked up, Aria. You're fucking innocent. Always have been. I protected you. I never knew about that night. If I had, we wouldn't be here now. But they're coming after you because they think you'd out Tyler if you got your memories back, not just for his tastes, but for the entire night. Tying you up to a tree for attempted rape and forced copulation. The girl in the picture standing between Rainer and Tyler is Ava Cross. She went missing two weeks ago. She was at the bonfire that night after you had already been taken back to the car. Apparently, she came to pick up Tyler but caught him and Rainer moving your limp body into the car. Tyler kept her quiet by keeping her around. Rainer said she stopped cooperating and then disappeared. His story is that he came back for you."

A chill runs down my spine. "You think he came back to hurt me?"

Spencer finishes his drink before saying, "He claimed he was back to help you, but that doesn't add up, because he tried to run at Holden's. When my flight arrived, I ran into Rainer at the airport, which caught him off guard. In hindsight, I don't think he planned on making his presence known. He had nothing with him, no luggage, not even a backpack, and was acting very skittish the entire way over to Holden's. Either way, it doesn't matter. We dealt with it."

"What do you mean you dealt with it?"

He clenches his fist. "That's something you don't need to know. I'm not worried about Rainer. It's Tyler I'm worried about. That's why I'm coming to San Diego with you."

I can't help but balk at that. "So, what? You're my personal bodyguard now? Spence, you just landed your residency in Baltimore. I'm surprised you're even on this plane."

Rubbing his temples, clearly frustrated, he adds, "I know, Aria. I've got it handled. I'm just transporting you. Nate will handle it when we land."

My eyebrows shoot up to my hairline as my eyes go wide. "What the hell are you talking about? Nate and I broke up. I am not his responsibility, and I don't need a bodyguard. This is absurd."

"Damn it, Aria!" he yells, drawing the attention of a few surrounding passengers. Spencer doesn't lose his cool. The fact that he is now tells me I need to back off. "You don't get to know everything. Not this time. You spent the last year with Nate. He's a good guy, and he's Connor's cousin—"

"What does him being Connor's cousin have to do with anything? You didn't even know Connor until last night."

"I'm just saying, Nathan Keller isn't a bad guy to have around until you figure out your shit with Holden. He has already agreed to pick you up from the airport and will stay with you and Olivia. I'm not giving you anything else, so leave it. If you want more, try talking to him." I decide to drop it, for now anyway. By the way things are going, all I'm going to accomplish is further pissing him off, and I'd rather spend this time catching up. It's been months since I saw Spencer.

"When we land, you're catching a plane back to Baltimore?"

His body visibly relaxes, grateful I'm heeding his demands. "Yes. I only planned on dropping in for the night to surprise you,

Mom, and Dad. It's been five years since they had both of us under the same roof. Clearly, that didn't go to plan." He gives me a sad smile before resting his head against the seatback and adding, "I don't hate him, you know."

I fidget in my seat, unsure which him he's referring to, Rainer or Holden, but then he continues. "Holden fucked up, and I wanted to blame him because it gave me something tangible to fault and hold accountable for the suffering I witnessed while you were in the hospital. I'm not over it. He's not getting a free pass. The fact still remains that he broke my sister's heart, but there is no denying he cares about you. I knew that back then, and I believe it's still true now."

A tear falls down my cheek. Throwing my arms around him, I give him a giant bear hug. "Thanks, Spence. That means everything." Pulling back, I wipe my eyes before adding, "The ball is in his court. I gave him everything before; it wasn't enough then, and while I'd like to believe his words now, I need more."

Furrowing his brow in confusion, he says, "He all but proposed to you before we walked out of the house. What more could you possibly want?"

Without pause, I answer, "I need him to put me first."

I'm not signing up to be the housewife who gives up her goals and aspirations while her man puts his career ahead of home and family. I want it all. Don't get me wrong, I want it all with him, but I'm not settling. He'll either figure it out, or he won't. I know what I'm asking, but I also know I'm worth it.

~

It's been two days since I returned to San Diego. I've spoken with Holden on the phone every night, and we text each other constantly throughout the day. I miss him so much it hurts. It's a real struggle daily not to book a ticket and fly back to St. Louis, but I don't. When he broke up with me the first time, he told me that I didn't deserve to be put on the back burner. His choice to prioritize baseball then didn't bother me, but, for some reason, it does now. In the back of my mind, I'm competing with a sport for his heart. Maybe that's because it was the reason he gave for pushing me aside before, and even though it wasn't true, some part of me still believes he'd do it again—no matter how much his words might say the opposite. I can't stop loving him, but I won't settle for less than I deserve. He said he'd chase me to the ends of the Earth. So far, that hasn't happened.

"Aria, are you borrowing my white dress tonight?" Olivia calls out from her en suite bath as I rummage through her closet. She always has the best stuff. I've never been one to skimp out on my clothing either, but nothing in my closet spoke to me tonight, so I'm taking a peek inside hers.

"I don't know. Nothing is calling to me. Do you think I should wear white? I thought that black dress with the low dip in front would be perfect for tonight since it's a cocktail party."

Coming around the corner with a towel on her head and one wrapped around her torso, she says, "Yes, that one would be perfect. Check the closet in the guest bedroom. It's been a while since I wore that one." *Great.* Now I have to see Nate.

Nate has been staying with us for two days since I got home. We don't talk. When he picked me up from the airport, his expression was sympathetic until it wasn't. It's been one of indifference ever since. I feel like I screwed him over, but the truth is, we did that to ourselves. He clearly had his own secrets, which he never felt compelled to share, but because I had my own as well, now I'm the bad guy.

Steeling my spine, I knock on the door to the guest bedroom that he's occupied since we arrived. But, of course, when it opens, I'm smacked in the face with his alluring cologne. The man has always smelled amazing. It didn't matter if he was just lounging around the house; he always had on a captivating scent. Nate likes to take care of himself, and I can't fault him for that, but when I'm trying to forget that he isn't mine anymore, it sucks.

Giving me a once-over, he gives me a sexy smirk before asking, "Is there a reason you're knocking on my door in a silk robe instead of tonight's attire?"

Rolling my eyes, I push past him and into the room. "You can stop flirting, Nate. You're my date tonight regardless. We both know you more than hate me now, and I deserve it. I'm just here to rummage through the closet, and I'll be on my way."

I'm just opening the closet door when his hand finds my hip, and he asks, "Can we talk for a minute?"

He sits on the end of the bed before gesturing for me to do so as well. Once I've sat, we both sit there in silence, drinking each other in. I feel shitty about how I ended things with Nate. Basically, I saw my ex, jumped on his dick, and told Nate to fuck off. It's pretty messed up, and I'm not proud of it. But I can't change it. It is what it is, but that doesn't mean I don't regret how I acted toward a man who only ever showed me kindness.

"Aria, I don't hate you. Over the past week, I've wished I could do as much, but I can't. I've replayed Holden fucking you countless times, trying to find the hate inside of me, but all I can do is wish it was me."

Pulling in a deep breath, he pauses, and I start, "Nate, look I'm—"

Shaking his head, he cuts me off. "No, don't do that. Don't say you're sorry. You shouldn't feel sorry for going after what's in your heart. I have my own regrets too. Over the past year, I never tried for more. I was content letting you call the shots, and I told myself it was out of respect for whatever sordid past you went through. We both had our secrets, Aria. I'm not fucking innocent in all this."

I reach out and place my hand over his in comfort. It's evident that he's struggling with something. Staring at my hand atop his, he says, "I felt safe with you, Aria, for the same reasons you felt safe with me. The only difference is my mind never hid my ghosts from me."

Those words are like a knife to the heart. Memories of the past year we spent together come rushing back, and scenes that felt so intimate then feel even more powerful now because I know the pain he was fighting. I know without words, intimacy was his weakness too. That's why he never pushed. He more than understood. When his eyes find mine, I say, "That's how you knew."

Pulling my hand to his heart, he says, "No. I could never know that, but I spent years in counseling when I was younger. I saw the signs. I listened and watched. At the end of the day, it was a suspicion, one I never hid from you, Aria, but one I would never push on you. Your mind dealt with it the way that it did for a reason. The day you shared yourself with me in the shower, I was terrified that I'd shattered whatever barriers you had built."

Before he can utter another word, I'm in his lap, curling into him like I would when we were together. I need him to hold me, but what's more, I want to comfort him, because while I don't know the details of his past that haunt him, I'm sure my reaction was more than jarring. "I'm sorry, Nate. I didn't know." I never would have suspected any of this.

He holds me tight, and we stay that way for long moments before he finally says, "You should probably get ready. It's getting late." I nod against his chest and pull myself out of his embrace for what I'm sure will be the last time.

Stepping out of Nate's Mercedes AMG, it's hard not to feel bougie. We are attending a party at a celebrity's house, and my dress cost nearly two thousand dollars. I feel like an impostor, but I'd be lying if I said seeing how the other half lives isn't intriguing. While I've been to the Harrisons' many times, I've never attended a social event like this.

Party planners have clearly taken over the entire property. It's almost unrecognizable. My nerves must be showing because as Nate rounds the car to walk with me, he clasps my hand and gently squeezes before asking, "Are you okay?"

I give him a half smile and say, "I'm good; this is just crazy. I've never been to something so elaborate—at a house, for that matter."

We both turn toward the yard and take in the sight. Tree trunks are wrapped in white lights up through their limbs as round Edison bulb lights hang from their branches alongside Spanish moss, creating a truly breathtaking whimsical ambiance. White roses overflow dozens of lit glass cylinder vases that now line the property's perimeter. The entire scene is indeed decadent.

As we walk up the staircase, servers are holding trays of pink fizzy cocktails that appear to be smoking. Nate grabs two, and we both take a drink as we continue through the front doors. We've barely made our way through the door when Maggie screeches from the top of the staircase. "Aria Montgomery, get your sexy ass over here!"

Nate places a kiss on my cheek before nodding down the hall. "I'll be around."

I give him a soft smile and answer, "Okay."

Apparently, Maggie didn't want me to come upstairs because she is already halfway down the grand staircase when I look up. I meet her halfway, and we hug. "Maggie, you look absolutely breathtaking tonight." Maggie has long red hair, fair skin, and the biggest brown eyes I've ever seen. "This dress looks amazing on you." It's black with a nude underlay only covering her private parts. Very sexy.

"You're one to talk. I'm still not convinced we share the same past. Aria, I swear on my life you are one of the prettiest people I've ever met. If Nate doesn't put a ring on it soon, I have an entire room full of men out there who would be more than happy to fill his shoes." I don't correct her. Tonight isn't the time to get into everything that has happened over the past week.

Linking arms, we stroll toward the back of the house, and I ask, "How are you doing?" She gives me knowing eyes that say everything. She's nervous as hell and dying inside.

"I have taken two Xanax, but now that you're here, I'm starting to feel more relaxed." I squeeze her arm. There's a lot to be said about the moral support of a friend who shares the same traumas. They know without words everything you're feeling, because sometimes you don't want to talk about it; you just need someone to understand that you feel a certain type of way, and no words can make it better. For that reason, there was no way I would have ever missed out on tonight.

Heading out the back door and into the garden, it's every bit as beautiful as the front, but amplified. The trees are all adorned with the same lighting, but there are private cabanas in a few nooks, while the middle of the yard houses a low-sitting table that almost runs the length of the property, embellished with giant cushions for seating. It's very intimate.

"Let's get cocktails." She pulls me over to the bar set up out in the far corner of the yard and orders two glasses of pinot. Maggie has just handed me my glass when a hand caresses my lower back, startling me until I turn to find Nate. We haven't been here that long, and typically, he would be networking at a function like this, so him being at my side is somewhat perplexing.

Tilting his head, he signals for me to follow. I excuse myself. "Maggie, I'll be right back."

She calls out rather loudly as I walk off, "You better be proposing since you're stealing my date." Nate thins his lips but doesn't respond as we walk toward one of the empty cabanas.

"What's up? I'm surprised you're not networking. Do I need Maggie to go find Tom?" He doesn't say a word, just stares at me with an unreadable expression, giving me pause. What feels like long moments pass before I finally ask, "Should I be worried?" Nate's been staying with Olivia and me for protection, which spikes my awareness.

My eyes quickly scan the yard, but when he pulls me into him, I know I've read it wrong. "No, Aria, you shouldn't be worried. I just wanted to say goodbye."

My heart skips a beat, and I'm sure confusion mars my face when I question, "You're leaving? We just got here."

He tucks a loose strand of hair behind my ear before he says, "In case I didn't tell you earlier, you look breathtaking tonight."

Placing a kiss on my forehead, he releases my shoulders and walks away, leaving me mystified by his sudden and abrupt departure. When my feet decide to move and follow after him, my eyes lock onto a set of pale blues that stop me in my tracks.

He came.

## 23

# UGLY TRUTHS

## HOLDEN

Fate is a twisted, sick bitch. I can't believe the hand I was dealt this week. The love of my life rolled back in without warning, turning my life upside down in the best and worst of ways. I got my girl back only to discover we shared the same night of horrors. It doesn't matter how many times I remind myself that I wasn't at the bonfire that night or how I would have never let that shit happen, I always return to the fact that I killed my best friend and couldn't save the girl. I've carried that guilt with me every day until, finally, she came back and released me.

The detailed account of what happened that night doesn't absolve me from taking my best friend's life; that pain will forever live inside me, but she is my light in the dark. For years, I tried to understand what Luke was thinking that night. The guy I knew would never have treated a girl that way, and now I finally have answers. Finding out Aria's truth led us to Rainer, who was a key piece of the puzzle for her and me.

After Tuesday night's game, Connor filled me in on everything that went down when he and Spencer left. Rainer's fuck buddy, Tyler, was the supplier of the evening, and the joints he passed out were laced with PCP. PCP caused Luke to lose his mind and do shit that was entirely out of his character. Knowing that he didn't consciously sign up to take street drugs and tie a girl to a tree was groundbreaking. I feel like I got my best friend back in a way, and I could breathe again.

Living out our shared dream wasn't just for me to feel better about taking his life and doing what he could no longer do for himself. It was about redemption for the guy I knew every day before that horrible night, and now that I have all the pieces, I know he hasn't been cursing me from the grave I put him in. He'd want me to live my life to the fullest, and that's what I plan to do.

I've been losing my fucking mind the past few days we've been apart. I'm unsure how I managed to pitch in Tuesday night's game after she left. I was sick to my stomach with regret the entire time, wanting to do nothing more than walk off the mound and fly to California to get my girl. The rest doesn't matter if she's not by my side.

When she walked out of my kitchen, I wanted to chase her down, but I couldn't make my legs move because I didn't understand how the woman I loved could walk away after the breakthrough we had just had. I was taken back to five years earlier when I broke her pretty heart the first time, and she didn't fight for me, for us. It wasn't until Connor showed up and knocked some sense into me that I understood.

Sitting in the car outside the Harrisons' elaborate cocktail party, I'm a ball of nerves. Sure, we've talked every day on the phone, and I feel like I've heard the pain and longing in her voice, but I could just be hearing the things I want to hear instead of what's really in her heart. She left.

"Get out of the car, prick! We've been over this. She fought for you the other night and did exactly what you asked. You told her to dig, and she did, like a fucking champ. Now it's your turn. Stop being a chump and go get your girl. If not, I have no problem filling in."

Reaching over, I punch him in the arm hard. "Dick." Connor is constantly fucking around when it comes to Aria.

"Did it work?"

I shake my head and mumble a few choice words before saying, "Yeah, it worked." He pulled me out of my doubts. I have never been insecure, but when it comes to Aria, I'm more than apprehensive; I'm scared shitless. She's all I want. *Damn it.* I'm doing it again. "Remind me again why I'm not the guy that gets to fuck up the asshole who dares to hurt my girl?"

"Holden, I know you want a piece. I know you want to take him down for attempting to hurt Aria, but your face is too well-recognized. You'll draw attention that I don't need. Tyler will be handled, and if for some reason he's not, that Glock needs to stay on your person. Let me handle this. You're not done playing your part."

I run my hand over my jaw, extremely perturbed by all of this. Aria is my girl. Mine to protect. Not to mention, the guy who managed to breach my walls lied to me. "I'm always packing, but for the record, I'm not over the fact that you've been leading this double life. I mean seriously, Con–this shit is crazy."

He can tell I'm unnerved by all of this. No one would have ever suspected how layered the Callahan's history with Aria was, let alone the depth of their work. I was livid when he got to my house, and he filled me in on all the details of what went down with Rainer. Connor should have told me immediately that Aria was in danger not hours after I let her leave my side unprotected, but he had his reasons.

The only reason I didn't get on a plane minutes after Connor filled me in was because he needed me to keep up the charade. According to Rainer, who I plan to strangle with my bare hands, Tyler hasn't come after her because he knew she didn't remember. However, Tyler is fully aware of my part in that night, and our connection—has been from day one, along with Rainer. Aria and I getting back together would trigger Tyler to come for her. Of course, this comes from Rainer, whose intel and intentions are still questionable. Regardless, he's been chained in the basement of Connor's house for the past week.

"You're going to walk in there and get your girl back while I take care of Tyler Marx." My jaw clenches of its own accord, fucking pissed that any of this is necessary. I swear, if anything happens to her, I'd murder everyone involved. I already have blood on my hands. What's a little more? "Get out, bro! I need to go," Connor urges.

"Yeah, yeah, I'm out. Let me know as soon as it's handled. I'm fucking serious." The second I'm out, he says, "It's what I do, Holden. Get out of the car." I slam the door, and he takes off.

I suspected Connor had dealings on the side; I just didn't realize their extent, depth, or importance. After I shared my picture and story with Connor two years ago, our friendship changed. Suddenly, I saw a side of him I had no idea existed. Connor always seemed way too outgoing and charismatic to have any darkness inside, but I've always said that dark calls to dark, and I've yet to be proven wrong.

This week killed me. Knowing Aria was with Nate cut deep. All I could think about was her taking him back because he was there, not me. Were it not for Con filling me in on his past and the fact that he's involved in the family business, I would have said fuck devising a plan. I only stayed away so we could set the trap.

On my way up the stairs, I slam two pink fizzy drinks the attendants offered, trying to calm my nerves. I told the woman I'd fucking marry her and that I want her to have my babies. I fucking told her I wanted everything, and she left. But I know what she wanted. Hell, I knew what she wanted before she left my house, and I didn't stop her.

Truth be told, we both needed to take a breather. I have no doubt that she's it for me, but I think the space was needed to solidify what we both already know. We are meant to be.

Now, the only thing standing between me and my girl is me.

Walking through the house, I keep my head down to avoid drawing attention. More than half the people here would recognize me, and I'm not in the mood for small talk. I need Aria. Connor texted Nate when we arrived, and he confirmed they were outside. Passing through the back doors, I stand on the back patio, scanning the yard for Aria or Nate, until I see both of them standing off to the side in a cabana. My chest tightens with anxiety. I want to storm across the yard and pull her into my arms, but I also need to watch this play out.

I know Aria cares for Nate on some level. Hell, I think he might have ended up being her man if I hadn't shown up. She spent the past year with him. He made her feel safe, but I need to know if the past few days changed anything for her. Nate rubs her shoulders before pulling her in and kissing her forehead in a nonsexual way that still manages to spike my anger. He knows I'm here for her. Then, before I get a chance to boil over, he walks away, leaving her standing in the cabana alone. I have no idea what words were exchanged, but she looks confused.

For a second, I wonder if she regrets ending things with him —until her head snaps up and out of her daze. When those beautiful brown eyes land on mine, they knock the air out of my lungs because it's then that I see it. *She's mine.* This is precisely what she wanted. Me.

We both start crossing the yard at the same hurried pace and meet in the middle, where she throws her arms around me, nuzzles her face into my neck, and says, "You came." *Fuck.* Those words pierce my heart.

Pulling her head back, I make sure her eyes are on mine when I say, "Did you think I wouldn't?" I have my answer when she sucks that bottom lip into her mouth. Once again, she doubted me. Taking her hand, I lead her around the side of the house and away from prying eyes.

"Holden, stop. I can't leave. I'm here for my patient, remember?"

"Aria, I'm here for my girl, and that's you. I'm not leaving, but I'll be damned if I'm going to be interrupted kissing you." Before she can process my words, my mouth is on hers, parting her lips and taking what's mine. When I feel her kiss me back with the same vigor, I'm a goner, groaning into her mouth and rock hard. Her hand slides down my chest, blazing a trail of heat in its wake.

She momentarily pauses when she hits my belt, before reaching down further to run her hand over my erection. A deep, heady moan fills my mouth when she feels how turned on I am. "Fuck, baby, you want me to take you right here?" In response, she starts unbuckling my belt. *Shit.* That's when I feel my Glock begin to slip. *Damn it.*

"Baby..." I place kisses down her neck as she slides her hand into my pants, grabbing my cock to stroke it. "Fuck, that's good." Clutching her hand, I halt her movement. Her eyes snap to mine and narrow in question. "Don't look at me like that, pretty girl. You can feel every fucking inch wants that sweet pussy." I feel a bead of cum drip from my dick at the mere thought of her sheathed around my cock.

"Then fuck me. I'll be quiet. I need you." My mouth covers hers as I lean down and lift her. Her legs instantly wrap around my waist, and I walk toward the side of the house. As long as my pants don't come down, I shouldn't have to explain the gun tucked in the back and ruin the moment. "Not here, Holden. There." She points to a shed.

"Pretty girl, you're a genius." I carry her over to the shed, ensuring my lips never leave hers, and swing the door open before placing her on a workbench. "Baby, you're so beautiful, but you're never wearing this dress again. No fucking bra." I easily slip a tit out of the exposed deep V that runs down the center and pop it into my mouth.

"God, yes, Holden. I love how you suck my tits." She holds my head against her chest as I let my hand trail up her leg until I reach the apex of her thighs and find her bare, and I'm instantly mad.

Releasing her tit, I find her eyes and growl, "No fucking panties!" to which she bites her lip, raises her knees so that her feet rest on the bench, and spreads her legs.

"Fuck me, baby." I'm so fucking pissed and turned on all at once.

Her pretty pink pussy is glistening and ready for my cock.

Bringing my index finger to her pussy, I run it down her center, keeping my eyes pinned on hers. Dipping one finger in, I pump her until her mouth goes slack. "You like that, pretty girl?"

With her eyes still on mine, she answers, "I'd like it more if you'd use that thick, hard cock." Fuck, that's hot. Withdrawing my fingers, I slap her pussy, and she startles before moaning out the pleasure from the hit.

"Tell me, Aria, how am I supposed to punish you for thinking it was okay to wear nothing underneath this dress or for doubting I'd come for you if you like it when I smack this pretty pussy?" That's when I know exactly what I'm going to do.

Bending down, I run my tongue through her folds, making her cry out, "Yes, baby, don't you dare stop." She's playing hardball now. Aria knows exactly how those words from her mouth unravel me. I spear my tongue into her as she grinds her pussy against my face. When I add a digit, I feel her clench, and I know she's getting close. I pump her a few more times before pulling out altogether.

Her chest is heaving, her cheeks are flushed, and her breasts are out and heavy with need from where she's been squeezing her nipples. "Why did you stop? You never stop." God, she's beautiful. *Fuck it.*

Withholding orgasms doesn't only punish her. It punishes me, and I need my girl. Pulling my cock out, I align it with her entrance and dip the head in. A whimper escapes her lips, and I pull back and say, "This is mine, Aria. If I'm not with you, this pussy...." I push into the hilt, "and these tits," I nip, suck, and kiss them before coming back to her mouth, "are covered. Do you understand?"

"Yes, god yes. Just fuck me already."

I bite her bottom lip before sucking it into my mouth and saying, "Hold on, baby. My cock missed you." She grabs the bar above her head used for hanging tools as I start pounding into her. Her tits are bouncing wildly as the sound and smell of our arousal permeates the tool shed. "Aria, you are so perfect, baby. You going to marry me and have my babies?" I look down, slowing my pace to watch my cock disappear inside of her, hoping to knock her up right now. When my eyes snap back up to hers, she's watching me, and I can't help but ask, "Is that a yes?"

Her eyes are heavily shrouded with lust, and she's on the cusp of coming when she pants out, "Are you seriously proposing while fucking me on a tool bench?"

Bringing my lips to her neck, I suck the spot she loves before saying, "Baby, I think I've proposed to you every time I've been inside you. I'm just hoping this time you say yes." Slowing my pace, I hit that spot deep that drives her crazy before adding, "Don't I give it to you good?"

I stroke her slowly, edging out her impending orgasm, dragging my tip over her bundle of nerves buried deep when finally she says, "Yes, god yes. I'll marry you, just don't—"

My mouth collides with hers before she can finish the sentence, making sure she knows without words the depth of my sincerity. I'm balls deep in the woman I love and on the brink of orgasm. I'll give her all the words she wants, but right now, I can only give her my body. Her pussy clenches down hard as she climaxes, and I roar out my release right behind her, holding her tight and not wanting to pull out. I want to lock every piece of this memory away forever. I want to live in this moment as long as I can.

Her hands sink into my hair as she drags her nails over my scalp. "Holden Hayes, I love you so damn much, but I need to get out of this shed. It's hot as hell."

I can't help but laugh because it is a fucking sauna in here. Reluctantly, I pull out and tuck myself back in, but not before catching a glimpse of cum dripping out of her, and fuck if that doesn't make me hard again. "Maybe you should lay down for a minute."

She's adjusting her breasts and tucking them back in when she asks, "Why do I need to lay down?"

My hand finds her pussy, and I rim my fingers around her

tight hole before pushing my seed back in. "I don't want this coming out."

Then, bringing her lips to mine, she kisses me long and deep before pulling back to say, "We have time for that. Besides, I'm on the pill. I already told you that."

When she hops off the bench, she quickly scans the shed, finds some paper towels, and uses them to clean herself up. Watching her wipe away my juices pisses me off. "Aria, I want you to go off the pill."

It's as if she doesn't hear my words or chooses to ignore them because she continues cleaning herself off before fixing her dress and saying, "Let's go."

As she attempts to exit the shed, I clasp her wrist. "Why are you ignoring me?"

Her eyes search mine with a pained expression before she says, "I'm not trying to. I just don't want to talk about this here. Can you please respect that?" Pulling her into me, I hold her tight as realization sets in. The last time she was pregnant, she lost the baby. She might want to have a baby with me, but it scares her.

No more words are spoken as we exit the shed and head back to the party. But, before we round the corner to enter the backyard, I take one last glance at the shed that made my dreams come true. Aria Montgomery said yes!

~

"I feel like these are all things you should have mentioned before we ever fucked in the shed, Holden! Like, oh hey, by the way, Tyler is in town for you, and your ex and Connor are out taking care of it!" She's stomping off down the hallway of my hotel, ready to bolt. I charge after her, grabbing her around the waist and carrying her back to my door.

"Aria, I didn't tell you at the party for this reason. Look how you're reacting."

"Holden, I swear to fuck, you better put me down this

instant. It's not just the party; you knew shit was going down all week and you didn't tell me!"

Flinging my door open, I gesture for her to walk in. "Can we please do this inside instead of in the hall?" She crosses her arms like a petulant child and stomps by me. *Thank fuck.*

"Aria, I'm telling you everything now; that should count for something. I never planned on keeping any of this from you. The plan was always to tell you everything. Did Nate happen to fill you in? Because he knew all along as well what was going down tonight."

She pulls out a chair from the counter and sits. "That's different. I didn't agree to marry Nate." I walked right into that one. I'm across the room faster than she can blink, pulling her into my arms.

"Baby, I wasn't trying to deceive you, I swear. We promised no more secrets, and I meant it. I was trying to protect you until I could be here in person."

"Tell me everything, Holden, and I mean everything!"

I eye the mini fridge across the room and say, "I promise, but let's get a drink." I nod across the room, and she agrees. As I go to the fridge, she heads to the couch, kicking her heels off and folding her legs under her as she sits. I pull out two beers, twist the tops off, and pass one to her before taking my seat across from her. After taking a long pull, I say, "I'm not sure where to start. I know Spencer told you things. What did he have to say?"

She quirks a brow before snapping back, "Nice try, Holden. Tell me what you know, and then I'll share what I know."

I can't help but shake my head in annoyance. "Aria, I'm not trying to leave things out."

Nodding, she says, "Good, then just start talking." This feistiness of hers is new. It's a part of her I always knew was there, but she was too conflicted to let out. I'd like to say I hate it, but I don't. It makes me want to bend her over and remind her who she's talking to.

"Aria, when you left Tuesday, I was stunned, completely

shocked by the events that had unfolded over the weekend. Reconnecting with you and getting my heart back was part of it, but then learning how intertwined our fates had always been was mind-blowing. Finding out the details didn't change anything for me. The only thing that could ever make me leave you is you. If you wished it, if you wanted it, I would leave. After everything, I would bow out if it was what your heart wanted. However, my not following you here immediately had nothing to do with any of that and everything to do with what Connor laid on me that night. He needed me to stay and play the part of making it look like nothing between us had changed, and there was no chance of you recovering your memories."

Pausing, I take a long pull off my beer, collecting my thoughts. While I don't want any secrets between us, a lot of what's left to say isn't for me to tell, and as much as I fucking hate it, I respect it. After all, it's what kept my girl safe for all these years.

"I'm assuming that since Spencer joined you on the plane, you know about Rainer keeping tabs on you, but the part that you might not know is that he wasn't the only one. Running into Garrett at the coffee shop all those years ago wasn't a coincidence. It was purposefully orchestrated—"

A loud knock at the door cuts me off. Immediately, I jump up and say, "Go to the bedroom, Aria," before reaching for the Glock tucked at my back.

"I fucking knew it!"

I turn and glare at her for her outburst, putting my finger to my mouth. "Shhh, go to the back room."

"No. I'm staying right here. You have a gun for crying out loud. Use it!"

Now would be one of the times when her feistiness pisses me off. "Damn it, I swear to fuck, if you don't get in that room..."

"Holden, open up. It's me." Relief floods my body as I reach for the door, knowing Connor is on the other side. I check the peephole before letting him in.

"Groupie! You hanging in there?" He comes strolling in like

we're not in the midst of a fucked-up situation. Aria stands and greets him with a hug.

Walking back to the couch, I say, "Con, drop the crap. What's going on? I just started sharing some details with Aria on what's been happening behind the scenes."

Connor knows I wouldn't air his shit, but I feel he'd tell Aria anyway. The two have always had this instant closeness that drives me crazy. Releasing Aria, he walks over to the mini fridge and pulls out two vodkas and a can of Coke before making his way to the kitchen, searching for a glass. I sit on the couch, but this time, Aria surprises me and joins me on my sofa, curling up into my side. Instantly, I throw my arm around her, pulling her in tight and kissing her head. She picks up my free hand and laces our fingers together as Connor walks back to sit opposite us.

"So, you'll never believe what fucking happened when we got to the airport to tail Tyler. Nate and I were posted up, making sure we both had eyes on him, when I noticed two other suspicious motherfuckers with full-arm tats waiting outside the airport coffee shop right outside Tyler's gate. I couldn't take my eyes off them. That's when I caught a glimpse of a star tattoo on the back of one of the guys' arms. I knew I'd seen it somewhere but couldn't place it. So, of course, I pulled my phone out and started googling star tattoos and gangs. I finally found it. They belonged to the Lost Vargo motorcycle gang."

Pausing to take a drink of his vodka and Coke, he looks at me like I should know what the hell he's getting at, but I don't, so I ask, "And that's a good thing?"

"Let's just say I didn't think it was coincidental that a major syndicate known for helping traffickers was waiting outside the plane Tyler was deboarding. For a second, I thought I would have to call it off. I assumed Tyler was potentially meeting them, but Tyler got off the plane with his head stuck in his phone, unaware anyone was trailing him. Nate and I watched the two bikers follow him out to the parking garage. Before he could get to the rental car area, a black van pulled up in front of him, and the two bikers knocked him out cold and shoved him in. Nate got the plates and is looking into the details, but from the looks of it, we won't have to worry about him. I would be surprised if he's not swimming with the fish by the end of the night. An hour after we saw him shoved into a van, Ava Cross posted a picture of herself in a string bikini in Antigua. We are double-checking, but I'm sure she posted that picture because she knew Tyler wouldn't be coming after her."

Aria shifts beside me and says, "This is all so fucking crazy. I can't even begin to wrap my mind around it. What about Rainer? Spencer wouldn't tell me what happened with him."

My eyes lock onto Connor's. I want to tell her, she deserves to know, but that also shares Connor's business. He gives me a subtle nod, assuring me he's good before saying, "Aria, Rainer is your family, and, I think, the same as you. Spencer can't wrap his mind around the fact that someone he was close to hurt his sister, and he never knew. The only reason Rainer is still breathing is because he kept himself useful. Whether that was out of self-preservation or genuine remorse is yet to be determined. Rainer is currently in a cell in the basement of my parents' house."

Aria's hand flies to her mouth, and when I look over, her eyes have practically bugged out of her head.

"My family has been working for years behind the scenes, battling sexual violence. It's an underground operation meant to be kept secret to protect the people operating it and the victims it serves. I'm only telling you this now because you were on that list."

Her body stiffens, and when I look at her, I can see that she's trying to process everything that's happened over the past decade. "Are you telling me that Garrett and Colton knew what had happened to me all this time? You knew?"

"What? Fuck no, Aria. Look, back then, I didn't have all the details of what my family did. I had pieces and half-truths. Your retelling of how you landed the job with my uncle Garrett only further confirmed my suspicions, but nothing added up when I dug. You weren't the type of person that needed my family's help. You didn't fit the script. Rainer was the missing link and the piece that put you on my uncle's radar. Essentially, Rainer was Tyler's boyfriend, and Tyler has been known to do his father's dirty work as it relates to the sexual exploitation of women. My family was watching them, and they were watching you. That's why he wanted to keep you close."

I notice she starts fidgeting with our combined fingers before asking, "What are you going to do with him? Do you kill people?"

Connor finishes off his vodka and Coke before giving a vague response, which doesn't surprise me. "People disappear all the time."

She bobs her head in understanding, but I can tell she has more on her mind, so I squeeze her hand and say, "Now is not the time to hold back, baby. Ask what you need to move forward."

Her eyes hold mine briefly in thanks before she turns back to Connor. "Is Rainer going to disappear?"

Connor's eyes narrow on hers like he's trying to get a read on her before he asks, "Do you want him to?"

She shrugs before answering honestly. "Does it make me a bad person if I said I don't know? That I don't think I ever want to know."

Connor stands and walks over to the mini fridge, grabbing more vodka and Coke before returning to refill his glass. As he makes his drink, he says, "How about you leave it to me? I'm not convinced that Rainer isn't a victim himself."

Aria doesn't respond with words, but when his eyes lock on hers, I know she's giving him her trust, and I can't help but be envious. Leaning back against the couch, she sips her beer, still deep in thought. When Connor's phone pings with a text, she slightly shifts forward, clearly on edge, and I know why.

"Are you worried about Nate?" I ask.

She pulls in a stuttered breath and clasps my hand tightly. "Not because I want him back, Holden, but he was a part of my life for the past year, and I care about him."

Connor cuts in, "No worries, groupie. That was Nate now. He just sent me pics of a body bag being taken out on a fishing boat with the caption, 'Swimming with the fishes.' He'll be fine, Aria, and to answer your next question, yes, Nate is involved in the family business. He is one of the reasons we do what we do." I don't miss their silent conversation, which leads me to believe Nate shared something with Aria that is his story to tell. Dropping my hand, she slams her beer on the table.

"Hold on, was I a job for Nate?"

Connor's eyes go wide before he answers. "No, Aria. You've been in California for five years and only spent the past year with Nate." He bites his lip and gives me a cocky half smile before adding, "I'm not convinced you weren't supposed to end up with a Callahan. First Garret, then me, and finally Nate." He shrugs, "This asshole wasn't the only man fate kept thrusting into your life." I fly out of my seat, ready to beat his ass, but Aria stands up and puts herself in front of me.

"Sit down. You know he's fucking with you."

Cocktail in hand, Connor shoots me a wink, crosses his leg over his knee, and sinks back into the couch. I have yet to reclaim my seat when he asks, "So, when are you coming home? Summer hasn't shut up asking about you and the mermaid you promised."

His harmless question only adds fuel to the fire because Aria and I have had zero chances to discuss shit tonight, and I'm about to explode until she runs her hands across my chest, drawing my focus to her, and says, "I don't know. I guess when Holden decides to put a ring on it."

My heart just about beats out of my chest from her retort. She's reiterating that she said yes to marrying me earlier, not just to me but in front of an audience. Pulling her into me, I nuzzle my face into her neck and breathe her in before grabbing her ass and pulling her on top of me to the couch.

Aria squeals, "Holden, my dress!" *Shit.* If Connor sees her pussy, I'll be furious.

"Connor, what the fuck are you still doing here?"

Spreading his arms wide on the back of the sofa, he says, "I'm crashing on the couch. I didn't book a room." Aria laughs out loud, a deep belly laugh that resonates in my soul. I haven't heard her laugh like that in years, and it's intoxicating.

Swatting my chest in jest, she says, "Relax, big boy, you have forever."

Grabbing her chin, I make sure her eyes are on mine when I say, "Then, now, always, pretty girl."

# 24

## HOME

### HOLDEN

"Aria, what are you doing in here? You can't be in here, pretty girl." It's the bottom of the fifth, and I just overextended my middle finger fielding a ground ball that came straight to me off the pitch. It was a fluke. The ball popped up and hit my hand at just the right angle. I'll be out for the next few games.

"You got hurt, and I wanted to see you. I don't like sitting in the family area talking with catty women. I'm not trying to be a bitch, but most of those wives have zero personality."

The doctor just finished wrapping my hand, and I started changing out of my uniform, so of course, I'm standing here in my boxers now with a raging hard-on at the sight of my wife wearing cut-off jean shorts, my jersey, and a baseball cap. When she stops her aimless perusal of the locker room and her eyes land on mine, I say, "If you're determined to break the rules, how about you come over here and help me out with this." I lower my boxers so she can see my raging boner.

Biting her lip, she starts unbuttoning her jersey before commanding, "Sit."

"Yes, ma'am." My woman doesn't have to tell me twice. For the most part, I dominate in the bedroom. I know what she likes, and I more than give it to her, but for the past few weeks, she's been pulling stunts like this and being demanding as hell. First, it was in the half bath at Connor's family picnic. She dropped to her knees, eager as fuck to suck me off before letting me take her from behind while she watched me fuck her in the mirror. Then, this past weekend, we went to a club for a co-ed bachelor/bachelorette party, and she hiked her short dress up and sat on my lap as I fucked her in the booth. That had to be one of my all-time favorite fucks. My god, it was hot. Now, this. I'll pay a hefty price if we get caught in here, and that clearly doesn't bother her in the slightest, but I know why I don't care. The reward is so worth it.

Once her jersey is unbuttoned, she unclasps the front of her bra, letting her full tits fall out before straddling my lap, pulling her shorts to the side, and sinking down onto my throbbing cock. We both release a euphoric hum of sheer ecstasy once she fully seats herself. Aria's mouth finds mine as she starts her pace. Parting my lips, her tongue runs up against mine in long, slow strokes the same way her pussy is grinding on my dick. I can feel her wetness dripping down my balls. She's soaked and horny as hell.

While my gut tells me I know why, I need her to see what I see and feel what I feel because it's sexy as hell. Breaking our kiss, I palm her heavy breasts and flick my thumbs over her nipples before sucking one into my mouth, immediately making her pussy squeeze my cock. "Fuck, baby, do that again. Don't stop, Holden." She grinds her clit against my pubic bone as her nails dig into my shoulders. My cock pulses from her eagerness, and I have to try hard to stave off my orgasm.

"Pretty girl, look at me. Do you feel how wet and swollen you are, baby? Your juices are dripping down my balls." She bites her lip and picks up her pace, loving my dirty talk. "These tits," I suck the other one into my mouth, and her pussy clenches tight. "Damn it, baby, let me see your eyes."

When her dark gaze finds mine, I bring my hands to either side of her face. "You're pregnant, pretty girl. I know this body like the back of my hand. These tits are so full and perfect. Your slick, swollen pussy is dripping down my cock, and I fucking love it. You're growing my baby. I love you, Aria." She stops riding me and shakes her head in disbelief.

"Holden, you can't know that. I haven't taken any tests. We've been off the pill for months, and nothing has happened."

Pulling her face to mine, I rest my forehead against hers. "Aria, I'm here. I'm not going anywhere. I love you with everything that I am. You are my home. You and this baby are my whole world."

A tear trails down her face, and I kiss her lips before saying, "You're not alone this time, pretty girl. Whatever happens, good or bad, we're in this together. Don't be scared."

I rock my hips, trying to pull her back to me and out of her worry, and she kisses my mouth gently before saying, "I love you, Holden, so damn much." And like the little sex fiend she's been over the past few weeks, she quickly resumes her rhythm, riding my dick like she fucking owns it, which she does, and I love it. Her tits bounce as she slams and grinds her pussy down on my dick.

"Fuck, baby, I'm going to come."

"No, don't come. I need more." Her pussy is strangling my dick. She doesn't fucking need more; she's scared to stop because she doesn't want to talk about what I said. Grabbing her hips, I slam her down hard, ensuring she gets every inch as I roll her hips, grinding her pussy on me, and she shatters, milking every last drop from my cock.

"Damn," I rasp out. My wife is the hottest fuck of my life. "Always perfect," I murmur against her neck as I kiss her gently.

When she doesn't immediately move to get up, knowing she needs to before we get caught, I say, "Aria, can you bring me my bag?" I feel her nod before she lifts off my lap, and the mixture of our joined arousal drips down my dick. There isn't a thing she can do that doesn't turn me on. We've been married for six months and still fuck daily. We can't get enough of each other. The woman is truly the other half of my soul, and I'll be damned if I'm going to watch her suffer in silence. I wasn't around the first time, and it kills me, but I'm here now.

While she retrieves my bag, I pull on my t-shirt and joggers before slipping into my slides. We need to get out of here before we get caught, and I need to take care of my girl. I meet her across the room before she has a chance to return to me. There is no doubt in my mind that Aria is carrying my baby, which means there is zero chance I will be letting her hold my bag.

Throwing my arm over her shoulder, I take the bag and say, "Let's go home, pretty girl." When her eyes find mine, they're glassy with unshed tears. "Baby." I pull her into my chest. "Don't cry. You're killing me." Her arms wrap around my back, and I swear she holds me tighter than she ever has, and it feels like I'm being stabbed in the chest. I hate that she feels any pain over something that is supposed to bring joy. "God, I'm so damn sorry I ever hurt you, Aria. If I could take it all back, I would."

"Holden, it's not that. I just know you want babies so bad, and, I don't know, I don't think—"

We married the same weekend I came to California, eloping with Connor as a witness before we ever headed home. Neither of us wanted to wait–we didn't need validation. We just wanted to start making up for all the time we'd lost. Not every day has been easy. Pain changes people. We both spent years shutting people out, overthinking every aspect of our lives, and now we have to find the courage to trust each other with the parts we locked away from the world.

"Stop, Aria. Yes, I want to have babies with you, but if it's not in our cards, that's okay too, as long as I have you. I love everything we have, and that's all I need. You're my whole world, pretty girl."

She literally starts climbing up my body, wrapping her legs around my waist and kissing her way up my neck and face. "I know what love is because of you, Holden Hayes." Her pretty mouth finds mine, and I kiss my wife, the person who holds my heart and owns the other half of my soul.

I've been sitting on the bathroom floor for ten minutes with Aria wrapped around me. I swear she'd crawl under my skin if it were possible. "Baby, it's been ten minutes. I think it's time to look." I slowly drag my fingers up and down her back in a soothing motion, trying to calm her anxiety. After we left the stadium, we stopped at the drugstore and bought ten pregnancy kits. I bought one of each brand, ones with plus signs and ones with words. There will be no denying whatever the outcome is. She peed in a cup, and we dipped three sticks.

With her head resting on my shoulder, she says, "I already know what they will say."

I kiss her neck and say, "Talk to me, Aria."

I feel her nod against my neck before she says, "I know I'm pregnant, Holden. I can feel it, baby." Those were not the words I was expecting. I pull back.

"Aria, look at me." Releasing me, her big brown eyes find mine, but I don't see fear or regret; I see certainty.

"I'm okay, Holden. I want this. I've never stopped wanting it since it was taken from me six years ago. I'm just scared of the unknown. I don't want to feel that pain again. I instantly loved something that I no longer had." Her eyes fill with tears again as I grip her face.

"Baby, I can't guarantee that won't happen again, but I swear on my life, you will never go through it alone. You told me before that we can't change the past but can choose not to live in it. Come back to me, pretty girl. Be with me here and now, and let's do this one step at a time, together, the way it always should have been."

Her lips find mine, and she kisses them softly before popping up and saying, "I'm ready." I watch as she crosses the bathroom to the sink, where the tests have been laid out.

I haven't moved from my spot on the floor when I see her hands fly to her mouth as her shoulders sag. For a second, I take that to mean they're negative until she cries, "We're having a baby." I want nothing more than to run across the room and pull her into my arms, but I can't move. My head falls into my hands, and I cry as a million emotions attack my senses.

"Holden?" Her arms wrap around me. "Baby, are you okay? I thought you'd be happy."

My head instantly snaps up as I pull her onto my lap. "Pretty girl, I am so fucking happy. You're my whole world, and now you're having my baby. It's surreal, Aria. I can't believe that I'm here with you. I love you." I hold her so damn tight, with no desire to move from this spot or let her go. I could sit on this floor for the remainder of the night and still not feel like it was long enough. I want to spend forever in this moment with my wife.

For the past twelve years, I've felt my fate was cursed and that nothing good could ever come my way. I was destined to pay penance for the life I took and the one I couldn't rescue. I never dreamed that the life I couldn't protect would be the one to save mine.

## BONUS EPILOGUE

Did the story end too soon? Are you anxious to know what happened with Aria's pregnancy? For a peek into Aria and Holden's happily ever after, scan the code below.

SCAN ME

## ALSO BY L.A. FERRO

Want more of Connor Callahan? Holden and Aria weren't the only ones with secrets. Read his story now in:

Fade Into You - An Arranged Marriage

Trope list: Arranged Marriage, Sports Romance, Small Town, Single Dad, Mistaken Identity, Unrequited Love

Rewriting Grey: A Small Town Romance

Trope list: Reclusive Author, Small Town, Siblings Ex, Secret Identity, He Falls First.

The Delicate Vows Duet - A Billionaire Romance

Trope list: Billionaire Romance, Off-limits, Age-gap, Secret Virgin, Different Worlds, He Falls First.

Wicked Beautiful Lies - A Taboo Romance

Trope list: Taboo/forbidden, Mistaken Identity, Enemies to Lovers, Dark Secrets.

Sweet Venom - A Why Choose Romance

Trope List: Taboo, Enemies to Lovers, Friends to Lovers, Dark Secrets, Different Worlds, Unrequited Love.

# ACKNOWLEDGMENTS

I'm not sure I'll ever stop thanking this woman for inspiring me to put pen to paper, but to, Mrs. TL Swan, your reach and the value added you are to this world extends far beyond the pages of your books.

To my fellow Cygnet's, you guys are fundamental to my success. I could go on for pages about how so many of you have contributed to my journey, whether for industry advice, the fire under my ass to do the things I procrastinate, or simply an ear to bend when everything feels overwhelming. You guys are truly irreplaceable.

To my phenomenal ARC team: Lori Rivera, Laticia Beymer, AK Landow, Terry Wilson, Leah Edwards, Victoria Wyatt, Ashley Townsley, Amanda Epp, Emily Cherry, Keli Moore Bruce, Layla Towers, Brittany Vitu, Kaylen Swedberg, Brittany Morrow, Olivia Rose, Kandace Allen, Claire Blanche, Alysha Adams, Kelly Streeter, Spice&Coffee, Tracey White-Griffin, Nicole Marie, Shannon Tori, Kara Weidner, Brittany Fraser, Kaylee Kleisley, Christina Rybka, Niyati Sachdeva, Aliyah Smith, Peggy Hogan, Kate Schaeffer, Kelsey Jenkins, Jess Berry, Court Anne, Heather Creeden, Victoria Shelton, Serenity Somers-Day, Tiffany Kinchen, Kat Schumacher, Tracie Mattingly. You guys are the best group of readers an author could ask for. I hold so much gratitude in my heart for all of you. Your support, kindness, and friendship have truly been an unexpected blessing. Thank you, for helping me share my voice with the world.

## ABOUT THE AUTHOR

L.A. Ferro has had a love for storytelling her entire life. For as long as she can remember, she put herself to sleep, plotting stories in her head. That thirst for a good tale led her to books, where she became an avid reader.

The unapologetically dramatic characters, steamy scenes, and happily ever afters found inside the pages of romance novels irrevocably transformed her. The world of romance ran away with her heart, and she knew her passion for love would be her craft.

When she's not trailing after one of her three crazy kids, she loves to construct messy 'happily ever afters' that take her readers on a journey full of angst, lust, and obsession with page-turning enchantment.

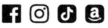